Praise for Delle Jacobs' *Sins of the Heart*

Rating: 5 Ribbons "This story has it all, a touching romance, an intriguing mystery and plenty of adventure. I loved this book."

~ *Christina Rodriguez, Romance Junkies*

"I found myself completely immersed in this vividly-written story. SINS OF THE HEART has it all...passion, danger, secrets, cruel guardians, true friends, and a tormented knight. It is a keeper, one that I recommend very much."

~ *Vi Janaway, Romance Reviews Today*

Look for these titles by

Delle Jacobs

Now Available:

Aphrodite's Brew

Sins of the Heart

Delle Jacobs

A Samhain Publishing, Ltd. publication.

Samhain Publishing, Ltd.
577 Mulberry Street, Suite 1520
Macon, GA 31201
www.samhainpublishing.com

Sins of the Heart

Print ISBN: 978-1-60504-175-9
Digital ISBN: 978-1-60504-035-6

Editing by Linda Ingmanson
Cover by Dawn Seewer

First Samhain Publishing, Ltd. electronic publication: June 2008
First Samhain Publishing, Ltd. print publication: April 2009

Dedication

To:

The Beau Monde

The Wet Noodle Posse

Rose City Romance Writers

The Golden Heart Finalists of 2001, 2002, 2003, 2004 and 2005

Sophia Johnson

Alexis Harrington

Heather Hiestand

And my wonderful editors at Samhain, Jennifer Miller and Linda Ingmanson:

You've believed in me and my stories through hard times and good times.

My love and gratitude forever.

Chapter One

Looe, Cornwall

April 1813

There was no place on earth like the Cornish Coast at sunrise.

Breathing in the briny sea air, spiced like cloves by the sea pinks on the cliff sides, Jane stood beside her friend and scanned the ripening stripe of dawn. Gulls swooped and screeched as they dove and circled, and on the horizon, silhouettes of ships in full sail headed out to sea. Her pulse quickened, imagining distant adventures in exotic ports, with unknown dangers...

But for her, there would be no adventure. She was plain Miss Jane Darrow, safe in her quiet haven. She had nothing more daring to do than to stand at the edge of a cliff, her pale curls whipping in her eyes as she looked down to the surf pounding on the rocks below. All the same, she loved to let the wind toy with her imagination as it fought her for possession of her wide-brimmed bonnet.

Jane turned, leaving Lydia at the cliff's edge. Smiling to herself as her gray skirt billowed in the wind and exposed the secret Belgian lace on her petticoat, she spread the pink Welsh shawl with a flick of her wrists and anchored it with the willow basket.

"Shall we eat, Lydia?" she called.

Lydia glanced back, a smirk playing on her lips. She turned again to sweep her brass spyglass along the horizon.

"Lydia," Jane called again, but it was useless to talk against the stiff April winds.

She smiled, watching Lydia's sky blue dress whip about like a flag. Blue was Lydia's favorite color, and once had been Jane's, too. But the plain dove gray of a lady's companion was good enough for her now. She was lucky, in fact, to have that much, for if it had not been for Lydia and her mother...

She shuddered.

"Halloo," said Lydia, her voice suddenly hushing. She crouched into the gorse at the cliff's edge and twisted the scope to adjust its focus on the secluded cove below the cliff.

Jane pruned her mouth, hiding a giggle. Who but Lydia could be so excited about coots and cormorants?

"Now there's a flock for you, Juliette. Marvelous plumage."

Jane frowned. "Don't call me Juliette. You forget too easily, Lydia."

"Hmm. No more easily than you, my dear. If you insist on being Jane, then I shall have to be Lady Beck to you, and that is silliness if I ever heard it. My. Magnificent wingspread. Mmm, look at that breast. Struts like a peacock, that one. But that one back by the trees, I'd say, looks like a ruffled grouse."

"Grouse?" Jane reached into the basket for her sketchbook. "Don't be silly. Even I know one does not find grouse so close to the sea."

"Ah, but you should see the peacock."

With a sigh, Jane gave up her thoughts of breakfast and picked up her sketchbook. She crossed the crest of the promontory to the leeward slope where a rosy sweep of sea pinks flowed like a bright blanket down to the crescent of golden sand in the tiny cove.

"Anyway," said Lydia, "I did not say he was one, only that he looked like it. Then, perhaps, more of a puffin, but a rather flubberdy-dubberdy one. A gannet, maybe, with that yellow tuft sitting on his head like a bad wig."

Whatever was the matter with her? If anyone knew the difference between a puffin and a gannet, it would be Lydia. Even Jane, for all her studied ignorance of birds, knew better.

"Shh," said Lydia as she approached. Her hand waved Jane back. Lydia knelt on the rock, balancing herself on a twisted limb of scrubby oak, spyglass still trained below. She patted the rock beside her.

Jane's curiosity mounted. Following Lydia's beckoning hand, she scooted in, balancing her sketchbook in one hand and tucking her skirt up with the other as she moved.

"Such elegant plumage," whispered Lydia. "I do believe it's a godwit," she said, and giggled. "He does look as if he has the wit of a god, although clearly he lacks the black tail."

Puzzled, Jane edged closer and peered around Lydia's shoulder. She gasped.

Plumage indeed! Or a lack thereof. At the strand line stood three men. One, the yellow-tufted one, had the posture of a servant. The other two, completely nude, dashed headlong toward a rushing wave, whooping and screeching like raucous gulls as the whitecap slammed into them.

The wave flattened and receded, and Jane blinked and looked again, just to be sure she was not deluding herself. The two discernibly male nude bodies pranced about on the wet sand, slapping their thighs and dancing as if they had stumbled barefoot into a snowdrift.

"Oh, my!" Jane snickered, sketching as fast as she could as the lean male bodies dove beyond the crashing waves, only to be carried tumbling back to the sand. Involuntarily, she shivered, thinking of the frigid water. They thought that was fun! She wondered if they understood the danger. Waves like that, or even bigger ones, were known to wash a grown man out to sea.

"Oh, my, indeed," Lydia responded. "I should like to see him take flight, wouldn't you?"

"Which one?" Jane reached for the spyglass.

Lydia jerked it back. "Not yet. I want to see if—"

"Lydia! You are spying on them!"

"Of course I am, darling. How many opportunities like this does a widow get? You don't get all that many occasions to watch men dance about in the altogether, either, you know."

"Really. I thought you didn't want anything to do with men."

"Not men, darling. Marriage. There's nothing wrong with looking, especially at such finely plumed specimens. You should take a look."

"I don't see how I can if you insist on keeping the glass to yourself. Give it to me, Lydia. I need it to catch the detail."

"Not until I'm finished. Be still. They'll see us. And then where would we be?" With a muted squeal, Lydia yanked the spyglass beyond Jane's reach. She shifted sideways closer to the edge and propped it on a thick branch of the scrub oak.

Jane huffed. Lydia never did anything by halves. "Be careful. You're awfully close—"

"Silly. Oh, you should see this." Lydia scooted forward again, elbows propped on the crooked branch.

"If you would just let me have the glass—"

A faint crackle, like damp wood on a fire, turned into a loud snap as the limb splintered.

"Oh!" Lydia pitched forward and caught handfuls of scraggly limbs. The limbs cracked. The spyglass spun through the air, tumbled down the slope and disappeared.

Jane's heart screeched to a halt as she lunged after blue cloth, but the muslin slid through her fingers like water. Lydia plunged into the gorse, arms flailing, rolling, bouncing through the springy brush. For a fragile moment, Lydia seemed suspended, then the frail shrubs shattered again, and she rolled on.

Jane screamed and screamed and screamed.

Lydia lay still, on a ledge halfway down the slope.

"Lydia!" Jane screamed again, searching the jagged face of the cliff for a path down. "Help! Someone help us!"

Something in the far corner of her mind mocked the absurdity of crying out to naked men for help. But Jane didn't care. Spotting a break in the shrubbery where gray granite poked through, she tossed her shawl aside. Heart pounding in her ears, she swung around the jutting stone and probed with her toe until she found a crevice.

Please God please God please God...

She edged downward, nightmarishly slow, brush snagging her dress and scratching her arms. Gravel crumbled beneath her boot as she clung to the snags of gorse, praying they would not break and send her tumbling like Lydia down the cliff. As she found her footing again, the breath she took burned in her lungs like thick, hot smoke.

She could see Lydia where she lay and heard her moan.

“I’m coming, Lydia! I’m coming!” she cried, and shouted again for help, but had no notion if anyone was still there to hear her. She dared not waste her time hoping.

The slope gentled to a narrow ledge, wide enough to walk along. To her left, Lydia rolled to one side, but then shrieked and fell back, clutching her arm.

Heart pounding, ankles twisting, her skirt tangling, Jane scrambled through clumps of wild pinks. At last, she knelt beside her friend.

Lydia groaned, cradling her arm. Scratches covered her face and arms. Somewhere on the slope above, her shawl and bonnet had disappeared, and the sky-blue dress she loved so much was torn in a hundred places.

“My arm,” Lydia whispered. “I believe I’ve broken it. My head. Oh, Juliette, my head.”

“Don’t try to sit up.” With ginger touches, Jane tested the scrape on Lydia’s head. It didn’t seem too bad, but what did Jane know? What if her neck was broken? How could she tell? The arm certainly looked broken at the wrist, for it was beginning to swell, forcing Lydia’s hand to jut at an awkward angle.

How she might get Lydia out of here Jane couldn’t imagine, but until she wrapped the arm, she couldn’t do anything. Jane fingered the ruffle of her petticoat with its Belgian lace trim, remembering briefly how dearly it had cost her. She hissed in a deep breath and, gritting her teeth, she ripped it off.

“Oh, Juliette, not your Belgian lace!”

“It was torn anyway,” Jane said. She smoothed the gathers out of the ruffle, then wrapped it round and round the bleeding arm, densely enough to form a fabric cushion and serve as a crude splint. The last of it she made into a sling, and slipped the knot behind Lydia’s head.

“How stupid of me, Juliette.” Lydia winced as she tilted her head toward the little cove below. “I don’t suppose we escaped their notice.”

Jane truly hoped they had not. She would never manage to get Lydia off the cliff alone. Maybe they would just go for help instead of parading their bare bodies up and down the cliff.

Behind her, she heard a rustle in the gorse and glanced back, feeling relief flood her as she spotted a man, complete in garments, working his way up the cliff.

She sat back and turned to call to him.

Cold fear slammed into her.

Edenstorm!

Dear heavens, could it get any worse? She ducked her head, tugging down her bonnet's wide brim to hide her face. Maybe he didn't see her. Or remember her. But he would. Just as she could never forget those icy, soulless silver eyes.

Run! Hide!

But she couldn't hide. There was no place to go, and she couldn't abandon Lydia.

She tucked her chin down, trying to look meek. Perhaps the enormous brim that so often made her feel like she wore a sail would hide her face until she could get away. He might pay attention to the lady and never notice the little mouse of a lady's companion. Men were like that.

Maybe. Edenstorm had that sort of arrogance. If there were a bible for propriety, he could have written it.

Jane bent over Lydia. "Jane," she whispered. "Don't forget I'm Jane."

"Oh—" Lydia blinked. "Who? What—"

"Edenstorm," Jane whispered. "He's one of those men. Oh, Lydia, don't give me away. Don't let him know it's me."

The vagueness in Lydia's eyes suddenly sharpened.

Jane could hear the crashing brush behind her.

"Pardon me, ma'am," he said, brushing by her where she knelt between Lydia and a large clump of sea pinks as if she were just one more bush.

He smelled of the sea as he passed, and his fawn colored breeches were stained dark where the water had soaked them. Beneath the unbuttoned knee placket, great, bulging muscles of bare calves were covered with light golden hair. Squeaking wet shoes covered his feet. Jane fought the urge to glance up to see if the face with the haunting silver eyes was the way she remembered it.

He knelt beside Lydia. Jane ducked her head and fixed her gaze on the jagged slope above.

"I'm Edenstorm, ma'am," he said, in a voice lower and gentler than the harsh, metallic one Jane remembered. "Are you hurt?"

"Not too badly, I think. I met you once, sir," Lydia replied. "I am Lydia, Lady Beck. You knew my husband, I believe."

"Sorry to hear of his passing. What a surprise to find you in this remote corner of England."

"My mother's home." Lydia took a trembling breath. "Lady Launceston. She has lived here most of her life. I sought the peace of the seashore after Lord Beck died. My— companion, Miss Jane Darrow, is with me."

Edenstorm glanced back. Jane had the sense to look away just in time and reached up into the brush, pretending to unhook Lydia's shawl.

"Your arm is broken, then?" asked the male voice behind Jane.

"Yes, I am quite certain."

"What about your head? That was quite a fall."

"It took a bump, but it's all right, I think. It was rather like rolling on a mattress, actually. The gorse is quite springy."

"Fortunately for you."

Jane peered beneath the bonnet brim as Edenstorm placed an arm behind Lydia's back and gently helped her to sit. Lydia caught her breath, then smiled weakly as she stood. She trembled and turned even paler, and for a moment, Jane thought Lydia might faint.

"Miss Darrow," Edenstorm called. "Come and help me with your lady."

Jane thought her heart rose into her throat and stuck there.

Please, please remember!

"Jane, you must get my shawl for me, please," Lydia countered. "I should hate to lose it. It is my favorite paisley, you know."

Bless her. "Yes, ma'am," Jane replied, and started climbing up through the rocks and gorse after the lovely red patterned shawl.

"Very well, Miss Darrow, if you are sure you can make it," Edenstorm said. "Now, ma'am, let us see if we can get you the rest of the way down. The slope is much gentler from here on. It will be easier to go down than up."

As he guided Lydia through the uneven footpath between the rocks, Jane climbed upward into the brush and stretched until she could touch the Paisley's long fringe. She gave it a tug and said a silent prayer of thanks when it did not give way, so at least she had some good reason to be busy elsewhere. She climbed higher, fighting the gusty breeze that taunted her sail of a hat while she loosened the tapestry-like cloth from each tiny snag.

"Miss Darrow," Edenstorm called, his voice dragging out the sound of her name. A shiver climbed up her spine. "Do come down. It is quite dangerous. I shall send my man for the shawl."

She buried her face in her task. "Oh, I am quite all right, my lord. I have it now. And I believe I shall go on up to the top and fetch the dogcart, if it is all right with you."

"No reason to do so, Miss Darrow. I have already sent my friend for it. Come down before you are hurt, too."

He would likely come up after her if she did not—the very last thing she wanted. She knew him too well. He did not brook disobedience. Yet if she went down, she could not avoid him.

Mentally patching her nerves together, Jane eased her way downward, slippery foothold by flimsy grip on gorse, descending as slowly as she dared. By the time she returned to the ledge, Edenstorm had worked Lydia down the slope almost to the beach. Beyond them, the other man drove Lydia's yellow-spoked dogcart onto the sand and stopped when he reached the gannet-like servant.

The sea had already become brilliantly blue and sparkling in the early morning sun, and the stiff offshore breeze teased her bonnet. Jane held down the wayward brim, more determined than ever to keep it under control. It was easy to shield her face now, pretending it was from the brightness and the blowing grit.

Perhaps she would get away without being recognized, after

all.

The other man brought the dogcart up to the slope of the cliff, and Edenstorm, moving with a gentleness Jane would never have expected of him, eased Lydia up onto the seat.

"Rokeby will see you home, Lady Beck," he said. "I will see to your companion."

Before Jane could protest, the other gentleman, who had managed to dress himself more completely than Edenstorm, no doubt having had more time, cracked the whip, and the pony sprang to a trot.

Edenstorm turned to face Jane.

Jane felt her mouth go dry. She ducked her head and turned, folding the bonnet's ridiculous brim over her face. "You needn't worry about me, my lord," she said, her words shaking as if she had the shivers. "I am accustomed to seeing to myself. So I shall be on my way now, if you don't mind."

Heart pounding, lungs burning, Jane trudged through the sand as she fought the voice inside her brain that screamed run, run, run! She forced each foot with agonizing slowness to move, one pace at a time. One, two, three, four. He hadn't seen her face. She was going to make it. Five, six, seven, eight. Count the paces. Safe, safe, safe, safe. She would go home and close the door and then, then she could sit down and somehow figure out what to do next. One, two, three, four. Safe, safe, safe, safe.

Without warning, Edenstorm stepped in front of her. Jane thought her heart stopped cold. Against her will, her eyes scanned upward over his tall body. Wet breeches clung indecently to his hard male form. His linen shirt was all but transparent where it stuck to his skin. Up and up her gaze climbed, to stormy gray eyes, no longer the icy silver that once had seemed to have no soul behind them, but cold and heated at the same time as if lit by the fires of Hell itself. As if they burned the very garments from her body, they stripped her bare to the wind and sun.

Jane planted her feet and clenched her fists to keep her hands from shaking.

"How astounded I am to see you here, Lady Juliette," he said, his voice as hard and brittle as his metallic eyes. "The last I heard, you were dead."

Chapter Two

Deuce!

His pulse hammered in his ears as Edenstorm stared at the woman standing before him. Here she was, haloed by the shimmering sea behind her, the ghost he'd long ago lain to rest, come back to haunt him.

She dropped her gaze to the sand at their feet and, for a fleet second, Edenstorm almost believed the meekness she portrayed. But just as quickly, the lush green eyes flitted back to him with a directness no mere lady's companion would dare.

This was no specter.

"Jane Darrow, my lord," she replied. A minute tremble shook her words. "Just plain Miss Jane Darrow."

The devil she was. Edenstorm brushed his wet hair away from his eyes and bored his angry glare into her. She had changed. She was hardly the dazzling coquette fresh from the schoolroom, for she was dressed in a dull gray muslin Juliette would never have allowed on her lovely body. But this was Juliette and none other. And she still took his breath away.

How? Where the devil had she come from? She sure as hell was not at the bottom of the Irish Sea!

His tongue was so thick he thought he'd choke on it, but he fought his betraying face and pulled on a mask of cool disdain.

"How odd," he replied. "You resemble Lady Juliette Dalworthy so closely. Identically, I would say."

Eyelids fluttering, she attempted a smile, but crimped her hands together so tightly she was in danger of breaking her own bones. No, he wasn't wrong. She knew exactly who he was and knew he was not fooled by her lie. But what the devil was the daughter and sister of earls doing posing as an impoverished lady's companion, under an assumed name?

"You're mistaken, sir. I—I must be going. Lady Beck will be needing me."

Edenstorm stepped closer, almost to touching distance, looming over her. "I shall escort you home."

She eased back a step. "No, you need not, sir. I can manage. Thank you— For your concern for my lady."

"It is my duty." Again, he stepped closer.

Stark fear widened her eyes as she glanced around her and backed another step over the sand. "Thank you, my lord. Surely you wish to make yourself presentable before going anywhere." Her tongue swiped over her lips. "I—shall be going now."

She whirled around and sped toward the sparse grass and the rocky slope beyond, the sound of her footsteps digging into the dry sand muted by the roaring tide at his back. Even the swish of her skirts in the brush faded away as if she climbed in a silent dream up the steep trail to the narrow road above.

She's alive.

Frowning, he shut out the unsettling thoughts that made his heart race. Something akin to rage boiled up in him to replace it. Shock, no doubt, that was what it was. Of course he was angry, after what she had done to him.

Yet...

She was alive.

No matter how she denied it, this was Lady Juliette Dalworthy, daughter of an earl and sister to Cyril Dalworthy, sixth Earl of Harlton.

One death, at least, that could not be laid at his doorstep.

Did Harlton know? Damn him to hell for a liar, of course he knew. He had to know. But why? They had hushed the scandal early enough, so there was no need to send her off and bury her socially. Or had it worsened? Had there been a child?

The memory flared with sudden brightness, like a flash in a musket pan. He slammed his mind shut on it before it could fully form. Hell. Half a war ago, but it still nagged at him like deeply imbedded shrapnel.

The chill wind blasted him, mercifully pulling him back from the assaulting image. Edenstorm swiped at his dangling hair and looked down at the doeskin breeches that alternately bagged and stuck to his wet skin. She was right about one thing. He could hardly go after her until he dressed himself decently.

A sheet of water from the last wave rolled over his shoes, reminding him once more of the cold sea behind him. It spread out over the sand, and where it left a line of foam as it receded, it deposited a bent tube of brass. Sunlight reflected on the fractured lenses of the spyglass as it rolled in the lee of the wave.

He bent to retrieve it, frowning at the mangled tube that was now about as worthless as a hound that couldn't smell. It would be his duty to return it to Lady Beck, anyway.

A spyglass, a cliff and two ladies at sunrise. One of them clearly not who she said she was. And what the devil had they been doing up there?

Devil it. That was the smallest of his problems. He had more to worry about if they started asking why he was here. He should leave. Now, before everything else went to hell.

He'd been a soldier too long, and he'd never run from a battle yet, but if ever he'd caught the scent of battle in the air, it was now.

"Nance!" he called, and scattered the sandpipers and gulls as he strode across the beach to the scraggled gorse and boulders where he and Rokeby had stripped off their clothing.

Nance waited with the horses. Only the tiniest flare of the valet's nostrils betrayed his dismay at the stained doeskin breeches Edenstorm peeled down his thighs so he could don the smallclothes he had omitted in his haste to climb the cliff.

The cold wind against his bare body brought back memories of other far more bitterly cold days and icy rivers in the Peninsula, and he wondered why he had ever thought to brave the frigid surf in April. The minute he'd hit the water, he'd known himself for the perfect idiot. After a stunt like that, a man ought to worry about his future ability to produce offspring.

But the wild swim in an even wilder sea was meant to give

the impression of a pair of foolhardy English gentlemen on holiday with too much money and not enough to do. He laughed bitterly. Anything for the good of the mission. Another thing he hadn't got out of his blood.

In minutes, Nance had him restored some sort of order, although Edenstorm would not have liked to look in a mirror to be sure. He sent Nance back with Rokeby's horse and the soggy remains of their exploit to Pendennen Hall, the little manor they had rented that was by any civilized man's standard little more than a stone cottage that happened to have a slate roof.

Leading his horse, he climbed the trail where he had last seen Lady Juliette who claimed to be Plain Miss Jane Darrow. Instead of following the narrow lane back to the village of West Looe, he turned left and followed the track to the promontory. He dropped Hector's reins and walked to the bare granite point that jutted out into the sea.

Edenstorm scanned the bright blue sky and puffy clouds above a brilliant sea. It was a spectacular view, he'd grant them that, but it was beyond his imagination that two proper young ladies would be out at dawn without even so much as a male servant to accompany them. Not even a groom to drive the dogcart. He would never have allowed it of his sister.

But the women clearly had been there. A basket with foodstuffs weighed down one corner of a pink plaid blanket as its other corners fluttered in the wind. Among the still-packed boiled eggs, ham and uncut bread, he found half a bottle of wine. He popped the cork and sniffed, nodding at the quality. An interesting picnic breakfast for two ladies, which he suspected meant they had intended to spend the entire morning. He folded the blanket and carried it with the basket as he walked to the cliff overlooking the spit of sand.

A light-colored shawl had blown into the gorse, and he plucked it from the tangled branches. It was soft and thick in his fingers, an elegant woven wool in a subtly complex checkered pattern of shades of gray, a contradiction to the vibrant memories of Lady Juliette's red-splashed cashmeres.

Almost against his own will, he lifted the fabric to his face, drinking in a nearly forgotten fragrance that sent him whirling, mind and body, into a torrent of vivid scents and colors, memories, and a violent ache of heart and body.

The bed. Kirkwood. Fury formed bright red in his mind.

He threw down the shawl.

For a moment, he just stared at it.

No. He was a man of reason. He would not be ruled by such base emotion.

With a brutal exhale of disgust, Edenstorm swiped up the wad of gray wool and folded it in precise squares. Gritting his teeth, he jammed it into the basket.

The scent was hers. It mingled with a different perfume, a simpler one that hinted more of earth and herbs, but beneath it clung the essence that was unmistakably Juliette.

Damn him for a fool to have trusted her.

A flash of white caught his eye, pages of a book shuffling in the wind. Dragging in a deep breath to clear his head of the nonsense, Edenstorm set down the basket and worked his way down the slope until he was within reach of the flapping paper. A sketchbook snagged by the gorse.

Edenstorm retrieved the book, folded it closed and climbed back to the promontory. He picked up the basket, meaning to stick the book in it, but halted when he saw the name carefully penned on the green baize cover.

J. Darrow.

The pages compelled him. He opened the book. He thumbed through sketches of the two villages that nestled on either side of the Looe Pool, with the rough surf beyond its harbor, but smooth as glass within the breakwater. Ships and coastal luggers sailing into safe harbor. A river scene at night, with a full moon dancing through dark clouds and lacing its reflection on the wide waters below. Birds of various sorts soaring against tousled clouds. And page upon page of people, carved out in clean, swift lines, capturing faces and spirits so well, he could recognize some of them. There was Lady Beck beside an older woman who seemed all perfect sweetness. And there, a sharp-featured young man who laughed at the artist. Edenstorm had seen him. He was one of the more prosperous boat builders in West Looe.

He turned to the last sketch.

Hasty graphite slashes formed two figures, in full, blatant, male nudity, cavorting like gangly marionettes in a lunatic dance with the surf. The very perfect idiots he'd known them to be.

Hell. Edenstorm slammed the book closed, crammed it into the basket and stomped across the jagged surface of the promontory toward the dusty road. He was going home to take a long, hot bath. Scrub away the itchy salt and sand drying on his skin and turning his hair stiff.

He'd scour away the memory of this entire morning if he could.

❧

With shaking breaths, Jane pivoted a bit too fast and stumbled. She forced herself to take each step slowly, while her mind screamed at her to run. Her backbone prickled as if waiting for a knife to slam into it at any moment. The man could destroy her with a word! But no steps pounded behind her, not so much as a squish in the sand.

She scrambled through the sparse sedge beyond the sand to the dirt path that led up the slope. She thought briefly of the basket full of their breakfast that remained on the granite promontory above them. But she dared not return for it.

No sound behind her but the roar of the tide coming in.

At the very moment she stepped into the narrow path that ran along the cliffs, she turned toward the village and lost any semblance of calm.

She ran. All the way to the road and down it to the edge of West Looe as if the devil were behind her. One named Edenstorm.

Seeing the square gray stone pillars that braced the gate of Launceston Hall, she slowed, but only to catch a breath and glance behind her. She pushed through the wrought iron gate and staggered up the cobbled pavement to the steps and the shade of the portico.

Jane pushed open the red door and stumbled inside, the room around her turning dark before her eyes as if she were close to fainting. She gripped her chest, her lungs burning, as she leaned against the back of the door.

"Miss Darrow? Are you all right?"

Slowly, Charles coalesced out of the grayness as the darkness faded away.

"The gentleman said you would be brought home, miss."

"No, there was no need—" she gasped. "Where is Lady Beck?" Her lungs still heaved. Charles must think her addled.

"In her chamber, Miss Darrow. Perhaps you should rest."

Jane shook her head and aimed herself down the corridor for the stairs, and by the time she reached them she'd caught her breath again. She took the stairs slowly, pausing on the first and second landings. She was almost breathing normally by the time she reached Lydia's chambers, and paused a moment more until the gasps ceased. Her pulse still pounded.

The room with its sky blue walls and sprinklings of all the colors of spring flowers, had a cheeriness that was like Lydia herself. Lydia was propped on pillows, with Mrs. Trelawny hovering over her, fluffing and plumping everything, then going back and doing it all again. Lady Launceston stood by, wringing her crinkled hands, worrying as she undoubtedly had for every day of her beloved daughter's life. But today she had more reason.

"Jane!" Lydia's eyes widened from a sleepy state that indicated a dose of laudanum already setting in. "Goodness, are you all right?"

"Never mind me," Jane replied. "How are you?"

"Oh, a bump or two. We were right, my arm is broken." She winced as she lifted the arm in its white sling.

It wasn't the one Jane had put around Lydia's neck. She glanced back at the boudoir chair and saw her ruined Belgian lace hanging limply over the floral tapestry of the chair's back.

"Oh, Jane, I'm so sorry about your lace," Lydia said. "You shall have more, I promise."

"It's not important. Have you seen the surgeon yet?"

"He is coming. But I don't think it needs setting. It's not at all crooked, just swollen. What about you? Did he—"

Jane glanced about the room. "Just out of breath," she interrupted before Lydia could let something slip. "I hurried back as fast as I could."

"Oh. Yes." Lydia gave a weak smile and dropped the subject. She probably would have blushed at her forgetfulness if she were not so subdued by the growing effect of the laudanum.

"You're quite sure you're not hurt worse? It was a terrible fall. I've never been so frightened in my life."

"No, quite all right, really. Do go change now, dear. I think I shall rest, if everyone will just allow it."

"I think I shall sit here a few moments if you do not mind. Just to reassure myself that you will be comfortable."

Mrs. Trelawny sniffed. Jane thought she heard a faint whimper, but then Mrs. Trelawny always sounded like she was whimpering. Soon the housekeeper left, followed by Lydia's maid and finally her mother. Jane lingered as Lydia's eyes grew ever sleepier. The door shut.

"Now, they are gone," said Lydia, and her hazy eyes brightened a bit. "Well? What about Edenstorm? He didn't recognize you, did he? I'm sure he didn't and we'll just keep you out of sight until he leaves. Mr. Rokeby told me they are only here on holiday, so they won't be long."

Jane bit her lip and pulled the blankets up for Lydia, carefully working them around her injured arm. "Everything will be all right, Lydia, don't you worry."

"Oh, dear."

Jane winced. "No, really, it will all be fine."

"You always say that whenever the world is about to erupt into madness. Oh, Jane, what will you do?"

"We shall manage. You need to rest now, Lydia. When you awake, you'll see it's not so bad."

"Never you mind, dear. We'll find something. I know. You shall marry Davy. That will do the trick. Cyril could not do anything to harm you, once you are another man's wife. It would certainly make Davy happy. Do be a dear and adjust this pillow? Mrs. Trelawny has it much too high."

Jane eased the lower of the two pillows from under Lydia's arm. Yet even as she moved slowly, she saw Lydia wince.

"I can't, don't you remember? It wouldn't be legal unless I used my real name, and then Davy would have to know the entire story."

"Oh. Yes. I wasn't thinking, I suppose. Well, someone else then. I'm sure we can think of someone."

Jane tried not to frown, although she doubted in Lydia's foggy state of mind that she would notice. It was all just a bit over Lydia's head at the moment. No, she might find a different man for a husband, but the problem wouldn't change. A marriage under an assumed name was not a legal marriage. And Jane had had enough of dealing with men who believed they had been played false. She couldn't take that chance.

"Truth to tell, I suspect Davy is even more rigid than Edenstorm. He would never tolerate a wife with the remotest blemish to her name."

"Hm. Certainly a staunch Methodist, that man. Handsome enough, and good family. Wherever it is he goes, he's always back for Sunday services. And well fixed. You would not have to play the companion, nor worry about mingling in higher society where someone might recognize you. "

Davy was handsome, in a jagged sort of way. He never went anywhere without women following him with their eyes. He was more than attentive. Persistent, in fact. As a boat builder and merchant of all goods who occasionally went to sea for reasons Jane knew better than to ask, he was wealthy enough. Nor did it hurt that he was related to Lady Launceston, who had married a baronet but never forgotten her family roots in Cornwall.

Yet Jane had somehow never been able to imagine being married to him. She had been turning him down for over three years, and wished he would stop asking, so she wouldn't ever have to explain why. A gentleman of the seas might play fast with the laws of the land, but every self-respecting Methodist in Cornwall knew a lady with the slightest question to her name was not a respectable one.

"I'm happy enough as I am," Jane replied.

"I had rather hoped not to let Mrs. Trelawny in on things, but we may have to. She has connections, you know."

Yes. Jane knew. She also knew to whom those connections really belonged, and Lydia did not. "I am sure everything will be all right, Lydia. You rest now. I'll see to everything."

The laudanum was settling in. Lydia's eyes became dreamy and her smile beatific, with no more than a hint of pain lingering in a furrow on her brow.

Lydia sighed lightly. "Just till your birthday, Juliette, and you'll be of age. Then you'll be safe." And then she drifted off.

Jane quietly dropped her face into her hands, at last left alone to contemplate her unraveling secret. She would never be safe from Cyril, even when he was no longer her legal guardian, because she would always pose too much of a threat to him.

Chapter Three

There was also the matter of her sketchbook which had gone over the cliff. It would not be good for anyone else to find it.

When Jane was certain Lydia was asleep, she checked to be sure the broken arm was safely cradled in pillows and slipped out of the room. As Jane expected, Lady Launceston waited in the corridor. She was not one to be far away when her beloved daughter was in pain.

"She's sleeping," Jane said. "She seems to be reasonably comfortable, although I think we should keep watch for a while. Don't you agree?"

"Oh, yes. They say head wounds are dangerous," answered Lady Launceston, her white brows folded into a deep frown. "Do you suppose we ought to wake her from time to time? To be sure?"

"Perhaps. We shall see what Mr. Saunders says when he comes. But I suspect the laudanum will wear off rather quickly."

"We did not give her very much."

"As long as she is fretful now and then, I think we can be sure she will not slip away."

"Oh dear."

Jane winced. She shouldn't have put it quite that way. "But that is only to reassure ourselves, I think. She will be fine. We just worry overmuch. I'm sure Mr. Saunders will say so."

"Yes, no doubt. I shall sit with her for awhile. You will be here, won't you?"

"I shall hurry back. I must go back to the cliff and retrieve what we left behind."

"Couldn't a footman do it, Jane?"

Jane thought of what she had left behind and gulped. Oh, no, not a footman! The last thing she wanted was for one of them to see the sketch. Well perhaps not the last thing, but certainly close to it, for she would die of embarrassment if Lady Launceston happened to see it.

"It is my fault. I did not think even to go back for our things, I cannot conscience having someone else do what is my task."

"I do so worry when you girls go to the cliff. You know, when I was a girl, a young man fell from the cliffs, and the tide swept him away, never to be seen again."

Jane nodded. She'd heard the story so many times she could have told it herself. She smiled. "I shall be careful. I promise."

"That nice Mr. Rokeby was so kind to bring my Lydia back, don't you think?"

Jane nodded.

"And that other man. Was he—"

Jane nodded again. Lady Launceston would never condescend to pry, but she knew Jane's story almost as well as Jane did herself. "Edenstorm."

Jane watched the wrinkled lips tighten. "Oh dear," Lady Launceston said again.

"Don't worry, my lady," Jane replied, and patted the older lady's hand. "Everything will be all right. You'll see."

Lady Launceston gave back that sweet smile that belied her great intelligence. "Yes. We shall see to it. You know, Jane, we shall take care of you."

Yes, she knew. Jane felt warm inside just knowing that. Lady Launceston and Lydia were her true family, the ones who could be trusted. She would do anything for them and knew she could expect complete loyalty from them.

"I shall not be long."

"Change your dress, dear."

Wincing, Jane looked down at the tattered skirt of her

favorite walking dress and had to admit the lady was right. Nor was it worth raising a fuss, not that Jane ever did. Lady Launceston was her employer, after all. Jane often thought of the old woman as a tiny tiger.

So the moment Lady Launceston slipped inside the door of Lydia's chamber, Jane hurried up to her chamber and changed quickly to her other rambling dress, a simple brown print muslin. In minutes, she stepped outside Launceston Hall and hurried over the cobbled pavement toward the gate.

She needn't have bothered. Passing through the gate was a small carriage drawn by a pretty brown cob.

Edenstorm. And she was trapped. There was no way to avoid him without committing an unpardonable social error. Her heart began to beat faster. She fixed her eyes in a modestly lowered fashion, clasped her hands in the way a good lady's companion ought.

The smart, cane-sided whisky drew up before her, and Edenstorm jumped down. Here he was, once again towering over her, in spite of all her wishes to the contrary.

Her breath caught. He was huge, even bigger than she remembered. He filled the space around him as if his very presence forced the air to compress and make way for him. No mass of sodden clothes and dripping hair now. Edenstorm wore a coat of dusky gray, cut to perfection for his massively broad shoulders, a waistcoat of a pewter-colored brocade. His perfectly turned out cravat a brilliant white that made his silver eyes even more startling. His hair had darkened to bronze in the four years since they had first met, but streaks of gold played through its waves, and his skin had changed to a golden shade that still spoke of his years at war.

"Miss Darrow," he said.

The ice in his tone made her shiver, but his eyes blazed fire. She nodded back.

"I've come to ask after Lady Beck's health."

She studied the toes of her boots to hide the uncontrolled fluttering of her eyelids. "She is sleeping quietly, my lord. We have sent for Mr. Saunders, but he is attending someone else. I think the bone does not need setting. The break seems clean."

"I am more concerned about her head. I saw her hit. I

thought surely she would be dead before I could reach her."

"You saw—"

"Your scream was unmistakable. Going back to the cliff, are you?"

"We left some things."

"I'd prefer you not go back there. I have no wish to repeat this morning's experience."

"Nor have I, sir. I assure you I am not in the habit of falling off cliffs."

"I'll wager Lady Beck is not either, but that does not seem to have stopped her. I took the time to gather your things for you."

Her mouth turned dry. She licked her lips. *What things?*

Edenstorm reached behind the seat of the whisky and lifted out the basket with the pink Welsh blanket laid across its top. "Fortunately the wind had not yet carried away the blanket," he said. "A pity your little repast was interrupted."

She managed a jittery smile.

"What were you doing up there?"

Those ghostly silver eyes pinned her as if he nailed her to a wall. Jane squeezed her eyes shut to break the trance and sought out the scuffed toes of her boots again. "We go there often at dawn, sir. To watch the birds. Lady Beck is fond of birds."

"Ah. Then that explains this."

As he pulled it from the floorboard of the whisky, Jane recognized the remains of Lydia's spyglass, bent like a dog's hind leg. She winced before she could stop herself, but accepted the mangled brass tube. "Yes. The birds."

He started for the door, basket hanging over his arm. Jane followed, craning her neck just so to see into the little carriage, but saw no sign of the sketchbook. Maybe he hadn't found it. She bit her lip.

"Cormorants, marmosets, that sort of thing?" he said as he opened the door. She gritted her teeth. No chance of fobbing him off now. Obviously he intended to enter whether she liked it or not.

"As you say, sir." Eyes lowered as properly as she could

make them go, she passed through the door he held open for her. Seeing Charles belatedly appear in the entry, she nodded toward the parlour. "We'll have tea, please, Charles," she said, handing the butler her bonnet and allowing Edenstorm to divest himself of the basket. Edenstorm followed her into the parlour, but made no move to sit when she did not.

His gaze roamed about over the walls and furnishings, taking in every detail, from the bright yellow walls Lydia had insisted on painting when she returned to live in Launceston Hall to the old porcelain figurines on the mantle where they had apparently sat since the day of Lady Launceston's wedding so many years ago.

With a smile that took only half his mouth, Edenstorm assessed her, and Jane felt heat gathering in her once more, from scalp to toes.

"A marmoset is a New World monkey, Lady Juliette," he said. "Not a bird."

"Kind of you to remind me, sir, but I had no wish to embarrass you with your error. And I do wish you would not call me by that name."

"You were born to the manor as much as I. Oh, and I believe this is yours," he added. He reached into his waistcoat and pulled out the green-bound sketchbook, which she would have thought too big to fit there comfortably.

A strange noise gurgled in her throat as if she were being choked. Jane gulped as she reached for it. "Thank you. I feared it was surely ruined by the wind." She took it from him, opened it, but then slammed it shut. Had he seen—

"I retrieved it right away. Fortunately, for I believe a storm is approaching. Some interesting work you have done, Miss Darrow. The landscapes are quite nice, especially the moonlit scene and the portraits. I recognize a few of them."

Jane managed to mumble something resembling a thanks.

"I kept the last one," he drawled. "I hope you don't mind."

She felt the hot flush deepen and grow, as if any minute it would reach all the way down to her toes. Odious man! No true gentleman would ever embarrass a lady so.

But then Edenstorm didn't consider her a lady. And she supposed she had just proven his own point to him.

The situation was getting worse by the minute. Couldn't he be a gentleman just for once and leave? She hated that he so easily assumed power over her simply by standing there, towering head and shoulders above her. On the other hand, if she sat down, he'd be compelled by his own rigid social rules to sit, too. She'd never seen a man succeed in intimidating a woman while sitting...

Taking in a breath as slowly and evenly as she could, Jane squared herself and lifted her chin. She smoothed out her skirt and sat in Lady Launceston's favorite cabriole-legged chair with its petit point seat. Although she did not allow a single muscle in her face to move, she was quite certain her mouth pruned in a ridiculously imperious way as he realized he was forced by the rules of that propriety he so greatly cherished to sit politely across from her. Now they were on more equal ground.

Edenstorm leaned back and let his silver eyes rake over her. He steepled his fingers. "What fascinates me most, I think, is how you managed to survive drowning in the Irish Sea."

Despite her resolve, her jaw dropped open. She shut it quickly. Irish Sea? Wherever did that notion come from? "Possibly by never going near it, sir."

"Indeed? Lady Juliette Dalworthy is said to have gone overboard on a crossing to Ireland to visit relatives and has never been seen again. There is a memorial stone for her in the parish church at Maidstone. I have seen it myself."

Sudden despair struck her, then sank into the deepest pit of her stomach. So that was how Cyril had explained her disappearance. It washed through her like water through wine as she realized her brother had planned that explanation from the moment he had decided she must disappear behind the walls of whatever lunatic asylum he had arranged for her. All these years, she had always hoped that somehow, someone in her family had longed for her or hoped for her return. Might welcome her back.

Now, that last hope was dead. And apparently, so was she.

A tear formed its poignant sting in her eyes. She blinked it back and tossed her head.

Well, then, that was how the game was to be played.

"I have never been near the Irish Sea, and I am quite

certain I have never drowned. It should be obvious to you, sir, that Lady Juliette Dalworthy is dead to all who might have cared."

His eyes held a strange look. Steel-hard, yet— Could it be said that steel could soften?

"Odd, though," he said, his voice suddenly quiet, "how much you resemble her."

Her mouth twisted bitterly. "It is amazing to me how much interest you show in a woman you insist has died. Perhaps you merely seek to replace the dead with the living. I have heard some people do that sort of thing. Perhaps that would be asking too much of you, but certainly some men are known to replace their old dogs when they die."

His nostrils flared minutely. "She meant little to me."

It was another little stab, yet with all the other bloodier ones he had given her, she hardly felt it. What had she expected of him, anyway? She had known he hadn't cared. He hadn't even liked her. If he had felt anything at all, it was surely no more than pale distaste.

She tightened her jaw and stiffened her spine, setting herself ramrod-straight and steel-hard. "Then perhaps that is the problem, sir. But as she meant little to you, and I certainly do not have any importance to you, then you really have no reason for your concern."

"I was to marry her."

"Marry a woman for whom you felt so little?"

"It was my duty. I knew her too little to have affection for her."

"You are of course a man who always does his duty."

That piercing gaze made her want to crawl beneath a stone and hide, the way it had years before.

"Always."

The lump in her throat hardened. He had never shed a tear for her. He was such a bastion of propriety. He had probably been glad to believe he no longer had any connection to the scandalous Dalworthys.

He had not changed. This was still the man who had so coldly left her in her brother's study. His anger had turned from icy cold to flesh-searing hot, but it was the same terrifying heartlessness. His words came back to her, as clearly as they had been that humiliating night.

"She might be as lovely as Helen of Troy, and I assure you she is not, but I have no use for tainted beauty."

The stiffness she had forced into her spine began to fail her as she remembered the pain of that moment. When he had found her, she had thought him her knight in shining armor, rescuing her from rape by the man who had stolen her from her home to force a marriage. He had come to save her. She had even excused his anger as she had ridden beside the sullen man for several hours, the curricle bouncing carelessly in and out of ruts, racing through the night to return her home before dawn. Until that very moment, she had hoped, still allowed herself to believe he had come for her. She had not understood his only purpose was in covering up the scandal.

But in that single brutal moment, the truth had hit her like a vicious slap. He had not come for her sake at all. He had not believed her. He had thought her as guilty as the man who had stolen her away. No, he had merely come to save her brother's honor. And his own. For never had the Edenstorm name been sullied.

"Fortunately for you and me, Harlton, the embarrassment has been concealed. But I suggest you announce her engagement to Kirkwood immediately."

With that one statement he had sealed her fate, condemned her, whether he knew it or not, to die. And for that, Jane would never forgive him.

As if her forgiveness meant anything to him.

Her heart turned to stone as she relived those horrible moments. They were alike, Edenstorm and Cyril. Appearances were everything. Truth mattered not. She doubted, in fact, if either of them actually recognized that truth and appearance were not always the same thing. Likely, Edenstorm would rejoice as much as Cyril in seeing her locked away with the lunatics.

In fact, that was probably why he was here. To assure himself she did not create some inconvenient embarrassment for him.

Jane's breathing grew long, hard and even to replace the ragged pace that had been driven by her frantic heart. She felt the last of everything that was Juliette Dalworthy draining away from her. From now on, she would be fully and forever plain Miss Jane Darrow. Never again would she care. About any of them.

"I should be surprised to learn, Lord Edenstorm," she said, "if you ever felt anything for anyone. Perhaps it has not occurred to you that your intended, Lady Juliette, might have thought you the coldest, most soulless man she had ever met and would have preferred the frigid depths of the Irish Sea to marriage to you."

She saw the gleaming fire in his eyes go out as ice froze it over. The old chill ran through her spine. So he was the same man after all.

"Then, Miss Darrow, if that is the way you wish it, so shall it be. But if it is my silence you want, you will earn it."

"How?"

"Who is Guinea Jack?"

Her blood ran cold.

Chapter Four

Jane's hands clenched into fists so tight they hurt and she had to force them to uncurl. What did he want? How could he possibly know—or care—about Guinea Jack? Whatever it was, it couldn't be good, but it wouldn't help to show her fear.

"I do not think I know anyone by that name, sir."

"Don't toy with me. The man's a smuggler. I'll wager every man, woman and child in Looe and the surrounding countryside knows who he is, including you."

"You, a Preventive? I can hardly believe a man of your position would stoop to such employment."

"I'm looking for a traitor. Thousands of British soldiers are dying in a war, and this Guinea Jack helps fuel it, running gold to France so Napoleon can pay his troops. He is growing rich off the blood of English lads, and I intend to stop him."

"I cannot believe it. Cornishmen fight in the war, too. They are as loyal as Englishmen."

"They do not even think of themselves as English. They speak of us as foreigners. They even introduce us as the gentlemen from England."

"Nonsense. We are simply isolated here. It is a rare thing to see an Englishman so far across the Tamar, especially in such a remote place as Looe. Life is harsh here, Lord Edenstorm, and if Cornishmen indulge in fair trade, 'tis only what they do to survive."

"So you are one of them?"

"You know nothing of me or who I am, Lord Edenstorm."

"Indeed," he said, his lip rising in a curl. "Well then, Miss

Jane Darrow, I shall give you three days to decide your loyalties. Thank you for the offer of tea, but I shall be going."

His bow was mocking. He pivoted with military precision and the heels of his boots clipped a sharp cadence as he marched out of the parlour.

Almost before the door shut behind him, Jane ran up the stairs to the window in the upper parlor and watched as he leapt up into his carriage. The ribbons cracked and the brown cob sprang into a trot, and she watched until the last flash of color from the whisky's yellow spokes disappeared behind the trees.

She could hope she had seen the last of him, or maybe that it was all just one of those rare dreams she had when everything went wrong, and she would suddenly wake up feeling foolish.

Or she might hope that angels would swoop down and carry her off to be Princess of the Nile, too, and it would be no more unlikely.

She plopped herself onto the ancient sofa close to the chimneypiece and dropped her face into her hands. What was she going to do now?

If she didn't give him what he wanted, he would tell Cyril where she was. It was nearly three months until her twenty-first birthday, when Cyril could no longer have any legal hold over her. This time, no matter how much Lady Launceston believed she could protect her, Jane would not escape. Cyril would never forgive her, nor let her humiliation be exposed and endanger his political goals. This time he would see her locked up where no one would ever find her again.

No one could stop him. And she would die.

She had been taken to Bedlam as a girl. The smell of the filth lingered in her nostrils even today. The screams of torment and the echoing laughter of those who had come to ridicule the poor creatures clanged like bells in her memory. Jane had tried to hide behind her governess's skirts. But that was why Miss Whittle had brought her there, to show her what happened to girls like her who behaved badly.

One young woman, Jane would never forget. Jane could see her even now, the way she sat on the floor, slumped against a wall, her garments disheveled and torn, her head bowed, unmoving. Someone kicked her. She never moved. Jane could see what she thought were long lash marks on the woman's exposed arm. Miss Whittle told her most of them died. Jane knew in her heart it was true. Even now the terror shook her to her bones.

Hopelessness. That was what killed them. Jane had known it then, even though she was only a child. Jane was not strong. It would kill her, too. She had been such a good girl after that, for the longest time.

Jane jumped up from the chair and scrambled back to the window. She mustn't give up now.

She had to make a plan. Jane always had a plan. She had escaped from Dalworthy Hall, right under Cyril's nose, because she had dared to do it. Surely she could get out of here before Edenstorm could stop her.

No. Again she dropped her face into her hands. That wouldn't work. Then Edenstorm would just tell Cyril, and Cyril would find it easy to hunt her down because she had no one else to hide her. But if she told Edenstorm what he wanted to know, everyone in Looe would suffer. And even if he didn't tell, he still might find out about the *Nightwind*.

Edenstorm's very curiosity could get him killed. She didn't know of any such happenings around here, but who knew what ordinary country folk would do when their necks were threatened? She might not like Edenstorm, but she didn't want him dead.

All right, then. Where was the middle ground? She went back to the sofa, but instead of sitting, returned to pacing. Nothing came to her.

All right. Something would come to her. She just had to keep busy until then.

She left the little upper parlour and ascended another flight of stairs to Lydia's chamber, where she found Lady Launceston quietly stitching her needlepoint. For a question, Jane raised an eyebrow, and the elderly lady smiled and nodded, holding a finger to her lips. Jane nodded back, closed the door and rounded the turn in the corridor that led to the stairs and her own bedchamber.

Jane had always thought this was the best room in the house, although both Lady Launceston and Lydia scolded her for it and worried that she might catch cold. She could have chosen another more comfortable one, but this one suited her most.

It was in the oldest part of the house. Occasionally the stucco on the walls crumbled a bit, and the casement windows were quite small. Sometimes it was chilly, but this old manor was cold everywhere in winter. But the room made Jane feel like a princess in a tower.

On a clear day, she could swing open the diamond-paned window. And far out to sea, she could watch the Plymouth-bound merchantmen, or the frigates sailing off to the war in Portugal. Now she saw the first line of the storm she had seen at dawn was coming upon them, and they were soon to be drenched.

She hoped Edenstorm was out when it struck. Give him his first taste of a good Cornish blow.

She picked up a book. *The Mysteries of Udolpho*, and sat down to read. She had read it many times and probably would read it many more, for she loved Mrs. Radcliffe's novels with their dark mystery and marvelous villains. She had been meaning to read it to Lydia and Lady Launceston on a day just like this.

She did not get past the first page before she realized she was not reading at all.

She went back to the window and watched the blow roll in.

But something called to her, nagged at her mind. Demanded its due. Jane picked up a piece of foolscap and a stick of charcoal. As if it commanded her, a single line slashed from her hand to the paper, a hauntingly sensuous line that curved back and forth down the paper. As it appeared she knew it for what it was: the curve of a man's muscled back, undulating from the neck, along the shoulder, then down, curving inward to form a waist, out again to outline one hard, round buttock. It screamed virility. Blatantly sexual. Instantly, the next stroke filled her mind, a sweeping curve to form the muscled shoulder and biceps.

And the next, that would mark the enticing indentation along the spine. Her fingers ached to draw it.

No, to touch it. To trace her fingers down its length.

The most dangerous man in the world. Her heart pounded like a drum roll at an execution.

She leapt up and dashed across the chamber to bury the paper at the bottom of her stack of drawings.

Deliberately slowing her steps, Jane carefully returned to the window seat and sketched glowering clouds and gulls swarming inland on the back of a ruined letter. But clouds and gulls could do nothing to keep her frightening thoughts at bay. She set down the paper and went back to brooding.

There was only one thing she could think of doing. Deceive him. Send him in a different direction from the one that would betray her friends.

But why would he suddenly believe her? He had already made it clear he didn't believe a word she said. Unless of course she let him think she was lying. When she wasn't.

Outside Pendennen House, which Rokeby had dubbed the cottage that pretended to be a manor, rain slid down the window panes in sheets that warped the darkness behind it. It had been two nights since Edenstorm had confronted Plain Miss Jane Darrow, and the rain had poured from the sky every day since then.

Across from him, Rokeby settled into one of the wing-backed chairs flanking the fireplace and sipped his brandy. "I do believe this is the smallest house I've ever lived in, Edenstorm."

Edenstorm snorted back. "You should try a tent sometime."

"Rather not. Don't care for discomforting myself if it can be avoided."

Edenstorm peered over the rim of his glass as he sipped. That did not surprise him. Rokeby had been his friend since they'd met at Eton as very young boys away from home for the first time. Both of them had been frightened, but only Rokeby had let it show, and that had laid him open for rough treatment by some of the older boys. But he'd grown up a strong man despite it, and never lost the touch of gentleness that made him such a valuable friend. He could never have survived a siege like Rodrigo. It would have destroyed him to see his cherished friends blown apart.

"It's small, true," Edenstorm replied. "But it was the only place available on such short notice, and it's furnished. And we don't have to worry about servants to watch where we go at night."

He let his eyes wander to the fireplace mantle and the wall above it that held a collection of old swords and armor a museum would envy. "And we'll be well fixed in the event of a swordfight."

"Not planning on one. Are you? When's the last time you were in a swordfight, Edenstorm?"

"Salamanca, I'd say. Make that 22nd July, last year. None since then."

He watched Rokeby's Adam's apple bulge beneath his cravat as it rose, then slowly descended. "I suppose you killed the fellow."

"Which one? Well, it doesn't matter, does it, since I am still here?"

"By damn, you are a cold one."

Yes. He was. "A good thing. Or I'd be dead."

He was being obtuse, knowing it confounded his friend. It was unfair, and he knew it. Yet somehow he seemed compelled to push Rokeby back a step or two, now and then. Right about now, Rokeby would give a harumph and change the subject.

As if on cue, Rokeby cleared his throat and set down his brandy. "You're sure it's her, then?"

Edenstorm didn't glance up. For a subject change, it was not much of an improvement. "Without a doubt."

"But you could be wrong. It is four years, and surely Lady Juliette would have changed somewhat. You said yourself she does not look entirely the same."

"Some things cannot be concealed. It would be odd if both ladies had a mole where the right ear meets the face."

"What are you going to do, then?" Rokeby asked in a hushed tone.

"We'll see," he responded, equally as quietly.

"Surely her family would want to know."

Edenstorm leaned back and rubbed his thumb along his chin. "I'm not so sure. Likely, they conspired with Lady Beck to seclude her here. If I recall, Lord and Lady Beck lived near Dalworthy Hall in Kent. Perhaps she was taken into confidence and a way found to send the troublesome sister into seclusion. Yet if that is so, then why is Lady Juliette afraid? It makes little sense."

Rokeby fingered the stem of his snifter. "Or perhaps they would like to know in ways we cannot imagine."

"Likely, Harlton put it out that she was dead to cover the scandal. She would make quite a stir if she suddenly reappeared. Harlton would not like being made out a liar. Think of what the whole thing would do to his political aspirations."

"Hmm," said Rokeby. "I hear he sees himself as the next prime minister. He's not well liked, but he's powerful, and that's what counts."

"And it is most definitely Harlton she fears."

They drank their brandy in silence. Edenstorm supposed he ought to feel glad for the rain since he had a snug place to avoid it, but somehow it seemed wrong to be dry and safe. In the same sort of way, he missed Eden's Vale and his family, but it didn't feel right to be there. Robert was the firstborn. He should have lived and been the one to inherit Eden's Vale and the title. Edenstorm had difficulty even thinking of himself as an earl. He was the second son, and like many a younger son had always seen himself as a soldier, an officer, accustomed to sharing the hardship of war with his men. This wasn't the way things were supposed to be.

Finally the rain ceased. Edenstorm had been standing by the window, thinking the evening a loss. But the clouds cleared away, leaving behind a sparkling black sky with a half moon rising. He trained his spyglass along the horizon.

"No more rain for tonight," he announced. "Let's go."

Rokeby groaned. "I was looking forward to a quiet night for a change."

Silence returned as they donned their greatcoats and the floppy woolen Cornish hats. With their lone lantern, they slipped out the door and headed up to the top of the steep hill. Soon they were walking across slippery grass, onto the rough, rocky slope near the cliff to their usual crevice, a sheltered spot that hid them from curious eyes.

The slide of brass against brass hissed as the spyglasses expanded to full length.

Edenstorm followed the horizon with his spyglass, but saw nothing but more darkness. The moon had advanced in the sky and risen above the highest lines of clouds, but it did not brighten things all that much, for the sea still merged into inky darkness, too dark to tell where sky ended and sea began.

"Why not simply leave well enough alone, then?"

"Because she can also be of assistance in this endeavor."

Rokeby frowned. "This is dangerous business. I am not at all sure we should involve a woman."

"This woman ruined herself years ago. She's no sweet, innocent lady."

"But she has been leading an exemplary life since then. Don't you think you should give credit where it is due?"

"She is as deceitful as a woman can be. Who knows what she has really been doing all this time?"

"Then that would make both Lady Beck and Lady Launceston either liars or incredibly stupid. Why would they take in a woman of doubtful reputation?"

"All I want from her is information, Rokeby," Edenstorm replied with a growl. "I'm not planning on turning her over to the hangman."

For hours they sat in the narrow niche in the rocks. For hours nothing happened, except that the air grew steadily colder. It was often that way after a storm. His years in the Peninsula had taught him that.

The opportunity they sought could only occur within a few days. The moon was waxing, on its way to full, but not so bright that a man, honest or dishonest, might find his way around with ease. Such a night might please a smuggler more than one so bright everyone could see his business.

"Cold out here," said Rokeby.

Edenstorm nodded. Rokeby said that every time.

Edenstorm had spent many a night in the Peninsula on colder ground, with an icy wind whipping up wild rain. But Rokeby was not a soldier and not used to such things.

Something to his left caught his eye, and he swung the scope toward it. But then before the spyglass reached the something, it was gone.

"Did you see that?"

"No. What?"

Perhaps he had imagined it or it was an illusion created by his eyes as they continued to adapt to the darkness. Rubbing his gloved fist over the annoying stubble forming on his chin, he frowned and arced the telescope back to the distant horizon of the sea.

No— There it was again. Something lightened then once again became dark as everything around it. But he knew where, now, and focused on the spot. And waited.

"There. See it?"

"A flash. A reflection, I think," said Rokeby. "Someone lit a candle. Or pulled back a drapery."

"Maybe." But draperies of any sort in a cottage would be rare. He waited, concentrating on the place where a small cottage with peeling white-wash clung to a precarious existence near the inlet. He knew that cottage. It would be a prime place for smugglers. No one lived in it these days.

"Watch the sea, Rokeby. I'll watch the shore."

"I am. There. A blink. No more than two miles out, I'd say. Near the island."

The temptation to turn to hunt for the ship tugged so hard, Edenstorm almost couldn't resist it, but, gritting his teeth, he kept his focus on the cottage.

"Three blinks together." Almost so quick he could have missed them. In fact he realized he wasn't meant to see anything, but the senders apparently did not know the faint light reflected off the white-washed wall of the cottage to seaward of the abandoned one.

"A delivery tonight, then," said Rokeby in a whisper that held the excitement of a soldier preparing for an attack. "Shall we go?"

"Let's go. But I doubt we'll learn anything."

"Why not?"

"It's a signal. A code that tells the ship where to land. Or more likely where to go to meet the boats. But we don't know the code, so we don't know where that is. They'll probably row out to meet it, then bring their booty ashore. Wherever it goes, it won't be in the middle of West Looe."

Edenstorm collapsed the spyglass with a singing snap. Pulling the floppy woolen cap down over his forehead, he frowned and started for the path that led back to Pendennen house, then quietly down the lane that led into East Looe.

They'd have to move stealthily because anyone else they found out at this hour would be one of those fellows known euphemistically as Free Traders. The Gentlemen of the Seas.

The pirate drew his sword and advanced across the deck toward her, his silver eyes gleaming. Her heart beating rapidly, she pushed the whimpering child behind her and lifted her chin as high as it could go. The evil-eyed pirate came within inches of her, his vicious grin widening, and he laughed, a wicked, horrible laugh that boomed like thunder, and she trembled. He lifted the sword until its tip reached her throat.

"Give him to me, me lady, or I'll tell the world who ye are..."

She came awake to the hissing of a voice and the tiny pinpoints of light from a tin lantern.

"Miss!"

Jane scowled against the light that hurt her eyes and looked up to see Annie, the scullion. Or smelled her rancid breath, more like.

"Miss! 'Tis the *Nightwind.*"

"Tonight? But it's too early."

"No, Miss. 'Tis come tonight. You got to go, miss. They're dependin' on ye."

Jane groaned. She'd hardly fallen asleep before dreams of the savage silver-eyed pirate had begun to taunt her. She pushed herself up and sat on the edge of the bed. Rising, she stumbled to the clothespress and pulled the brown fustian dress from the bottom of the stack, and her thickest wool stockings, for the night was cold.

"I've left ye a lantern in the passage, miss. I'll be going t' cove now. Got to meet a genn'lman, ye know." With a smile that betrayed one over-long front tooth, Annie gave a buoyant curtsy and disappeared out the door.

Jane pulled on her warm stockings, then her dress and tied the ties, then, groaning, bent over and pulled on her half boots. She reached to the bottom of the pile in the clothespress and eased out a dark shawl that was much like one Annie would wear. It was nearly threadbare and provided little warmth, and she already shivered with the chilly night air. With a sigh, she chose instead her gray one because it was warm. No one would see her, and it did not look all that different in the dark.

As quietly as Annie, she slipped out of the chamber and down the corridor to the servants' stairs. Old though the house was, not a board creaked to betray her as she descended two flights of stairs and walked the long way around to the servants' courtyard to the kitchen wing and down the corridor to a weathered old door with long iron traces. On any other day, it would have appeared blocked and unused, but tonight light shone through cracks in the wood.

Jane pushed, and the door swung in silence, as well oiled as the doors to Lydia's parlour. There, on the top step of a stone staircase that descended into darkness, sat the promised tin lantern, three sides shuttered, the fourth showing mere pinholes of light. She could lift the shade when more light was needed, but Jane had become accustomed to the darkness and kept it closed to protect the candle's flame from any breeze.

Counting the stairs as she descended gave her an odd feeling of security, until she reached the tunnel. For what seemed hours, yet was barely minutes, she walked along the tunnel and she came out in the light of a waxing moon sliding in and out of long clouds that striped the night sky. She was past the village now, among the rocky country paths and stunted coastal oaks and heather.

She pulled the shawl over her head to cover her hair and pinched it tight at her chin for warmth. The path squished with mud. Ahead, tiny pin-pricks of light shone from other lanterns and cast long, faint shadows of other walkers. She joined them in silence, and they plodded along the path.

Closer to the cliffs, they met the first ponies climbing up the slopes to the lane, pulling carts heavily laden with ankers of brandy and crates of goods.

The walkers descended the hill around the bluff and came upon the little cove where the waxing moon struck the sand with silver light. A huge lugger, sails furled, tossed beyond the rough surf, and smaller boats were pulled up on the sand.

"Evenin', darlin'."

"You're back," she said, managing a smile, for Davy was a man to be smiled at by everyone, even when the night was cold and one wished to be in a warm bed, sound asleep.

"Aye. Most of the time, I come back." He grinned. "I've got a petticoat for ye."

She stifled a grumble as she watched him riffle through the oilcloth-covered bundles and remove one that was flatter than the bundles of tobacco above it. He slid his knife beneath the cord and unwrapped the heavy cloth, revealing a plain muslin petticoat and several small, flat packets wrapped in muslin.

Jane let out a resigned sigh. She pulled out the needle and thread she always brought and sat down on a rock to baste the muslin packets onto the petticoat, a task so well-practiced she watched the men and ponies trudge up the steep slope into the darkness. Within an hour, the last keg and bundle would be gone, and before dawn all would be tucked away in secluded caverns, cellars and perhaps even buried in the sand. She remembered the old church near Angston they had used. It had collapsed from the weight of too many ankers placed on one side of the foundation.

She grimaced as she sewed, thinking of the way the packets would chafe against her legs on the journey home. Once, she had tried pinning the packets to the skirt to save herself some time, but that had been a disaster. The pins had pricked her legs all the way back, and some of the packets had worked loose and dropped to the road. Fortunately, riding officers never troubled the people of Looe these days. Nobody challenged the Free Traders of Looe. Except Edenstorm.

Once the last packet was sewn into place, she stood, turned away from the group of men and lifted her skirt to step into the petticoat. She tied it about her waist, then turned back, whining to herself at the sudden largeness of her shadow.

"I'm not going to do this anymore, Davy," she said.

"Don't go saying names, darlin'. The wind carries them to distant ears. And 'tis not for me to say, ye know that."

"It's getting too dangerous."

Davy laughed. "'Tis no more dangerous than it always was. I've got to meet my contracts, ye know. Would ye be knowing something I don't?"

Jane stiffened, her throat tightening. Yes, it was worse now. But she dared not say a single word more or she would be pointing a finger directly at Edenstorm. No matter how much he threatened her, she could not be the cause of harm to him. Yet if she didn't warn Davy, he could be caught in Edenstorm's trap. And if Edenstorm caught her here in the moonlight, it would be the last she saw of daylight.

"It's just frightening," she responded, looking down at her bulbous skirt.

Davy's grin danced across his face. "There's a way, ye know. Ye've only got to marry me, and ye'll never lift your skirt to the moonlight again."

She wondered if he ever feared anything. "Maybe I won't do either one."

"Aye, ye will. Ye know ye're needed. Don't forget your lantern, darlin'."

As if she would. Jane sighed as she tugged her shawl tighter about her shoulders. She climbed the trail up the hill from the inlet to the road. Other women, already on the road, trudged silently along, walking back to places about which Jane did not wish to know. Beside her, Annie grinned, showing her long tooth. Jane pulled her shawl over her head as protection against the morning air and to hide her from the first rays of dawn that would soon break over the hill.

Edenstorm frowned and adjusted the scope to get a clearer focus. The faces were hidden in darkness. The bodies too large. What was it?

"Deuce."

He hissed the word into the silent air and extended his telescope to focus on the two women coming around the bend in the narrow lane leading back to West Looe.

Rokeby jerked to alertness. Edenstorm had been aware of his companion's dozing by the way his breath buzzed in and out like the sound of bees. Edenstorm waved him back to warn him of the need for silence and nodded toward the women.

"What?" whispered Rokeby.

Silence was as heavy as the fog in the morning air. Edenstorm watched as two heavy-set women in rough brown dresses and thick shawls climbed the road with weary steps.

"I know that shawl," he said. "It's the one I found on the cliff."

Only two days before he had held it to his face, inhaling the scent that could belong to only one woman.

"But they're too fat," Rokeby replied. "She's not a heavy woman."

"There's not a fat woman in this village, haven't you noticed? They're all thin as rails. No, it's what they have under their skirts that makes them look fat."

Rokeby grunted. "But why women?"

"It's illegal to search a woman."

"Do we follow them?" Rokeby asked.

"No. We'd be seen by anyone else coming up the hill. And they will come, you can be sure."

"What, then?"

"Go home. And go to church tomorrow."

"Church? Why?"

"To see who's sleepy."

Chapter Five

The vicar yawned for the fifth time.

Half the congregation were nodding, heads jerking suddenly back to consciousness. To his left, Rokeby appeared to be no better off. But then, Edenstorm once again reminded himself, Rokeby did not have a soldier's discipline and hardening.

He sat beside bright-eyed Lady Beck, whose arm was still in a sling, for she had cheerily invited her saviors to sit in the family pew. Her mother, Lady Launceston, beamed at the vicar as if she had no notion of her community's nighttime activities.

And all the way to the far end of the pew sat plain Miss Jane Darrow, who was neither Jane Darrow, nor plain with her face so drawn in tension she couldn't have nodded off if she'd been kept awake for the past week of nights. But he'd willingly wager the sum of his great-aunt's dowry that she'd like to.

Edenstorm felt like laughing, although he had never in his life done such an improper thing as to laugh out loud in church. But it did amuse him to think that the very delectable Plain Miss Jane Darrow was not only distraught, but about to become more so.

The vicar's sermon was mercifully brief, likely because of his own suffering. Soon the congregation flowed out through the Gothic pointed doors into the bright sunshine. Wary villagers eyed the two foreigners as they tipped their freshly donned hats or curtseyed to Lady Launceston and Lady Beck, who chatted back like happily singing birds. Miss Darrow looked more like a downed pheasant that wished simply to curl up and become pleasantly deceased.

Lady Beck beamed at him like warm sunshine. “I am so pleased you joined us this morning, Lord Edenstorm,” she said.

He nodded politely. At least one of the ladies thought him worthy of a smile. Lady Juliette—Miss Darrow—looked like someone had pinched her face at her nose and drawn it in like wadded fabric. Edenstorm made the extra effort to provide a nod and smile to Lady Launceston who beamed back at him even brighter than her daughter. He’d always liked older ladies. So much less trouble, and pleasant to everyone.

“I am pleased you have recovered so well, madam. I trust your arm is healing?”

“Oh yes, Mr. Saunders tells me it should heal quite straight. I cannot tell you how fortunate I feel, Lord Edenstorm. Though I daresay I shall not be watching birds for awhile. Mr. Saunders will not allow me to take any chances until it has healed.”

“Certainly. I suppose you will not be riding.”

She sighed. “He has expressly forbidden it. And this is such wonderful country for traipsing about on horseback. Jane and I have had so many lovely rides into the country. Have you been into the moors yet?”

A wicked idea sparked in his mind. “Just what I had in mind. But I suppose now I shall have to ask Miss Darrow to join me instead.” He slid a glance sideways to Miss Darrow and watched the sleepy eyes pop wide as her mouth dropped open. That should wake her up for a bit.

“But perhaps later,” he said. “You look a bit tired, Miss Darrow. Perhaps too many late nights, worrying about your lady. Or whatever it is you worry about.”

He watched her jaw quiver as if she couldn’t find words, and he squelched a wicked grin. Let her wonder about how much he knew.

“Oh, yes,” she replied. Her words had a funny drag to them. “I suppose you are right. Now that Lady Beck is getting about, I am much relieved. Of course I still have my responsibilities, so I’m afraid I would have to decline.”

Lady Beck shook her head. “Oh, Jane, you enjoy riding so much. I would not wish for you to miss the wonderful fresh air simply because I cannot go. Someone must show the gentlemen about, don't you think? Perhaps tomorrow would be a good day to ride if it does not rain."

Miss Darrow's mouth clamped down tight as she stared at her employer. Then she glared at him. It warmed that wicked place in his heart that enjoyed watching her get what she deserved. "Well, then, tomorrow, Miss Darrow? If it does not rain, of course?"

"Very well, sir," she grumbled. "If it does not rain."

"I'm sure that will be fine," said Lady Beck. "We do not ride on Sundays, and Jane likes to spend her Sunday afternoons drawing, so she would not wish to go today."

"She has a fine talent for catching detail," Edenstorm added, and all but had to suck in his cheeks to keep from laughing as the color rose in her face. "What will you be drawing today, Miss Darrow?"

Her eyes narrowed fiercely. "Perhaps I shall sketch you, my lord. Perhaps I shall make an attempt to catch you as you really are."

He gathered from the glare, she meant with horns.

"Unfortunately," she continued, "I lost my pencil. I don't suppose you found one with the sketchbook."

"No." He frowned. "Why?"

"It wasn't important." But he could see the hopeful look fade to disappointment in the slight downturn of a mouth that was meant to show nothing at all.

His frown deepened. From the looks of her sketchbook, drawing was a passion with her. Yet he did not remember her as anything more than a flighty young girl who was overly enamored with herself.

The memory flashed back to him like a picture.

She was Lady Juliette; she was a haughty flirt.

He had come to Harlton Hall, knowing he must make a marriage to please his father and brother. He was like a walking skeleton, moving almost dreamlike in a world that didn't fit, as awkward as the remnants of war he still wore on his gaunt frame.

He stared dumbly as the saucy green eyes assessed and shredded him. With a toss of her head, she flung her elegant, brilliantly colored cashmere shawl over her shoulders and walked away.

Merritt stared dumbly. Just stared. Oddly moved, yet too numb. Just as oddly, struck dumb.

And the next day, she had run off with Kirkwood. To be more exact, had slipped though the kitchen door in the middle of the night. He wondered how he could blame her. Yet he did.

He snapped back to reality. "Why do you care?" he asked, and too late tried to stop the growl in his tone. "Get another one."

She winced as if he had slapped her. "Of course." She pulled together a bare smile that all but bared her teeth. "Well, I thank you for my sketchbook. It would have been ruined in the rain that night."

What the hell? It was as if she had sliced his skin with ice. He frowned, but managed a polite nod as she turned away. Could a damned pencil be that important?

"Jane's pencils are expensive, Lord Edenstorm," said Lady Beck. And they come from France, so of course they are impossible to find now."

"A pencil is expensive?"

Miss Darrow tossed her head in exactly the same haughty way as the Juliette he had known in that faraway life. "It was a Conté. All pencils are expensive for some people, my lord. Contés are even more so. But you need not concern yourself. I shall contrive."

Edenstorm resisted a sneer and considered suggesting she just ask her friend Guinea Jack to pick up one on his next shopping trip, but he decided that bordered on being cruel.

He caught her gaze and forced her to hold it. Oh, yes, this was Juliette. Did she think he would have forgotten the fine curve of her cheek? Or that by pulling her hair back so extremely she could disguise its luster and curl?

But there was something else, and he began to feel his gut twist in a way he didn't like.

Something in her eyes.

No, was not something in her eyes, but something in the way she didn't look at him—the way she focused at nothing at all.

It was pain. If he understood anything, it was pain. Something he had said had hurt.

Over a pencil? Hell. How was a man to cope with a woman, anyway?

"Lord Edenstorm?"

He was jolted out of his strange reverie. It was Lady Beck trying to retrieve his attention. Edenstorm grimaced as he hunted up a properly polite smile to hide his wandering thoughts.

"Come, Lord Edenstorm, Mr. Rokeby," said Lady Beck, and she took his arm to pull him in the direction of other worthies of the community, where she began to introduce them.

Edenstorm scolded himself for his childish desire to needle Miss Darrow and did his best to pay proper attention to the introductions.

"Yes, my lord," said a man introduced as Mr. Jack Tremayne, an MP Edenstorm had met a few years before. "Time ye came back, to be sure. 'Twas all the talk in Town. Such a tragedy for your poor mother, losing all her kin at once, and ye being gone."

Edenstorm nodded, frowning. "It was, indeed," he replied. "I regret that I could not be with her to console her."

He saw Miss Darrow's eyebrows rise. Yet she had to know he could not have inherited the title unless both his father and older brother had died. But perhaps a bit more explanation was needed.

"My younger brother's loss at Albuera was an unexpected tragedy," he added. "And my father's death was most unexpected." From the corner of his eye, he noted that the lady was putting the pieces of the puzzle in order.

"And what'd ye be finding so interesting about Cornwall, me lord?" asked Tremayne.

"Investments."

Miss Darrow blinked sharply.

"And a bit of touring. It's the thing, you know, to tour England these days. A man can't see the Continent the way our fathers did. So I thought I'd see what I can of England and look for opportunities while I'm wandering about. Cornwall being so full of enterprising men like Trevethick, it seemed a good place to look."

"Ah, ye'd be thinking about the mines, then. Copper's good, nowadays. Tin, of course."

"Maybe. Or perhaps something more speculative."

He hoped Miss Darrow didn't swallow her tongue.

Lady Beck cleared her throat daintily. "You know, Mr. Tremayne, it was Lord Edenstorm and his friend Mr. Rokeby who rescued me when Jane and I went bird-watching and I fell from the cliff."

"On the contrary, Lady Beck, it was Miss Darrow who came first to your aid," Edenstorm said. "I merely assisted. It was quite brave of her, climbing down the cliff that way."

"To be sure," replied Tremayne. "But ye ought not to be down on the sand, with the sea being so high. 'Tis dangerous, this time of year. What would ye be doing there, sir?"

Damn. He didn't want to explain that. It might have been all right before, even good for their mission to look like inane idiots, but not if it became known two ladies had spied upon them with their telescope.

"Seashells," said Miss Darrow, all but shoving the word into the conversation. She was deliberately avoiding his gaze. "I believe Lord Edenstorm has an interest in seashells."

"Seashells?" Tremayne frowned. "My word. What would ye be wanting with seashells?"

"Cocklewinks, actually," he replied. Now he saw why she avoided his eyes, for if they dared to share a glance, they would both burst out laughing. "They're quite rare. Small, hard to see. More common in the Mediterranean, but can't go there these days."

Tremayne's eyes widened as he rubbed his hand against his chin.

"Collected shells as a boy," Edenstorm added. "Always wanted a cocklewink, but never found one. Best time to get them is after a storm, with a high sea."

Miss Darrow covered her mouth with her hand, but she made not a sound.

Fortunately, Lady Beck smiled her continuously sunshiny smile and offered up a small dinner party to help the visitors become acquainted with the finer folk of the neighborhood, to which, quite naturally, all of them agreed. But Mrs. Tremayne thought Lady Beck ought to rest up a bit first, and offered her own house instead.

God. He hated dinner parties. Well, it would be a good time to listen. No telling what one might learn. So he resigned himself to the boredom. He gave a final nod to the ladies, squared his top hat on his head.

As he and Rokeby started toward the horses, he saw a young man in a starkly somber brown coat standing at a distance near the low wall surrounding the churchyard. It was the man she had drawn, the one with sharp features who seemed to be laughing back at the artist. But this man wasn't laughing. His dark eyes bore down fiercely on Edenstorm.

Edenstorm's senses snapped to attention. His nostrils flared, catching the scent of coming battle. A scent he would recognize for the rest of his life.

The air hung thick with it.

It was as if the air exploded. Jane gasped. It was the last thing she wanted, for these two men to meet, but there was not one thing she could do about it. Then, as smooth as a glassy sea at sunset, Edenstorm's gaze slid past Davy and he kept on walking. Davy Polruhan shoved himself away from the stone wall around the church where he had been leaning.

"Morning to ye, ladies," said Davy, but a hardness tarnished his customary wide grin. "'Tis a beautiful Sunday morning the Lord has given us."

All the ladies returned their best Sunday smiles and walked toward the lane up the hill. Davy took Jane's arm on his without her asking, the way he always did.

Her jaw tightened. She adored him in a friendly sort of way, which was not surprising, for everyone loved Davy Polruhan. She supposed he would make a good husband, as Lydia so often said. She admired his energetic nature and cheerful approach to life. Any wife he took would have his protection forever. But even if she wanted to, she would not marry him and dared not tell him why. The guilt of it twisted inside her, yet she bristled at his assumption that it was only a matter of time before she gave in to his continuous proposal of marriage.

"Who is he, darlin'?" said Davy. The jovial tone of his voice had the edge of broken glass to it.

Jane felt her back stiffen. The last thing she wanted was for the two of them to meet. Everything about him was a warm as Edenstorm was cold. The air between the two of them had sparked to fire the very moment their eyes had met.

"Oh, that is Lord Edenstorm," she said, tossing it off as unimportant. "He is the one who saved Lady Beck on the cliff, you know. So of course she would want him to join us in church."

"'Tis ye he seems to be looking at, darlin'. Who is he to stare at ye like that?"

"He was a friend of my brother's, I believe."

Davy frowned, "Your brother? Ye've never mentioned a brother before. I thought ye had no family."

That cold chill chased up her spine again. That was a bad slip, and she'd better not let it happen again. Davy was too quick. "Not anymore."

"Of course. Forgive me, darlin'. 'Twould be a painful thing for ye. But 'tis not the stare of a friend. Who is he to ye?"

Jane contrived a huff, but it sounded shaky. "Really, Davy, I cannot think why it is anything to you."

"If I'm intending to marry ye, 'tis something to me."

"That's your intention, Davy, not mine. I've told you I have no plans to marry."

"Would it be something wrong with me, then?" She saw the smile had returned, but it did not sparkle in his eyes.

"Only that you're marriageable."

With his laugh, his face softened. "All the same, I'm wondering what he's doing here."

"I suppose everyone does. Being an Englishman and all that. And an earl, too. Well, I have not precisely asked him, but he has mentioned investments. I suspect he merely means to have a pleasant holiday. He's quite the war hero, so Mr. Tremayne says. But he came home to take the title when his father died. He was the second son, but the older brother died before the father. And there was another brother who died in the war. They discussed that, too. Now that's all I know. I hope it satisfies you."

Davy's grin reappeared so suddenly, it was like a flash of sunlight. "'Tis enough, to be sure, when 'tis only ye I want to know about. I'm thinking I'd better come calling more often."

"Davy, really. He's an earl. He is far too important for the likes of me. I'm nothing to him."

"That's what worries me, darlin'. There's only one thing a man like him sees in a pretty woman with no family or fortune."

"Davy, you're insulting me. I'm not a schoolgirl and I do not harbor fanciful dreams."

"Aye, ye're not. But it always seems to me there's more to ye than meets the eye."

"Nonsense. My greatest fortune is that Lady Launceston and Lady Beck have been so kind as to take me in. Without them, I would have no consequence at all."

"I'm wondering, then, what would an earl be doing being friend to the brother of a lady so impoverished?"

This time her huff was genuine, but hid even more fear. "Well, my dear Mr. Polruhan, the great Lord Edenstorm was once a nothing, too, you see. Nothing more than the Honourable Mr. Merritt Winslow. Quite within my brother's touch at Eton." Jane let her nostrils flare. "It's Sunday, Mr. Polruhan. Do go home and take a rest. You must be terribly tired after your hard night's work."

"So haughty, me darlin'," he said, chuckling. "I'll be calling again tomorrow."

With that, he grabbed the marvelous black lock of hair that always fell down over his eyes and tugged it as if he were the meanest servant, when he was a man who could buy and sell Lady Beck's properties thrice over. She laughed and watched as he sauntered away, his step swinging to the tune he whistled.

He was a good man. In the daylight at least.

Edenstorm launched into Hector's saddle and turned away from the church, riding along the Looe River toward the sea.

Rokeby clucked at his horse to catch up. "Where are you going now?"

"To the cove."

Which cove he meant, Rokeby didn't question, although it might well have been the farther one where they suspected the smugglers had landed the night before. The narrow road, mostly dirt and crushed rock, rose up into the hills along the west bank of the river and as it reached the top of the hill, he caught his breath at the brilliant deep blue water. They paused, still astride, and looked out at frigates and ships of the line out of Plymouth Harbor, moving far out to sea, destined to man the blockade or transport supplies to Portugal.

"Still miss it, Edenstorm?"

He frowned at his friend. "I suppose so," he replied. How could one miss the bloody chaos of war? At least in a war something seemed to make sense, seemed to matter.

But here? He wasn't meant for this life.

They traveled the short distance to the cove, but instead of descending to the sand, they followed the road to the promontory where the women had been watching birds. Close to the cliff, near the one solitary stunted oak, they dismounted and left the horses.

He walked to the cliff and squinted, looking down at gentle waves lapping lazily against a thin band of golden sand.

"What are you looking for?" Rokeby asked.

"The pencil." He spotted a freshly broken branch of a knotty shrub and walked to it. "Lady Beck would have fallen here."

Rokeby grunted at the obvious deduction.

Edenstorm took a few steps to his left and pointed into the gorse. "I found the sketchbook there. Miss Darrow is right-handed, and the last sketch had a dark line across it, as if the pencil slipped in her hand. I doubt she could have done anything without falling over the cliff herself, but I am certain she would have tried. So if the pencil slashed across the page, then the book would have gone to the left and the pencil to the right. Therefore, we should search to the right of where Miss

Darrow was sitting. It would probably fall down the steepest part of the slope, possibly to where Lady Beck landed."

"We are going to look for a pencil? In this?" Rokeby pointed to the tangle of gorse, bracken and sea thrift.

"I am. You may join me or go find some other activity that better suits your fancy."

"How the devil are you going to spot a stick of wood in all this mess?"

Edenstorm ignored him. He studied the edge of the cliff and found a space where the gorse had been broken away. He climbed down through gray rock and green gorse with its fading yellow blossoms, sidling toward his left, until he reached the level spot where Lady Beck had landed. Now that he took the time to look, he saw how difficult that descent must have been for a woman, for the brush seemed to take up every inch of ground.

The cove was still a good twenty or more feet below. She must have been terrified to climb down a cliff face. But her devotion to Lady Beck was obvious. At least the remainder of the journey downward hadn't been so difficult.

Edenstorm looked back up the cliff to reclaim his bearings and saw Rokeby down on his knees, parting the brush as if he might find something that way. He got down on his knees, too. Nance was going to have a fit. They should at least have gone back and put on rambling clothes.

Assuming gravity had pulled the pencil downward, he concentrated on the lowest point. It could have caught anywhere above, too, but it seemed to make sense to start here. He combed through the brush at the ledge in a wide arc. Nothing. He widened his search, checking crevices where it could have gotten stuck. It could be almost entirely obscured by brush.

"Why don't you just buy her a new pencil, Edenstorm?"

"Wouldn't be the same. Besides, we probably couldn't find the right kind."

"What's so special about this kind?"

Edenstorm stopped and looked back to the top, where Rokeby was now lying face down, his long arm pawing over the edge, down into the craggy gorse.

"I don't know. I'm no artist."

Edenstorm grappled about and climbed higher. He combed his fingers through the sea pinks. Hell, this was impossible. It could be anywhere. Had it bounced and gone all the way to the surf, where the tide had carried it away? He could picture a pencil bouncing, end over end.

"Edenstorm!"

He grabbed two handfuls of gorse and leaned back so he could see Rokeby. "What?"

Above him, Rokeby sat back on his haunches, his right hand waving in the air. "This it?"

Hell. He'd wanted to find it himself. "Does it look like a pencil?"

"Piece of wood. Graphite in the middle."

Edenstorm gritted his teeth and returned to the ledge, then climbed back up, boots slipping and scuffing. By the time he reached the more or less flat top of the promontory and dusted himself off, he had become utterly disrepaired. He frowned.

"What?" said Rokeby, holding out the object of their pursuit. You want me to give it a toss and give you another go at it?"

Edenstorm grabbed the little stick of polished wood and turned it over in his hands. It looked like any other pencil to him. "Just don't know why all this fuss for a stick of wood."

"Seems to me you're the only one making a fuss."

Edenstorm sneered back.

"You're welcome."

With a snort, Edenstorm turned back to his friend. "All right. Thank you."

"Damned if you aren't the hardest man to figure out, Edenstorm."

They walked up the slope of pocked granite to the horses and mounted. He'd agree with that. He'd never figured himself out. But most of the time he didn't bother. It was a waste of time.

Did most men figure themselves out, and only he was left to puzzle over his fit with the world? Did Rokeby have himself figured out? The man was so damned ingenuous. So damned pleasant and at ease with the world. Odd traits for a man whose position in life required him to ferret out facts people didn't want others to know. But maybe that was what made his work possible.

He remained silent all the way back into West Looe.

He left Rokeby in Lady Beck's parlour and followed a footman's direction out into the garden. When the fellow started to announce him, Edenstorm waved a hand to shush him. Out in the bright sunshine, Miss Darrow sat at a small table, poring over her work as if it meant more to her than anything else in the world. He was beginning to believe it did.

For a moment, he only stood and watched her, so focused on her task that she had no sense of his presence. Yet the air between them seemed to grow thick as he moved in closer, a quiet footstep at a time, until he stood behind her and could see over her shoulder.

Of a sudden, she sat erect and turned, mouth gaping, and she threw her arms over her drawing.

"Too late," he said. "Well, you said you would draw me. But I expected to see horns."

The girl turned fiery red. "Horns?"

"As in those of the devil. Why would you be sketching me, I wonder?"

She tossed her head as if dismissing his annoying ignorance, the same haughty gesture he remembered from his first meeting of her in Harlton's drawing room. "I sketch everyone I know," she replied, her nostrils making a minute flare. "I find faces fascinating, and they are ever so much more difficult than anything else."

"Indeed? Why not draw Rokeby, then?"

She pursed her mouth and reached for the top sheet in a pile of papers and held it out, letting it dangle from her fingertips at full arm's length. "He was easy. He is who he says he is."

Edenstorm grunted as he looked over the drawing. It was Rokeby to the inch.

"You, on the other hand, are giving me quite a fit. Drawing, that is. Something about the eyes is not quite right. They are so light. Any stroke I make seems to darken them, and that is not at all the effect I need."

"Try this." He held out the Conté pencil that had consumed a good portion of their afternoon in searching.

"Oh! You found it!" Her eyes turned bright as emeralds as she took it.

"Rokeby, actually. It was in the bushes just below the cliff edge."

"But you went and looked." Her face turned suddenly solemn. "Or was it just Mr. Rokeby?"

The devilish woman utterly confused him. She got her damn pencil back, didn't she? "It wasn't where I looked," he said.

"Well." She blinked. "In that case, my thanks to both of you. Now, since you are here, I would like for you to sit on the bench for a moment and perhaps I can find out what is wrong with my drawing. Perhaps I had need of my favorite pencil."

"I have no wish to be drawn."

"Of course. But you are here, and I find that convenient, so please sit."

"I do not wish to sit."

Her brows puckered into a studious squint and the tip of her tongue breached the bounds of her lips, licking over the lower one. Edenstorm's body jolted into unexpected hardness. He stiffened and frowned. He supposed he might as well sit, so he did, his back straight as a ramrod, hands folded before him to obscure the sudden unwanted erection.

Her face contorted into a nearly hidden grin and she snickered.

"What is so funny?"

"Cocklewinks."

"Really. You started it, Miss Darrow."

Her eyebrows shot up, green eyes wide, and she let loose a girlish giggle. "That's it!" She grabbed up the pencil and began sketching furiously.

"What's it?"

"The dimple. Aha, I had not realized it, but that changes everything."

"Men do not have dimples."

"Of course they do. But I venture to say men do not see them on other men."

"Perhaps they call them something else."

She shook her head, not even looking away from her project. "They're dimples. And do not think to fool me, sir. I saw it before you could hide it. It changes everything entirely." She snatched up the ball of rubber and scrubbed at the paper. "And it makes the cheeks higher and more rounded. And the eyes just a bit more closed at the outer corners. A touch of wrinkle..."

He started to rise. "I do not have wrinkles, Miss Darrow."

"Ah, ah," she scolded and pointed imperiously to the bench. "Sit."

And for some reason he could not comprehend, he felt compelled to obey. He sat.

"Very well, then, creases. Men have manly creases in their faces. Women have wrinkles. When they are of a certain age, of course."

Edenstorm stifled a grin and sat very still, mesmerized by the swift movement of her hands and noting she used both of them, one drawing, the other erasing or smoothing or whatever she might need done. Her fingers were long and moved elegantly, like a dancer on a stage.

She smirked. A tiny, one-syllabled giggle escaped, and her eyes darted back and forth between his face and the paper. Her hand swiftly stroked a line, and she frowned, erased it and stroked again, a slow, soft, doting touch to the paper.

She sat back, and a small smile crept onto her face. "There," she said, hands on hips. "That will do it."

Edenstorm began a slow rise to his feet and was almost surprised not to be ordered back to the bench. He almost made it to the table before she turned it face down on the pile of papers.

"What's in the pile?" he asked.

"Mistakes, mostly. But a few good ones." She gathered up her tools and reached for the papers.

"May I see it?"

The wariness of a doe about to be shot seeped into her eyes. Not taking her eyes off him, she peeled the top page off the pile and held it out.

He took the foolscap in his hand and stared at the image on the page. His gut twisted into a sudden knot, and an unfamiliar lump caught in his throat and began to swell. This was not him. It was a pirate, a wild man, a warrior, a creature reeking with danger, yet there was a gleam in the eye that said mischief, joy, something that was not him. It tore at something deep inside him, something he wanted. Something he hated. He knew this man—had known him, once. But he had been dead for more years than Edenstorm could remember.

And besides, he had no dimple. Frowning, he shoved it back at her. But that knowing gleam in her eye dug deep down inside him. He turned away before she could burrow deeper.

"What about your mistakes?" he asked as they walked back along the stone-laid path through the garden toward the house. "Do you erase them?"

She shook her head. "Little errors I can correct, but the rubber is more costly than paper. But not to worry, sir. I try to make my mistakes on already ruined paper first, before I move on to anything better. Poor Lydia—Lady Beck—is never allowed to throw out so much as a scrap of letter paper until every corner of it has been used up."

"Do you paint, too?"

"No."

"Too expensive?"

"And I have no training, only some in watercolor. But perhaps someday I shall teach myself."

"And I suppose even watercolors are too expensive."

Only a tilt of her lips answered him. It was a tilt he remembered, the barest curve upward at the corner. A funny ache grew in his throat.

Tell me you are Juliette. Only say it, just once.

He shut down the thought. Damn, but he hated it when things like that crept up on him. He had not loved her then, so why should it matter now?

But he had begun to think of her as his.

And that is over, you bedamned fool. Long over.

He had no business toying with a woman he knew to be so tainted.

As he reached past her to open the door, his hand brushed the sleeve of her dark green Spencer, and old urges surged through him again. He felt her pull away, just the tiniest inch from him. As she always had.

The door was opened instead by a footman of smallish stature, and Miss Darrow stepped through, Edenstorm following. Just inside the hall, as if they had been watching out the mullioned window overlooking the garden, stood Rokeby and Lady Beck. With the strangest looks on their faces.

What the hell?

Whatever it was, they were both thinking exactly the same thing. It occurred to him that the smell of conspiracy was an awful lot like the smell of battle.

Chapter Six

"Shall I call for tea, gentlemen?" asked Lady Beck, returning to her usual sunny, sociable smile.

"We ought to be going," Edenstorm replied.

"That would be marvelous," said Rokeby at the same time.

Edenstorm glared, but nobody seemed to care, and Rokeby's pleasant demeanor all but reeked of conspiracy. And as Lady Beck signaled the footman, Edenstorm was left with no choice but to take a seat like any polite gentleman would. He chose a straight-backed wooden chair slightly aloof from the others.

"I must thank you for finding my pencil for me, Mr. Rokeby," said Miss Darrow.

Rokeby cocked his head, looking puzzled. Well, what did he expect, that Edenstorm would take credit for it? He did have standards, after all.

"It was really quite by accident, Miss Darrow. We divided up the territory, you see. More efficient for searching. It just happened to be where I was looking. But it was Edenstorm's idea to go looking. Credit must go to him."

"Oh, how nice of you both," said Lady Beck. "Did you finish your drawings, Jane?"

"Yes, I am pleased. A good day's work."

"She's captured you quite perfectly, Rokeby," Edenstorm said. "And you did not even have to sit for her."

"Really." Rokeby beamed, and Edenstorm had the most inexplicable urge to cold-cock him. "Might I see, Miss Darrow?"

Miss Darrow nodded toward the table where she had laid

her pile of foolscap, and Rokeby stood and crossed the room.

"I say, Edenstorm, you're right."

Lady Beck rose and helped him examine the drawing. "Oh, indeed, Jane. You have such a way of capturing the spirit as well as the flesh. Did you finish the one of Lord Edenstorm?"

Jane emitted a funny squeak and nodded.

Rokeby all but bounced on his toes and picked up the next drawing. "Egad, what a talent, Miss Darrow. You have captured Edenstorm to perfection. You have caught something there I have not seen in a long time, and I have known him, what, twenty years?"

"I don't have a dimple," Edenstorm growled. Now he really was going to plant the man a facer.

Lady Beck laughed. "But of course you do, sir. Jane would not put it there if it were not there."

And so it went, Edenstorm clutching a delicate teacup so tautly he expected it to break in his hands, while the jovial folk about him discussed the merits of the dimple he most assuredly did not have. He sucked in a breath and endured. He was a proper man and he would remain one if he had to bite his own tongue in two. And if Rokeby didn't wipe that ridiculous smile off his face, he was unlikely to survive the night.

Finally the last cup of tea was drunk, the last nicety exchanged, and the gentlemen rose to leave.

"I shall call for you tomorrow for our ride, Miss Darrow," he said as he took his hat and gloves at the door.

"If it does not rain, sir."

"Yes, if it does not rain."

"Where do you wish to go?"

A sardonic twist came to his mouth, and he allowed it to show. "Perhaps there are places you would like to show me."

"Perhaps I shall not go, then, if you have no particular place in mind."

"But you did agree."

"If it does not rain."

"Yes."

A smile as wicked as his own cocked up one corner of her

mouth, jabbing through him like a shaft of lightning. "Have you looked at the southwest sky, my lord? It will rain."

"Perhaps sooner than you think." He pivoted and turned away and walked to the groom who held their horses waiting at the cobbled driveway.

"What was that about?" Rokeby asked as he mounted.

Edenstorm frowned and shrugged. Rokeby didn't need to know everything.

But he rode home in silence, and they entered the cottage and ate the evening meal with nothing exchanged between them that did not require saying aloud. Still in silence he studied the play of the fire dancing like demons in the sitting room's small fire grate. Rokeby lit his cigar. Edenstorm flared a nostril but said nothing else about the habit he detested. Rokeby already knew his feelings.

"You're quiet, old man," Rokeby said at last.

"Thinking."

"About what?"

"That sketchbook of hers. She is incredibly accurate with details. I suppose you noticed."

"Aside from the mythical dimple."

Edenstorm sneered. "There is a scene in the sketchbook. The Looe River, I'd say, looking down from a hill somewhere out in the countryside."

"So?"

"Moonlight scene."

"And?"

"I thought you were supposed to be so good at deduction, Rokeby. It's a marvelous scene, done with a full moon, with clouds draping around it."

Rokeby scratched his head. "So?"

"What was a lady doing so far out in the countryside so late at night?"

"You don't know it was late."

"I'll wager it was. Very late."

"A smuggler's landing."

"I believe I shall ask her to take me there tomorrow."

Rokeby grinned. "And I believe I shall rise late and saunter about the village."

"Looking for gold, I presume."

"Indeed."

Edenstorm was in no hurry to head up the creaky old staircase to his chamber, but then he never was. But eventually he had to follow Rokeby up the stairs. Nance was there waiting, even though Edenstorm had asked him over and over not to wait up. What was the point, when Edenstorm never knew himself when he would finally give in to the sin of sleeping? He stood submissively as Nance undid his cravat and helped him out of his coat and shirt.

Edenstorm glanced at the mirror hanging on the wall above the nightstand and thought of cocklewinks.

Hell. He did have a dimple.

"Oh, very nice," cooed Lydia's voice behind Jane.

Jane jumped, heat already creeping into her cheeks. She had been so engrossed, she had not even heard Lydia come into her chamber. There was no hope of covering her work. Jane was left with mere shrugging as she stepped back from the sketch, which was now much more than a few curving lines.

"I believe we can say our Bird of Paradise is no plucked chicken. Amazing what one can see in such a short time. Oh, my dear, you are not embarrassed, are you? Not after all our little talks."

Jane winced. It was not the nude male she had sketched that made her blush. It was the particular nude male.

Lydia pointed to a location where the buttocks joined the back. "There is a sort of dimple right here. A triangular sort of shape. In a muscular sort of man, at least."

"I doubt you'd know about any other sort."

"True. Sculptors don't seem to choose fat men as their subjects."

"Not when they can find one like this." Jane smeared the

lead of the pencil in a small triangle.

"A little larger." Lydia reached past Jane's shoulder and ran her finger over the smudge, which smeared into a more linear streak. "Oh! Yes, I believe that is just right," she said. "Dear me, it feels rather odd to touch it, as if I were actually touching him."

Jane frowned. "It's just a drawing."

"And better to look at than the rain."

She had been utterly lost in her sketching and had not even noticed the rain, which she had hoped would not come before tomorrow. "I'm sorry. I have not been at all companionable tonight."

"Well, we are always quiet after Mother goes to bed. You are not angry with me, are you?"

"I do rather wish you had not told him I would ride with him tomorrow."

Lydia rose from the sofa and walked to the window, absent-mindedly cradling her broken arm. "Sorry. It did seem the two of you were getting on passably well, so I thought perhaps it would give you an opportunity. If he comes to know you for the person you are, surely he must see he is wrong. If he understands how vicious Cyril is, he will not want to see you hurt."

But that was only one of Jane's problems. How could she possibly tell Lydia about Edenstorm's demands when Lydia was probably the only person in all of Looe who did not understand the consequences? She had been gone too long and she had been back less than a year, not long enough to know. Jane did not want to be the one to tell her. Lady Launceston must do that.

"You don't know him, Lydia. He is not a man who brooks any misconduct in a woman. He will never believe me in any case."

"You don't know until you try."

"And if I dare try, he can use what I tell him against me."

"Do you want me to make an excuse for you, then? I could say you are ill, or you must stay with Mother who is ill."

Jane watched the gusts of wind toss about the branches of

the tall pine outside the window, and for some reason felt a strange tug of compassion for creatures or persons caught out in such a storm.

"No." She sighed. "I think I must find a way to work this out, But I think I did discover something about him today."

"What is that?"

"I suspect he has a soul after all. I saw it in his dimple."

Lydia smiled. "Oh, yes, my dear. He does."

❧

The horse was swimming. The stupid horse was swimming after the ship. Go back, you damn horse!

Go back, Betsy! Go back! Johnson was screaming at the horse. Russell, Weatherford, everybody was screaming at the horse. Go back!

The horse swam on, pewter gray waves slamming into it, but still it swam.

Why the hell didn't the dumb beast go back? Couldn't it see it was going to drown?

Go back! Go back! Go back!

Who would have thought a horse could swim as fast as a ship could sail?

Tears were streaming down Johnson's cheeks. But he couldn't do anything. Nobody could.

The shouts faded.

The horse still swam, its dark round eyes huge with fear. The waves overtook it. It slid beneath the gray water.

Edenstorm jerked awake. He sat up, shaking the dream away. He scrambled out of bed and dashed to the wash stand and threw the icy water on his face.

God, he hated sleeping.

Why the horse? Why the cursed horse, for God's sake? The dumb animal was not even his.

He leaned over the washbowl and poured the whole pitcher of water over his head. Why at least not Edward? He'd seen

Edward fall. That was the most damnably awful moment of his life, so why didn't he dream about that? It was always the horse, and every man on board the ship begging God to make the creature go back and watching helplessly until their hearts were broken.

Edenstorm rubbed a towel over his head and breathed and breathed and breathed. There was no fire, and he couldn't see his watch. The night was black as the depth of a tin mine, and rain thudded dully on the soaked ground. Water would be gushing along the road in front of the manor like a wild mountain stream. He grabbed for his clothes and threw them on in a manner that would make Nance want to cry. He went out the chamber door and down the creaking stairs.

"Sir?"

It was Nance who stopped him at the front door, candle in hand, still in his dressing gown and cap.

"Just going out," he replied. "Go back to bed,"

"Yes sir."

Nance would not question. Not even if it were a blizzard beyond the door. Perhaps he thought his master insane, but he never said so.

Edenstorm snatched up his greatcoat and hat and reached for the door handle.

"Wait, Edenstorm." It was Rokeby, tucking in his long shirttail, his coat slung over his arm at the elbow.

Blazes. He'd hoped to get by Rokeby this time. "You don't need to come."

"I'm coming anyway. The dream again?"

Edenstorm tightened his jaw. There was no point in answering. Sometimes he wished Rokeby hadn't come with him to Cornwall, but there was no telling him so. He jammed the spyglass into a pocket inside his coat as he waited, watching Rokeby's clumsy movements as he crammed his arms into the coat sleeves. Nance held out Rokeby's greatcoat, then hat.

Out in the darkness, the hard rain fell like it was thrown from a bucket. Edenstorm took off his hat and let the cold water pelt his face and drown his hair, turning it to dripping ropes before his eyes. It felt cleansing. Washing away the sins of the night.

"Don't you ever sleep, Edenstorm?" asked Rokeby, pulling up the collar of his heavy wool coat tighter around his neck.

"Sometimes it's necessary." But if he had his way, he'd abolish sleep altogether.

"You'll never see anything in a storm like this."

"I know. Go back to bed, Rokeby. There's no need for you to be up. It's my dream, not yours."

"But it's my friend who has the dream."

Edenstorm shrugged and crammed his hat back on his head. He was going to hate that in the morning because his favorite hat would be as wet inside as it was out. He started up the hill, which was as good as going down when he had no particular destination in mind.

They walked in silence. That was the best thing about Rokeby. He didn't demand talking all the time.

"Why the hell a horse, I don't know," he said at last.

"You like horses."

"Why Johnson didn't shoot the thing as he was ordered—damn, he knew it would starve if he didn't."

"He was a fool. You couldn't help that, either."

He knew that. He knew that! He'd told himself that a hundred times. He would have shot the horse himself if he'd known. It was godawful watching it drown that way. It was just so odd that he never dreamed about Edward, and he couldn't imagine anything worse than seeing his own brother die.

"Edenstorm, you've got to find a way to let it go and get on with your life."

Oh, he knew that, too. "When we're done with this," he replied. When they were done, he'd go back to Eden's Vale and live in peace.

But he knew that wouldn't work either. He'd already tried it. There would never be peace for him. But he had to do something to bring some peace to the rest of the world.

They turned around. Perhaps the rain had cooled him enough so he could finally sleep. Neither of them said a word as they trudged along, not even taking the trouble to avoid the water running like a stream down the muddy road. The rain eased to a light patter.

Down the hill they strode to the cottage. They turned into the gate and walked toward the house.

Something dark moved across the even darker line of the stable. He stopped cold, his hand out to hold Rokeby back.

"See that?"

"Let's go."

Edenstorm and Rokeby sprinted the distance to the stable. The shadow vanished.

"Footprints," said Rokeby, pointing to the muddy ground. "Maybe it's just the groom."

"Maybe it's not."

They lifted the bar on the stable door and entered. Nothing but darkness greeted them. "Hector," he called.

The horse nickered back.

They checked the horses and the coach. Nothing.

He called out to Trevenny and the groom came down from above the stable, tucking in the long tail of his shirt, his dark hair standing up like the bristles of a broom. "Me lord? Anything wrong?"

"Did you hear anything?"

"No, me lord."

"Go back to sleep, then."

"Maybe I did, sir, earlier," Trevenny said. "Heard ye go out first. Then a noise near the house. Thought ye was back, but then I thought, maybe not."

"In the house?"

"Maybe, me lord, but I'm not sure. Maybe we oughta see."

Edenstorm frowned. "Thieves, then?"

He headed toward the house, with Rokeby and Trevenny following, but as he neared the front door, Nance came running out in his brown dressing gown with one of Edenstorm's pistols in his hand.

"Oh, it's you, my lord," Nance said, lowering the pistol. "I heard noises and I thought you were back. But then I heard voices outside and I didn't find you in the house."

"You heard noises inside?"

"Yes, sir. But I don't see any signs of anything."

The four men entered the house and fanned out through the ground floor, looking for anything out of place. Edenstorm dashed for the kitchen. The cupboard had all its pewterware and the huntboard all its knives and forks. But something wasn't right. Glowering, he turned about slowly in a full circle. Just as he started to give up and search elsewhere, it dawned on him.

The door to the cellar was ajar.

"Nance!" he shouted.

Nance, Trevenny and Rokeby all came running.

"My lord?" asked Nance.

"Did you open the cellar door?"

"No, sir. You know it's been locked since we got here."

"It's not locked now."

Edenstorm lit a candle from the kitchen hearth and started down the stairs, but examined the back side of the door before the others could follow him.

"Devil it!" he said. "You can bar the door from the backside. Why the devil would anyone want to do that?"

"More like, how the devil did they do it," Rokeby added.

"Then there's a way in from below," Edenstorm replied.

He rushed down the crude wooden stairs to the cellar, which seemed mostly bare.

"I expected to see some of the owner's possessions here," Rokeby said. "Something a man might lock a door for."

"But it wasn't locked. It was barred." Edenstorm walked slowly around the cellar, carefully shining the candle around the walls. There were some shelves with oddments of things on them, an old, broken chair and some loosely piled crates and kegs, but he saw nothing that indicated a way in or out of the cellar. The walls were solid stone blocks.

Belatedly, he looked at the floor for footprints. He should have thought of that before. But not even their own showed on the hard stone floor.

"We'll look outside in the morning," he decided. And he sent Trevenny and Nance back to their respective beds.

"So it wasn't the groom," Rokeby said. "A thief, most likely."

"Or someone who is very curious. Feels like a declaration of war. And I have a feeling I know who's making it."

ಹಿ

The next morning, Edenstorm rode Hector into the boatyard on the west side of the river, dismounted and dropped the reins to the gravel. Two Cornishmen looked up from their work of cramming oakum into the planks of a small dinghy. Nearby, a small lugger was being fitted with its mast, and inside a covered yard, he could hear hammers and saws and other boat-building noises.

Those held little interest for him. He headed straight for the quay and one of the sleekest boats he had ever seen. The *Nightwind*, it said on her prow. She hadn't been there a few nights before.

She was more than twice the size of the little two-masted luggers that sailed out from the harbor to fish, and she sported two tall masts and a bowsprit. Her sails were furled, but he had seen her sail in, and she was tall and proud, her hull smooth, not like the lap-sided boats around him. Even her colors spoke of pride: bright blue and yellow above her black hull. She had no peer all the way to Plymouth.

Nor did she appear to have a practical purpose. And that seemed strange in this part of England, where everything seemed to be geared toward simplicity and utility.

"And would it be his lordship, the Earl of Edenstorm?" The voice behind him had a curiously lyrical tone, but was sharp enough to slice meat.

Edenstorm ran his gaze up the full length of the high masts with their furled sails, then slowly turned, gauging the man from the tip of his tousled coal-black hair and rough linen shirt sleeves to boots that gleamed as if they belonged to a gentleman. "You would be Polruhan."

Polruhan snapped a nod. "What would his lordship find so interesting about a humble Cornish boatyard?"

Edenstorm saw nothing humble about the man. More like a

cocky ring fighter. And uncommonly wealthy for a merchant with a little boatyard. "A fine boat there. Looks fast."

"She'll run with the best of them. Better, if she's got a Cornishman to love her well and treat her right."

"You built her?"

"My design."

"Looks French."

"Aye, she's got a touch of that."

"Lug-rigged, but a topsail on the main mast. But she looks too tall. That's a lot of sail for her hull."

"She's tricky. She's a Cornish boat built for a Cornishman. A lubber'd lose her in a storm. What would be your interest in her? Me lord?"

Edenstorm caught the slur and knew it for a challenge, like the slap of a glove on the face. And now that he knew he had a dimple, he stopped it from forming. This was obviously a man who read faces well.

"Investment," he replied.

"Look to the mines, then. There's profits in tin and copper. China clay, they say's the coming thing."

"Maybe I want to look elsewhere. Maybe shipping and ships are more to my taste."

"Go to Portsmouth, then. Or Plymouth. They'll take an Englishman's money."

"And Cornwall?"

"Cornishmen take care of their own. Me lord."

"Do they?"

"Aye, they protect what's theirs with their last drop of blood."

"That so? And what would be yours that you'd be protecting with your blood?"

Polruhan's eyes hardened and his fists set high at his waist, elbows spanning broadly, reminding Edenstorm of an eagle preparing to launch. The corners of his mouth rose up in a hard snarl. "Everything ye want."

Edenstorm let a narrow smile reply for him as he assessed the man, head to toe. A wiliness, hard as steel. Equal to him in brawn, if not quite in height, and the kind of cold-blooded determination that made a soldier great. Or a smuggler. The scent of battle, blood and gunpowder, sweat and fury heated his blood. It was all the same, facing this man.

"Then you're a man I understand, Polruhan. I do the same."

He slid his scathing gaze over the man, then back to the tall boat. "She's a beauty. I have a mind for a boat like her. A man with a brain could learn well enough to handle her."

"'Tis bright thoughts like that could get a man killed."

"Ah." Edenstorm nodded slowly, and he let his brow lift a touch. "But what's a bit of death to brave men? Let me know if you're of a mind to sell her."

The Cornishman folded his arms and a slow smile crept onto his lips, belied by a gaze as hard and sharp as steel.

"Aye, I'll be doing that, your lordship. And ye'll know when the time comes. That'll be when angels visit Hell."

Edenstorm mounted the bay that had so patiently waited where its reins had been dropped. "You'd be surprised, Polruhan, how many times they've already been there."

He rode out of the boatyard and up the hill to Launceston Hall.

Chapter Seven

The rain that had fallen hard in the night left only a few puddles by mid-morning. Hardly enough mud to prevent any passable horseman from riding out.

And Edenstorm, true to his rigid nature, appeared at Launceston Hall precisely at the appointed hour. The fates were conspiring against her.

Jane would have jumped up into the saddle from the mounting block herself, but Edenstorm wouldn't permit it. The heat of his hands at her waist sizzled her skin, all the way through the deep green wool of her riding habit, her stays and shift.

He had worn green that day, too, a beautifully tailored double-breasted superfine in bottle green that made his silver eyes seem bright. His doeskin inexpressibles expressed a great deal more than she wanted to know, snug over the blocky muscles of his thighs. He had never seemed so muscular, nor so blatantly male, when she had known him before, when he'd had a spindly adolescent look to him. But he did now, and it made her feel oddly heated.

He mounted his horse Just at that moment, he turned his face to hers. Her breath caught at the shocking effect of his silver eyes, hauntingly full of mystery even when he smiled. So different from the blank emptiness that had frightened her so many years before. She almost could not look him full in the face without gasping.

Something dangerous lurked in the way his mouth lifted at one corner. "Where shall we go, Miss Darrow?" he asked.

"Go?" she asked, shrugging, and she tossed her head as if

it all meant nothing to her. "Wherever you wish, my lord. I am to be but guide and companion, I understand."

"There is one place I would like to see. But I don't know where it is."

"Then how would you expect me to know?"

"It's in your sketchbook, Miss Darrow. Show me the place you sketched by moonlight."

Jane licked her lip. Silly of her, but she had almost hoped he was going to set aside their differences for awhile. She clucked to her little brown hack and started up the hill.

From the river to the hilltop, the road was steep, but above, the hill spread out flat and almost level. They rode out of West Looe, where she had been safe for so long, and Jane looked back almost wistfully.

"Long way around?"

Now why would he ask that if he didn't have any idea where they were going? "This is the road to Liskeard. We usually go this way. If we followed the river, we would have much farther to go. There are few crossings and many branches."

Jane led them past the old quarry and up through the shrubby woodland that capped the hill.

"This is called West Looe Downs," she told him. "It's an interesting view." If luck stayed with her, she could keep on playing guide and never get to anything important, although she didn't expect anything so easy.

He nodded. "I've seen the sea, Miss Darrow."

Jane returned an acid smile. "Always lovely, isn't it?" She turned to her right and rode toward the wood.

The sea breeze felt cold, even through her wool habit. But soon they rode beyond the ridge and looked down on the river's mud flats, with its dark ribbon of water flowing between them. Jane always felt odd here, with the steep slope to the river on one side, yet gently rolling downs to the other side. It was like being on the edge between two worlds.

"Where are you from, Miss Darrow?"

"Halford, in Cheshire."

"Really. Who is your family?"

"The Darrows and the Ipswiches. Country squires, vicars, an occasional knight. Not at all your sort of fellows."

"Never heard of Halford, nor the Ipswiches or Darrows."

"Surprising. It's famous for its cocklewinks."

"Not telling, then?"

She sidled a sneer at him.

"I do hope your lace survived the escapade at the cliff," he said as he studied the countryside.

That was the least of her worries. "A little mending and it will be usable again."

"An odd place for a woman to wear something so exquisite. Most would trim a neckline or skirt, rather than a petticoat."

"I cannot think I have met another man who would discuss a lady's undergarments with her."

The dimple flashed momentarily on his cheek. She almost laughed at the shock of it. It was so odd that she had never noticed it before, yet she thought she had always known it was there. It made her pulse race, the way his oddly haunting eyes did.

She took a sharp breath, suddenly catching the direction her thoughts were going. The Earl of Edenstorm was the last man she should allow herself to admire. Still, it was a marvelous dimple. She'd just have to remember it was nothing more than that.

He let loose a chuckle, but she heard no humor in it. "When they are in full view, it is hard not to notice. Expensive lace, I'd say. Far beyond the reach of a lady's companion."

"I inherited it from my grandmother."

"Oh? It did not seem particularly old."

"My grandmother was old. Her lace was not."

For a moment, he was silent. "I must admit, Miss Darrow, I found your courage admirable. Unusual for a woman to risk her person for the sake of a friend."

"Lydia is deserving of that and far more."

"She is a friend, not simply an employer, I have no doubt."

"I suppose I should say thank you or something."

"Not necessary. We understand each other far better than

we admit. It is nice to see you wearing color."

She drew in a slow breath, finding the compliment chafing like sandpaper. "Lady Beck insists I abandon my gray when we ride, so I made up this riding habit."

"I suspect she would be happy if you abandoned gray altogether."

"She detests it. But it is suitable for a companion."

"But you are more a friend."

"We have a strong affection for each other, but my position is not changed by that."

"Gray is unsuitable if you hope to find a husband."

"I have no such hopes. Or desires."

"I have the feeling Polruhan fancies you."

"He does. He has made it clear. I consider him a fond acquaintance."

"No one else?"

That almost made her laugh. "No one would consider it. Whatever Davy Polruhan says he wants, everyone smiles and lets him have it."

"And you?"

"I just smile."

Below them, as the trail descended, the river sprawled outward like the branches of a tree.

"He does not bully you, does he?"

"Davy? Of course not. Nobody bullies me. Except you."

"I do not bully you."

"Really, Lord Edenstorm? You have already threatened me."

Silence was his only response as the shoes of the horses clipped on the rocks of the path.

"That will be Polruhan down there in the boatyard."

Yes, that was Davy. From here, only a small stick of a figure, his hands upon his hips as he stared up the hill. They would be only small stick figures to him as well, but she would stand out in her green riding habit and her little hat with its wispy green ostrich plume. The one Davy had seen her wear so many times beside Lydia in her brilliant blue as they rode out together over the hills. She was going to pay dearly for this ride.

"You could do far worse for a husband, Miss Darrow. I'm surprised you haven't married him already."

"So is Mr. Polruhan," she replied.

"Fondness is enough reason for many a woman. You would be well taken care of."

"Not good enough reason for me,"

"Still with the romantic notions, Miss Darrow?"

"I don't know what you mean."

"Yes you do. Still intending after all this time to find that great love?"

"Is that such a terrible notion, my lord? I suppose it would be to you, since you appear to have no feeling for anyone. If I were ever to choose to marry, I would value nothing else as highly as love, and since men do not marry for love, I have no desire to marry."

"Men marry for dynastic reasons, Miss Darrow. Ultimately more practical. Affection can come as surely to two people chosen carefully for each other as it can to those who swoon before they think. I have nothing but contempt for such a poorly thought out reason for anything as important as marriage."

Jane gritted her teeth, her hackles rising like bristles on a hedgehog. "A rather nice slap in the face," she responded. "Thank you, Lord Edenstorm, for reminding me of one more reason why I find marriage distasteful."

"Why?"

She tossed her head as haughtily as she could manage. "Because men are who they are. Poor creatures, darlings in many ways, to be sure, but they are hurtful to women and don't care a fig about it. They give no thought to what a woman thinks and proceed immediately to tell her her own mind."

"Women don't think. They haven't the brains for it."

"Then why hold a conversation with a woman about what a woman thinks?"

She gasped. Heaven help her, she'd done it now! Cringing, she glanced his way as she waited for the deluge of rage. Her fingers gripped the reins, resisting the urge to slap them against the hack's neck and ride as fast as her poor animal could take her. Beg Lydia to ship her off to Northumberland. Scotland, maybe.

Instead, to her horror, the dimple formed and melted into a lopsided grin. "Welcome back, Juliette. For a while there, I almost believed you were gone."

God help her. She'd just given herself away, completely. And all it had taken was a little bit of baiting.

"Don't call me that," she snapped. God help her, and not let this day last an eternity.

He leaned back and roared a laugh at the sky. He spurred his bay gelding to a canter, which she was forced to follow. Jane could swear the man sat at least three inches taller in his saddle.

She had never seen him smile before.

If one could call that a smile. It looked more like part of a teeth-baring, gawky victory dance by some primitive tribesman somewhere in Tongarora. Or Roratanga, or whatever it was called.

As she caught up with him he slid a sideways glance at her, the whole side of his face caught up in a twisted grin.

"You have a devil in you, Lord Edenstorm," she said.

"True."

Jane sniffed and urged the brown hack past him to begin the descent to the spring that fed the main branch of the West Looe River and led the horses across a narrow footbridge. Past the Ten Acre Wood they reached the overlook above the fork of the East and West Looe Rivers. Jane reined in the hack and slid down from the saddle before Edenstorm could dismount to help her.

"This is what you want," she said, waving a hand over the expansive view.

"Are you sure? It's not quite the same," he replied.

"The tide is coming in. In an hour the mudflats will be covered, and it will look entirely different."

"Then there is the moonlight."

"We shall not be around for that."

"But tonight's moon would be much the same, would it

not?"

She nodded.

"The moon was high in the sky. I wonder what a lady was doing so far out from the village in the middle of the night."

Jane narrowed her eyes at him. She was already ahead of him. "Do you think an artist can only record what he sees in front of him? Do you give us no credit for imagination, sir?"

Edenstorm studied her as he rubbed a knuckle over the dark shadow already forming on his chin. Was it rough? She had always wondered what a man's shaven cheek must feel like against a woman's.

Stop it. She jerked her head away and poured all her attention into the view.

"So you made the scene into a night scene?"

"Simple enough. Shall I do another? I have brought my book."

"I like to watch you draw. But do something else. Can you do Hector?"

"Hector?"

"My horse."

"I've never tried horses. I suppose I should."

His face warped upward in that feral, lop-sided grin again. He returned to the bay, who had remained exactly where his reins had dropped, and pulled a brown blanket, a bottle and some foodstuffs from his saddlebags. He picked a spot where the view spread out beside them and fanned out the blanket beneath an oak tree.

Jane watched him with narrowed eyes. She'd thought he was dangerous before, but she'd had no idea just how dangerous. This was another way to distract her, like his needling intimidation, so she forgot to think. She didn't dare let him irritate her that much again.

So she would be at least outwardly compliant, but she resolved to think out everything she said before she said it. Jane pulled out her sketchbook, pencil and ball of rubber and sat on the blanket with her feet tucked up under her skirt. Edenstorm poured two glasses of wine into goblets which he seemed to have produced from nowhere.

Jane opened the sketchbook, grateful that her sketching would give her an excuse not to look at him. "Would you like the horse to be on a barren hilltop with a lightning storm behind him?" she asked.

"Lightning frightens him. I'd rather not do that to him."

"And I should not like to have him suffer a rainstorm. Perhaps a bright summer day with a pasture in full bloom. Or might he like a little stream to pause for a drink?"

"He'd like the stream, I think," Edenstorm said.

He handed the goblet to her. Before she could raise it to her lips, he held out his own. "To Juliette," he said.

Jane raised her glass, holding her breath. "To Juliette," she said. "May she remain in her grave." She took a sip and set down the goblet, and began her sketch, roughing in the horse and the imaginary stream.

"Why?"

"Lady Juliette is dead. Let her lie in peace. There is no one who wishes her alive."

"I do."

"She was nothing to you. Why should you care?"

"Because at least she is one person who is not dead."

Her hand clenched the Conté pencil. Jane hunched into her work, frowning. She scrutinized the horse, furiously drawing leg and muzzle, her lines hard and incautious. Drawing, erasing and drawing again, she forced her mind to think only of the horse. But the man beside her moved closer, leaning over her shoulder, his breath like hot cinders against her skin.

"It makes me happy that she is not dead," said the voice from behind her, tickling at her ear with a whispery softness. "It makes me happy to know she is flesh and blood after all. She is all rapier wit and high-blooded, and her cheeks glow with fire and her eyes spark like emeralds in sunlight when she is angry."

"You have a great deal of imagination."

She felt something touch her cheek lightly, like a feather. She turned. It was his hand, sweeping back her curls and tucking them behind her ear.

"I'm not imagining the mole that tucks so perfectly into the groove between her cheek and ear."

She jerked away. "Let her die, Lord Edenstorm. You do not want her. You only want to be annoying."

"Perhaps. Or perhaps not. But you are right, of course, I do enjoy being annoying sometimes."

Jane sneered without looking up. She turned her attention back to the sketch, which was just about the worst thing she had done since taking up a pencil at age four. It had no life to it.

"What's the matter?"

"It's wrong."

"Looks good to me."

"Because you don't know."

Frowning, she resolved to study the horse more carefully, to find that spark she was missing.

"Oh!" There it was! There before her, Hector was munching with great relish on a patch of buttercups and the golden blossoms dangled from his teeth in a way that almost made her laugh.

Swiftly, she flipped to the next blank page, and her pencil flew in wild boisterous strokes over the page. The head of the horse, not the whole animal. The flowers were already gone, but they had been there long enough to imprint on her mind. She caught the jawline just so, and the perfect round darkness in his chocolate-colored eye, the narrow blaze streaking down his muzzle, and his funny shock of forelock that somehow did not fit with the sleek smoothness of his mane. With the tip of her finger, she smeared the graphite to haze in the color of his coat.

It was done in mere minutes.

Hector, she wrote in the corner, bold, square letters.

"May I have it?" he asked, his hard voice suddenly soft and quiet.

She shrugged and carefully tore the page from the book.

"Sign it," he said.

"I never sign my work."

"Sign it."

She shrugged again.

J. Darrow, she scrawled into the corner below the horse's name.

She didn't take the time to see what he did with it when he stood and walked away. Instead, she returned to the bigger sketch and made a few more notes about the horse's musculature, then shut the book. He wasn't looking, so she slipped the pencil into its safest place, down her stays between her breasts.

"I have decided I was wrong about this place," he said.

She looked up. He had come back and he reached out a hand to help her to her feet. "I suppose you want to explain that."

"It is beautiful here. I see why you would want to draw it. Perhaps you have not been here at night, although I do not believe that. But there are really not such great possibilities for smugglers here, are there? All the little inlets would make for marvelous landings. But they would have to pass the bridge at night, and that would be quite brazen of them. The tide would have to be high, or they could be stranded on the mudflats."

Jane watched him, waiting. He was up to something again.

"On the other hand, is there anyone who would bother to stop them at the bridge?"

"You really don't know what you are stirring up, Lord Edenstorm. It could get you killed."

"So I've been told."

A chill ran down her spine. "You've been threatened?"

"I'd consider it a warning. But there are many ways to die. None of them frighten me. I have already been through hell, Juliette. Death has nothing that frightens me."

"Have you thought of what happens to people who snitch?"

"Are you afraid of them, Juliette? I can take care of you."

"No, I am not afraid of them."

"But they are your friends, and you do help them, don't you?"

"Friends always help friends."

His breath felt hot against her shoulder, and he brushed

back a dangling curl that he tucked behind her ear. "You would do well, my love, to remember you are buying my silence."

She shrank away from his touch. "Then perhaps, my lord, you should listen to your own words, and you might realize for yourself why your lady fled the scene."

Edenstorm rose up abruptly from his elbow to sit. "Fled the scene? And all this time I've been assuming she was exiled by her family."

Jane clamped down her lips. Damn the man! Was he going to weasel everything out of her? Even when she thought she was being so careful?

"What was her great crime, do you suppose?"

"Trusting men, I'd wager," she grumbled.

"Ah. The voice of experience."

"Men, sir, seek only their own ends, at a woman's expense if it suits them. As you do now."

"How very worldly of you. But, Miss Darrow, it need not be that way. You could have all the Conté pencils you want. Paints, a master to instruct you. You would want for nothing."

The implication hit like a slap. She pushed him away. "You cannot be saying that."

"No? How shocking it is; the flamboyant Juliette wearing dull gray, folding her hands demurely in her lap, quietly taking orders simply because they are couched as polite requests. You were meant for silks and cashmeres, fast waltzes, elegant carriages and beautiful horses to ride."

"Why do you want me to be this woman when she is the very one you hate?"

"Not hate. Perhaps she merely made my thin blood race more than I knew how to manage. Perhaps she still does."

Jane stared, open-mouthed, for a minute feeling like Juliette again.

Passion? Oh, no, she remembered him all too well. There had not been a trace of emotion in him then. He had terrified her with his soulless eyes.

"You are offensive, sir," she said, forcing herself to edge away from him, resisting the urge to let her eyes engage his, for that was when she had the most trouble resisting him.

"You are refusing my offer?"

"That was an offer? I misunderstood. I thought it was a threat."

"You are a lady. I do not threaten ladies."

"You cannot talk as if I am a lady one moment, then the next treat me as something a lady would never be."

"Oh, you are a lady, Miss Darrow, but a very scandalous one."

"No doubt. A true lady would have slapped your face by now. But I am merely a servant, which makes striking my betters a dangerous thing to do."

He shrugged. "Your situation is a bit precarious."

"It was not before you arrived. It was comfortable."

"I cannot imagine Lady Juliette settling for mere comfort."

Her smile turned lethally narrow. "Then perhaps you are mistaken?"

"No."

She walked away from the blanket he had laid out for his nefarious picnic, but then whirled around to face him. "Tell me, sir, why any woman in her right mind would accept such an offer? In the end, and it would end, men being the inconstant creatures they are, she has nothing but a few baubles. She cannot return home. And indeed she has no home, nor family, nor friends."

"That is why most men are very generous with parting gifts."

"And well they might be, considering they have just ruined the woman's life. What kind of gift could compensate for that? She has no choice but to continue her life as a whore."

"Mistress."

"Mistress is the term men use to describe the woman they use. Whore is what they call the woman another man uses. What could possibly benefit a woman in such a relationship?"

"I could hardly marry you, Juliette."

"Ah. The taint again. But at least we agree, there is no basis for a relationship between us. And I am only tainted in your mind, sir. You can prove nothing."

"But I don't have to prove anything, Juliette. I think it will be enough merely to let Lord Harlton know there is a woman in West Looe who looks very much like his sister."

The old terror slammed into her again, tightening her chest so that she almost could not breathe. She sensed him moving ever closer to her again, and the hairs rose up on her neck as if she awaited the executioner's axe.

"This is what happens to bad girls, Lady Juliette. You will end up here, too, if you do not mend your ways."

Her mind still rang with the pitiful wails of those ragged women chained to the walls of Bedlam.

Shudders wracked her so badly, surely they betrayed her. What good did her denials do? Yet, no, she could not say it. She could not take even the slightest step toward the most frightening end she could imagine.

Jane forced in a breath, then another, and made herself look out over the deep Looe Valley so that she didn't have to look into his icy silver eyes. At least if she didn't look at him, she could think.

Perhaps the only way was to give him what he wanted.

But she couldn't. She pictured those who would end up dangling from the scaffold. She could not. No doubt Davy would mean nothing to him. Not snaggle-toothed Annie, who was so far below his class that she could not matter. Probably nobody but she cared much about what happened to Annie. But if he found out about Lady Launceston? She trembled at the thought. It was that sweet lady to whom Jane owed her own life.

No. Maybe he didn't care about them, but she did. She could never give them away. All she could do was to stall. Pretend.

"What makes you think I know anything?" she said. "The women of Cornwall learn very early to watch the walls, Lord Edenstorm."

"Perhaps they do. Some of them. But perhaps others walk the lanes carrying tin lamps early in the morning before the sun comes up. They fasten bundles beneath their skirts so that they look almost fat as they walk along. And perhaps some of them wear gray Scottish shawls with a subtle weave."

Her throat closed down and her heartbeat pounded in her ears.

"Might someone have borrowed your lovely gray shawl last Saturday night, Miss Darrow? The one with the delicate pattern woven in several shades of gray?"

Jane stared at the clouds, trembling all the way down to her toes. Damn the man. He was heartless.

"How do they do it, Jane?"

Jane walked along the hill, doing her best to keep her back to him, and as she walked, the shudder that ran down her spine and back up hardened it to iron.

No. He would not succeed. Neither Annie nor Lady Launceston would hang from a gallows, not on her word. Even if that meant she hanged there instead. It was her task to fool him. Somehow. She fumbled about in her mind for a plan and grasped instead only straws. But they would have to do.

"If you want to catch smugglers, my lord," she said, "perhaps you should learn to think like one."

Edenstorm had moved up behind her so silently, she had not heard him, but she felt him there. The heat of his breath stirred the hair behind her ear. She felt his danger. But she no longer felt him attractive. She was both hot and cold inside, raging with a passion to push him off a cliff or something equally violent, yet she felt she could do it with the utmost calm.

"Can the boats get past the bridge, Juliette?"

She would give him information. Not necessarily the right information, but she would give it.

"The smaller ones," she said, her voice so flat it sounded deadly. "Small luggers are not much different from other boats. They are built so their masts can be lowered to pass under bridges or the like, then raised again and sails re-set."

"Not the *Nightwind*?"

She shook her head, her jaw stiff, her mind flitting wildly with thoughts of what Davy might do to this man if he knew any of this, and for a brief second she contemplated letting that happen. If he got himself killed, it would be his own doing.

She resolved she would not help that happen, but she

wondered why.

“Have you seen its masts?” she asked. “They are twice the height of the usual lugger.”

“It seems to have no purpose.”

“It’s Davy’s experiment. It’s the boat he always wanted to own. It needs no other purpose because he can afford to sail it whenever he chooses, wherever he chooses. He behaves rather like a rich man, wouldn’t you say?”

“Surprisingly so. Considering his source of income.”

“He comes from a wealthy family. He might even have as much money as you. But he is not a gentleman, and does not care to be.”

Edenstorm’s narrow smile told her he didn’t care. So. He was the same man he had always been, ruthlessly cold in order to gain what he believed was right. No matter what it did to others.

“How do the small boats get upstream, then? With the tide?”

“The Looe is a tidal river, but waiting for wind and tide would take a boat till tomorrow morning, and by then, the tide would have changed twice. Small boats are rowed, my lord.”

“Rowing past the Customs House? Noisy, isn’t it?”

“It probably doesn’t matter.”

“Ah.”

She masked her urge to smile. He had made the deduction that the customs agent was bribed, but he would have found that out soon, anyway. As long as he didn’t find out about the large stash of brandy in the cellar of the house next to the Customs House. That would not be good.

“Oars can be muffled.”

“So then, they can quietly row upstream beneath the bridge when the tide is coming in. Small boats would be preferred, I’d think. Where do they go?”

“What does a smuggler need?”

“A secretive location to unload.”

“Hidden. What else?”

“Easy access where the goods are unloaded.”

"What else?"

He frowned. "What do you mean?"

"Who needs lace, my lord?"

"Ladies. Dandies. He needs a market for his goods."

"How does it get to them?"

"I gather they don't meet the smuggler at the dock."

Jane rolled her eyes. "What's in between the dandy and the smuggler? If you want a brandy at the pub, you can get it, can't you? If the dandy wants lace, where does he go?"

"The haberdasher?"

"Do you suppose the haberdasher has French lace? Not on his open shelves, but if he thinks you discreet enough, he will get it for you."

"So?"

"Who gets it to him?"

"A middle man. A distributor. But who?"

"Whoever is interested. Or whoever has the money to invest. And he will want his investment protected, so he wants to meet the smuggler in a safe place. If you were this dealer, where would you meet?"

"Someplace with a road nearby. To move the goods faster. But remote, where there is little movement. Away from a town. And maybe someplace where goods could be hidden quickly."

"Ah. Now you are thinking like a smuggler. Think in terms of what the riding officers would not think of."

"As in the way packets are hidden beneath women's skirts, the law prohibits searching women."

"Even then, a risk. A woman might fall down and expose her packets. Or they might fall out in the dirt. But that's the idea."

"Then, on the river, someplace where the water is deep enough to bring a boat ashore but not leave marks in the mud, except that the tide coming in would wash them away, so that probably doesn't matter. A small boat to go in with the flow and leave with the ebb. Allowing a few hours each way, the boats should enter about two hours before high tide. And land in the shelter of trees, to muffle the sound as well as conceal from sight."

He scanned the length of the river winding upstream like a crumpled ribbon. "But it would take a lot of people to move the merchandise, so it also has to be a site where a lot of people can move in and out quickly."

"With pack animals," she added.

"And easy access to other roads." He pointed off to the left of the river. "That little lane leads up to the ridge and to Liskeard."

"One other thing. Why not find who buys the goods and trace back where they got them? Surely you know dandies wearing lace on their cuffs. Or perhaps your sister or mother."

"I'll never involve them."

"Oh, no, of course not. Not the people you know. That would be disloyal, wouldn't it?"

"Don't be absurd."

"I should think it reasonable to sacrifice anyone who engages in the free trade."

"I care nothing about free trade, remember? I only want the man who drains Britain's coffers of its gold to aid the enemy. Where does the gold come from, Miss Darrow?"

"The gold?"

"Gold. The point of this endeavor. How is it getting to Cornwall, and how is it taken out of Cornwall?"

"I'm afraid you have me there, sir. I always assumed gold came from banks. But I never thought about it further than that."

"Then what else does Guinea Jack use for trade?"

"Well, I admit, I hadn't thought of that either."

"I'm sure some English goods make the trip. But think about it. Only gold is really worth it. And he must be bringing back nearly twice its value in French goods. Otherwise it wouldn't be profitable."

"Then I'd look to bankers and wealthy men, sir. You can do that far better than I. I have probably not had two gold coins in my pocket more than five times in my entire life."

Jane felt the touch of his hand on her arm, and gritted her

teeth. Did he think he had somehow endeared himself to her in the last few minutes? By threats to her and those she cared about? Now she felt nothing but contempt for him. She strode away through the lush green grass to the tree where her brown hack was tied. Let him think she would more willingly betray her friends than share his bed. That would put him in his place.

The horse was not all that keen to have her grazing disrupted, but Jane cared little. She just wanted away from him. She led the animal to a granite outcropping that was a bit tall for a mounting block, but it would do.

"If you will wait a minute, Miss Darrow, I'll help you up," he said as he gathered up the blanket, bottle and goblets he had left.

"No need, sir. I have no need of help from you of any kind."

He jammed the gear into his saddlebag. "Oh, yes," he said. "Lady Juliette is back."

Jane kicked her heel into the mare's flank and started off at a trot down the hill. She avoided his conversation all the way back to Launceston Hall, but noted, to her chagrin, he didn't make any effort to engage her, either.

Mr. Rokeby was in the drawing room with Lydia and Lady Launceston when they returned, and although it might have been more polite to stay and talk, Jane had had enough of both gentlemen, just from being with the one. She excused herself with a headache and went to her room.

When she saw herself in the mirror, she allowed herself a smile that was so angry it almost frightened her.

So now he knew all about smuggling on the Looe River. That might have been dangerous, for she had not told him anything that wasn't true. Except that no one had used the Looe River in nearly a hundred years.

Chapter Eight

"Turned you down, did she?"

Edenstorm snarled and jerked Hector's reins, something he hadn't done since he was a boy. He almost wished he hadn't met Rokeby in town as he was descending the hill from Launceston Hall. "Don't know what you're talking about," he replied.

"I'll wager she would know if I asked her."

"No doubt. You jump to conclusions about as fast as she does. I don't suppose you learned anything."

"Not much. To judge from the records, there's been no smuggling in Looe for years. Quiet little town, not much commerce in and out of the port at all. So quiet, in fact, there's no need of riding officers anywhere near Looe."

"In other words, the customs officer is bribed."

Rokeby shook his head. "Eighty-seven years old and blind and deaf. But his deputies all are."

"And gold?"

"Not a peep. You'd think they never heard of the stuff here. You can get the usual amount at the bank, but I see no signs of any unusual movement. In fact, the gold is one thing that is conspicuous by its absence. Yet we know it gets to Looe. But from where? And how?"

"It could come down river. Just as goods could go up it."

"Oh? She did tell you something, then."

"In a manner of speaking, she told me without telling me. But I don't believe her."

"You're very puzzling, Edenstorm. She did, but she didn't

but you don't believe her."

"She only told me things that would lead me to draw my own conclusions."

"Perhaps she is simply being oblique, then. To let you know without actually having to say it."

"She's cleverer than that."

"I don't like this, Edenstorm. Have you thought about what could happen to her? Smugglers tend to be rather blunt about their dislike of people who rat on them."

He had. He'd thought about a lot of other things. Mostly about the slime he'd felt growing on his soul when he put pressure on her to betray her friends like the proverbial rat. Never had he used a woman quite so disgustingly. And worse, something about it had actually been pleasing. Then her icy rejection had brought him back to reality. He got nothing he hadn't deserved.

That was strange. One minute pressuring her into giving him information, but the next, sabotaging everything by his lurid proposition. What the hell had he thought he was doing?

Had he honestly been so foolish as to think she would find such behavior charming? Or had he deliberately provoked her rejection? Hell, he never knew why he did anything anymore. Other than that he liked to watch her quietly spitting fire.

He turned away from Rokeby with a growl. "Don't tell me she's charmed you into believing in her virtue?"

"Don't tell me you don't find her attractive."

"Never said I didn't. But I know how to draw the line, and I'm not so sure you do."

Rokeby didn't respond, but then he usually did not when Edenstorm let loose with one of his jabs. Devil it, but the man had been his good friend since they were boys.

"She said something, though."

Rokeby cocked one eyebrow.

"Something she didn't intend. About Lady Juliette fleeing the scene rather than marrying someone like me."

"Girl has a barb on her tongue, I see."

Edenstorm ignored that. "I'd assumed she had left home with her family's consent, or perhaps been exiled to Cornwall by them."

"And?"

"If she fled, then that explains why she doesn't want Harlton to know where she is."

"Afraid he'll find her? Why?"

"Do you know Harlton?"

"Evil-minded bastard."

"My thoughts, too. She isn't just afraid of him. She's terrified. So I'd put money on it she ran away and Lady Launceston and Lady Beck have been harboring her."

"Which they would not do lightly, as I have said. I don't like this, Edenstorm."

Edenstorm turned his bay off the bridge and headed up the hill toward Pendennen Hall. "Not sure I do either. She had a sizable dowry. Wonder what happened to it?"

"You think Harlton got his hands on it?"

"He claimed she was dead. But I'd think he'd have to prove it before the courts would let him have it."

"Now I really don't like this."

"Doesn't make sense, does it? I doubt she's living as a ladies' companion simply for the pleasure of it."

"I think you should let the whole thing go, Edenstorm. You could have no idea what you might be stirring up. At least attempt to discuss it with her."

"I tried. She doesn't trust me enough even to admit she is Lady Juliette. I suppose I can hardly blame her for that, since she sees me as her brother's friend."

"Harlton has no true friends, that I know of."

"But she believes men stick together."

"And you have not exactly won her trust lately."

There was that. "We could be making something of nothing. Maybe Harlton kicked her out, and passed around the story to protect his political reputation, and she's afraid of his anger if she lets the truth be known. I say we see what we can uncover before we say anything more."

Rokeby gave him a sidelong glance as they rode into the driveway in front of the little manor. Edenstorm laughed to himself at its ugliness every time he rode up through the gate. It was built in the typical Cornish fashion of a two-storied box with a plain slate roof, but with a comical attempt at half-timbering such as could be seen in the Shires, and behind it a stable that really seemed to be more of a barn. But it did well enough for his purposes.

As they dismounted, both Nance and Trevenny came hurrying up to them. Trevenny took the horses, but Nance looked worried.

"There's a red-marked letter come by courier, Mr. Rokeby," he said. "I was about to send Trevenny to find you, but we saw you riding up the road."

Rokeby took the letter, which Edenstorm could see was wrapped at an angle in a second paper. He held the letter to the fading daylight, studying its edges in his accustomed way. "Looks clean," he said.

Once inside the manor in the parlour, Rokeby lifted the seal with a pen knife, checking carefully the way the seal came loose from the paper. But he made no more comments, so Edenstorm concluded there were no signs of tampering. He unfolded the bias-folded paper, then the letter inside it. A frown furrowed his brow as he read.

"Bad news, old chap," he said. "I've been called back. We'll have to fold the mission."

"Deuce. We were just getting started. If we quit now, we won't be able to re-establish our connections."

"And Miss Darrow might take the break to disappear. Sorry. It's that other matter. The one involving the contact at Deal. Much greater priority."

"Why don't you go back, then, and I'll stay? Try at least to get some more information before I leave. I think we're close to something here."

"Not good to work alone. Things happen."

"I can take care of myself."

Rokeby hummed softly. "Well, this won't take long, I don't think. I should be back in about a week. What about her? Don't hurt her, Edenstorm."

He'd never meant to hurt her. Make her think he might, maybe. "Have you forgotten we're talking about treason? That's not for me to decide."

"And you're not going to find her at the bottom of it. I'll want that promise from you."

"I'll do my best to protect her. But this is something I've got to do, Rokeby. While you're in town, you could check with Equity Court about the dowry. And maybe find out something about Harlton or what he's up to."

"I'll give it a try."

"And buy her some paints, will you?"

Rokeby huffed. "Paints? I don't know anything about paints. What kind?"

"How should I know? I'm no artist. Ask someone."

Rokeby grinned and sped up the stairs to pack his things. With a quick arrangement on how they would contact each other, he was soon gone.

Edenstorm stood in his bedchamber watching Rokeby ride down the hill toward the river. There would be no coach passing through Looe until Wednesday, so Rokeby would ride to Plymouth and catch the mail from there, and by Wednesday morning he would be in London.

Edenstorm was left alone with the night. The moon was nearly full, and he ought to be out on the cliffs watching. But he knew the smugglers had already made their delivery, and another so soon would be unlikely. So he merely stood by the window in the parlour, watching the starry night over the sea.

When he'd believed she was dead, he'd always thought it was his fault, somehow. There were so many he had lost. Like Edward. If he'd never boasted about a soldier's exploits, maybe Edward wouldn't have followed him into war. So he'd wondered, time after time, if he had done something different, maybe she wouldn't have died. Yet he couldn't have married her, not after what she had done.

What if Rokeby was right? What if she was killed this time? It really would be his fault.

Having his fill of staring out the window, he sat in his favorite wing-back chair by a fire gone cold, holding the drawing of Hector with his mouth full of buttercups. He touched the page to his nose, remembering a scent he could not quite smell that filled his mind with images of a saucy girl with flashing green eyes and vivid red shawl, of Jane so plainly dressed, yet as vivid in her dark green wool riding habit. Of the woman she had become, something he could not picture, yet knew, deep in that place inside him that had been so long vacant.

Again and again, he traced the tip of his finger over the lines of the drawing.

❧

The ladies were settling down to their evening, looking through the books they had taken from the lending library in Liskeard, when the butler entered the library, clearing his throat in his usual fashion.

"Yes, Charles?" Lydia said.

"'Tis Mr. Rokeby, ma'am, to see Miss Darrow about a private matter."

"Me?" Jane squeaked. Why would he want to see her?

"Yes, ma'am, he was very specific."

A jumble of strange ideas tossed about her mind. Had Edenstorm been injured, or perhaps arrested for unconscionable rudeness? Maybe died of terminal arrogance?

Or, she thought with a secret inner smile, perhaps Mr. Rokeby was seeking her complicity in courting Lydia. She could see him doing that, for there was something very romantic in the man's soul. And he was certainly to be found in Lydia's company whenever the opportunity arose.

She scurried off to the sunny yellow parlour that was Lydia's favorite place in the entire house, thinking that might remind Mr. Rokeby of his interest, in case he needed bolstering. She smiled as she entered the parlour, but her smile abruptly faded, for Mr. Rokeby's anxiety overwhelmed his face. Gently bred though he was, he held his top hat tightly in his hands and looked as if he might bend its brim completely out of shape.

"Mr. Rokeby?" she said. "Won't you please sit? I can call for some tea."

"No, thank you, Miss Darrow. I've been called back to town, you see. On business. I must leave immediately."

"Oh." She couldn't think of anything else to say, not having any notion why he would be speaking to her.

"I am employed, you see," he added. "With the Home Office. Although I may not tell you my duties, may I say my position is important, and I have a reasonable salary."

"Um. How very nice for you."

"Not that I need employment, you understand. I have a reasonable competence from my grandfather, who was the sixth Earl of Cranston. I have reasonable family connections, too, you see."

Ah. She couldn't help the hint of a smile on her face and hoped she didn't embarrass him. He did mean to seek her assistance for Lydia's hand. How sweet.

"What I mean to say, Miss Darrow, I mean to ask, will you do me the honor of becoming my wife?"

Jane's jaw fell open. She couldn't even squeak out a reply.

"Even though I must be leaving immediately, Miss Darrow, if you will just say yes, then I may be assured you will be safe in my absence."

"Safe? I don't understand, Mr. Rokeby. I thought you were, I mean—"

"I am aware that we do not know each other well yet, Miss Darrow. But please do rest assured that I am cognizant of your true situation, and I shall not hold anything of the past against you. What's past is past and shall stay that way. Nor am I such a mild-mannered fellow that I cannot be your protector."

"Protector?"

"Oh, I did not mean it in quite that way, ma'am. Please understand I have only the greatest of respect for you and I assure you I have the most honorable of intentions. And although I must be leaving immediately, I assure you my name itself may be your protection until I return. If you will only give me my answer so I may be on my way."

"I see." But she did not. Only that he must be concerned about Edenstorm's manipulations. His very anxiety gave her a chill. Did he perhaps think if she agreed to marry him, then Edenstorm would have no hold over her? Whatever it was, a warmth stirred in her for the man, for his kindness.

She clasped her hands together, and studied her interlocking fingers. "Mr. Rokeby, you are the kindest, most caring and finest of men, and I thank you for your offer, which I am sure is meant for the best of reasons. But there are circumstances, I'm afraid, that prevent me entirely from marrying. I cannot explain to you, I'm sorry to say. But I cannot. I cannot marry anyone."

"I see," he said, and his face seemed to fall ever so slowly. "Surely, it could be worked out."

"No," and she shook her head. "It cannot. And I have reason to believe your heart may be elsewhere engaged, sir."

"Oh. Not really. I mean, it is of no importance. Two people who have high regard for each other must surely be able to make a go of it."

"I could not do that to you, sir. I am so grateful for your offer. Just knowing that you thought of me so kindly will lift my spirits."

"But if there is something you might tell me, something that I might be able to do for you, Miss Darrow, perhaps a task while I am in town, something you might want to know? I would be so glad to be of assistance. If you might need legal assistance or the sort..."

She frowned. "No, I don't think so, sir. My only wish is to live my life out quietly, here in Looe."

Mr. Rokeby drew his lips into a tight line. "Yes. Well. Perhaps if while I am gone, you will not go outside..."

"Oh, but I must, sir. My duties and all. Really, Mr. Rokeby, I am sure everything will be fine."

"Yes. I do hope so, Miss Darrow. But if you should have need of me, you will send for me? I shall come in all haste."

"Thank you sir. I shall do that."

"Well, then, I must be going. I must be in London by Wednesday. And I shall be back within a week, two at the most. You will take care, will you not, Miss Darrow?"

Jane felt her skin crawl as she saw Mr. Rokeby to the door. Did he also fear Edenstorm, so much that he was willing to sacrifice his own feelings to marry a woman he didn't love?

Chapter Nine

On Wednesday morning, Jane no more than stepped beyond the gate of Launceston Hall when she saw Davy sauntering up the hill, whistling a sailor's tune. Perhaps she should have expected that. And at least there was no sign of Lord Edenstorm lurking to surprise her.

"Good morning, darlin'," said Davy in his usual presumptive way. "'Tis a fine day the Lord has given us."

"It is indeed, Davy." And in her usual way, she could not help but smile back at him. But for all the sunshine in his smiling face, she spotted a dark spark lurking in his eyes. She had known the minute Davy had seen her riding with Edenstorm yesterday that she would hear about it no later than today. And she could no more tell Davy what Edenstorm was up to than she could tell Edenstorm of Davy's mysterious voyages into the night.

As smoothly as silk sliding over satin, Davy turned and joined her in her direction down the hill, taking her arm on his. She might as well have objected to the direction the river flowed, for she would have had as much effect. So Jane shrugged and spent a few minutes with the niceties, such as inquiring after Davy's slightly dotty mother and listening to how her usual aches and pains were somewhat better this morning. Jane made her usual observation that it might do the elderly woman good to be outside on such a bright and cheerful day, to which Davy made his own usual observation that she would not go beyond her own garden and was probably too old to change her ways now.

"Was it a good ride ye had the other day, darlin'?"

She stiffened. Not because she hadn't expected the question, but more because she had.

"It was a nice day to be riding," she replied. "Too long since the last rain to be muddy, but not so long that we kicked up a dust. And the view from the Downs is magnificent."

"Did it take so long to see the view from the Downs?"

"I only do it for Lady Beck, Davy. It would be Lady Beck's social obligation to ride with a man such as he when he visits her community. But since neither Lady Beck nor Lady Launceston is able to ride these days, and no other ladies about who care for riding, I must substitute. It is expected of me."

"I'm thinking ye see a lot of the man."

Jane sighed, trying to make it sound natural. "And I suppose I'll be seeing him again tonight at the Tremayne's dinner. Although since his friend Mr. Rokeby had to return to London so suddenly, I suppose I could beg off and Mrs. Tremayne might be pleased. Must keep the numbers even, you know."

"I never understood that about the Quality. I invite who I please to dinner."

"As long as it pleases your mother."

"Aye, there's that," he agreed with as grin. "Which means I don't have dinner parties."

"It's just that way, Davy."

"I suppose ye'll dance with the man, too."

Her entire body tightened. It was not dancing, but waltzing Davy found so immoral. But Mr. Tremayne was noted for his waltzing parties, a scandal in the eyes of the good Methodists of the community such as Davy. And she had no doubt Edenstorm would demand a waltz of her.

If she didn't find a way to pacify Davy—well, she had never been altogether sure what the man might do.

Yet he was too kind in his heart to be sinister. Wasn't he? Or did he simply charm her too easily? He was altogether too much like his great-aunt, Lady Launceston, who was so unusually fond of him.

"Mr. Tremayne must always have his music, you know. I'm sure there will be dancing. I suspect Lady Beck will even give it a go tonight, if it doesn't jar her arm too much."

"Ye know what I mean, Jane. It's not proper to be seen so much in the man's company."

"But for the *ton*, it's nothing, Davy. I'm only a spare. I am merely brought along on the train of Lady Beck's skirts by the necessity of a lady to have a companion such as I. A woman may not live alone, so they allow me to fill up space and it solves a problem for them. But I'm nothing."

"Ye don't need to live that way when ye could have a good home among your equals, where ye'd be appreciated."

She drew her lips into a line so thin she thought they must surely have turned white. She wished he did not care so much for her. Odd, how not so very long ago she had almost wished she could accept his offer. She supposed she should thank Edenstorm for clarifying that for her.

Jane sighed without realizing it until the sound was already out. She wished she could tell him the truth, but she had heard him speak against loose women and the men who used them. She could not keep denying him without a better explanation, but when she told him, she would have no choice but to leave Looe. Something a woman with no place to go could not do.

Davy took his own deep breath, and she could hear it rush out. He turned to her. "He's got a hold on ye somehow, Jane. Is he a bother to ye?"

Her laugh had a funny jitter to it and she tried to look him in the eye, but glanced down too soon. "Of course he does not, Davy. He is naught more than a jaded dandy seeking a lark. But we know, don't we, Cornwall will not charm him long. You know how Town gentlemen are, in such a hurry to get to the country, and then once there discovering the country is too quaint for them."

As if Edenstorm had been summoned by their talk, Jane spied Hector coming up the hill toward them, heading toward Launceston Hall. A frisson that must surely be half fear raced up her spine. Edenstorm, resplendent in deep blue with fawn inexpressibles and gleaming black boots soon looked down at them from his high perch on Hector's saddle. Just the sort of thing to set Davy's teeth on edge.

"Good morning, Miss Darrow," Edenstorm said. "Polruhan," he added as if it had just occurred to him to be kind to his inferiors.

"Good morning to ye," responded Davy. "Me lord," he tacked on. "Ye'll be going up to the country alone today, I see."

Edenstorm's silver gaze sliced from Davy to Jane, and the corner of his mouth lifted with a hint of disdain. "Going too far afield for a lady's comfort today. Hector needs to stretch his legs."

"'Tis no more'n thirty miles across Cornwall to the Irish Sea, me lord. Ye can't be going far enough."

Jane cringed, but Edenstorm hardly narrowed his eyes and the innuendo slid over him as if inconsequential. The innuendo was not lost on him, just ignored. "Won't be back before nightfall. I'll be seeing you at Tremayne's on Friday, Miss Darrow."

Jane nodded as he tipped his hat and rode away up the hill. And if she'd felt a frisson before, now her spine fairly shimmered with dread. She wished these two had never met. Even more, she hoped they never met with her caught between them.

"Something could happen to him."

The gasp caught in her throat and she thought she'd choke. "Davy, you wouldn't! You are a good Christian man."

"Now, darlin', I never said I'd harm the man. But he asks too many questions. People are talking about him, Jane. They say he walks the streets late at night and goes out to the cliffs. They say he's got a haunted soul. And whatever it is he wants here, he's got no business knowing about. Do ye answer his questions?"

"Don't be silly. I know how it is here, an outsider is always an outsider. But I owe so much to you and everyone of Looe. 'Tis my home now, Davy."

"Hmm. Be sure ye remember that. There's some who don't forget ye come from afar."

"Truly, Davy, you worry for nothing. I know my own tongue. The man will be gone soon, off on another lark with the whole of East and West Looe forgotten, no more in his mind than a tiny town divided by a river."

Davy walked in silence for a few moments, leaving Jane feeling oddly tense. She had never misled him about her intentions never to marry, but no one had ever challenged Davy's right to possession of her before. No one ever challenged Davy about anything.

No one like Edenstorm had ever come to Looe before. She felt the danger like a stifling shroud coming down on her face.

"I don't trust him, Jane," Davy said at last. "But could be ye're right. Sometimes 'tis best not to stir the dust if the tracks are to be hidden. But I'm thinking maybe we could make use of this. Maybe ye could keep him busy. Say, on next Monday morning. Away from Looe."

Her eyes widened. "Davy, you're not to do anything dangerous or harmful."

"Never said such a thing, darlin'. I'm a good Christian man, as ye say. But 'twould be good not to have prying eyes about on Monday. And there's ways of dealing with a man, even a powerful lord, without hurting a soul."

"But I promised Lady Launceston we'd—"

She suddenly brightened, piecing together the rags of her quandary into a whole, like a country quilt. "Oh, yes, I think I could do that, Davy. Monday. All day."

Davy nodded and touched the tip of his gloved finger to her nose. "Ye be taking care of yerself, lass. I want no harm coming to the woman I'm to marry."

Jane snorted.

Davy laughed back at her.

&&&

True to form, Mr. Tremayne made his dinner party into an evening of music and dancing. The rugs were rolled back and more candles lit until the smell of burning wax laced the air.

Equally true to form, Edenstorm turned his compelling silver eyes on her and without saying a word, held out his hand, demanding a dance. Jane felt her heart battering her chest with its wild rhythm. His hand on hers felt like fire burning through her, and his hand at her waist burned more like ice. She was as stiff as an ancient oak in his arms.

"You may relax, Miss Darrow," he said in a low whisper. "I shall not devour you before all these good people."

The frisson shimmered through her. She ought to be getting used to it by now. No, he wouldn't eat her alive here. Just roast her in the flames in preparation for his later private feast.

Jane decided to retaliate with his own weapons. She lowered her lashes demurely, then suddenly looked directly into his eyes and slid on her most dazzling smile.

He missed his step. She allowed herself to relish the moment in secret.

"It's just that I fear you will step on my toes, sir," she said sweetly.

"Minx," he growled.

From that moment, he paid perfect attention to the dancing. Jane pursed her lips so she would not break out laughing.

Nor did he surprise her when he made sure they were standing amongst her friends when he asked, politely of course, that she ride with him on Monday to show him the Old Barbican up on the hill, as he had an interest in antiquities. He was in some ways a very predictable man, and she intended to use that for her own benefit.

So of course, it was also no surprise when Lady Launceston, in a manner to be expected by all who knew her, flashed her best silly schoolgirl smile at Edenstorm. "Oh, Lord Edenstorm, you know, Jane has promised to accompany me on a little trek up to Tregorney Hall to visit Mrs. Tregorney. She does not get out much since her husband went aloft and she is so glad for a bit of company. But we would be so pleased to have such a handsome man as you doing the driving. No doubt you are a dab hand, as they say."

Jane fought her tendency to lick her lips, which then led to a battle against a catlike grin. Eventually she gained control. With a perfectly proper social smile. "It would be delightful," she said. "All those daily rides must require a nice diversion from time to time."

Edenstorm rewarded her with a smile so brittle she was

afraid his jarring footsteps would shatter it and, following a bow of perfect politeness, he turned and walked away.

She laughed to herself. *One does not always get one's way, my lord. Especially when a mere earl is up against the formidable Lady Launceston.*

If there was anything good about the man, it was his rigid adherence to his social obligations, for he prized propriety more than anything. He appeared at Launceston Hall precisely at nine of the clock on Monday morning. His nod to Jane was icy, but more than warm to Lady Launceston. And he expressed proper regret that Lady Beck felt the ache in her arm too deeply after the previous night's dancing and had decided not to make the journey with them. In perfectly proper fashion, he climbed up onto the driver's seat while a footman assisted the two ladies into the carriage behind him.

Out of the corner of her eye, Jane saw him take note of the long, flat packet a footman surreptitiously slipped into the narrow boot beneath the driver's seat. She pursed her lips to keep from grinning in an untoward and unladylike manner.

She had to admit, he did the pretty uncommonly well. He was the perfect escort, showing attention to Lady Launceston, who was of a certain age that commanded more than the usual respect from a gentleman. When they arrived at Tregorney Hall, he treated the elderly widow with uncommon kindness and gentility. He might be the man she thought best suited to write the bible for propriety, but his genuine affection for the two elderly ladies couldn't be denied.

They took tea in a parlour that was delicately fitted out in lovely shades of soft blue, and he did not so much as wince or squirm through an entire discussion of the Gothic romances which the two older ladies had just exchanged. He could, in fact, discuss them intelligently, which made her wonder if he might actually have read them. But that would not be the Edenstorm she knew. He would instead have picked up information from his mother and sister, or even gone to the extent of having his secretary read the books and produce a report on them. She could imagine him doing that.

When they had been more than two hours into the discussion, Mrs. Tregorney finally noticed the time and invited them to join her for supper. At last Jane caught Edenstorm wincing, but it was so slight, she was sure no one else saw it. Fortunately, Lady Launceston came to his rescue and insisted they must be going back, for the roads were quite crude and dangerous to negotiate at night, even with so fine a driver as Lord Edenstorm.

When they returned to the carriage, Jane noted his eyes sought out the packet that had been beneath the seat. It was, as she expected, not there.

"Jane," he said when he was sure no one else was close enough to hear, "what happened to the packet?"

"Packet, sir?"

"The one beneath the seat."

She looked. She cocked her head with a puzzled frown. "There's nothing beneath the seat, sir."

"I know that. What happened to it?"

"To what, sir?"

"The packet, Jane."

"What packet, sir? I confess, I have no notion what you are talking about."

He glowered, his nostrils flaring so widely, she was reminded of a bull about to charge. "Under my very nose, Jane?"

She turned up the corners of her mouth prettily.

He had no chance to probe further, for Mrs. Tregorney was saying a nearly tearful goodbye to Lady Launceston and Jane, and expressing her profuse delight at meeting such a fine gentleman as Lord Edenstorm. He had no further chance to say anything on the return journey, for Jane and Lady Launceston chatted gaily all the way back to Launceston Hall, where they arrived shortly after sunset.

"All right, what was it?" he asked as she saw him to the door to leave.

"What, sir?"

"The packet. What was it?"

She shrugged, but knew her eyes were twinkling. "How big was it?"

"Flat, narrow, long." He measured out the dimensions with his hand. "Perhaps the size of a package of Belgian lace?"

"Perhaps French gloves?" she proposed.

"Ah."

"Or perhaps a few ells of watered silk?"

His eyes narrowed and one corner of his mouth lifted in a mild sneer. "Too small for that."

"Then not an anker of brandy."

"Of course not."

"Nor fine-rolled cigars. Nor a bundle of tea leaves."

He fisted his hands at his hips, elbows spread wide. "Under my very nose, Jane."

Jane cocked her head and laughed. "Ah, not to worry, my lord. Your nose is not so very huge that it can accommodate a large number of objects beneath it."

She smirked as she watched him mount Hector. *And you have no idea, my lord, what else is going on beneath your very nose.*

❧

Edenstorm took back his horse from the stable boy and rode down the hill, across the Looe River bridge, then up the hill into East Looe to his cottage, thinking about how pleasant the evening ahead would be with none but the very terse Nance for company.

As he rode into the small park and up to the stable, Trevenny hurried out to take Hector by the bridle. "Best hurry inside, me lord," Trevenny said. "Nance is in a stir."

Why? There was scarcely even a film of dust for Nance to brush off his coat. But he nodded and strode to the house, where Nance greeted him at the door.

"Welcome home, my lord. I do hate to bother you so soon, as you've just arrived, but I'm afraid we've got a problem."

Frowning, Edenstorm followed Nance through the house into the remotest corner of the kitchen, where that crude staircase led down into the cellar. As they reached the lower stairs, he saw the problem for himself.

"What the devil?"

It was rather obvious what the devil it was. Stack after stack of small kegs, the little ankers only smugglers used because a man could carry two of them.

"Fifty of them," said Nance. "Precisely."

"How the devil did they get in here?"

"Don't know, sir. I suspect I'll have to move all fifty of them to get to the answer." He rubbed his back in such a way that Edenstorm guessed he'd probably already been shifting the little kegs around.

"Where were you while this was happening?"

"I went down to the village, sir. A little shopping for dinner and some champagne to put in my bootblack, and came back to find the cellar door barred. I thought someone might have come up into the house and went looking about, but didn't find anything missing. Came back, and the door was open."

"I see. Where was Trevenny?"

"It was his day off, sir. To visit his ailing mother. He's just returned. Looks like someone is telling you to leave well enough alone, sir."

He gathered that. Either leave well enough alone or get a visit from the Excise Officer from Fowey. Who, unlike the local customs officer, had not been bought off.

But it also occurred to him no one would have bothered delivering such a message unless his investigation was getting uncomfortably close to something. Therefore, it was time not to give up, but to raise the ante.

A quick inspection of the cellar revealed nothing more than they had found a few days before, yet it was obvious all this brandy hadn't come in through the house.

With a snort to express his frustration, Edenstorm went back up the stairs with Nance, where he accepted a glass of claret, brandy being the last thing he wanted. He stood in the parlour looking out through the rectangular panes of the front windows over the steep-sloped tiny park toward the sea.

There was another message that came with the kegs below, a more sinister one. Whoever they were, they could get into his house anytime they wanted and do what they wanted.

And worse, a message that had not been intended, but that he had put together from many pieces of his own.

Rokeby was right. Jane could get hurt, and it would be his fault. No matter how much Jane was involved with the smugglers, she did not deserve what could happen to her if she got caught in the middle of something ugly that he had started.

She had been pushed too far and she was fighting back, perhaps with the help of her smuggling friends. Perhaps all of them had had enough of his meddling, but he knew he had gone beyond the pale with her. Just as he had years before, he had given her a very ugly taste of himself, and her message to him was very clear.

She had lied to him, deceived him, misled him, distracted him, done everything else but help him, all while pretending to meet his demands. But he knew in his heart there was no threat large enough to make her betray those she loved. Nor would she willingly trade herself. She would instead sacrifice herself rather than submit to him or give them over to him.

As he leaned back in his chair, he thought of how she would laugh when she learned of this. How the rest of his life he would hear the sound of it chiming in his mind like silver bells.

Maybe he wouldn't tell her.

The devil! She probably already knew. She knew all about it, just like she knew all about the French kid gloves that rode so insidiously beneath his seat all the way to Tregorney Hall.

He'd been a cad. Nothing less. He'd have to find another way to hunt down Guinea Jack.

Edenstorm groaned. How in damnation did one get rid of fifty ankers of brandy, fast?

Chapter Ten

"Fifty ankers?" Jane made no pretense of even hiding her giggle.

She could have laughed, too, at the way the sunlight bounced in the window of the bright yellow parlour and danced in the waves of his golden bronze hair. But that laugh would have been one of delight.

Edenstorm winced and that only made her laugh harder. Davy had never said a word about it, but she knew exactly how those little kegs had gotten into Edenstorm's cellar. The old Pendennen manor had an unusual tunnel, and everyone in Looe knew about it. Everyone except Edenstorm.

"Exactly fifty," he grumbled back. "Precisely what do you know about them?"

"Why, absolutely nothing, sir, only that smugglers prefer to use ankers instead of larger kegs."

"I'm aware of that, Miss Darrow. I find it fascinating that they happened to appear in my cellar at the same time you had me traipsing off into the country with a pair of contraband French kid gloves beneath my seat."

"French kid gloves, sir? There you go, making assumptions again. And we did not traipse. We went for a visit to a dear old lady. I believe you may be referring to Lady Beck's needlework. She likes to keep her hands busy, you know."

"Lady Beck has a broken arm, and in any case she did not accompany us."

She tittered again. This was such fun. "Yes, I noticed."

"Miss Darrow," he said, standing abruptly, his irritation

showing in his jutted jaw. "Enough of that. I have come to say something."

His sharpness startled her. Perhaps her teasing had gone too far. She shrugged, for it was not anything he didn't deserve. "Then do get on with it, sir, for I am sure you cannot be prevented."

His scowl deepened. She could not tell when he was all about bluffing or not, but she had made her decision. He was not going to get the best of her, no matter what mischief he had in mind.

"I have decided you are of no use to me as an informant. Your information cannot be trusted."

"Would you be saying I am a liar, sir?"

"Most definitely. Nevertheless, in your case it is understandable. A matter of loyalty. That, I find, I must honor. It does not change my goal, of course, but I shall not coerce your assistance."

She blinked, her mouth slowly dropping open. Was that an apology? If so, it was a rather lame one.

"Well," she replied, thinking she must choose her words carefully, for there might be some sort of trap in them. "I suppose I am rather glad to be useless, for once."

The silver eyes held her gaze in a silent moment, strangely glowering, yet, she thought, searching, evaluating, in a way that puzzled her. Should she have thanked him? Perhaps acknowledged what she wasn't even sure was meant to be apologetic? Whatever it was, she didn't seem to have met his expectation. Never had she met a more mystifying man.

He cleared his throat, which she had learned was a sign that he was finally getting to his circuitous point. "However, I would like for you to ride with me today."

"But I thought you said—"

"I only ask you to ride with me, Miss Darrow, not conspire."

"Then if you have nothing to hold over my head, why should I ride with you?"

"Because I want to ride with you. Just to ride. Because it is such a perfect day."

Jane saw in his eyes a different kind of intensity. Not the

chilling coldness she had first known in him, nor the blazing heat of his fury. It had a depth and warmth that made her question herself, wonder if she had always been wrong about him, and perhaps the icy gray had never been there. Made her think, perhaps, yes, the man inside was not soulless.

It drew her like the pull of a magnet.

She should say no. Just to show him she could.

But it was a perfect day. So she joined him. They rode and rode and rode, then walked to rest the horses and let them graze, and rode some more. They stopped for a glass of claret beneath the tall oaks in the forest, and tasted slivers of fine Cheddar cheese he carved off a wedge with his knife. They rode along the river, along the tall cliffs and at last, along the beach.

The sea was yellow gold as the sun dropped toward the horizon, a quiet plane of precious metal that melted into silvered sand, and as far as the eye could see, changed from gilded sea to brilliant amber sky. All the world was silver and gold.

The horses paced across the wet sand, their steps muffled, disturbing the metallic sheen that settled back to serenity in the little rounded puddles they left behind. Only the quiet huffing of the horses' breath and the faint screech of gulls far out from the shore broke the silence.

She had long ago loosened her bonnet and let it fall behind her, to feel the delicate breeze in her hair as they rode. Beside her rode the man with silver eyes and golden hair, his face dark in the shadow, as silent as the quiet water. It had been his idea to ride along the shore, taking advantage of the long beach created when the tide ebbed. But low tide was a curious thing that made one believe in the forever of an instant. She had come along, appeasing him because...Was it because she must keep him occupied, to keep him from making discoveries about the people she loved?

Oddly, though. She had come to expect, almost to want his companionship. Never knowing when he would turn the quiet of the moment into some strange demand that ruined all that was beautiful. Or if he would not. Perhaps today was one of those times when he would remain silent, or trade the silence for small, beautiful words.

He was, in so many ways, a strange man. He did not court

her. But he shared beautiful things with her, often in silence, as if he accepted or believed they saw them the same way. She wondered if they did. Did he see and feel the colors with the sort of passion that invaded her?

They reached the headland that separated this beach from the next, and he pulled ahead. Here, their ride must come to an end.

"Don't go there," she said, and reached for the bridle on his bay.

"Why?" But he reined in his horse.

"It isn't safe beyond this point."

"Is that a cave?" His head inclined in the direction of the sharply jagged cove tucked between two cliffs.

"Yes. But you can only see it when the tide is out."

"Then I want to see it."

"No. It is dangerous. There have been too many rockfalls into the sea, and it's hard to go around except when the tide is very far out. And if you stay too long, the tide will trap you."

"I could climb out."

"But your horse could not."

For an answer, he stroked the bay's mane. She knew he was fond of Hector. Something about him told her he had a fondness for all horses.

"Is it a smuggler's cave?"

"It's called Colliver's Cove. They say it was used by Robert Colliver, but they also say Robert Colliver left Looe in his youth and never returned. Both could not be true. They also tell tales of men who drowned because a high sea came up and caught them inside. When the tide comes in, the cavern floods."

"Is there another way out?"

"There is a hole near the top, but it cannot be reached from inside."

"So you have seen it."

"Yes."

"You got out safely."

"I went when everything was right. I did not stay."

Edenstorm leaned forward in his saddle. He planted a fist

on his hip and narrowed his eyes as he studied the small, dark opening that marked the top of the cave. "If I were a smuggler, I'd think it ideal. Drop ropes through the top. Hide the ankers, strung together inside the cave. Let them float. But pull them through the top when there is no one around to see."

"But you are not a smuggler, and you do not know everything you would need to know."

"And you do?"

"More than you, and that is not enough. They say once the kegs floated out to sea and the entire cache was lost."

"So they have used it. Do they use it now?"

"There is no need for it these days."

"Why?"

"There is a war. No one pays much attention to free traders these days. You have never seen a riding officer near Looe, have you?"

That deep dimple formed in his right cheek. "No."

"Don't go in there," she said again. "There are many ways to be killed on the Cornish Coast. That is one of them."

His ghostly silver eyes studied her for a moment, then he dismounted. He held his hands up to her and she slid down, his hands catching around her waist. They turned back to the beach they had just left.

He stopped, scanning the distant horizon where the sun dropped lower in the sky and began to tinge the gold with pink.

"If you painted, how would you paint this?"

"Rapidly. Soon the sun will go down and we will never see it quite this way again." She swept her hand in an arc along the horizon. "It is not simply golden, anywhere. It is only the way the many colors work together that makes it so." She pointed to a distant promontory. "Look over there. Even the rock in the distance is bathed in gold, yet none of it is truly the color it seems."

He stood there, his eyes intense and hazy, darkening to smoky pewter. She was aware of the scent that was his, so close and mingling with the salt of the sea and flesh of horse, with leather and brawn.

"I could never paint," he said, his voice as soft as fine

doeskin. "But I could never forget this. If I could paint, I would paint you, bathed in gold, just as you are right now. The color of your hair gleams like tiny strands of golden light."

He took one of her curls into his fingers, then slipped a hand into her hair. A tangle of longing twisted and turned in his eyes. "I'd want to capture the light shining in your hair and playing across your face, the softness of your lips."

"How do you know they're soft?" she whispered.

"I just do." The pad of his thumb crossed over her lower lip. "Yes, soft."

She gasped as his lips touched hers, but not from fear or outrage, but because she had not known her own longing. Had not known the feel of his arms circling her and pulling her close to his body where she could feel all his firmness as if she flowed into it, his kiss deepening and stroking in ways that set her afire inside. Her heart raced with the pounding of an unexplainable wildness within her, the heat she had not understood that had been building from the moment she had first seen him on the beach.

Abruptly, he pulled back, frowning, and dropped his hands from her waist. His jaw took on that hard, jutting look it had when he was getting stubborn. He turned away and walked back to the standing horses.

The wildness drained out of her like water through a hole in a pot. Sometimes she wanted so much to slap him.

"Well, I would say I did that wrong," she said, and strode back to the gentle brown hack she had been riding.

"You did nothing wrong." But his face was hard like an iron mask.

"Oh, my," she said, and sneered. "I would never have known."

"I told you I do not feel things."

"You lie. You feel things as much as anyone else. You just lie to yourself about it."

His shoulders stiffened, and she could see his jaw jutting even more. He stormed across the sand, his bay gelding in tow, toward the line of brush and furze that grew close to the shore, and found a bush that almost could be called a tree. He tossed the reins over a branch, then turned and stalked back toward the promontory that separated the sandy beach from the cove that ended in Colliver's Cave.

Oh no! He wouldn't! But yes, she knew him all too well. And it was her fault, for she had told him not to go.

She left her brown hack and ran after him, feet slipping and squishing in the dry sand. "Lord Edenstorm, be reasonable," she called after him.

"Reasonable? Why do you tell me not to go there, my dear? Is there something inside the cave I should not see? Contraband, perhaps? You can go back. There is no need for you to go."

"No, if you are going, I'm going, too."

"No you're not."

"Yes, I am. I told you, you must not go, so naturally, then, you think you must do it, and it will be my fault if something bad happens."

"Then why did you tell me?"

"Can't you just believe me when I say it isn't safe? Oh, but no, I am forgetting, you do not believe anything I say. Well, look for yourself, then. When the sea enters a narrow cove like this, it rises swiftly. It is the sea boring against the rock that makes a cave, and think what power the waves must have to do that."

"The sea is as calm and smooth as glass."

"And what's beyond the horizon? You can't tell because the point in the distance obscures it. Storms are common here in the spring, and they come up quickly. You do not even have a lantern. How will you see what is inside?"

In the fading light, he stood on the narrow strip of sand at the end of the promontory and studied the cave, and the rock around it, his gaze following on either side of the cave and upward over the jagged rocks to the top of the cliff. The incoming sea lapped at the rockfalls, already beginning to cut off what little path lay around them. Surely he would see reason.

"Why do you know so much about it, then?"

"Because I draw. I pay attention to details."

He frowned. She watched his mouth twist in a funny way to one side. "Ten hours from now, then," he said.

"In the middle of the night? You are crazy, Lord Edenstorm. You could get killed on the rocks."

"Funny it doesn't seem to stop the Gentlemen in the middle of the night."

"Cornishmen know their coves and inlets. They know the sea. And still they are killed."

"It will be nearly dawn. And you will come with me."

Jane put her hands over her eyes. "Well, of course I cannot. I cannot possibly be seen climbing on the rocks with you in the early morning light. A lady does not go out at night alone, sir."

The dimple struck up on his cheek again. "Oh, but my dear, you will not be alone. And you are so very good at sneaking out. It seems to be a lifetime habit with you."

"What do you mean?"

"Or perhaps I was mistaken and that was Lady Juliette who was walking up the road with a shawl like yours around her head."

"You're despicable," she said.

"No doubt. But I'm also right. Tomorrow before dawn."

"No. We will do it my way or not at all."

"Why?"

"Because, you slackbrain, I don't want to die. Do what you will with your own life. I'll be sure to tell the beadle where I last saw you."

Edenstorm was amazingly silent, for once.

"Tomorrow afternoon," she continued. "An hour before low tide, on this beach. We'll still have more than an hour before sundown, enough time to get in and out safely and be back before it's too dark. No horses. We don't go if there's rain."

"It's a long walk."

"Only a few miles. But I'll not leave horses tied to a tree limb to starve if we fail to come back."

"We won't be hurt. We could climb down if the beach worries you."

Jane rolled her eyes.

"All right. I'll let you do it your way." A wry twist formed on his lips. "But I'll bring the gig. We'll leave them where they can't be missed, so you need not fear they will die of starvation if we should perish on the rocks."

She tossed a disgusted look at him and strode to her hack to mount. She needed little more than a good rock for a mounting block, but in that imperious way of his that took pride in the manly art of assisting a woman who needed no assistance, Edenstorm rushed up and laced his hands to take her step. She stiffened at the suddenness of his scent that assaulted her the moment he drew near.

The good thing about riding horses was he couldn't stay that close while they were riding.

In the same way their previous ride had ended, they returned in silence, with only an occasional remark competing with the calls of the gulls. The sun had dropped behind the horizon and the golden glow gone from the sea. They passed through the stone gate of Launceston Hall, and the imperious gentleman handed her down, his powerful muscles making nothing of her weight.

"Tomorrow," he said. "I will come for you at four."

She pursed her lips and frowned, stepping back to make more distance between them, but it only amused him. Jane spun around and hurried through the door.

She hurried even faster past Charles to the stairs at the far end of the corridor, barely noticing the glow of candles in the lower parlour as she rushed past.

"Oh Jane, dear."

She paused and sighed. Lady Launceston. Well, what did she expect? She was, after all, expected to mind her duties as their companion at least occasionally. She looked longingly at the stairs, but turned back to the parlour.

Would they see the kiss on her face?

She swiped her hand across her mouth as if she might belatedly wipe away its last trace like an errant speck of currant jelly.

~

At precisely four of the clock on Wednesday afternoon,

Edenstorm appeared at the front door of Launceston Hall, two fine horses at his command to draw a fine gig. Jane groaned, but she stepped outside the door before he could jump down. The sooner they were out of sight of anyone who might talk, the better, although she knew the impossibility of avoiding gossip in a tiny town like Looe. There was no hiding the fact that Edenstorm was acting as if he were courting her, and only Jane really understood he was not. Not even Lady Launceston or Lydia fobbed his attention off as boredom. She dared not tell them the truth of the man's intentions, lest it get back to the very men he was hunting. She might dislike Edenstorm, but she had no wish to bring him harm, and he seemed immune to the notion that his pursuit could generate interest in his activities.

In his usual way when he was of a mood to be silent, Edenstorm handed her up to the gig's seat, letting his haunting eyes do his talking. She felt a shiver go up her spine as his silver gaze slid over her, marking her as his own. She did not belong to him. She would not. The last thing in the world she wanted to be was a man's property. She'd had too much experience with that.

Jane rode along beside the silent man as they went up the hill, above the inlet where they had been the day before. It would have been easier to walk it than to suffer the jiggling of the gig on the rocks, but it was not a long ride to Colliver's Cove.

Edenstorm took the turn down to the beach where they had watched the sun set the day before and stopped beneath the cliff where the ground was higher than the highest tides. There he handed her down and unhitched the pair, staking them out where they could eat their fill of a small plot of lush grass.

"You see, I have given thought to the welfare of my beasts," he said. "If we should come to our doom on the rocks, they will be fat as country pigs when they are found."

Jane deliberately arched her brows.

As Edenstorm strode down the slope toward the sand, a lantern in his hand and a rucksack slung over one shoulder, she huffed and started after him, running to keep up with his long strides.

"What's in the rucksack?" she asked as she caught up with

him.

"Necessary things."

"What sort of necessary things?"

"Tinderbox and flint. A rope. Sausages and cheese."

"Really, Edenstorm, this is not the time for a picnic."

He stopped and turned her, the dimple dancing on his cheek as he mimicked the hand she placed on her hip. "I have never known you to turn down food. Really, Jane, you will have to watch your weight soon if you are not careful."

"Don't change the subject, sir. We are not here to play. We are to go in and out quickly. Do you understand?"

"That will depend on how large the cave is."

"Small."

"Good. Then it will not take us long. Provided we do not run into any pirates. But since I was already here at dawn, I have little fear of that."

"You are going to be very disappointed. I suppose you have already been into the cave, which makes me wonder precisely I have bothered to come along."

"I merely watched the tide flow. I must admit, I have come to the conclusion you are right. The place could be quite dangerous if one does not pay attention to the tides. I checked the back side, too, by the way."

"Because you didn't believe me. You don't have enough to do, Edenstorm."

That enticing but maddening dimple formed in his cheek, prompting a sudden desire in her to taste it with the tip of her tongue. As if a dimple might actually have a taste. How utterly silly.

"I have plenty to do, my dear," he said, still striding over the sand, "and good enough reason for it. I have to make it look like I am just a jaded dandy rusticating on a whim. Come along now. We do not have a great deal of time."

"As I believe I told you."

"Less than two hours to get all the way in, look it over and make our way back around the point. Otherwise we shall be obliged to climb the cliff, and it is not particularly amenable to climbing."

"As I also said."

"So you did. I have confirmed it. Let us be going."

Jane wondered if her eyes were emitting steam, for certainly her nostrils were. She lifted her skirt as they started over a rockfall at the very end of the promontory. She paused to check the sky out to sea, which had a gloom of blanketing gray clouds and the distant horizon looked darker than what pleased her. Not like yesterday, with its serenely striped sky and glassy sea. The wind was picking up. Something might be blowing in, but she couldn't tell, for the distant sea was obscured by the point of land to the southeast. Surely it would take more than a few hours for anything to arrive.

He would not believe her, in any case. In fact, that would only drive him to greater curiosity, so, best in and out as fast as possible. She huffed to herself and picked her way over the rocks, even allowing him to help her down the other side of the rockfall.

"Taking longer than I thought," he said as they once again descended to the narrow line of sand between water and cliff.

She thinned her lips and resisted saying she had told him so.

Three times, they climbed up and over the steep piles of rocks that had fallen from the cliffs, and reached the fourth one just as the tide receded far enough that they could clamber over it and into the low entrance of the cave. They crossed the sandy strip almost at a run, Edenstorm's giant strides bouncing in his eagerness.

He had to stoop to look into the cave. He frowned.

"I presume you will light the lantern now," she said.

The nostrils of his elegantly long nose widened, somehow making him look even more conceitedly superior than before. He dug into his pack and fished out flint and tinderbox. She leaned against the jagged dark rock of the cliff, arms folded, as he struck the flint repeatedly until she smelled the smoldering tinder.

It struck her as odd, not that he knew how to do such things, for surely even the most affluent of aristocrats could strike a flint. He was at ease with such things. He rode over rough country as if he knew it well when he did not. His garments, although they fit well, lacked the tightness of a dandy's perfect fit and seemed constructed for comfort and movement. He was an odd man.

She had learned to value the simpler things in life. Had he? Had being a soldier changed him? Many a man bought his colors but came back and took up his place among the rich and powerful, behaving much as if he had never suffered a single day's march or night's encampment.

The candle wick caught fire, tingeing the air with the acrid odor of burning wick and tallow. He raised the lantern, grinning. Edenstorm stepped inside the cave, ducking his head, and Jane came in after him.

Inside, the walls gleamed, still dripping with the water left from the last high tide. They could see the sand at their feet, but beyond the lantern's glow and the small hole near the cavern's roof that let in a shaft of failing daylight, all was blackness.

"I can't tell how big it is," he said.

Jane looked around the darkness and shivered. She hated this place. "No bigger than a small cottage, I suppose."

He lifted the lantern high, away from his face. "Is that a ledge?"

It wasn't a ledge. It was a huge slab of rock that had fallen from the cave's ceiling. "Don't go up there, Edenstorm."

"Why? Not safe?"

"We don't have enough time."

She might as well have been talking to the cave walls, for all the attention he paid to her words. He set the lantern on a rock above his head and scaled up the slope of fallen debris that led to the ledge several feet above the cave floor, moving the lantern as he moved upward until he reached the ledge and stood. "Coming?" he asked, holding out the lantern to light her way.

Jane grumbled and climbed. Not that it was hard, for it was not. The pile of rocks gave ample footholds. Soon she stood beside him, and he moved the lantern to shine light around them.

"Looks like a slab of rock that fell from the ceiling," he said.

"One more reason I don't care to be in here," she replied. "There is nothing stable about this place, Lord Edenstorm."

"But it fell a long time ago. There is a lot of moss growing on the surface."

"A lot of moss can grow in a few years."

He walked to the edge, then back to the cave wall, swinging the lantern in a slow arc. He stopped, reached down and picked up a stave from an anker and the rusted metal band that had bound it.

"So they stored their little kegs up here on the shelves. But that was long ago, too. The metal is almost rusted away."

"Why just one stave?" she asked.

His eyebrows rose. "The others were washed away?"

"Marvelous deduction."

"So the cave fills with water at high tide?"

"Sometimes during storms water has been seen spewing out the hole in the roof."

He shifted the rucksack off his back and dropped it to the slab, where he sat and began rummaging in it.

"What are you doing?"

He pulled out a blanket and spread it over the rock and set a wine bottle and two goblets, cheese and bread on the blanket. "A light repast before dinner. I'm hungry. Aren't you, after all that walking?"

"Not really." But she was. He was right about her. She did enjoy food, perhaps a bit too much for her own good. She sat on the blanket, for the sooner she got this little repast over with, the sooner he would be willing to leave this forbidding place.

Edenstorm poured dark red wine into the two goblets, and the aroma filled the air, sweet and fruity against the musty scent of the cavern. With a knife he sliced the cheese and bread.

Jane sipped the wine and set it down. "I cannot imagine one would bring glassware in a rucksack. Why not just a couple of tin cups?"

"Tin gives the wine an odd taste. I had enough of that in the Peninsula."

Jane shrugged back. “I suppose that is good enough reason. It must have been a harrowing existence.”

“There were hard times. Most of it was not so terrible.”

“I heard you say your brother died at Albuera while you were there.”

She heard the sound of his exhaling in the damp air, for she was not looking at him. Somehow it was too much question for the meeting of eyes. Would he answer? Or would he make nothing of it, in the way he had of shrugging off anything of depth?

“I saw him fall.”

Her gaze shot up to his face, but he was looking off into the darkness of the cave.

“The entire square fell before they could form it. They had no chance. Their powder was wet from the sudden storm, and it had rained so hard, they couldn’t see the Polish Lancers riding up on them until it was too late. But from where we stood, we could see it all.”

“Oh, I am so sorry! That must have been the most horrible thing that happened to you.”

“No.”

Jane’s mouth dropped open. What kind of man was he that he didn’t feel the loss of his own brother? “Did you not care for him?”

She saw it instantly in the seething pain in his eyes. “I was very close to my brother. But he was a soldier. He saw friends die almost daily, not from battles so much as from sickness, but they died. He knew to expect to die.”

Edenstorm snatched up the wine bottle and sloppily poured himself another glass, but then his mouth drew into a thin line, and he wiped at what he had spilled with a cloth. The glass he lifted to his lips rose as if of its own accord, and with a slowness that was almost exquisite in its deliberateness.

“Wait, I don’t understand. Do you mean to say it was all right for him to die because he was a soldier? Or that he asked to die?”

“No. It just was not the worst. At least he had some say in his fate.”

That soulless look came over his face again, the one that had sent shudders up her spine years before, and she felt that same urge to runaway. She took a deep breath instead.

"What was the worst, Lord Edenstorm?"

"You should eat, Miss Darrow. It will be hours before we return for supper. Cheese?"

"No cheese, my lord. What was the worst? You might as well say it, for I shall now not stop nagging you until you do."

Once again the exhaling of his breath echoed within the cavern, and she saw that dimple form in his cheek, but this time, she knew there was no humor in what he was remembering.

"Perhaps the baby."

"Tell me about the baby."

His voice became as flat and plain as the dull nothingness in his face. The man of the distant past had returned.

"We were retreating to Corunna. It was very cold, ice and snow everywhere. We had lost our supplies, and the men were in rags, some barefoot. They cut hide off dead horses and took skirts from the dead women they found beside the road to wrap around their feet."

"Dead women?"

He glanced at her, then swiftly away. "Don't look so shocked. The women and children die first. They have no one to protect them."

"They just leave them there?"

"What else can they do? They are barely surviving themselves, starving, carrying a heavy pack. I had my last horse, at least until he died. But the soldiers are afoot, and their shoes wear right off them.

"One of my men heard a noise and found a baby in the arms of a dead woman we recognized as the wife of a man in the battalion ahead of us. We had no food for the baby, but since I was still riding, I put him inside my greatcoat. But it was too late. After a little while, he died, so Thompson took him back and laid him in the arms of the next woman we came upon."

His eyes turned from raging pain to mockery. "Well, Jane,

now will you eat your cheese?"

"No, I think not, thank you. I don't understand how you could have dealt with such a thing. I could not."

"Yes, you could. You would do your duty, the same as everyone else. It is amazing what a person can deal with when he must."

"That is what you do. Your duty."

"That is my life."

Jane listened to the steady breathing of the man beside her. So this was the man she had thought had no soul. It was instead a soul shot through with pain. There was something in his eyes, in the hard set of jaw, the stiffness of shoulder that reminded her of herself after she had left Harlton Hall. She remembered her own pain, how she had tried to close it out.

But unlike her, he had succeeded.

"The baby would have died anyway," she said. "How wonderful that he died warm, in the comfort of your arms."

His head snapped around, and he stared at her almost in horror.

"I believe I'd like to have that cheese now," she said.

"The bread is very fresh." He laid the cheese on the bread and handed it to her. Jane bit into it, thinking it oddly pungently sharp, but tasteless at the same time.

They ate in silence, their eyes not meeting, and in silence, Jane accepted a second glass of wine.

"The current is strong out beyond the point, isn't it?" he asked, his words trailing back to where she sat.

"It's a cross-current and it tends to sweep into the inlet. You can see it in how the sand builds up in some places and not in others."

"But the inlet is very narrow. It funnels the tide into it so it rises higher than in the coves nearby."

"Imagine your smugglers rowing in while the tide is going out against them, depositing their wares, then hurriedly rowing back out, but this time with the tide coming in against them."

"I see your point. They must consider the time and height of the tides in conjunction with the phases of the moon. So it could actually be months between the times when the cave could be used."

"And why bother when they can simply row up onto an isolated beach?"

"There must be more than one place they use."

"Why do you say that?"

"There are signals given. They appear to be part of a code. So there must be more than one signal. They would signal safety, but also location."

"I suspect you do not need me to tell you anything, Lord Edenstorm."

He laughed and leaned in so close she could feel his heat. "Not telling again, then?"

She shivered as the caress of his breath trailed close to her ear. But no, it wasn't his breath, but the faintest exquisite touch of his finger sliding across her cheek. Her heart beat faster.

She should move away. No, stand up. Climb down off this precarious ledge. Gather her skirts and walk swiftly out of the cave. Yet the ache began to build inside her, remembering the silken touch of his lips on hers and how it had set something throbbing in her throat that sneaked down through her and coiled inside like twisting ropes of smoke.

Why— No. She knew why. He was using her for his own ends. Yet somehow she couldn't care.

Below, the hiss of foam sizzled on the sandy floor of the cave.

Jane jerked from her reverie, startling the man who was leaning toward her. "That's water."

He sat back, frowning. "What?"

Jane glanced up at the hole in the cavern's ceiling and saw only darkness. She grabbed the lantern and shone it on the cavern floor. "Water. The tide is coming in."

"Couldn't be. It's too soon."

"If you want to contradict me, certainly you may, but I don't think you can deny the tide. Because that's what it is."

He snatched up the blanket and goblets, stuffing them into the rucksack and discarding the wine bottle. "We'd better go."

Jane was already over the ledge and descending, not waiting for the light of the lantern. As she touched her foot onto the sand, water seeped through the soles of her halfboots.

Beyond the entrance of the cave, instead of the dying light of day, she saw only pale gloom.

As Edenstorm neared the floor, he handed her the lantern. "Head for the entrance," he said.

But she waited until he landed in the thin film of water over the sand, and they hurried across just as a new wave sloshed through the opening and spread itself thinly over the cavern floor. They ducked beneath the low opening and stood, staring at a glowering sky just as, with the force of a hammer blow, the storm hit, slamming hard, cold rain into their faces.

Chapter Eleven

"Blazes!" Edenstorm gaped at the black storm that rolled in like dense smoke, flashing lightning and driving a waist high wave straight at them.

God, what had he done? How was he going to get her out of here? She was right; the cave would trap them and drown them. But the cliffs around the cave were unscalable. They could climb a few feet, but no more. The only route to the top was across sand that had already been flooded.

But the water would recede with the wave.

"Up the cliff," he said. He grabbed her waist and shoved her up the rock face.

"We can't climb that," she protested.

He hauled himself after her, seconds before the next wave slammed against the rock, dousing them with the spray.

"When it recedes, jump down and run for that rockfall."

"But they're not stable. We can't get up there, either."

"It's the only place we've got. Maybe we can get up high enough for now." He waited as the wave lost power and receded until it was shallow enough to jump into it.

"Go!"

He leaped down, but she hesitated. He grabbed her waist and lifted her down. "Come on! There's no time to waste!"

She ran through the shallow water near the base of the scarp. He ran behind her, his eyes on the next wave coming in like a cliff of water. They had to reach the rocks before it hit or the sand would disappear beneath their feet, and they'd be helpless against the undertow.

"Run!" he shouted, as if his voice could make her run faster.

They splashed their way, each step slowed more as the water deepened, pushed inland by the oncoming giant wave. Only a few more feet to the rock slope. To seaward, the wall of water rolled toward them. He hoisted her into the air and thrust her up onto the rockfall. She climbed like a spider and wedged herself between two boulders. Behind her, he gripped crevices in the rock and started climbing.

The wave smashed against him, tall as his face, washing him away and banging him against the rock like a mere twig in a wind storm. One hand clung to a precarious hold, but the other was torn free of the rock and dangled uselessly. His footing vanished, tossing his legs with the surge. The rucksack hung like a boulder on his back, pulling him down toward the violent sea. He swung himself around as the wave receded and found a grip for his feet as he climbed higher, but a second surge rolled over him, submerging and whirling him, tossing him like jetsam in a storm. His last grip on solid rock washed free.

An odd calm descended on him as his doom rose up to meet him from beneath the waves. He'd always known his end would come to him in a fight, but he would not give in to it until his last chance was taken from him.

He'd done his best, she would make it... He would wash away to sea with the receding wave... It was the end and he had done his best...

Dangling by one arm, his legs driven in the force, first landward then seaward, he couldn't breathe beneath the wave, but he had done his best... Had done his best, would be at peace with it... She would be safe...

His head popped free of the roiling surface. Air, real air. He gasped violently, deeply, as the fierce water buffeted him where he hung, suspended by one arm. His eyes caught hers... Terror... Her arms wrapped around a pillar of rock, and her hands clenched his arm in a blacksmith-strong grip, fueled by the same stubborn ferocity that blazed in her eyes.

She'll be pulled in. She'll drown with me.

"Let go!" he shouted, or thought he did.

"No," he heard over the roar in his ears. Her hands clenched his arm so tightly, it hurt, but she couldn't hold his weight. She couldn't try hard enough. She would be pulled down with him.

"Let go!" The cold salt water sloshed and slammed his face and filled his mouth, cutting off his words.

"No!"

His free arm swung wildly as the retreating wave tossed him about, until he forced it toward the cliff and found a jagged rock to grasp. The frigid seawater inched down his body, baring him to cold wind as the savage slosh and pull eased. Waist deep, then down to his thighs, it dropped away until his legs were free and his slipping boots could fumble for toeholds. Cold, wet, salty grit filled his mouth, dripped from his hair. The monstrous weight of the rucksack had vanished, but his back ached where he had been pummeled with its weight.

He could breathe. He gasped, his chest heaving so hard he couldn't stop it.

He was alive. She still clenched his arm so tightly, she had to be leaving bruises. He almost laughed, would have laughed with the giddiest glee, if she didn't look so frightened.

"You can release my arm now, Miss Darrow," he said, trying to sound responsibly solemn. "I have my feet beneath me."

"You're quite sure."

"Yes, Miss Darrow. If you will release me, I may be able to climb up before the next wave hits me, which may be very soon."

"Oh." She lifted each finger free as if she had to pry them away separately to make them comply.

Edenstorm pulled his bruised and battered body up over the steep slope of jagged boulders until he stood once again, with blessed solid rock beneath his feet. His chest heaved, and he stared at the woman who stared back at him, her bodice transparent against the soaked skin of her breasts. Her eyes were round and frightened as her body trembled, and she was gasping as badly as he was.

He seized her by her arms, captured her in his embrace with all the wildness that poured from him, making her trembling his own as he bored his kiss into her. She tasted of anger, passion, fear, salt and sand, and sweet as the wine they had drunk. She became his whole world.

Somewhere in the depths of his mind, there was an awareness of another wave dashing against the rocks, throwing its spray over them and soaking their legs, and the rain was pelting them, slanting almost sideways. But they were safe, beyond the pounding surf. It merely drove his elation higher, knowing what almost had been, but was not. It was not!

Instead he still held her, thrust his kiss, his entire being, onto her, into her, as if he could make them one body.

Slowly, the violent beating of his heart and heaving of his chest eased, but his arms could not give her up. Not just yet.

Below and all around them, the black storm blotted out any sunlight that might have been left in the day. Only a dark haze showed through the heavy rain, not a trace of the cavern they had left behind. The next wave he could barely see and it was rising, rolling in. They would keep coming, each one higher than the one before, forced in by the driving storm. This would be one of those wild blows she had described that would send spray spewing out the hole in the cavern's top. How foolish he had been to think swimmers would be able to climb out the hole, buoyed up by the water! Now he understood if they had stayed there they would be drowning, smashed by the turbulence against the rocks. She had been telling the truth all along, and he'd been too suspicious, too stupid, to believe it. He'd seen the danger, all right. He'd just been certain they wouldn't be caught by it.

"We have to climb higher," he said.

"There's no place to go."

"There has to be. Even a few feet higher could save us. Come on, let's look."

"No lantern, of course."

God, he didn't even remember when he'd dropped the lantern. He shook his head. "Rucksack's gone, too." The wave must have torn it right off his back. But if it had not, the weight would surely have dragged them both down.

"We could have used that," she said quietly.

"The rope would have been nice, and the blanket. Better to

have our lives. Come on, climb. Just a little bit higher. We may spend the night clinging onto handholds on the cliff, but we can always go down later, once the tide goes out again."

"Eight hours at least, Edenstorm. I can't see anything up there."

"Wait for the lightning to flash and figure out where to put your hands."

"You go first."

"Not on your life. I'll stand behind you to make sure you don't fall. Step into my hands." He laced his fingers together, the way he would assist her in mounting a horse.

Jane obeyed, and he boosted her up against the slick granite, praying she would find with her hands what they could not see with their eyes and that it would be enough to get her up away from the tormenting waves. If she fell, he probably couldn't catch her, but they'd go down together.

The lightning flashed, not just once, but several booming strikes, not far out to sea.

"Found something," she said, and lifted herself out of his enmeshed hands.

"Describe it."

"Right hand, about as high as I can reach and off a little to the right. Left hand is lower, to the right of left center, but it's a better hold. Left foot has found a good place. Just up about a foot from your hand. I don't know how you're going to get up this high, Edenstorm."

"If you can, I can. Keep going."

"Ow!" she cried. Gravel slid down, pelting his face. He shut his eyes against the grit, praying she wouldn't come down with it.

"Are you all right?" he called to her.

"Yes. The rock is weak in places. I'm testing my way."

He could only see her now when the lightning flashed. The sea wouldn't get her now, even if she had to cling to the cliff all night. But he had to move, too. Just a few more incoming waves and he would be right back where he was, for the waves were crashing in taller than a man, maybe eight or ten feet.

Around him, he could hear the roar of the storm and the

fierce pounding against the cliffs, but only when the lightning flashed could he see the sea or rock below. Cold rain pummeled his back and poured in cascades down the face of the cliff. The surf slammed at his soaked boots.

"I've found a ledge," she said. "It's pretty small, but there's room for both of us. You can come up now."

He could reach higher than she could and found his first handgrip higher than she could have reached alone. He pulled himself upward, fumbling about for a place for his toe while groping around for the footholds and handholds she had described. He cursed himself as he began to comprehend how easily she could have lost her grip on the butter-slick rock and fallen. It was all his fault, all of it.

As if that mattered now. All they could do was climb, trusting to fate. He followed her directions as he ascended and finally crawled up onto the little ledge where she waited.

He sank down to the rock ledge, sitting with his back against the cliff face. Relief flooded through him, draining away the last of his strength.

It wasn't very level and in fact was jagged and rough and nestled back into the cliff as if it had been crudely nicked out by a giant knife. But that was good, for it gave some shelter from the driving rain. Some forlorn tufts of gorse grew in odd places and an icy rivulet gushed down the notch behind them. They'd not hurt for fresh water, anyway.

In the flashes of lightning, he could see her face, her golden curls turned to tight ringlets that hung like dripping ropes over her forehead. Kneeling at his side, she leaned forward, her face tight with worry, but all he could think about was that he was staring right at breasts that lay beneath soaked fabric so transparent, it might as well not have been there at all. Her skin was tightly pebbled with gooseflesh, and the hard nubs of her nipples poked into the cloth, the stuff of his reveries as he lay in bed at night, waiting for the sleep he dreaded. He'd wanted to make love to her from the moment he'd seen her again and now so suddenly craved it as if it were the very gift of life itself.

And damned if he wasn't too cursed cold to get it up.

He managed a smile. "Cold?" he asked, his teeth chattering.

"But you're soaked."

"So are you." He sat up and peeled off the clinging green coat that had once been Nance's pride. The perfect country garment, his poor valet had called it. It was probably a good thing Nance wasn't with them because if he could see the torn sleeves, he might jump off the cliff in despair.

Edenstorm set the coat on her shoulders. "Put it on," he said.

"You'll freeze," she said.

"I'm used to it. It's much colder in the Peninsula. Soldiers stop noticing it after awhile." It was a lie. But it was one soldiers often told themselves and their friends, so it didn't really matter. "We'll have to keep each other warm," he said, backing them as deeply into the crevice as they could get. "Sit in my lap."

He waited for her objection, but she just shivered, wriggled her arms into the coat sleeves that were so long they hid her hands. That was good. It would keep her hands warm.

Slipping his arms around her, he shifted her onto his lap with her bottom settling between his legs and he raised one knee for her to lean against. She pulled her skirt over her legs and tucked her feet beneath it. She opened the coat and leaned against his chest, but the coat kept slipping back down and he had to tuck it in between them instead.

Her cold hands slid beneath his arms, over his sopping shirt, to his back. His heart began to pound and the rush of passion started to flood his mind, beginning to warm him like a hot, red fog. Damn, but it was a weird thing, suddenly wanting so much to have her when he knew there was no way it was going to happen. His balls turned to hard rocks, yet the whole apparatus seemed to be doing its best to retreat to someplace warmer. Made him wonder if it had a mind of its own and meant to find a way to burrow inside him.

Now, that was not a comforting thought.

Being inside her would certainly be warmer—if he could ever get to the place where he was warm enough to accomplish that feat. It looked like he was going to be a perfect gentleman whether he wanted to or not. He ought to be laughing at himself, for as cold as he was, he felt the warmth from his heart radiating through him. There weren't many men who could say a woman had risked her life for them, and won the battle.

"You should have let me go," he said, suddenly feeling that giddy urge to laugh out loud again, but he squelched it. It was the funniest feeling, that wild elation he had not felt since boyhood.

"I couldn't." Her voice trembled.

"I know." He kissed the dripping wet curls on her head. "Honor and duty and all that."

"That's what you're all about, isn't it, Edenstorm? Honor and duty?"

"Yes." He had hesitated briefly, and wondered why, for it was true. What else did a man have? His duty now was to somehow see her back to safety, alive and well, no matter what happened to him. Yet the intoxicating joy that rushed through his veins demanded fulfillment.

"I will never, ever, ever go anywhere with you again, Edenstorm. I mean it. Never."

He smiled, for even as she said it, she burrowed more deeply into his embrace, perhaps, like him, unable to think of separation even for a fleeting moment. She was his world, and he, hers, and their world was a precarious perch on a slippery cliff in a beating rain. But they were alive, and together. And his mind was swimming in the glory of it.

"Because I didn't believe you," he answered. "But if you hadn't come, you knew I would have gone in the cave alone, and I wouldn't have known to get out in time. I would have drowned."

"You said you didn't care if you died or not."

"No, I said I wasn't afraid of dying. Not the same thing."

"Maybe you're too much of a hero."

"Maybe you are."

"Not me. I'm too scared."

He knew that too—how scared she was. Something thick and alien shuddered through him, and he squeezed the hug in which he held her. The ache in his throat hungered for another kiss, but he massaged his hands safely over her shivering back instead.

"Heroes are always scared," he said. "They just get a damn-you gleam in their eyes and do what they have to do anyway. And you, my love, are a very formidable hero."

"I don't feel like it."

The wave of hunger and longing washed over him again. It was funny how it came in waves like that. He rested his lips lightly on her damp hair, let his kiss caress. Oh, God, how he wanted her.

"Thank you for my life," he whispered.

She whimpered and buried her face against his shoulder, then was silent. He let the quiet moment be, wishing almost that it could last forever. How odd it seemed to him, yet how wonderful, that from the first moment he had seen her climbing down the cliff to her friend, he had recognized her, and from that moment on, his every thought had centered on her. The forgotten joy of being alive was snaking its way back into him. Showing him the man he'd forgotten he was.

It was not all joy. It hurt, hurt like the very devil. He ached so much with longing and desire, yet he knew she could not be his. He couldn't marry her, yet he had to. No lady could spend the night on a cliff face in the pouring rain and not be ruined. Yet he had a duty to his family, and the moment she reappeared to society, the scandal would devastate the family name. There could be no good reason for four years of absence, having been thought dead. Nor would she ever be his mistress. She had made that very clear.

Hell. Honor demanded that he marry her, but duty said he must not. A load of shrapnel in the gut would feel better.

"Is it really this cold in the Peninsula?" she asked.

"Colder." He was glad for the distraction. Maybe he'd quit thinking about a nice warm bout of love-making on the face of a cliff in a raging storm, since the closeness of her body was warming him in more ways than one.

"But Spain is so much farther south. It seems like it would be hotter." Her warm breath tickled the cold skin beneath his chin as she spoke.

"Colder in winter, but hotter in summer. It's hot and dry and dusty, but with sudden cloudbursts that soak everything."

"Like Albuera."

His muscles went stiff. That squelched his rising desire. His mind made a quick dive back to the safer haven of his sexual desperation. But it didn't work. The haunting memory had found its way in, an image he couldn't shut out. He had choked it back and buried it for nearly two years. But he had opened that door when they were in the cave, and now here it was, coming at him in a flood, twisting into a thick knot in his throat.

If he shut out his pain now, much as he wished he could close it off, he knew he might never learn how to open it to joy again.

"I can still smell the dust in the air," he said. "Two armies marching toward each other raise a lot of dust. The air was thick and choking, and we didn't see that storm coming."

"Like we didn't see this one today. We should have been paying attention to the birds. They come inland before a storm."

"We didn't see the signs that day, either. There were lots of tall clouds, but that happens a lot. The storm just seemed to come from nowhere. It changed everything, but everything was wrong anyway. I still wonder why we won."

"What was wrong?"

"Bad site. Beresford's a good man, but he makes mistakes Wellington never would. There was a rise in the ground, but not enough to slow the French down. Then the storm hit. I saw Edward's square fall. With their powder soaked, they were completely helpless. Afterwards, I found him, his eyes still open. His hands were cut through where the lance had been pulled back."

"What did you do?" she whispered, so quietly he almost couldn't hear her over the roaring of the surf and rain.

Edenstorm swallowed past the thickness in his throat. "I closed his eyes. I took everything I thought he would want me to take and left him to be buried with the others. He would have wanted it that way."

"Did you talk him into going to war"?

"In a way. Men tell stories. Young boys listen and believe."

Jane snuggled her head into his shoulder, her forehead rubbing against him like a caress. "I'm sorry."

"I know." Once again he reassured her with his hands

stroking over her shoulders. "But war is like that. A soldier has to expect it."

"You didn't have to go back in '09. Why did you?"

For a moment, he thought he couldn't breathe. Why did she have to keep asking these questions? These things he didn't want to remember? Then his breath came back, slow and hard. How could he say it to her when he didn't even understand, himself. He had come back from Corunna so numbed, nothing had meaning.

He had not loved her then. He had felt nothing at all. He returned to the war feeling nothing. But damn it all, if he had felt so damn little of anything, so why had her betrayal hurt so much, enough to send him back into the chaos of war for relief?

He let out a sigh that seemed to echo against the rain. No, it was a lie. Another one of many he had told himself over and over until he believed it all the way to his heart. That he felt nothing. It wasn't true. Yet it was. He didn't understand. He had wanted her then, even though he had only just met her. From the first instant he'd seen her, he had begun to dream.

Maybe he hadn't known how much. He'd just known he'd stood there, staring at her like a bloody bumpkin, feeling her disgust of him wash over him like a scalding, humiliating wave. Feeling the pain of desire so badly that he covered it up, buried it as deeply as he could. Not letting anybody, even himself, know he cared.

And why did he want her so damn much now, when he knew she found him even more contemptible now than she had then? Perhaps she was being kind, understanding, to him now, but eventually they would find their way off this cliff and she would remember how she really felt about him. The gradually warming body in his arms would flee the moment they could be safe and dry again.

He sighed. She deserved at least an answer. "I couldn't stand not going, I suppose. My father was angry. I'd never disobeyed him before."

Her head rose off his chest. "Never?"

"Never. He was like a god to me."

"Did he forgive you?"

"Of course. He even forgave that Edward followed me."

"Even after Edward died?"

Edenstorm rested his hand on her hair and urged her back to rest her cheek against his chest. He needed it there. "He just asked me to please come home."

"Did you?"

"When I got the letter, I didn't know he'd already died. We were retreating from Burgos and things were bad. We'd lost most of our supplies and mail."

"And then you came home."

"Too late." He frowned. Was that what he thought? Hell, how did he know what he thought?

Jane sat back from him abruptly, leaving cold, dark emptiness where her warmth had been. She turned, slipping one knee between his legs to face him, fanning the fire inside him again.

"You are just like him, aren't you?" she said, for it was not really a question. "Duty and honor above all. Aren't you?"

He had never thought of that before. Yes, he was like his father, so very much like him. He nodded, almost glad that it was so dark, she probably could not tell it.

"Do you think he didn't understand? Maybe you don't understand, but he did. He knew you had to go."

"How do you know?"

"I just do. He's like you, the man you'll be someday, the man of his youth you have already become."

There were tears stinging his eyes. They were warm. They hurt. They were there, yet almost as if they were not his own, as if they had been given to him from someone else.

But no, they were his. They were the tears he had lost somewhere on the dusty plains of Spain and had never found again.

Just as suddenly, she placed her hands on his cheek, the softness of her palms gliding against the roughness of his beard, and before he could see it coming, she descended upon his mouth and pressed an urgent kiss to his lips.

He groaned as blood-red passion surged through him again, and he rose to his knees and pressed their bodies together. His tongue teased until her lips parted for him. He searched every nook and cranny of her mouth, tasting every delicious corner as he turned his hands loose on the soft orbs of breasts that had been tormenting his dreams, night upon night.

She gasped and whimpered, inflaming him more. But God help him, something told him he had to stop. How the hell could he make love to her, now, here, in a rainstorm on the side of a cliff where they barely had room to sit?

But damn it, he wanted her, and now.

His mind whirled with wild sexual thoughts. He could make her his mistress. Somehow he had to talk her into it. He could take her now, on his lap. He could...

No.

His body screamed its outrage as he forced himself to take his hands off her breasts and stop kissing those soft, pliable lips. But he had to. No sense going over the reasons once again.

Hell and damn, he was a responsible man and it was about time he started acting like it. Taking a deep breath that shook like Vesuvius in his chest, Edenstorm compelled his hands to obey and, instead of fondling her indecently, wrapped his arms around her. He could hear her impatience in her sigh as she withdrew her hands, and he was almost glad he could not see her face clearly. The green coat began to slip from her shoulders again, giving him another needed distraction as he pulled it back to cover her.

What was her question? He rummaged through his mind until he finally remembered. "You're right," he replied, so belatedly, he almost wondered if she had forgotten it, too. "Father understood. He understood everything, I think."

She rubbed her cheek against the wet linen of his shirt, and though he almost wished she wouldn't, she slid her arm behind his back again. He could feel each finger that seemed to fidget in its place, as if they each had longings of their own to touch him. "How much you must miss him."

He felt the painful ache in his throat. The longing and hurt. "Yes," he said. He couldn't manage anything more.

Quietly, he slipped his arm behind her and scooped her into his arms. "Lie down with me," he said. "Put the coat over you backwards and lie down with your back to me. We need to keep each other warm."

Silently, she complied, too silently. But there was a roughness in her breathing as she lay down, facing the edge of the precipice overlooking the roar of wind, rain and surging waves, with the lesser darkness giving a faint hint of the outline of her cheek, the curve of her thigh. Edenstorm resigned himself to his hard erection as he pulled himself into a more perfect fit against her, accepting instead the comfort of her warmth and presence. She was probably right, that when they got out of here, she would never go anywhere with him again or even tolerate his presence. But for now...

For now, he held her in his arms and pretended it would last forever.

Only silence fell, with the steadily dripping rain, that at least was no longer being slammed into their faces by a driving wind. She was still so long, he began to wonder.

"Are you sleeping?" he whispered.

"No. Just listening to your heart beat."

His body jerked back to full sexual awareness. God, what a story that beat must be telling her. Just that quickly, he could feel his pulse hammering in his ears.

"How long has it been, do you think?" she asked.

He could not tell. From the hardness of the rock biting into him, it might have been days. "A few hours, maybe. It was nearly dark when we came out of the cave."

She sighed and shifted closer to him, if closer were actually possible. He wrapped his top leg over hers, remembering a time he had done this in making love to a woman. The woman had all but passed from his memory, but the lovemaking had not.

"Stay awake," he said. "Tell me a story."

"A story? What one?"

"Doesn't matter. Maybe tell me a story about Lady Juliette. When she fled her brother's home. How did she do it? How did she make her way to Cornwall?"

She was silent again. Her body became taut in the same way his had when she had asked him about Albuera. Would she finally tell him, or would it be too much for her to dare? Would it be safer for her to tell it, disguised as a fanciful tale?

"There was a woman named Lady Juliette who had a

brother named Cyril," she said quietly. "When she would not marry the man he chose for her, he became very angry with her. So he locked her in her chamber and wouldn't let her have any food."

Edenstorm jerked. His gut twisted into a knot. Was it he she meant? No, surely not. It must be Kirkwood, for by this time Edenstorm had already withdrawn his suit. Would Harlton really have starved her into submission? He'd always known the man had a cruel streak, but his own sister?

Her voice was almost wistful as she continued. "The servants were worried and slipped food to her. When she still refused, her brother decided to take other measures. One night a footman came into Lady Juliette's chamber and waked her, and told her she must escape because her brother meant to lock her away in an asylum."

Edenstorm shook his head. "Surely it's not that easy. It requires a doctor and a judge."

"Who was there to stop him? He was Lady Juliette's guardian. He could do anything he wanted with her and no one could stop him. Lady Juliette sent the servant to a friend, and the friend agreed to help her escape.

"There was a chamber adjoining Lady Juliette's bedchamber, and a servant's stairs ran behind it, but the door was locked. That night the servant removed the hinge pins from the door, and Lady Juliette squeezed through the opening. Then he put the pins back, and she escaped down the servant's stairs. They crossed the countryside at night until they reached a waiting coach that took them to Cornwall."

"The servant, too?"

Her head moved in a slight nod against his shoulder. "His name was Charles. It was the only decision he ever made in his life on his own. It cost him everything."

And Charles had become the vapid-minded butler at Launceston Hall.

"Why didn't she want to marry Kirkwood?"

There had been no mention of Kirkwood between them. Again she wavered. Her voice had a shake in it, with words that didn't quite form. "He—" she said, and then stopped. "He was a cad. He was...cruel."

The bile rose into Edenstorm's throat so quickly, he almost choked on it. He held her tightly, feeling her shiver. No wonder she was afraid of Harlton. God, but he'd like to kill both of them, Harlton and Kirkwood. Nothing she could have done would have justified that treatment.

"Lady Juliette will be safe," he said, and he kissed her damp hair. "She will always be safe. I promise it. I will never let him know where she is."

Jane turned onto her back and looked up at him, her cheek and the corner of her mouth outlined in dim light from the fading storm. Her hand, so tiny and comical the way it peeked out from his absurdly big green coat, reached up to his face, and she stroked her fingers along the bristle of his beard.

His mind turned to mush.

Chapter Twelve

In the soft light and dark shadow, his lips found hers, tasting the sweet warmth of her mouth. His hand slipped down through the clinging wet fabric and lifted one breast from her stays until the nipple popped out above the low-cut bodice, and he abandoned her lips to take it into his mouth, flicking it with his tongue, sucking and kissing like a wild, untried boy.

Red and gray haze whirled in his head. Somehow his falls had been undone, but he couldn't have said how, for all he could think of was burying himself inside her. So hot he could hardly breathe, he surrendered to the demand, snuggling into the crevice between her legs, pushing slowly toward her soft, tight heat.

"I want you," he said hoarsely. "I want you so much, I don't care about the rain and the cold and the hard rock. I just want to make love to you until I explode."

"Is that what it's like?" she murmured, and her tongue trailed around the rim of his ear. "Exploding?"

"Sort of." Damn, did he want to explode. Go off like a Congreve rocket into the sky.

"I want that."

Vague little clouds of guilt began to float about in the red-gray haze of his mind, growing into a tangle of confusing threads. Had she ever had a decent man in her life?

He remembered... He was sure... Damn it, no, he knew she'd been with Kirkwood. He'd seen them. That was what everything had been about, the reason he hadn't married her. The reason for her disgrace. Had that damn Kirkwood been so crass he'd never even considered her needs? But why be surprised? The man was a snake.

So what did that make Edenstorm?

A snake.

Here to take from her what she could not afford to give. Quick to meet his own needs. He was what she said men were, creatures interested only in themselves, who leave women behind with ruined lives. But damn, it was easy when the blood was heated to ignore or forget what a few moments of bliss could cost a woman.

With a moan of true pain, Edenstorm pushed himself up and backed away, grazing his head on rock he had not noticed protruding from the back of the ledge. Good. Maybe it could knock some sense into him. He squeezed his eyes tight to shut out the faint light and shadow that delineated the woman who had been lying beneath him just seconds before. He must not. Could not. Not here and now, when they were still driven by the elation of their survival and the emotions they had shared.

He could hear her breathing with a raggedness to it like his own, see her profile when she turned her face upward, her eyes cast down and the fringes of her lashes catching faint glints of light. She seemed poised as if she, too, sought to find rational thought to overcome passion. If both of them fought off passion, how could they possibly manage to stay in each other's arms until the storm passed?

But she needed his heat, and he needed hers, red haze of passion be damned. He'd think about something else to distract himself. The war. Remember how cold he'd been there. Think about the horse. The baby. Edward.

Yet all that seemed suddenly so far away, as if in a distant, hazy world he could not reach or feel. All he could think about was the woman beside him and how badly he wanted her.

Come on, Edenstorm, it wouldn't be the first time you've had to endure a little suffering.

Gritting his teeth, he tucked her breasts back inside her stays and folded the fronts of his green wool coat over her once again. He lay down beside her and pulled her next to him, thinking by now she must think him a completely incompetent lover, or perhaps worse.

"Nothing happens right now," he said. "When we are safe

and warm again, that will be a different time. Then we will choose what we choose."

"I know. Yes, you're right," she whispered. The faint sound she made was little more than a murmur. She turned her back to him. Did she think he was rejecting her? He must let her know he did not. Edenstorm slicked back her dangling curls and tucked them behind her ear.

"Sometimes when I was in the Peninsula, I was so cold, I'd dream of a woman in my arms, to help keep me warm," he said. "In a small room, with a roaring fire to heat it, and a soft bed with draperies opened at the foot to trap in the heat, so there was no need for bedclothes."

"Then you lied," she replied. "You said you got used to the cold."

Yes, he'd lied. "We lied to ourselves a lot, when it helped us stay alive. It gets to be a very bad habit."

"Who was she? This woman of your dreams?"

"She had green eyes, and her long blonde hair curled down her back. I couldn't see her face, but I can remember the outline of her cheek." He traced his fingertip along the line of her cheekbone.

She reached up from beneath the coat and imitated his gesture with a finger along his jaw line. "You're not fooling me, Edenstorm. I know you didn't want me."

"Not then. I couldn't allow myself to want a woman who didn't want me. But I didn't know. I did lie to myself. A lot."

She shifted a little, but he moved in closer.

"That's what I'd want for you, Jane. A warm cozy bed. I'd snuggle you in down covers and prop you up on a mound of pillows and make love to you in the golden light of the fire.

"I'd kiss and taste every inch of your flesh and find all the places you love most to be touched, and make love to you. We'd spend all night finding each other's pleasure. And our own."

"Just the thought warms me."

He watched how the profile of her face changed with her cheek rising ever so slightly, and he knew it was because the mouth he could not quite see was smiling. He smiled in response, even knowing she could not know. "Then keep thinking it. Imagine all the ways we could make love, because we'd not have to worry about being cold or wet, only so wonderfully warm and wildly passionate."

"I'm afraid I don't know enough to do much imagining."

"Then everything will be a new and wonderful discovery."

He tightened his embrace around her, suddenly aching deep inside as he soothed her with soft kisses to her cheek and the wet ringlets of her hair. She said nothing, only lay very still, one hand resting atop the hand he held at her breast.

He imagined a house somewhere for her. With footmen who were big as mountains to guard her. He owed her that. And he could go there, where she would be waiting for him.

No, he had to get to the root of the problem. She wasn't insane. She never had been. So he had to prove she wasn't. When Rokeby got back, they'd know about what happened to her dowry, and she'd just claim it, then her life would be hers again. She was almost of age now, just a few months more. Then Harlton couldn't claim guardianship. As long as they proved she wasn't insane.

They'd get out of here and back inside a nice safe place where moonlight and rain were a roof away.

She turned back to him, and with a jerk, raised herself on her elbow. "Edenstorm, I can see your face."

He looked past her. A nearly full moon stuck its edge out from beneath the band of black clouds. Together, they sat up, watching in awe as it untangled itself from the strips of clouds.

"The moon isn't as high as I expected. It must be around eight or nine o'clock. The rain has stopped, too. Maybe we can climb out of here now."

"I don't think so. The sea is still rough and we're several hours away from low tide."

"I'd rather go up than down if we can." He rose, straightening legs that had long since gone stiff and stepped back as far as he could to study the cliff above them.

"It's not all that far," he said. "We climbed higher than we thought. I'm going to give it a try. If I make it, I'll come back for you."

"If you go, I go."

Edenstorm turned a hard glare on her, which instantly softened when he caught the equally hard determination in her eyes. It would do no good to tell this woman she was a girl and shouldn't take chances.

"All right," he said. "You first, then."

"I'll let you have the honor."

Something in him started to protest that he needed to be there to catch her if she fell, but he knew that was a false premise. If she fell, they would both fall. If he fell, same thing.

He laughed to himself as she removed the ruined bottle green coat and handed it back to him. Yes, it would get in her way, he realized. He shrugged it on, past the gaping holes in the armpits, and began to climb.

"Very slick," he said. He began to describe the handholds as she had done.

"Move to your left," she said. "I see places that look like good grips."

Edenstorm sidled to the left, finding what was another ledge, wider and more comfortable than the one where they had clung together for hours. Regret seized him for a moment, but then he remembered they could not have found it in the intense gloom of the storm. He called out to her, and she began to climb and quickly reached the little platform. The same disgust showed in her face.

He laughed. Would he have had so many wild sexual delusions if they had merely sat beside each other?

He had room enough to broaden his perspective, and he saw a narrow gap before them that dropped nearly to the beach. If they could cross it, they would be only a few feet farther up, but it would be the beginning of the path to safety.

"Can you make it?" he asked.

She studied it. "I think so."

"Maybe you should wait here."

"No. You go first. You have longer legs. You can catch me if I slip."

There was a wildness in her eyes. He almost decided to sit down and wait for help instead. He could make it, but he would know better how safe she would be if he made the jump himself.

Edenstorm jumped the narrow chasm. "It's all right," he said. "It's not slick."

Before he could encourage her more, she leapt, and he caught her in his arms. With no more than a brief embrace, he directed her to the sloping climb up to the top, slick with mud and frilled with broken-limbed gorse.

Grabbing handfuls of the woody shrubs, she pulled herself upward, like walking on hands and feet, until she stood erect above him, silhouetted by the moonlight against the dark velvet of the sky. He followed and soon stood beside her. And all he could do was stare at her.

"You're a beautiful man, Edenstorm," she said.

He laughed, knowing he was as rumpled as she was, and she was a sight. "You're not so bad yourself," he said.

Chapter Thirteen

He was. Truly the most beautiful man she had ever known. And now, despite all she had ever thought about him, he had become the most precious.

Nothing had actually changed. She knew that. But something about the horror of the night had also made it, and him, memorable in ways she would always treasure. Somewhere in the night, he had found his soul. She had, too.

They followed the ridge inland until they reached the muddy lane that rimmed the cove. Edenstorm left her on the road and took the path that led down to where he had left the horses. Soon he rejoined her, the two horses in tow.

"Too muddy to get the gig up the slope," he said.

She could see that. In addition to having been soaked to the bone most of the night, he was now slathered in mud up to his elbows.

"I guess we'll walk," she decided, looking at the drearily sodden beasts. "They look like they're ready to collapse from fear."

"Not Peninsula-hardened beasts, for sure. Too much storm for them."

Exhausting as the night had been, she felt elation fill her as they slogged along the muddy path. The air had turned crisp and sharp and felt like inhaling stars.

"I wonder how you are going to explain this," he said.

"I shall simply tell them I am never, ever going anyplace with you again, for you are a walking disaster."

The dimple danced on his cheek. The air that entered her

lungs felt suddenly even sharper.

"You will be fortunate if Lady Beck does not call you out."

"I'd prefer not. I should dislike shooting a lady, and she has suffered enough pain lately."

"She will be frantic. She will never forgive you."

"But you will."

"I shall not. You will suffer my indignation for the rest of your days."

"I shall do my best to bear the burden. But I believe I shall call upon you in the morning anyway. To assure myself of your good health."

She widened a nostril in a one-sided sneer and watched his dimple deepen as it folded into his grin. She forced herself not to laugh. On the cliff she might have frozen to death if he had not so utterly heated her up with his lovemaking.

She would never forget that. Any other woman might be embarrassed or ashamed, but she wasn't. Not in the slightest.

When the road forked just before West Looe, she stopped. "You can leave me here," she said.

"I'll see you to your front door," he protested.

"This is better. It leads directly to the servant's quarters. It's a tunnel."

"Does every house in Looe have a hidden exit?"

"Probably. I'm less likely to be seen, going in here."

"I'll call on you tomorrow."

"It's best that you don't. I shall not go with you again."

"So you said before. But things have changed."

"No. They are the same as they always were."

"Did all that mean nothing?"

Nothing? It overwhelmed her, consumed her. "I—thank you for everything. Everything. But you know there can be nothing between us. You are all about duty. I understand that, truly I do. You must marry a wife who will bring no dishonor to your family, for you would never bring shame to them. And you know what kind of life I would lead if I married into the *ton*. They would never accept me. I cannot imagine how I could deal with that. But here I am comfortable. I have friends and kindness around me."

"Will you marry Polruhan, then?"

"No. I cannot. I simply cannot imagine being married to him. A legal marriage requires a legal name, which I dare not give, and he is not a man to tolerate a woman's indiscretions any more than you are. I must be content with what I have."

"There could be something else. I would always take care of you, and you would not ever have to work again." His eyes searched hers as if he hoped to find some sort of salvation in them. But she could give him no such hope.

"No. There couldn't. I could not bring myself to be any man's mistress, especially not to a man who was married to another woman. I am not capable of that."

Her throat began to choke up, and her eyes to burn so that she knew any moment she would burst into tears. "Good night, my lord," she said, feeling as if the very words caught in her throat. "Thank you for saving me. And keeping me warm. I shall be warm in my heart for the rest of my life."

Jane whirled around, surely too abruptly, sped for the tunnel hidden in the trees and ducked beneath the low entrance. Once inside, her eyes grew hot with tears that flooded down her cheeks, and she walked briskly through the blackness she knew altogether too well.

How had she let that happen? The very man she had detested for so long? And he wanted to make her his mistress! Had she not fallen far enough in his eyes already?

She neared the staircase and slowed, for no light came down the shaft to tell her exactly where she was. With one hand on the rough stone wall, she eased along, grateful to concentrate on something besides her pain. At last, her toes stubbed against the bottom stair. She took each step carefully in the dark, counting to herself the usual eighteen steps, and pushed against the weathered oak door. It swung, silently as ever, on its oiled hinges.

The servant's quarters seemed to be deserted, but across the courtyard, in the main hall, candles blazed. She dreaded that. Lydia and her mother would be frantic. Charles would be pacing, unable to decide if someone ought to be going out to search or if they ought to stay and wait.

She sighed and combed her fingers through her salt-stiffened curls. She pulled, tugged and fluffed her dress in a futile attempt to prevent it from clinging to her skin.

How *would* she explain this? What if they had called for Davy, to come and help search? If any more animosity flared between the two men, disaster was sure to follow.

Lady Launceston would make noises about Edenstorm's obligation to salvage Jane's ruined reputation, for she was more than sly enough to come up with such a devious plot. What in the world could ever be worse than marrying a man who didn't want her, just because he felt some sort of obligation?

She stopped and breathed in deeply to fortify her flagging courage. There was nothing for it now but to get on with it. The sooner done, the sooner she could get to the pitcher on her washstand, clean herself up and crawl beneath a cozy blanket.

She slipped through the north door and tip-toed down the corridor toward the lighted parlour. Voices came from the room, their timbre sharply punctuated, but she could not quite make them out. She drew closer and spotted Lydia with her firmly erect posture, sitting on the curve-backed sofa.

Something was wrong. She sat too far forward, almost to the point of rising, yet she did not.

Jane moved in closer, one quiet step at a time.

"You will not hear the end of this, John Gates. You will never be beadle in Looe again."

"Now, Lady Beck, ye know I got no choice. Ee's got a writ, 'ee does. I got to honor it."

"You've no such thing. You know it is falsely obtained. How many years have you known her? Four? Is there a single member of this community who would concede she is insane?"

Jane froze.

"You'd best comply, Lady Beck, or I shall have you charged with interference of custody. You have been concealing her from her lawful guardian all these years. I know you are hiding her now."

Cyril!

Jane whirled around and sped back down the corridor.

"There she is! Seize her. Catch her, you fools!"

Heavy steps pounded behind her as she ran out the north door and across the servant's court. She had to make the tunnel.

"Catch her! Don't let her get away!"

Fire seared her lungs and she drove her legs faster and faster. The pounding feet behind her drew closer and closer and she begged God to help her, please. Hot breath scorched her neck. *Please God!* Arms clamped around her chest like hard bands of iron. Jane screamed as she panted and kicked. A rough hand closed over her mouth, tasting of grime and sweat. She wriggled, but the bands tightened. She couldn't breathe.

"You monsters! How dare you! Leave her alone! Get out of my house!"

Cyril stepped in front of Jane. "Too late, Lady Beck. The game is up." Manacles clicked onto Jane's wrists, and the key twisted in the locks. "Take a look at her. You don't think she looks crazy? Well, little Juliette, at last we have found you. Now we shall take you home. Safe and sound."

Chapter Fourteen

Edenstorm left the two weary horses with Trevenny in the stable and trudged the last few steps up the hill to the manor's front door. Before he could open it, the door opened for him.

Nance's face exhibited all the signs of a man who had just been gut shot. "My lord! What happened?"

Edenstorm staggered inside and began removing the battered green coat, Nance jumping in quickly to lift the rags of superfine from his shoulders. "It's rather much to say," he said. "We are both simply happy to be alive. I don't suppose you might have a spot of tea about at this hour? Or a bit of brandy would do as nicely."

Edenstorm pulled his gold watch from his pocket by its fobs and flipped open the case. With a sigh, he snapped it closed again. "I can safely say the wave hit us at precisely forty-two minutes past five of the clock." He handed the watch to Nance.

"I shall take it to Plymouth immediately in the morning, my lord. Might I ask, is the lady—"

"In somewhat better shape than I am, Nance. She is amazingly strong when pushed. She put sizeable bruises on my arm, keeping the wave from taking me. We managed to escape up the cliff in time when the storm came in. But after this she may not be speaking to me."

"But how will you obtain information from her then, sir?"

"I won't. That's done with, Nance. I'll not use her against her will again. I should not have in the first place. That brandy, please? And perhaps some warm water to wash up."

"There's a letter arrived from Mr. Rokeby, sir. Red-marked."

Edenstorm's ears perked and he watched Nance pick the letter out of a silver tray.

"I should be happy to prepare you a bath, sir."

"No. It's too late." He started to break the seal, then thought better of it. Better to clean up a bit, then read the letter with a spot of brandy. "I can't imagine you have not retired for the night. I've told you not to wait up for me."

"Yes, my lord. But with the letter seeming so urgent— I'll find you some brandy. Then we'll just get you out of those clothes."

Edenstorm noticed just the slightest hesitation in Nance's voice, as if he found it hard to call the shreds of garments clothing, but he didn't wait for Nance's help. He took the stairs two at a time up to his chamber, unloosing his garments as he went, and had himself down to his smallclothes by the time Nance returned with the brandy.

"I'm going down to light a fire now, my lord. I'll have the water hot in no time."

"No, bring the water cold. I just want to get the salt off my skin now."

Soon he was passably clean again. Encased in his favorite blue and gold striped banyan, he sat before the blaze Nance had built in the grate of his chamber and sipped the glass of brandy. As its fire slid down his throat, he lifted the glass in gratitude to the Free Traders who provided the substance. Tonight he had a greater respect than usual for the Gentlemen who tackled the Mother Sea for their living, regardless of what the government thought of their trade.

What was he going to do about Jane? It was his fault as much as anyone's that she was having to hide from her brother, but she had refuse his offer of assistance.

However, he had put some rather tight strings on his offer. Tainted though her reputation was, she was still a lady, and he should have expected her to turn him down. It was clear she wanted no more of her past sins, and who was he to stand between her and her chance to make a new life?

But devil it all, he couldn't marry her. She was right about that. It was his duty to protect his family name. No Winslow had ever even stained the family name. He could not be the first.

But damn, his blood was all but boiling just thinking about making love to her.

He took another swig of brandy, this time a big one. No, damn it all. He owed it to her. Any way he looked at it, he was the one who had made such a mess of her life. She had made a mistake with Kirkwood, but by damn, he, Edenstorm, had not even made the effort to find out what had happened between her and Kirkwood. She hadn't said exactly what that was, but he could imagine a lot. He had just been so damn sure he was right, he hadn't even asked.

Now he owed it to her to make it right. He had to convince her somehow. And somehow he had to make it work, scandal or no.

What? What in damnation did he want, to make her into something she was not? She was right, the *ton* would make her life miserable if she tried to re-enter society. Here she was safe, comfortable, with friends who loved her. She would have none of those things with him.

Hell. Did any of that make sense? It didn't to him.

Edenstorm reached for Rokeby's letter lying on the table beside his winged chair. He broke the seal, and his eyes slid quickly past the salutation.

I shall have to remain in Town for a while longer, as certain new information has surfaced. In the meantime, I have learned some things regarding that other matter that have caused me to write you urgently.

You are correct, there was a substantial dowry. More importantly, it was a large, unexpected inheritance, and I believe our friend does not know about it. Further, there has been an unsuccessful attempt to establish to the court that a certain death did occur. Obviously, it appears a fraud has been perpetrated on the court which, if discovered, could pose a considerable threat to the litigant.

Do what you feel is best. I cannot help but feel we have been mistaken in many ways, and the situation for our mutual friend is very dangerous. Whatever you choose to do, remember your promise to me and protect our friend.

R.

His heart slammed like cymbals in his chest. Good God. Harlton wanted her dead. It was not simply a matter of concealing a scandal, not realizing the attempt could create disastrous harm or even death for his sister. He had meant for her to die all along.

He had to do something, fast. The best thing was to marry her, quickly, before Harlton could find her.

His ears picked up noises below and the sound of the front door creaking open.

"His lordship has retired for the night, my lady." It was Nance's voice.

Edenstorm sat bolt upright in his chair.

"Then you must wake him. Miss Darrow is in serious danger. He must help her!"

Lady Beck! Edenstorm leapt from the chair and dashed to the stairs, his silk banyan fluttering in his wake. He ran down the stairs and dashed to the entry, every step like an eon in the terror of his mind.

Seeing him, Lady Beck broke past Nance and ran to him. "Lord Edenstorm, you must help her! You must!"

"What? Tell me!"

"Her brother, Lord Harlton. I realize you must know who she is now, but you do not know what he has done to her. He will surely see her to her death now."

Devil! How had Harlton learned? Had Rokeby's probing done it? "She told me some of it. Tell me the rest."

"Harlton forced his way into my house with the support of the beadle. I tried to persuade them she was not with me, but the beadle of course knew better. And then she came in, not knowing she was trapped. They have taken her, my lord! They manacled her and dragged her from my house. He will see her dead! He has a writ pronouncing her *non compos mentis*, and he is her legal guardian. He means to lock her away!"

"It's worse than that. There is also an inheritance. Did she know about that?"

"Inheritance? No. I can't imagine who— But there was a great aunt who was fond of her and did not care for the rest of the family. I'd heard she had died, but—"

"There's a letter from Rokeby. He made some inquiries. It appears Harlton petitioned the court to declare Juliette dead. A lie, and he obviously knows it."

"Of course he does. Oh, my lord, you must help her!"

He dashed for the stairs. "Nance, have Hector saddled quickly. Then load both my pistols. I'll want powder and more shot. Lady Beck, come with me if you will, and you may stand outside my door and give me details while I dress myself."

He took the stairs two at a time, Lady Beck close behind him.

"I assure you, sir, I am not squeamish concerning men's garments, or men. I will assist if it will help at all."

"Thank you, no. If you will remember, my lady, you have a broken arm. I imagine I can best handle it myself."

Edenstorm yanked clothes from the clothes press and threw them. Stockings, drawers, trousers he pulled on beneath his banyan, which he then jerked off over his head.

"Where did they go?" he asked as he pulled on a shirt that he tucked haphazardly into the trousers before he buttoned them.

"I heard him tell her he means to take her home, but that could have been said for the sake of the beadle who was not at all comfortable with his task. They put her in Harlton's coach, and left. That is all I know."

The boots. Damn, but he never had been able to get them on without Nance's help. He reached for a brown coat and tugged it on.

"So they will head for Plymouth on the post road, then take the post road to Kent. They'll need at least one change of horses before they make Plymouth."

"The usual stop is the Bear and Lion, at Hesson Ford. Would they not try to go farther?"

"Depends on the speed they need. But the roads are terrible after tonight's storm." He tugged fruitlessly at his left boot. "Lady Beck, are you adept at men's boots?"

"I'll do it, my lord." Nance came running into the chamber and snatched up the boots, which he expertly guided onto Edenstorm's feet. "If you could spare a moment, my lord, we could manage a decent cravat."

"Give it to me. I'll tie it while I ride. See Lady Beck home safely, will you, Nance?" Edenstorm ran down the stairs and paused when he spotted the old armor and weapons above the mantle. He lifted a long saber that had to be at least a hundred years old, but that he knew to have a good, sleek blade, and draped the crossbelt over his shoulder. One never knew when such a blade might come in handy.

Out the front door he ran, and found Trevenny standing ready with Hector and a long-legged mare. Edenstorm raised an eyebrow.

"Let me go with ye, my lord," said the groom. "I know the land. 'Tis better if ye be crossing a Cornishman's land with a Cornishman, my lord."

"You know how to catch up with them?"

"Aye, my lord. We'll catch 'em before they make Hesson Ford."

With a curt nod, Edenstorm leapt into the saddle. "I'll bring her back safely, Lady Beck. I give you my word."

"Then what, Lord Edenstorm? If he has been granted wardship of her, what shall we do?"

"We'll undo it. Write to Mr. Rokeby everything you know, about Lady Juliette, about Harlton, about the entire thing. Nance, see that she has Rokeby's letter. She'll need it. And send a copy of everything to my sister, Lady Cadridge, in Norfolk. Tell her she must not give it over to anyone. Just in case."

Beneath the brilliant moon weaving in and out of the clouds, Edenstorm sent Hector flying over the top of the hill following Trevenny.

"They'll be on the post road, and 'tis the better one, me lord," Trevenny said. "But 'tis the longer one, and they'll have the mud on their hooves, same as us. And the wheels, too, I'm thinking."

It was muddy enough. The storm had done its damage, and the roads still ran with water. Edenstorm took one edge of the road and Trevenny the other, where the mud was not as deep and the cart tracks not so entrenched. There was little hope of speed. They were lucky enough not to be up to their necks in mud in the valleys.

"They could be stuck quite easily," Edenstorm said.

But the dense trees in the valleys hid the moonlight and made their going difficult. Edenstorm could only trust to Hector's sure hooves to keep them going, but if anything befell the horse, they were lost.

What if Harlton had not taken the post road? They could have gone north instead, to head for Launceston, but it seemed less likely. From what Lady Beck had said, Harlton had no particular reason to expect pursuit.

Up on the top of the next rise, the moon again gave light, but dropped behind the hill as they descended into the next valley. Trevenny was quick to find the best crossings of fast-running streams.

"Not to worry me lord," Trevenny told him. "At the worst, they can't cross to Plymouth till dawn, with the first ferry."

Edenstorm had thought of that. The thought of holding up a private coach with pistols at a public ferry landing did not particularly appeal to him. Catching them in the midst of changing horses at a post stop was bad enough. There'd be the devil to pay in court for that alone.

But he had to do what he had to do.

On they dashed with their sure-footed mounts. Edenstorm's mind rushed with terrifying images of Jane, trussed like a madwoman, held by vicious ruffians. He could picture her futile struggle. Picture Harlton's evil grimness. He swore to himself. He had to find her in time, recapture her by force if necessary, for once Harlton had her locked away, they could be too slow in their effort to free her. She could so easily die by some unwelcome chance. Such things happened in such places, all too often.

As they approached the post road, Edenstorm saw something, indistinct in the blotchy moonlight. The anxious neighs of horses and rough shouts of men cut through the still night air.

"It's them, me lord," said Trevenny. "Stuck, I'd say."

He'd reached the same conclusion. "Can you handle a pistol, Trevenny?"

"Yes, me lord. Better'n ye might think."

Edenstorm passed over one of the pistols and then the

cravat that he'd forgotten and left slung about his neck. "Cover your face. I don't want you caught up in this if it gets sticky."

"What about yourself, sir?"

"They'll know me, regardless. Approach at a normal pace as if we're merely travelers."

"Not likely they'll believe it, me lord."

"I don't think they're going far anyway. They don't know anyone of substance has an interest in Lady Juliette, but we'll rouse as little suspicion as possible."

"Likely they'll think we be highwaymen."

Edenstorm nodded. In this part of the country, yes, that's what they'd think. Reason enough to move up slowly.

He could hear shouting. That would be Harlton, standing beside the coach at the far edge of the road, away from the deep mud, railing against the men who pried at the stuck wheels. Edenstorm nodded to Trevenny, who urged his horse ahead.

The men stopped their work to turn to the noise of approaching horses.

"Stuck are ye?" Trevenny asked as they rode up.

One of the men grunted and leaned into the lever.

Edenstorm came up beside him. "Harlton, I presume," he said.

Harlton whirled around. "Edenstorm. What the devil?"

"Jane?" Edenstorm called. "Don't move, Harlton." He held the pistol at Harlton's face and urged Hector a step forward to position him between Harlton and the coach.

"Edenstorm!" The sound of her voice sent both relief and terror flooding through him. "I'm in the coach. I'm manacled."

"You there," Edenstorm said to the smallest man who had been working to free the wheel. "Get her out of there."

The small man nodded warily, let down the step and opened the coach door. He took Jane by the arm and helped her down onto the muddy road.

"The key, Harlton," he said, waving the pistol.

"The devil, Edenstorm. What's she to you? You made it clear you wouldn't have her. I'll wager you won't now, except as your doxie."

"She's not insane and you know it, Harlton. You've just found a way to get her inheritance for yourself. The key."

"I'll swallow it before I'll give it to you, Edenstorm."

Edenstorm pulled his saber from its scabbard, the steel singing, and swung the point between the cravat at Harlton's neck and his chin so that it touched precisely to the skin. "I'll enjoy slitting your gullet to get it. Go ahead. Swallow."

"It's in my pocket."

"Move slowly. You wouldn't want me to become suspicious."

Harlton's hand began to move upward and slowly slid behind the lapel toward the upper inner pocket of the coat. The point of the saber followed his hand. "Let's have that pocket pistol first. Carefully, so I don't get the idea you meant to point it at me."

"You'll pay for this, Edenstorm," said Harlton as the pistol came out of the pocket. "I'll have you up on charges."

"No doubt. As you try to explain to the court why you have kidnapped Miss Jane Darrow. It will do wonders for your political career."

Edenstorm took the pistol and tossed it toward the sea cliff. "Now the key. Unlock the manacles."

Jane held up her wrists as Harlton jerked the manacles around and fitted the key in the lock and released first one wrist then the other.

Jane smiled. "Thank you, Lord Harlton. I do hope you find your sister. The real one."

Edenstorm kicked his left stirrup free and held his right hand behind his back for Jane to grab. In seconds, she had her foot into the stirrup and swung up behind his saddle, straddling the horse, her arms latched around his waist.

Edenstorm rode forward to the team of horses, with Trevenny guarding the rear, grabbed the leader reins in one hand and sliced them through with his saber. He flung them toward the cliff, hearing the collective moan of the men he was leaving stranded. Then he whirled Hector around and the two horses rode off down the road toward Looe.

There would be no fast going with the mud, but Trevenny led them across the rocky countryside along narrow paths until they met the road past the Old Barbican, north of Looe. There they picked up speed. Edenstorm took one hand off the reins and grasped Jane's hands that encircled his chest, squeezing heartily. Her cheek rested against his back in response.

The smell of salt and mud still permeated her torn clothes and hair, and she still looked like she had when he'd left her at the hidden entrance. Damn Harlton to hell, the man had never even given her the chance to clean up. He must have nabbed her the minute she entered Lady Beck's home.

They reached the hill above Looe, and began the descent toward Pendennen Hall. Soon they rode up to the front door. Jane slid down, Edenstorm quickly following. As Trevenny took the horses toward the stable, Nance hurried out.

"A warm bath for Lady Juliette, Nance," he said, wincing as he realized how much he had over-burdened his servants this night.

"Just some washing water would be fine," she said.

"I hoped you'd find her, my lord. I have water heating and some useful things in the spare bedchamber. Lady Beck explained things, and I remembered your state when you came in, so I thought—"

"You and Trevenny are true treasures, Nance. I'll see you both well rewarded for this night's work. One more thing, though. Go to Lady Beck with the news. Tell her we are all safe for the night, but we will no doubt face legal challenge. And we must have a physician and judge to counter Harlton's claim. Tomorrow I will take Lady Juliette wherever she thinks it safe."

"Edenstorm—"

He ignored her and with an arm around her waist helped her up the stairs to the small chamber beside his own. Towels and a brown cotton dressing gown he recognized as belonging to Nance were set aside on the wing-back chair near the firegrate, and the slipper tub was close enough to the fire to keep her warm. "I'll see to her, Nance."

"I shall return in a few hours with Lady Beck's instructions."

Edenstorm dismissed any notions of what Nance might think. He knew exactly what he wanted tonight, and he would not settle for less.

Chapter Fifteen

There was a tall Cheval glass standing in the corner of the bedchamber, its glass crinkled with black spots and lines that gave a mottled pewter cast to the rosy glow from the fireplace.

Jane stood nude before the mirror, clutching a man's plain brown muslin dressing gown. Her eyes were pinched as tight as a miser's purse, and she couldn't make them open. She should look at herself. She must. But the minute her own image would appear in the mirror's dull haze, her eyes would close it out.

She had never felt so dirty. So ugly. She had leaned over the side of the little slipper tub and lathered and washed the salt and grime from her hair, scrubbing until she worried that her hair might come out. Then she had sat in the tiny tub, her legs hanging spider-like on either side, and scoured her skin until the bruises, scrapes and scratches hurt worse than they had with the salt imbedded in them. Then she had scrubbed herself again.

If only she could make her eyes open, she could surely see the dirt was gone. But they would not. This was the kind of dirt that could not be washed away. Once, four years before, she had scrubbed her skin until it was raw. She had thought she was beyond that.

Jane touched the deep bruise on her wrist where Cyril had clamped his hand when he'd dragged her to his coach. Funny, though. It was not the bruise that hurt. She had thought there was nothing Cyril could do to hurt her again.

Tears welled up in her pinched-tight eyes and seeped through the cracks, and she couldn't make them stop. Jane never cried. Never, ever cried. But she couldn't keep the tears from pouring out. She could only stand there in all her ugliness, trying to make herself look at what her eyes couldn't bear to see.

All she had ever wanted was to be loved.

A door squeaked behind her and she knew from his masculine scent it was Edenstorm. In the mirror she saw him, his blue and gold silk banyan flowing as he moved toward her.

Quickly, she dabbed at the tears she didn't want him to see, but knew he would see her wiping them, and just as rapidly, she converted the movement into something that resembled an attempt to slip her arms into the muslin dressing gown's sleeves. There would be redness in her eyes, and she must not let him see it. She lowered her lashes, hoping the dim firelight would help her.

Edenstorm stood behind her. His blunt-fingered hands touched her arms and slid upward to her shoulders over the brown cotton. "You don't need this," he said, the whisper-soft words tickling her ear. "You need never hide from me again."

Jane closed her eyes and leaned back against his chest, feeling instead of seeing as the gown fell from her shoulders, slid down her arms.

"You're dressed," she protested.

"Undress me," he whispered back. His silvery eyes were darkening with wildness she had never seen in them before.

Yes. It was what she wanted most in the entire world. It would be her gift to him, for tomorrow she would give him an even more important one, for she valued all that made him who he was. Loved who he was.

Tomorrow would be a different thing, but tonight, she would give him this gift, knowing she really gave it to herself. She would love him, memorizing every inch of him, making memories she could cherish forever.

Jane turned to face him, her eyes still lowered, appearing to watch the movements of her hands as she fingered the golden frogs on his banyan. She slipped the knots free from their loops, one, two, three, and maneuvered her hands inside the silk, to the fine cambric of his nightshirt. She smiled, looking down, to see his bare toes beneath the cloth. Such strangely ugly feet with funny, snaggle-toes, for such a beautiful man. But she would love them, too. Later. When she finished with the more interesting parts.

In her hands, which seemed so small touching his huge body, the soft striped silk fell away from his shoulders. She let it drop to the floor, puddling on top of the plain brown dressing gown.

Following the hard lines of his body, then his legs, she bent and ran her hands downward to grasp the hem of the nightshirt. She gathered fistfuls of the cambric as she slowly rose, grazing her thumbs over his thighs. She leaned her head back, her eyes closed, absorbing the feel, learning the crispness of the golden hairs on his legs, imagining what it would be like rubbing against her legs.

Slowly as she straightened,, the fabric rose, up past his hips, and she heard the soft hiss of a sharp, deep breath. Yes. She would get back to that, the groin area that Lydia had so carefully described. She kept moving her hands upward, the fabric collecting in bunches so thick, she opened her grasp and hooked it on her thumbs. Up it moved, exposing his chest, and now she could see the male arousal she had grazed before.

She didn't know what it was called, only the occasional vulgar term she had over-heard accidentally a few times. It seemed wondrous, powerful, this focus of his passion. Something zinged and sang inside her, wanting to stop and test it in her hands, but she wanted the nightshirt off his body first.

Upward, she moved her hands, skimming her thumbs over two hard, small nubs of male nipples. He arched his head backward, and a shudder ran through him as he moaned in that same way she had heard before when they were on the cliff. It sent a shiver through her that wound like a spring inside her.

As she reached the sleeves, she hooked her thumbs into them and continued moving up. His arms rose until the cloth passed his elbows, and he pulled his arms free. His male scent, clean, yet like the musky hint of leather, the feel of his flesh, the sight of his golden hair, all blended, made her hungry, a hunger that had been awakened on the cliff and grew beyond any she had ever known before. In a flash, he had both hands wrapped around her, sliding down her back to hold her against him, the hard unnamed part of him pressing against the flesh of her stomach. The nightshirt cleared his head and dropped behind him.

He bent down to capture her lips with his, the shiver still wracking through him. Gleefully, Jane embraced him as tightly as he did her and let her hands run wild over his smooth skin and muscles, loving their shape, feeling their hardness. Down his back, the marvelous indentation where his spine ran and joined to hard buttocks that were nothing like hers. Nothing, in fact, was like hers. She closed her eyes again, sneaking a hand between their bodies, drinking in the sensations of the crisp hair on his hard-planed chest and exploring downward over his belly which was not soft and forgiving like hers, and found the intriguing part of him which had no name. And according to Lydia, was the focus of a man's desire.

She smiled, remembering, grateful that Lydia had insisted on educating her, even if Lydia didn't always know what to call something. Lydia had mentioned gentle strokes, and later as the man became more aroused, more vigorous ones. That left a great deal to the imagination, but Jane figured her fantasies were up to the task. She heated up, just thinking about it.

The skin was silkier than velvet, and hot, sleekly covering the rigid thing that had grown even in the little time since she had felt it pressed against her. It moved at her touch, and he moaned, not releasing her from his kiss, but arching inward to give her hands free access. She wanted both, both to feel his body tightly pressed to hers, and to explore his marvelous maleness.

With one of his big hands cupping her buttocks, he slipped the other between her legs. Her heart sped as he slid his hand between her thighs up to the juncture with her body, and then between those lower lips. Something wild sprang free inside her. Whatever he was touching made her want to beg for more. And as he began to rub back and forth, she gasped, arching backward, her whole body screaming for more.

"My Juliette," he rasped out.

Jane. But he didn't understand that. She wished she could be what he wanted, wished everything for him, but it was only Jane who could give him this, and this was so very little, for the man who was giving her so very much.

His finger slid inside her. Jane lost her mind. The world

became only him and her, and what was passing between them.

He stopped. Her eyes flew open.

"Jane, you're a virgin," he said.

"Well, yes, I knew that," she replied, sort of shaking her head to dislodge some of the cobwebs that had bound her mind into some sort of mysterious muddle. "Does it matter?"

"Yes. Are you sure you want to do this?"

"Yes." That much was clear to her.

Edenstorm lifted her into his arms and carried her to the bed. He parted the bed curtains with an elbow, deposited her against the stack of pillows and went to the foot of the bed to open the curtains and let in the heat from the fire. Then he climbed onto the high bed beside her.

"It's like your dream," she said.

"It is my dream." He fanned her damp hair over the white pillows, meticulously arranging it. "The golden curls splayed over the pillows. Green eyes turned dusky in the firelight. Rosy lips awaiting my kisses. And now my dreams have a face, not just features. You are my dream."

Stretching out his full length beside her, he leaned over her, seeking her lips again. "Do what you were doing before," she said. Such a request should make her blush with shame. But she didn't care. Wantonly, she opened for him.

Edenstorm splayed his hands over her belly, caressing the curves. In the golden glow of firelight, his pale eyes were soft and smoky, his golden-bronze hair dusky, with the one errant wave dangling over his forehead, unmasking that secret part of his soul that had suddenly decided to rebel and show itself. Two desires warred inside her, wanting both to drink in every inch of him with her eyes, yet to close them and find all his beauty by touch.

The hand that had inflamed her desires before roamed down to the brown curls and slid between her legs, and her body opened, wildly anticipating the coming pleasure. As he leaned over her, stroking the place between her legs, her mind was spinning out of control, and she wanted the same for him. She recalled the male nipples she had touched before and she found one, rubbing her thumb over it. Groaning, he captured her nipple in his mouth and teased it with his tongue.

She was lost. She moaned, whimpered, bucked against the hand that sent her into some savage, demanding world of desire. She was taut and hot, desperately pleading for something.

"Juliette," he said, hoarsely. He spread her legs and moved atop her, still stroking her as he had been.

The yearning to pull him close to her all but overwhelmed her as she felt him place the male thing where his hand had been. Then she felt the stretching, and it seemed she was too tight, yet then was a perfect fit. It was too much, just right, perfect, as he eased in, relieving yet building the passion that glowed red hot within her.

A sharp pain pricked. "Oh!"

He stopped.

Jane grabbed a breath, and the pain faded away. It was only like a pinch, then it was gone, and he was inside her.

It was the most wonderful thing in the world. She wanted him to stay there forever. But no, he slid even deeper. Deeper, until she felt him touching all around. She wrapped her legs around him to imprison him.

The wonder began to change. He began to pull away and she felt an emptiness. No, she wasn't ready for him to leave yet!

And then she discovered the true wonder, as he stroked in, slowly, so slowly, and she thought she'd found heaven. Nothing could ever feel so good. Yet she wanted more.

Quickly she learned the rhythm of the strokes of his hand and the strokes of the male part within her and began to move with them, but the more she did, the more she wanted, and her body bucked to keep up with him. She grasped his buttocks, trying to drive him deeper into her. She gasped and whimpered, and begged and didn't even know what for.

Then suddenly— And he suddenly—

Jane's body thrashed. Ripples of beautiful colors swirled like whirlpools and flashed and splashed like fountains. With a massive shudder, he plunged deeply into her, convulsing, ramming his last strokes home.

They floated together, on a silent, quiet sea, their bodies still entwined. Now she had found perfection.

“Ah, Juliette,” he said at last, his voice as soft a caress as the long, blunt fingers that trailed gently over her flesh. And after awhile, he raised himself and placed his palms on her cheeks. “My Juliette,” he said.

She was Jane. He did not understand that, nor that Jane could never be his. But for tonight, he was hers.

“I’m sorry I hurt you,” he said, rolling to his back and heaving a huge sigh.

“You didn’t hurt me. It wasn’t any more than a pin prick.”

“That was no pin pricking you, my dear.”

“Well, I know, of course it was not. But it didn’t hurt any more than that.”

“I wish I’d known before. A man should be more careful with a virgin.”

“But why wouldn’t you— Oh.”

“That was my fault. I haven’t trusted you, when you’ve been telling me the truth all along.”

“Well, not entirely, but it didn’t seem to make a difference.”

“You do seem to know more than most innocents, I’m afraid.”

“Women do talk. It’s only men who think they don’t. Lydia had a wonderful marriage, and it must have been hard for her to accept my attitudes sometimes. She did make it seem rather nice, if one had a decent husband.”

He laughed, and it made her smile at him. For him. She’d never seen him laugh so much, and it was a beautiful laugh that seemed to come from deep in his soul. It was like an echo, the way it resonated inside her.

“Odd,” he said. “I had the feeling she didn’t want to remarry.”

“Oh, she doesn’t. She doesn’t think she’ll ever find a man to equal Lord Beck. I suspect she won’t, at least until she stops missing him so much, but she rather likes men anyway. Not that I mean she behaves like some widows do, but she does seem to appreciate men. I’ve found that hard. But the men around Looe are good men.”

“Like Polruhan.”

“He is. Really. He would make a good husband for some

woman if only he'd look a bit further."

"I'd be happy for him to do that, but I can't blame him."

Jane blushed and looked away. What she saw was the male organ that intrigued her, now at rest and completely different. Lydia had explained that to her, too.

"What is this called?" she asked, stroking a fingertip lightly over the object that puzzled her. It jumped at her touch, startling her.

"A penis," he said, smiling.

"That's a strange word. It doesn't sound at all English."

"It's probably Latin. There are some vulgar words some people use."

"You mean people talk about it?"

"You and Lady Beck did. We are now. Men talk about it all the time."

"I heard some men in the stable using the word cock, and I don't think they meant the rooster."

"Why?"

"Because then they saw me and their faces turned red."

"You're right, then. But the word probably came from the way the rooster struts about so arrogantly."

"Like men do sometimes."

"Some men call it a rod, or a pecker. Or a prick."

"Then that's why you didn't like the pin-prick idea."

"No man likes to be considered small."

"I didn't mean that. Really. And I don't think you're small. You aren't, are you? For a man, I mean."

"Men don't go around comparing, usually. But I don't think so. Do you mean to tell me, Lady Beck taught you about making love but she didn't tell you what a penis is called?"

"There may have been a few gaps in her knowledge. I don't think she knew what to call it, either. Although once she did refer to it as the device for sexual transmission."

His jaw dropped open, and he fell back, chuckling when his elbow slipped from beneath him. He pulled her on top of him.

"Then you'll have to correct her when you have the

occasion again."

Jane lost her smile. She dragged the palm of her hand over his cheek, memorizing the faint bristly feeling. "Do you think there will be an occasion?"

He rolled, taking her with him, until he was once again on top of her. "You are mine, Juliette. What's mine, I protect. He will never harm you again."

She just smiled.

"Tomorrow, we will find a physician who will counteract your brother's claim. I told Lady Beck he must be someone of significant reputation, so we may have to go to Bath. Portsmouth is too much of a risk. But that will be of little good unless we can keep you hidden until your birthday."

"But how? That's still two months away."

"We'll go to Scotland."

"Won't he follow us?"

"Maybe. We could hire a boat. Sail to Ireland, then take a packet from Northern Ireland to Scotland. I've also had Lady Beck write to Rokeby to explain what has happened, and to send copies of everything to my sister, Lady Cadridge, just to be sure there is documentation of what your brother has done."

"You don't need to do that, Edenstorm."

"Merritt. I'm Merritt to you, from now on. And yes, it is necessary. Harlton might try to contest the physician's certification. And he could demand custody of you while it is being wrangled in the courts. But once you reach your majority, it's highly unlikely any court will actually hear the case, and no chance they will force you back to his care while awaiting the outcome."

She lowered her lashes again. So, he really meant to do it. And he was carefully omitting the part where Cyril would charge him with interfering with a guardian's custody. The images of the coming scandal flashed in her mind. She couldn't let him do this, but she didn't need to tell him that now. She leaned her head against his chest.

"You are so beautiful," he said.

"No." She felt the shame sneaking up on her again, grasping at her throat and twisting her stomach into a knot.

"You are. You are the most beautiful woman in the world. From the first time I saw you, you have left me breathless. Speechless."

"You said—"

"I said too many things I regret, and you have paid the price for them. Forgive me. I want another chance."

She licked her lower lip. She would give him whatever he wanted. She would be his mistress, even share him with a wife, for she could not bear to lose him.

But she would lose him. She knew that. She was ugly inside. Whatever he thought now, that would fade away, and she would become too much of an embarrassment. She would have to be satisfied with this one night, and then he must go away to lead the life he was meant to lead.

She said nothing, only smiled one last time and turned her back to fit against the curve of his body. She felt the penis growing hard, and in a way hoped it meant he would make love to her again.

"Are you cold?"

She shook her head. But then she feared he might pull away from her, for on the cliff, he had used his body to help her keep warm. But he stayed where he was, nestled against her, and pulled the blanket up to tuck beneath her arm, then cradled her breast in his hand.

She closed her eyes, wishing she could spend every minute of their last time awake. But she could not. Exhaustion was claiming her. She could fight it no longer.

❧

He slept, a blessed, dreamless sleep.

It was the soldier's instinct that woke him. He'd slumbered lightly, barely aware of the sounds of dawn approaching, for the first time in years feeling a certain peace, a contentment. The first chirp of birds stirred him, and with a touch he had assured himself that she was still beside him. He drifted off again.

Then the sharpness of silence jarred him awake. He got to his feet and in a smooth movement crossed the room to the window.

A flash of motion caught his eye. Something up against the low stone wall surrounding the house. Nothing else. But that one thing should not have been there.

He saw her sit up. "Get your clothes," he said, hurriedly grabbing his own, but realizing most of hers were still drying in the kitchen. He pitched her the cotton dressing gown Nance had loaned her.

"What?" Already running out the door, she wrapped the garment around her.

"They're out there. We'll have to go out the back."

"They'll be waiting there, too."

He knew that. He tucked one pistol in his belt and slung the saber's crossbelt over his shoulder.

"The kitchen," she said as they ran down the stairs. "We can get to the cellar."

"We'll be trapped there."

"There's another way. I think I can find it."

In the kitchen, he scooped up her garments, adding to his pile and she ran for the cellar door, tossed it open and started down, holding it open for him. He hurried past her and she shoved the door closed and threw the bolt.

Edenstorm stared and the door that had puzzled him so much before. "That's why, then."

"An escape route," she agreed. "Like a bolt hole in a castle. It will slow them down just long enough for us to open the passage. But no longer. It's not that strong. Hurry."

At the bottom of the wooden stairs, she turned and ran behind the stairs, Edenstorm close on her heels. She stopped, her face pulling into a frown.

Before them, he saw only the shelves he had seen before and the remaining ankers of brandy. It looked like a dead end. What the devil was she doing?

She studied it, running a finger along the stone joints. With a grim nod, she pulled one of the shelves forward and set it aside atop the casks. She pushed against the wall and a small hole opened. She climbed through.

Edenstorm shoved the garments through and followed her.

Above, the front door rattled, then banged. He could hear the heavy tromp of boots up the stairs to the first floor. Shouts rang out, and Nance's calm words responded. Nance wouldn't tell them anything.

She lifted the shelf into place and pulled the kegs back where they had been. The door, made of the same stone as the wall and hung on a perfectly mounted pivot, swung smoothly and silently closed. She slid a heavy beam into place and barred the door. He doubted the entire contingent above would be able to shove it open.

"How did you know?" he asked as they felt their way along the dark passage.

"There are things everyone in Looe knows," she replied. "The Pendennens were free traders many years ago. This goes beneath the stable and comes out near the St. Martins road."

"Beyond my property. We didn't search there."

"It belongs to the vicar's family now. Close relatives of the Pendennen family, who own your house. You wouldn't want to be making accusations."

She stopped and took her clothing from him. He chuckled as she tried to sort her clothes from his in the dark. But they got her into her stays and chemise, and pulled on the dress that had been so badly abused the previous day. He had lost a stocking of hers somewhere, but was of no mind to go back for it.

"If everyone here knows, then the beadle does, too."

"He's a weasel of a fellow, but he'll not reveal Looe's secrets unless they're already obvious."

"Can they hear us above?" he asked.

"Possibly."

"I really do hope you have your clothes on and not mine," he said.

"Really, Edenstorm, I don't believe you would fit in mine."

"Merritt."

He could almost feel her smile as her voice turned soft. "Merritt."

Suddenly he felt like he was king of the world.

Dim light slipped through a crack ahead of them and he

realized it was time to become more practical. She moved cautiously now, up to the wooden door, and put her ear to the crack. The only sound he could hear was the deep breath she took, then the rasp of the latch as she lifted it and pushed open the creaking door.

A shaft of early sunlight slanted into the little cellar through a broken door above. A ladder missing two rungs rested against a wall carved into rock.

Edenstorm moved her aside and started up the ladder, pushing the door upward as he climbed. They emerged in an old cottage that looked abandoned. He considered leaving her hidden while he went for help, but the chance was too great that the tunnel would be found.

She clambered up the ladder to stand beside him, and they eased the old wooden doors back into place.

If they could get across the river to West Looe, Lady Beck could help them escape, but already he could hear the clash of voices and footsteps of men spreading over the hill. They could get that far, maybe even to the other side, but anyone on either side of the river would be able to see them on the bridge. There was no other place to cross for miles before the river reached Liskeard, so it was the bridge or nothing. But what after that? They couldn't make it to Launceston Hall before they were caught.

The sounds were coming closer.

There was only one place she would be safe. The last place he wanted her to be. With Polruhan.

Chapter Sixteen

Edenstorm grabbed her hand and ran across the lane, behind a house, setting a little brown dog to barking from a few feet distant. Shouts behind them grew louder.

Peering around the corner of the house, he saw no one coming and dashed along the next street, heading down the hill toward the river.

"Where are we going?" she asked between gasping breaths as they ducked behind a small shed.

"The bridge." They moved out, once again running toward the river.

"They'll see us."

"They're going to see us anyway. We have to get to the other side."

"We can't go back to Lydia's. She can't protect us."

"I know."

"Then where?"

He didn't want to say, not just yet. "Shh."

He gripped her hand harder and held her back while he checked again for movement. Seeing nothing, they once again ran, following a narrow cobbled street that paralleled the river. Then they turned, moving in a zigzag that brought them closer to the bridge with each step.

"I know some places upriver," she said. "There's an old church where we can hide."

Edenstorm didn't reply. Let her think that. In the early morning gloaming, he could see the searchers swarming like bees all over the hill, arousing barking dogs. A horse neighed, and a man shouted. Soon the entire village of East Looe would be awake, if not already.

Most of the noise came from the southern slope of the hill close to the sea, but the pursuers seemed to be moving upward, as if they expected their quarry to move east toward civilized England. He sneered. Of course they would think that. Why, after all, would anyone escape toward the sea, where they would be trapped?

Because they wouldn't be. But Harlton wouldn't know that.

They reached the bridge as a cock crowed. The moon had set long before and dawn was only a gray strip on the horizon, out to sea, but this deep little valley would be dark for awhile yet.

"Go," he hissed, and gave her a shove toward the bridge.

Together they ran. Jane's footsteps pattered erratically, and he could hear her heavy panting. His boots clattered in his ears like horseshoes on the cobblestones.

No more than halfway across, the shouts rang out. Far enough away that he couldn't distinguish the words, but he knew the meaning. They'd been spotted.

"Run!" he shouted to her.

She was slowing instead, holding her side. "I can't."

"Run or I'll carry you!"

She paused, gasping, bending forward and clutching her arms over her waist. Behind them, men were running down the hill toward the bridge. He reached for her, but she straightened and, grabbing her breath, started running again.

She couldn't keep it up much longer. He couldn't carry her fast enough or far enough. But Polruhan's house and boat yard weren't so far.

She was staggering by the time they crossed onto the road that ran along through West Looe, along the bank. She started to the right, but Edenstorm took her arm. "No, this way."

"Not there."

Seeing she was nearly faint, Edenstorm lifted her and flung her over his shoulder. He ran again, down into the deeply shadowed the dip in the road. Maybe they had not been seen turning this direction.

But he was slowed by the weight and, gasping, himself, he finally had to stop.

"I can do it now. But there's no place—"

"Polruhan," he said between gasps.

"No, Merritt!"

"He'll protect you."

"No, we can't! Merritt, you don't know!"

Dark shapes of men emerged from darker shadows and came toward them. The long objects in their hands might be clubs or muskets, he couldn't tell.

"Oh, I think he does, darlin'."

"Davy!"

"I'm wondering why ye might be out running through the streets in the wee morning hours with the likes of him, lass."

"You've got to hide her, Polruhan," Edenstorm gasped out. That's her brother coming after her, and he means to have her dead."

"And why should I be believing the likes of you? Me lord?" Edenstorm could hear the sneer in his voice.

"Listen to him."

Edenstorm turned toward the feminine voice, one he didn't know, yet did, for he had never heard it with harsh tones.

"Lady Launceston! What are you doing here?"

He turned back to Jane who squeezed her eyes closed, pulling her whole face into a pinch. Behind them, he could hear the approaching shouts and pounding footsteps.

"About time you are redeeming yourself, Lord Edenstorm," said Lady Launceston. "But you've got more to answer for. Now listen to him, Davy Polruhan. If you're a true son of Cornwall, you won't let a fine woman like Jane Darrow be a victim to her cruel brother again. She is Lady Juliette Dalworthy. But if you let Lord Harlton capture her again, she will be Lady Juliette from beneath a tombstone, for he will kill her, one way or another."

Davy turned hard eyes on all of them, one at a time. "We'll talk on it. Trevenny, ye know where to put them."

Trevenny was here, too? Had he betrayed them? After

helping Edenstorm rescue Jane?

In the shadows of the house, he could see the whites of Jane's eyes as she looked up at him. "Leave, Merritt, while you can."

"Don't think so, darlin'. Your fancy lord knows too much."

Edenstorm felt and smelled the forms of rough men as they tightened the circle about their quarry.

"No, I stay with you," he told her. "There's no time for talk, Polruhan. They have to have seen us come this way. Take her and hide her. Or better, get us to London, by the sea, where they can't reach us. You want money? I've got all the money you could want."

Polruhan's dark shadow formed a menacing block as he placed his hands on his hips. "Ye'll go where I say, and now. And ye don't make a move or a sound unless ye're told to. Trevenny will see to it ye understand. Trevenny, take them."

Trevenny stepped up, glancing back at the ruckus on the bridge. "This way, me lord. Come along, me lady." With his head, he nodded toward Polruhan's house as the others with Polruhan, including Lady Launceston, walked on in the direction of the boatyard.

"You've turned on me, then, Trevenny?" Edenstorm asked as they walked.

"Doing what I got to do, me lord. Hurry." He started off at a trot across the narrow street, motioning for them to follow as he ran behind a large, boxlike house built of dark gray slatestone that blended with the hill behind it.

Then Edenstorm saw what Trevenny carried. A new Baker rifle, capable of picking an apple off a tree at a hundred yards. So escaping from Polruhan or his men was not an option. They were better equipped than most of Wellington's army.

Trevenny rushed up to the door at the rear and opened it, quickly shuffling Jane and Edenstorm inside, where a stern-faced footman glowered at them.

"In the hole," said Trevenny. His voice was brusk and gravelly.

The footman nodded. Without saying a word, he strode through the house toward a servants' staircase and up to the first landing. Edenstorm couldn't tell what was being maneuvered, but a wooden panel that looked just like the rest of the white-painted wainscoting came free.

"In there," said Trevenny.

Edenstorm crawled in first and helped Jane in after him. The tiny space expanded beneath the stairs, leaving them barely room to sit.

"Ye're not to move or make a sound," Trevenny said as the footman was closing the panel. "Think of yerselves as brandy, with the Exciseman coming to search."

Darkness closed in as the panel shut. Edenstorm wrapped his arms about Jane, keeping her in his arms, reliving their moments on the cliff when she sat on his lap. But there would be no making love now. Any sound would carry through that thin panel. She was heating heat him up like a baker's oven, but Davy Polruhan's house was the last place he wanted to be caught making love to her. He just hoped that panel was as inconspicuous to anyone else as it had been to him before the footman had moved it.

"What is he going to do with us?" she asked in a whisper.

"Shhh."

"He's furious, but at least he's hiding us."

Edenstorm slipped his hand over her mouth and laid a soft kiss on her hair to reassure her.

Soon, they heard voices in the house, and the sounds of servants moving about in the early morning, but soon the strident sounds of invaders searching for something. He could pick out the whimpers of terrified women and other low, calm voices, mostly male.

Harlton's voice was easy to distinguish as it grew ever more shrill from rage and fatigue, cursing the servants and railing at the beadle's incompetence. Men tromped up the stairs and over the floor above their heads, then soon came back down, followed by more of Harlton's outraged screaming. More footsteps pounding on stairs again, a different staircase. Then more sounds from below in a cellar. So probably Harlton believed they were in Polruhan's house and he was not about to give up.

A door slammed. Things grew very still.

Were they leaving to search other houses after all?

Edenstorm knew Jane had a lot of friends who might hide her. And likely, Harlton had demanded a search of the boats in the boatyard. Perhaps the men they had met behind Polruhan's house had been seen walking toward the boats at the quay, giving the impression he and Jane had gone with them. Edenstorm could imagine the men stationed outside to watch the surrounding area while others searched inside the houses.

Where had Lady Launceston gone? She must have been trying to persuade Polruhan to help Jane, even before they ran across the bridge. Had Trevenny been doing the same, even though he'd known Jane was already with Edenstorm? Or was it something else entirely? What was this group of men doing here in the early morning, all of them dressed like ordinary seamen? Even Trevenny had shed his groom's clothing, and Polruhan lacked his usual polished look.

Jane knew more than she had told him, but he couldn't ask until it was safe to talk. She only squirmed about occasionally, in the same kind of cramped discomfort he felt.

Damn, a chamber pot would be nice. But there wouldn't even be a way to use it in such a little space. He suspected that was why Jane was squirming so much. He caressed her cheek to remind her he was still here and still caring. As if that somehow meant he could actually do anything about their predicament.

At last, a crack of light penetrated their gloom as the panel came off. Edenstorm and Jane groaned as they unfolded their stiff bodies and climbed out of the hole.

Polruhan awaited them, glowering.

Chapter Seventeen

"Ye can come out now, me lord," called Trevenny. He sounded almost kind, giving Jane a bit of hope.

The light blinded her as she sat up. Every muscle in her body ached from fatigue, bruises and staying too long in one position, but all she really cared about was how soon she could get to a chamber pot.

Being closest to the opening, she crawled out first, with Edenstorm following, and unfolded her stiff legs as she rose to her feet. The first thing she saw was Davy at the bottom of the stairs, stance wide, fists planted on his hips, his dark gaze seething. She had the feeling she was about to find out what that dark current was that lurked beneath his good-natured grin.

Fear tightened like iron barrel bands around her chest. "Davy—"

The heavy muscles in his jaw flexed as his eyes radiated anger. He jerked a nod to the footman, then stalked away.

"'Ere, Miss Darrow," said gray-haired Mrs. Downs, Davy's housekeeper. "Ye're to come with me."

She glanced at Edenstorm, who attempted a reassuring smile as he was led off by the footman who had put them in the hole so many hours before.

Mrs. Downs was a harmless soul, at least. Jane followed her up the back stairs to the second floor and a small chamber with draperies tightly pulled. The room was stark and sparely furnished, but on the bed lay her brown fustian dress, gray shawl, and a brown pelisse she didn't recognize. A small valise sat beside the dress.

The housekeeper poured water into the washbowl and set a folded towel beside it. "Ye're to dress and eat, miss. Will ye be needing help?"

"No, thank you, Mrs. Downs. I customarily dress myself."

"Well, then, I'll be coming come back for ye."

With downcast eyes, the housekeeper bobbed a curtsy and left the room. A key turned in the lock.

Jane found the chamber pot beneath the bed. She let out an enormous sigh of relief, for she couldn't remember a time when she'd appreciated one more.

When they had left Edenstorm's house, she had put on her stays so sloppily that she was glad for the chance to remove and readjust them. They were simple, unfashionable wrap stays, but she had not cared about fashion for a very long time. She put on the fresh shift, stays and stockings, and brushed out the tangles of her hair that had not been touched since their abrupt wakening in the night. It felt good to be dressing in ordinary clothes, in ordinary ways. How long she might have that privilege, she could not tell, so she meant to savor it while she had it.

Davy was a good man at heart. He would not hurt her.

But what would he do to Edenstorm?

Your fancy lord knows too much.

Her knees went weak all over again. She dropped into a chair, fighting the rush of tears that threatened her eyes. Could Davy be no better than Cyril?

No. She couldn't give in to fear. She forced herself to stand, ignoring her shaking legs.

She picked up the old brown dress, and something heavy fell to the bed. Lydia's gold locket, the one that had held a tiny portrait of Lord Beck, painted before he died. Jane flipped it open. The portrait now was one of Lydia.

Jane smiled. *Thank you, Lydia.*

But she did not feel safe wearing it on a chain around her neck where it was visible, so she tucked it inside her stays.

Knowing Lydia, there would be more. She rummaged into the bottom of the brown canvas valise and found what she had expected, her sketchbook. Then the Conté pencil and several others. She tucked the Conté down the center of her stays with the locket.

She sat down to the tray of food that had been left, but all she could do was pick at it, even though she hadn't eaten since the little picnic Edenstorm had brought with them into the cave.

No. Eat. This was no time to be missish. She was going to need every bite she could get down.

If only Edenstorm had left when she begged him to. Why had he brought her here? Surely they could have made it farther up the road and then disappeared into the shadows beneath the little wooden bridge that crossed the creek on the way to Liskeard.

She sighed. She might as well have asked him to carry her on his back all the way to London. No, it had been her flagging strength that had doomed him. She should have found a way to make him leave when he first came here, instead of indulging in his stubborn curiosity. It was none of his business!

That also would have been impossible. It was his obsession with duty and honor that had brought him here, and if she could have dissuaded him, then he wouldn't be the man he was. Still, had she doomed him by leading him on, making him believe she would give him what he wanted to know?

The sound of a key turned in the lock again and the housekeeper returned, her wrinkled face struggling between the proper faraway look of a servant and one that spoke of some emotion a servant ought never to show. Jane pretended she didn't see it.

"This way, please, miss. Ye're to see the master now."

Jane nodded. She squared her shoulders and followed down the stairs, holding her head high as if she were back in the schoolroom with a volume of *Plutarch's Lives* balanced on her head. Brown fustian and all, she imagined herself as proud as Mary, Queen of Scots on her way to her execution.

As the housekeeper held open the door, Jane entered a study on the first floor, all browns and russets, with the clean, spare touch that spoke of Davy's way of living. Like the room where she had dressed, the draperies were pulled closed.

Edenstorm stood amidst nearly a dozen local men, most

wearing the simple clothes of seamen. All of them paused to watch her enter, and all but Davy glanced guiltily down to their shoes. Her heart lodged in her throat.

Jane subtly moved to Edenstorm's side.

Rage smoldered in Davy's dark eyes. She gulped and lifted her head high, mentally placing that heavy book on her head to remind herself to stand tall.

"So this is the lovely Lady Juliette Dalworthy," Davy said. "Shall I be bowing to ye now? Seeing ye're above my touch."

Jane clenched her jaw.

"This isn't her doing, Polruhan," said Edenstorm. "Let her go. She'll never turn on you, you know that."

"Ye think she won't?" Davy folded his arms and glared.

"Davy, I'd never betray you or anyone here. I never have."

"Have ye not, darlin'? I'm wondering what ye was saying on those long rides into the country."

"That was your idea. You were the one who wanted me to keep him busy and away from town."

"Oh, aye. The one time, it was, but not the others. But things change when a girl's head's been turned, and his mighty lordship's done more than turn your head, has he not?"

Her face turned humiliatingly hot.

Davy pushed away from the desk and walked toward her, his accusing eyes boring into her. "I'm wondering how ye managed to fool me all these years."

"I told you I wouldn't marry you, Davy. I couldn't, without telling you the truth. And that would have been the end of it."

"The truth. That ye aren't who ye say ye are. That the sweet, unassuming and virtuous Miss Jane Darrow isn't our Jane at all. I'm wondering, darlin', what ye did that was so wicked that your own brother would lock ye up for insane to hide it. I'm wondering why you'd spend four years hiding from the man who's your legal guardian. I'm wondering what other lies you've told me, or if there's anything ye've told me that isn't a lie. Ye haven't even been honest about your age."

Edenstorm stepped between them. "Leave her alone, Polruhan. I have more claim on her than you do. She was to marry me."

"Oh, aye, I heard that, too. But then ye didn't, did ye?"

Edenstorm didn't answer.

Jane jumped in. "I was the one who wouldn't marry him. Then I ran from my brother because he tried to force me to marry a violent man."

"Ye're such a victim, darlin'. I'm thinking your high and mighty lordship didn't believe ye."

"He didn't." Edenstorm's voice was as hard as Davy's.

"I'd say we have something in common after all, Edenstorm."

"And that makes us both wrong. Her brother wants her inheritance, which will go to him if she's dead."

Jane shook her head. "I don't have any inheritance."

"Yes, you do. Rokeby found out about it in London. He also found out your brother tried to have you declared dead and himself your heir. Listen to me, Polruhan. You know she's not insane, no matter what warrants her brother has."

Davy folded his arms, and one hand tapped a slow, steady rhythm against the other arm. He turned back to his desk to pick up a folded letter with the red wax seal popped open.

"The letter," he said, holding it up. "Thanks to Lady Launceston. 'Tis not a guess he wants her dead, and has the blunt to make it happen, but he wants a better job done of it this time. 'Twould be so easy to take her out to sea and let her vanish, but 'twouldn't satisfy the court. More like she's found floating face down in the pool. A tragic accident, y' see, but with a body to show the court, and with her lover found shot by his own hand."

"Damn you!" Edenstorm lunged at Davy, his eyes blazing. His fist caught Davy in the jaw, knocking him away from the desk to the Turkey rug. "Run, Jane! Get out of here!"

Jane screamed, but two hands seized her arms in a grip she knew instantly she couldn't break.

"No, me lady," said Trevenny. "Be easy."

Davy swung a leg to trip Edenstorm, but Edenstorm jumped free and sprang, just as Davy scrambled off the floor. Edenstorm hit the carpet hard, two men knocking him down. His fists came out swinging, but too late. Three rifles pointed at his head, while the other men held down his arms and legs with their feet or hands.

Davy landed on top of him, his eyes blazing and the tip of a knife at Edenstorm's throat. "Ye're a lucky man, Edenstorm. 'Tis a good thing I remembered I'm a God-fearing man, or I'd have slit yer aristocratic gullet."

"Go back and read your Bible again," Edenstorm growled back. "You're as murderous a bastard as I've ever seen, Polruhan."

"Now, maybe ye're right about that."

"Let her go. If it's money you want, I have more of it than Harlton will ever see."

Davy sat back, shaking his head. "Trouble is, ye see, she knows too much, and so do ye, ye bloody rotter. Ye come here sticking your nose in where it don't belong. Well, me fancy lord, ye're about to find out more'n ye ever wanted to know."

Jane moaned, shook herself free of Trevenny and ran to Davy. "Davy no, don't! I'll do anything you want!"

"Anything, is it, darlin'?" he said. Davy pushed himself off Edenstorm, kneeing him in the gut, and whirled on Jane. "Anything for his bloody precious lordship? Well, maybe I'll give that a thought."

With a swift glance around the room, he gathered in his support. "We missed the morning tides, lads, and we're running late for our appointment, but there's a strong tide and a stiff wind to blow us on our way tonight. Take 'em to the *Nightwind*. Trevenny, ye'll come along to keep his lordship from being too much trouble."

Chapter Eighteen

As the sun dropped behind the west hill, five Cornishmen left the Polruhan house and walked down the lane to the quay where the *Nightwind* was berthed. In their midst were Jane, her head hidden by an old, tattered shawl, and Edenstorm, wearing the plain shirt and coat of an ordinary Cornish seaman.

Davy walked next to Jane, his jaw clenched and dark eyes glinting, but rigidly focused on their route. It was odd that his anger gave her hope.

But it hurt. She felt like her heart had been torn in two. It didn't matter that she could have never loved him, for she had cared about him, admired him for his devotion to his community, enjoyed his company. And she wanted him to think well of her. She'd tried to turn his attentions away, but Davy Polruhan was a man who would have what he wanted. She doubted if it had ever occurred to him that she would not someday change her mind.

It was like that horrible night so long ago when Edenstorm had found her and driven her back to her brother's home. Her life had fallen apart then. Now it was falling apart again, but this time, far more dangerously.

Her mind raced, fear at its topmost. She'd made up her mind: she'd be Davy's mistress if it would save Edenstorm's life. That was all she had to give that he might want. He wanted to humiliate her, so maybe he'd do it.

Or maybe not. Maybe he hated her enough now that he'd see her and Edenstorm both dead and take Cyril's money for it to boot. She squelched the shudder that ran through her.

At the quay, the *Nightwind* bobbed in the high water as if in eagerness for its voyage. Davy took Jane's hand, his iron grasp another reminder of his control. She walked up the pier and stepped over the gunwale onto the deck.

She caught Edenstorm's eye and saw both wildness and caution. He would make no more attempts, for he'd figured out she would not leave him even if he made the opportunity for her.

Davy still wouldn't meet her eyes. She made another decision. Given her choice, she'd rather die at Davy's hand than Cyril's.

The other men, too, would not look at her. None of them would come to her defense. But she'd always known it would be that way. She'd seen it with snaggle-toothed Annie's poor mother, who had been condemned by all as a whore and not even been permitted a Christian burial. But they'd all used her. Men were like that. She'd been right to keep her secrets, for at least that way she'd had a chance for survival.

In a way, she was sorry she had ever thought to protect them, for they had no such loyalty to her. Cornishmen took care of their own, but she was not Cornish and never would be.

"Keep 'em in the cabin till we're out to sea," Davy said, his voice as icy as a January wind. "Too easy to see them from shore."

Trevenny led them to the cabin, built half above and half below the deck. "Down the ladder with ye, me lady, me lord," he said, holding open the hatch-like door to the cabin.

Jane exchanged glances with Edenstorm and climbed down the ladder. Trevenny handed down the brown valise. The cabin door closed above them, blocking out all the light except the dim refractions from a prism in the cabin's ceiling. Slowly she began to make out shapes.

Edenstorm's hand found hers and their fingers interlaced.

"There's a lantern hanging near the door," she said. "But I don't know where the tinderbox is."

"There aren't too many places to look," he replied. "Smaller boats like this are buffeted more at sea, so it has to be secure."

"Davy is proud of his innovations," she said. "He built a desk that folds away and has lots of compartments. It's to your right."

She joined him as he groped along the cabin bulwark, easily finding the unusual shape of the desk. She pulled down the legs and set the brace. Compartmented shelves and drawers folded out as the desk set into place.

Edenstorm searched through the smaller drawers, naming writing instruments, compasses and the like as he found them.

"What does a smuggler need with a desk?" he asked.

"You don't know he's a smuggler, Edenstorm."

"Of course I do. No one else could be Guinea Jack."

"Um, not exactly."

"Who else? He even has the perfect boat for it."

Jane hesitated. But he was as embroiled now as a person could get. He deserved the truth. "It's not so much a person. It's what we call the entire operation."

"But he's the leader."

"Not really."

In the dim light, he turned to her, and she could see the furrow in his brow, but little more. "Jane, who else could it be? He has the power, the money, and the boat. They even met together at his house."

"Well, yes, but— It's the group, not just one person. Davy takes charge at sea, but—"

The sudden silence was thick in the cabin air.

"Hell. Not Lady Launceston. That's why she was at Polruhan's house in the middle of the night."

"Guinea Jack has been around a long time. She was a part of it in the beginning, years ago, with Davy's father. Then after Thomas Polruhan died, there wasn't any trading going on for a long time. But a few years ago, they started it up again."

His sigh was rough and loud. "Damn."

"There was just too much hunger in the area, Edenstorm. I know that's hard to fathom. They used to ship their pilchard catch to the Mediterranean countries, but after 1806 and the blockade, the markets on the Continent were cut off. That's all the people around here had. She couldn't bear to see the little children starving. Davy's the same way. He's a firebrand reformer beneath that friendly smile."

"He's a smuggler, Jane, like it or not, and you and I are perhaps only hours from our demise because of it."

She opened her mouth to answer, but then her fingers touched the familiar shape of the little tin box they sought. "I found it."

Edenstorm took the lantern off its hook. He struck the flint and blew on its sparks until the tinder smoldered. Jane touched the candle wick to the glowing tinder at just the right second. It glowed, then flickered into flame. She set the candle back in the lantern and hung it on its hook. She smiled. It always felt good when a newly lit candle chased away the darkness.

"I still want to know why a smuggler needs a desk," said Edenstorm, as he continued opening drawers and sliding his hands into slots.

"Don't captains have to keep logs?"

"Of a vessel this small? Not really."

"Davy does. He told me."

"Hello, what's this?" From a low, open compartment, Edenstorm pulled out a tight roll of large sheets of heavy rag paper. He unfastened the string and flattened them on the desk, weighing the corners down with whatever he found handy.

"He has charts and maps," she said. "Wouldn't that be normal?"

"Men like Polruhan tend to know the waters they sail in, but charts would still be useful. But tell me why he needs to know about the west coast of France?"

Jane didn't reply as she looked around his shoulder at the chart and its obvious markings. There seemed to be no point.

Edenstorm pulled up another chart and blocked it on top of the one of the French coast, then another, and another, studying each one briefly then shifting it to the bottom of the pile.

With the sixth one, his jaw tightened. "Hold the lantern closer," he said in a very low voice.

Jane moved in closer, adjusting the lantern so its best light played over the map.

"Spain and Portugal," he said.

His large, blunt finger traced over lines drawn in red and blue ink over the map. She could see tiny numbers that appeared to be dates written at points along the lines.

"Tell me. Why does a smuggler know or need to know where Wellington is?"

Jane made a gurgling noise in her throat as if she were choking.

"Not just where he was, Jane, but everywhere he's been this past year and where he is right now. He knows more than Horse Guards. Not only that, he knows where the French are in Spain. All four armies."

"What's wrong with that?"

"What's wrong? Jane, not even the French know where the French are. Their reconnaissance is completely disrupted by the Spanish guerrillas. They can't send out anything smaller than a battalion without the guerillas wiping them out. Their couriers are captured so frequently, Wellington knows more about their movements than they do."

"But if Davy is on the French side, he wouldn't know, either, would he?"

"Unless he's passing on the information for them, while the British just think he's an ordinary smuggler."

"He wouldn't, Edenstorm. I just know he wouldn't."

Edenstorm's nostrils flared as he groped into more slots, hunting for other betraying documents. "If he'd sell British gold to the French, he'd pass secrets."

Out from a small drawer came two small books. The first looked to be a daily log. He thumbed through it. "Roscoff," he said. "And here's Jersey. That's a bold smuggler, to keep a log that could incriminate him."

He opened the second book. "Damnation!"

"What?"

"A complete list of troop movements. Detailed. Interesting, though. No names of the contacts providing the information. Locations, but no names. He's a traitor, Jane. Nothing less. And you and Lady Launceston are helping him."

Her throat was so tight, she could hardly breathe. "I don't believe it."

"I suppose you want me to ask him, then? 'Here now, Polruhan, do be a nice fellow and tell us you're not a spy for the French. We'll believe you of course.'"

"Explain to me, then, why he hasn't already killed us? He couldn't let us know this and let us live."

Edenstorm quietly rolled up the charts and maps, re-tied them and put them back in their compartment exactly the way they had been. The journals went back where they belonged, and he carefully re-folded the desk against the wall.

"Blow out the lantern," he said. "Maybe we'll be fortunate and he won't notice we've been snooping through his desk."

She blew out the flame. The darkness felt as thick as mud. But slowly their eyes adjusted and she began to get her bearings.

"I saw a bunk. Might as well sit there," he said.

"He calls it a berth. He doesn't like hammocks." Jane gripped his hand so tightly she doubted if he could have freed it, and in the new darkness, they eased across the cabin until they found the bunk, a long, narrow mat in a corner so tight, it barely counted as a crevice. He took off the brown wool coat. The worn shoes he had been made to wear clunked to the floor. Jane folded her shawl and laid it atop his coat and put her slippers beside his shoes.

"Well," she said, "at least we'll have some comforts. I do have my shawl. Even a hairbrush."

He wrapped his arm around her and drew her close. Jane laid her cheek against the coarse muslin shirt.

"I'm sorry," he said.

"No, I won't let you take the blame for this. If anyone is to blame, it is Cyril."

"He wouldn't have known where you were if I hadn't sent Rokeby to London to ask questions. Someone Rokeby talked to must have let the word slip."

"Always have to blame yourself, don't you? It's still Cyril who is to blame. But I wonder what Davy is going to do now?"

"If he were going to do something, I think he would have shown more signs of it. He wouldn't be so angry with us if I hadn't made love to you."

For a moment, she didn't answer. If she hadn't encouraged him, he would have stopped, and now his life wouldn't be threatened.

"That's his own fault," she said, but not quite sure she believed herself. "I've never given him cause to believe he has any claim on me. But he seemed to think what I wanted didn't matter."

"A lot of men make that mistake. I didn't even think about what you wanted."

She burrowed her hand beneath the muslin shirt for the reassuring feel of his flesh. He rested his cheek against the crown of her head, the day's growth of beard catching in her hair.

All around them the boat rocked lightly, and muffled footsteps and voices came down from the deck above. It seemed odd, how quiet they were, and yet the words carried clearly.

"Getting under way," he said.

She nodded. Once they were out of the river channel, they would pick up a breeze, and they would feel that, too.

"Polruhan said something about being late. I wonder who they're meeting."

"I always made a point of not asking those things."

He shifted on the narrow bed, stretching out lengthwise. "Lie down with me," he said. "There's not enough room to sit up."

Jane smiled, her hope fading. At least Davy was also tall and he had made the niche long enough for himself.

She responded to Edenstorm's tugs, nestling down into the crook formed by his body. She let her fingers forage around, delighting in remembering all those little curves and hardness of muscle, the indentation of his spine that she had memorized from the night before. How easily she had taken to the warmth of his body, the loving gentleness she had never suspected he could possess. She would not die without the wonderful memories they had created.

"Jane— Tell me what happened."

"What do you mean?"

"With Kirkwood."

She sighed, wondering why it had been so hard to tell him the remainder of the story. It was humiliating, yes, but perhaps it was more that she couldn't stand being shamed before him. Yet now...

No, even now, it was hard to say. But it had to be said. Funny how she had never thought before how much she had hurt him.

"He told me he loved me, and I foolishly believed it. Cyril had refused his addresses and wouldn't let me see him. He would not even let me attend an assembly if Mr. Kirkwood was there. I suppose he was just protecting me, but I didn't understand that then. Perhaps that was why he was in such a hurry to marry me off."

"True. He called on me and made me the proposition when I hadn't been home even a week."

"I knew nothing about you until you arrived at Harlton Hall. I was very angry, but I knew better than to thwart Cyril openly. He said he would never allow me a Season in London because I couldn't be trusted. The only way I could have one was by agreeing to the marriage. But you frightened me so much. I thought you would be like Cyril. I couldn't imagine him choosing anyone for me who wasn't like him."

"He probably thought I was."

"At first I agreed to elope with Mr. Kirkwood to Gretna Green because he said it was the only way we could ever be together, but then in the end I just couldn't do it. I knew it would hurt my mother, and she was so frail, I just couldn't. When I told Mr. Kirkwood, he said he understood, but he wanted me to meet him so he could give me the things he'd bought for me." She sighed her disgust. "I believed him. The worst part was I had decided I wasn't being fair to marry him when I didn't really love him. So I met him to tell him the truth, but instead, he grabbed me and threw me into the coach he'd hired."

"But I found you—"

"Making love? Willingly? No."

"I saw your clothes, all neatly folded."

Yes. She had taken the time to fold them, just the way she had seen her maid do for years. It had given her a sense of calmness and order when she had been so afraid.

"I thought I'd persuaded him to leave me alone until we reached Gretna Green and were married. He gave me my own room, so I thought I was safe, but I should have known by then not to trust him. After I was in bed in my shift, he came in anyway. That was when you arrived."

"I should have done more than break his nose."

"I didn't care about that. I thought you'd come to rescue me, and I wanted you to believe me. But you just came to save your own honor and my brother's. No one ever even asked me what happened, not even my mother."

"I'm sorry," he said again. "I couldn't manage the thought of a wife who hated me so much she'd run away with someone else."

"But you didn't want me," she protested. "You didn't even like me. Why did you want to marry me?"

In the dark, quiet, thick air of the cabin, she could hear only his breathing.

"I don't know. It wasn't that I didn't want you. I did, in a way. I thought you were the most breath-taking woman I'd ever seen, and I could hardly talk for gaping at you. I just couldn't care about anything then. I don't know why. I just did what I thought I ought to do."

"Which was to marry."

She heard the hard sigh he let out, and a ghostly caress trailed over her shoulder. "Before I left for Harlton Hall, my brother told me he wasn't going to live long and he didn't want to leave behind a young family. He thought the title should pass through stronger blood. I didn't expect to go back to the Peninsula then, so I didn't see any reason not to find a wife. But I didn't care."

She stiffened, preparing herself for words that would be like a blow. Yes, she'd known he hadn't cared, but it hadn't hurt then like it would now. The cabin felt like it was closing in on her, and she couldn't evade even his breath on her skin.

"Once you said you don't feel things."

"I didn't. For a long time."

"Do you now?"

"Too much. Maybe it was better not to feel."

"Was it?"

His fingers stroked her cheek and tucked her curls behind her ears. Her flesh seemed alive with desire, hungrily magnifying his touch.

"No," he said. "It was a hell of its own. It kills all the good along with the bad. We've shared so much these few days. I'll never let anything take it from me."

"Edenstorm," she said, screwing up her courage, "I was such an awful bratchet back then."

"You were just young. You weren't even seventeen."

She leaned into his caress, absorbing it into her memory to cherish for as long as she had left. "No. I treated you abominably."

The boat lurched again, throwing them roughly together. Edenstorm braced himself and steadied her. "Sails are set," he said.

"It's a good, stout breeze," she replied.

They listened. She could feel the choppy rhythm of the waves, and knew the *Nightwind* had hit the open water of the Channel. She snuggled into the warm niche Edenstorm made for her with his body, thinking only of how quickly and how much she had come to love being with him like this.

"You're mine," he whispered. "I'll take care of you. We'll get out of this, I promise you."

Yes. In her heart, she knew. But what would he say if he knew what she planned to do?

"Make love to me," she said.

The last of the dim light coming in through the deck prism was gone now. She could barely make out the shape of his face as he leaned over her and traced the line of her cheekbone with one finger. "It's too dangerous," he replied. "He's very angry with you now."

"I'm not afraid. I want one last time with you. We might not have another chance."

He stroked her hair, weaving the curls in his fingers.

"Anything could happen, love. We don't know how long it will be before they come looking for us again."

"But anything could happen, anyway. We could be stuck in the cabin for hours or days."

"It won't be a last time," Edenstorm said, trailing his finger down the length of her nose. "He's not going to hurt you."

But the truth was obvious. Edenstorm was trying to soothe her fears, but if Davy had taken Cyril's money, the chance of their coming out of this alive was next to nothing. Still, how would he do anything without implicating half of Looe?

"What about you?" she asked.

His chuckle sounded throaty. "He wouldn't dare. You'd never speak to him again."

She laughed back as she let her hands drift from his cheeks down his neck and over his shoulders, savoring his shape and feel. "I'm already that mad at him."

"He can't get money from your brother if he didn't carry out the plan. Why didn't he? Maybe Lady Launceston forced him to help us escape. That could explain why he's so mad."

But Davy could be lying. Maybe there was another plan and he hadn't told them. Maybe Davy had to meet his contact first. Maybe the contact would dispose of them. Did he have some horror planned for them, maybe drowning them at sea, and seeing that their bodies washed up on shore? She shook away a shudder, thinking of the darkness within Davy she had always sensed.

"No," she said. "Shut them out. Don't think about Davy or any of them. It's only us, and we'll not let them take that away from us. Make love to me, Edenstorm."

"Merritt," he said. His lips touched hers, that soft touch that reminded her of feathers brushing lightly.

He pushed back the scratchy wool blanket on the bed and pulled it up over their bodies, as if he might conceal their actions from prying eyes. They would fool nobody. Yet it felt good that he meant to shield her however he could.

No matter how much she wanted to touch him, body to body, she knew he would not take the chance of removing her garments. Beneath the blanket, she unbuttoned his falls as he pulled up her skirt, skimming his hand over the sensitive flesh of her thigh.

She loved the way his skin was different in different places, from the silken smoothness on the underside of his arms to the rougher texture along the shoulders. Her fingers remembered the scrub of hair she had found on his lower arms the night before, but it was beyond her reach beneath the billowy sleeves of the rough muslin. She found instead the scattering of hair between the two small nipples and followed it downward, past the drawers that she unfastened, to his navel.

There she found the silken tip of his penis, and she quietly smirked, thinking again of the word's odd, unforgettable sound. How marvelous it was! The night before, she had watched its thrilling change in size, hardness and even shape. Her smile broadened as she felt its movement beneath her fingertips and heard his soft moan, and her own body began to tingle in the exciting way it had then.

Cautiously, she slid her fingers downward, not quite sure what would please him, but feeling that haze of passion invading her, becoming wanting, yearning beyond words.

"Touch me the way you want to be touched," he said. He leaned his body over hers, leaving just enough room for his hands to skim over the flesh of her belly and trace every minute curve, the indentation between belly and thigh, her navel, the contrast of the triangle of curls. In the darkness, his touch became her eyes, her pleasure.

She had a thought. Something he might not allow. She remembered the friend of Lydia who had been rebuked by her husband for touching him the way a whore would.

As she started to move down his body, he shifted, and his greater strength and weight urging her onto her back. Puzzled though she was, she didn't object. After all, he might be teaching her something she really wanted to know.

Edenstorm instead moved his body down on her, and in the cramped quarters rose up on his knees, yet his head did not rise. Instead, he dipped beneath the blanket. His hands rested on her thighs, caressing them, then moved between them, gently parting her legs. She began to pant as his thumbs found the crevice between her legs. She must remember to ask him what it was called. She was going to need to know.

Pleasure warmed to desire as he stroked, and her hips canted upward toward him, pressing against his strokes, longing for more, harder, faster.

He peeked his head out from the blanket. "Whatever happens, love, whatever you do, don't make a sound."

She tried to nod, but was only hungrily begging with her body for him to continue every glorious touch. She wanted, begged, hoped it could go on forever, yet wanted too that wonderful crest in passion she'd had before.

He trailed the wet tip of his tongue down the length of her belly, and a moan escaped her.

"Shhh," came his voice from beneath the blanket.

How could she be quiet? It was so wonderful.

His tongue passed through her curls, slid into the slit.

She started to cry out. His hand came up and clamped over her mouth.

"Be quiet or I'll stop."

"No, don't!" she said between gasps. "Don't stop." She pushed on his head to urge him back to where he had been.

Obediently, he returned to his task. The touch of his tongue sent her passion reeling out of control, heated and wildly yearning. The world closed out. She wanted him inside her, yet couldn't bear for him to quit what he was doing. She combed her fingers into his golden hair, gripped his shoulders, arched into him, restlessly fighting yet yielding to the strain. The desire demanded to be eased. She wound tighter and tighter, craving fulfillment. Higher, higher, higher, she spiraled upward.

The force of passion gripped and writhed through her. She clutched his head between her hands, riding through the parti-colored waves. Then slowly descended, still gasping for her breath.

He was there. Beside her. Holding her in his arms. She felt the silkiness of his caress, the warmth of his body, the comfort of his embrace. Jane sighed softly.

Yes. It was worth the risk.

Edenstorm crumpled back onto the cramped bed, breathing hard, his legs scrunched up and his arm around her. His heart still pounded like a drum, but his ardor was finally starting to cool. He'd survived, but by damn, not by much. Now, if she would just lie still like a well satisfied woman ought, his body would calm down and he'd be all right. Fortunately for him she didn't know a lot about lovemaking, or who knew what would happen?

She'd drive him screaming through the roof of this damn cabin, that's what.

It didn't bear thinking.

She rested her head against his chest, sighing quietly. Her hand grazed over his side, lazily along his arm. He could deal with that.

Her hand strayed downward. She found his penis, still much harder than he wished it were. He startled and all but hit his head on the low ceiling of the bunk.

"Edenstorm, I don't believe your needs have been met."

"Don't," he said.

She propped up on one elbow. "Why not? You liked it before."

"Not a good idea right now," he said, thinking he sounded slightly strangled.

She dropped beneath the blanket, and he felt the moist warmth of her tongue caressing him. His mind spun with wild sexual thoughts, mixing like a whirlwind with the hazy blur.

She peeked out. "If it works for me, it ought to work for you."

Dear God! He'd be making more noise than an Irish banshee on All Hallow's Eve. "You can't trust me, love. I'll make too much noise."

"I can trust you completely, Edenstorm. You will never betray me."

Her head disappeared completely beneath the blanket again, and her little rear bucked up into the air.

"Jane, stop. You don't know what you're doing. You don't know what to expect."

"Yes I do. Lydia told me." She disappeared again beneath the blanket.

God help him. And God rot Lydia. His body was hardening so fast it hurt, every muscle turning taut as his groin leaped to readiness. Her tongue trailed lazily down his length, driving him to screaming madness as it reached his balls.

Wanting, yearning— Damn, if they were caught, who knew what Polruhan would do? He knew himself too well. When the crucial moment hit, he was as likely as not to yell so loud he'd bring every one of the smugglers down the ladder.

In the darkness, her searching caresses were like striking lightning, turning him to sizzling, fiery stone. He had to tell her to stop, but God help him, as he felt her mouth go down on him, he wanted it so much, he'd die before he could push her away. Blindly, he fought to keep his mind intact, but it was slipping away.

He had to do something, somehow to keep himself together. Desperately, he grasped at the only mental straw that came to him, and he clamped his teeth into the flesh between his thumb and forefinger.

Hell, that wouldn't work. He'd only scream twice as loud when the moment came.

But what? His mind was fading fast, losing to the splendor of a glorious haze. Her tongue stroked like magic making him fit perfectly within her mouth, every hot, engorged sensation turning him to mad mindless...

Bite something else. What? Soldiers bit on a knife or stick to keep from screaming during surgery.

Just in time, he crammed the edge of the blanket into his mouth. He bit harder and harder, his mind fighting his body as he dissolved into the violent convulsions of release.

He was in heaven. The heaven of total peace.

He was in hell. He'd lost his battle. He knew he had. He clenched the blanket with both hands, and his teeth locked into it between them, but he knew he had betrayed her. He didn't remember. He just knew he had. He cringed, awaiting the clamor of footsteps that would soon descend the ladder. He would throw her behind him. They would have to kill him first.

"Uhm, Edenstorm, do you think maybe you could let me out now? It's a bit stuffy under here."

Oh. Hell. He was an idiot.

He released the scratchy wool from his mouth and let go his hands, noting there were no screaming, sword-waving pirates or smugglers dashing down the ladder to lop off their heads.

She snuggled up beside him, wiggling in to make herself comfortable.

"I didn't make any noise, did I?" he asked, dreading her answer.

"Well, only a strangling sort of sound. I thought maybe you might have swallowed part of the blanket. Is that normal? To bite the blanket?"

"Not usually. I just thought it would help me keep quiet. It's hard sometimes, you know."

"Oh. I'm sorry. I didn't know."

"Not your fault, love." He let out a huge sigh of relief and stroked her soft curls, reminding himself of the way they had gleamed like gold in a golden sunset. He could imagine himself caressing her hair like this for the rest of his life.

She'd be safe now, a little bit longer.

Maybe. As the normal world began to return, hope began to fade again.

A sudden flare of danger flashed in his mind as his nose picked up the scent of their lovemaking. Edenstorm rolled out of the low bunk compartment, unfolded himself to full height and re-fastened his garments. In the dim light, he worked his way across the cabin and fumbled around until he found the tinderbox, then lit the lantern's candle. The acrid smoke of burning tallow filled the cabin's stale air.

"I thought you didn't want it lit," she said.

"Any man with a good nose could sniff out what's been going on in here. Maybe the smoke will hide it."

He lay down beside her again, for the first time in his life glad for the rank smell of burning tallow candles. It was a different kind of desire that flooded through him now, an ache that hurt all the way to his heart. He wanted so much more now. He wanted a lifetime of loving with her. He wanted her whole and happy and free from fear.

He was so damn helpless to give it to her.

He had to save her. It was nothing to give up himself. True, he wanted to live now, more than he could ever remember, but that made the sacrifice more real, more necessary. Whatever he had to do, he would do it. Whatever he had to give would be given.

He was the only real risk to Polruhan. If he could just find the way.

~

"Me lord? Miss Darrow—I mean, me lady? Cap'n says ye can come out now. We're out to sea."

Edenstorm roused from a sound sleep to the sound of Trevenny's voice and yellow lantern light shining down the ladder, and he became aware again of Jane in his arms as she frowned against the light.

"Thank you, Trevenny," he called back. "I suppose we might as well. Not so stuffy out there, anyway."

"'Tis a stout, cold breeze. The lady'd want to wear her shawl," Trevenny replied.

"Thank you," she murmured. "I'm feeling a bit queasy."

"Sea's a bit rough, ma'am, but the fresh air's better for ye."

Jane brushed her hair and braided it, and it occurred to Edenstorm she didn't have a bonnet. Not a good thing at sea, where the wind seemed to be constantly blowing, but he supposed her shawl would help. He held out the brown pelisse and she slipped her arms into it and fastened the frogs on the bodice.

Her eyes were a bit wild as she took a deep breath.

"Let me go first," he said. Perhaps if something happened to him, she could delay, get back into the cabin. And Trevenny did seem too concerned about her comfort to be planning to push her overboard.

"That would be very rag-mannered of you, Edenstorm," she replied. "A lady always goes first up the steps." Without hesitating the second time, she set foot on the ladder and climbed.

They stepped onto the deck into sharply crisp night air, with stars like crystals against velvet and a bright full moon. Polruhan stood at the port bow taking bearings on the North

Star behind them, too occupied with his business to take notice of his unwilling guests.

Two huge white sails billowed at angles from each side of the foremast. Edenstorm frowned, looking behind him at the peculiar configuration of sails. "It's a lug sail, but it's not. It's like the one sail split into two."

She nodded. "Davy calls it an Adam and Eve sail. He won't say why."

A sexual reference, then. Noting the way Trevenny rolled his eyes heavenward, Edenstorm gathered his guess was correct.

"He says it sails as close to the wind as a lug sail," she continued, "but it doesn't have to be lowered and shifted to the other side of the mast the way a standard lug sail does."

"Definitely an innovation," he agreed.

"Aye," replied Trevenny. "The closer to the wind she sails, the better the advantage, but we don't waste several minutes of luffing each time we change tack. Watch. We're going to shift her in a few minutes."

"So you're really Polruhan's man, then, Trevenny? I suppose you were when I hired you on."

"Just my job to see ye kept out of trouble, sir."

"Either you failed or I did."

Trevenny shrugged. "But that was some ride we took, wa'n't it, sir? I liked the part where ye tossed the reins over the cliff."

Edenstorm nodded back. "I'll always appreciate that, Trevenny. You saved her life, you know."

"Thank ye, sir." He lowered his head, almost shyly. "Cap'n says ye can stay on deck so long as ye're not in the way, sir."

Trevenny ambled away toward the mainsail behind them. The man was not acting like a cold-blooded murderer.

Neither was Polruhan, who had let his gaze slip a good dozen times from his supposed concentrated scanning of the horizon through his spyglass.

Edenstorm took Jane's arm and led her to the starboard side, where they watched out over the dark, choppy sea. Jane wrapped her shawl tightly about her arms. He watched two crewmen shift the fore sail from starboard to port, admiring how quickly it was done. Behind them at the main mast, two more crew shifted the main sail in the same way, and the *Nightwind* began a smooth turn to the right. Now the North Star hung in the velvet sky almost directly behind them.

"Heading for France," Edenstorm surmised.

"South or southeast," Jane replied in a low voice, but it seemed to carry in the clear air like bells chiming. "They go to the Channel Islands sometimes. That's legitimate trade, you know."

"Sometimes."

"Legitimate trade can be declared and can help cover for the other goods."

"When the customs officer is blind and deaf," he agreed. But he also knew the Channel Islands sat not twenty miles off the coast of France.

Jane frowned but said nothing.

"You're cold," he said, watching her shiver again.

"I'm fine, really," she responded.

"'Tis too cold for a fine lady," said a harsh voice behind them. Polruhan had come up so quietly, neither of them had heard him. "Ye're to go below now."

"No. Really, Davy, I don't mind," she protested.

"Now, me fine lady," he replied, his mouth drawn tightly, almost to the point of turning down. "Ye've two hours to sleep and then ye're back on deck till it's your turn again. Unless ye've a mind to share with the crew. We share equally here."

Edenstorm gave thought to planting a blow right on Polruhan's chin, but it would only make things worse for Jane.

Jane slanted a cutting gaze across Polruhan that would have sliced through any man. She turned to walk across the rolling deck, balancing herself by touching the low roof of the cabin.

Edenstorm started after her.

"Not you, Edenstorm. Ye'll not be breaking God's laws on my boat."

Edenstorm felt his spine go stiff and stopped his head from whipping around just in time. From the corner of his eye, he saw Jane stop, eyes suddenly downcast.

God help them.

The air turned taut around him, and Polruhan's hard eyes bore down on them.

Then the air exploded.

"Ye bedamned heathen!" shouted Polruhan. He stormed across the deck and his fist shot out, catching Edenstorm in the jaw, knocking him back against the cabin.

Edenstorm shoved away from the bulwark straight at Polruhan, throwing him against the main mast as he ducked the next blow, and launched his own fist into Polruhan's stomach.

"Stop it! Stop it!" Jane screamed.

The hell he would. He'd had all he was going to take from the rotter.

They toppled to the deck, scrambled back to their feet as the crew scattered. Polruhan had him by the neck, but he hooked the man's leg and tripped him. Twisting to the side, he slammed into Polruhan. They banged against the mast, then wrestled back against the cabin bulwark.

Polruhan slugged back. Edenstorm dodged, swung back and caught Polruhan in the stomach. The deck pitched. Edenstorm's feet slipped, and he staggered, grappling for something to steady himself. Polruhan's punch slammed against his chin, and he slid across the deck. He hit the gunwale with his back and lurched to his feet just as the next swell bucked the boat like an angry stallion. He went flying, out over the gunwale and toward the dark, choppy sea.

Instinctively he lunged for a line that dangled with him down toward the water.

He slammed to a halt.

The boat pitched and yawed, pounding him against its side. He clung ferociously, waves dashing over his legs and he climbed, but the line started playing out again. Jane was screaming. Polruhan stared down at him as he dangled halfway between boat and sea.

Their gazes dueled like swords.

"Cap'n, ye can't." It was Trevenny's voice.

"Damn ye." Polruhan leaned over the gunwale and grabbed

Edenstorm's arm and lifted him high enough for Trevenny to grab arms and lift. Polruhan hoisted him by the breeches to the gunwale, and Wilson grabbed Edenstorm's leg and pulled him onto the deck.

He landed with a thunk, nose down.

Jane broke free from whoever had been holding her and ran to him. All he could hear was that she was screaming his name, because his head was whirling like a waterspout. As he pushed himself up from the deck, she had her arms around him. He swiped water from his face, which felt like it had been used as a punching bag.

An adequate comparison.

Edenstorm glared at Polruhan. How did one go about thanking a damned villain, anyway?

"What kind of monster are you, Davy Polruhan?" Jane cried. "I'll never be your mistress! Never!"

Polruhan bristled, his chest heaving. His black eyes darted from Edenstorm to Jane, back and forth.

"The divvil wi' both of ye! Fornicatin' on my boat!" Polruhan spun around, stomped to the ladder and disappeared down it.

Trevenny helped Edenstorm to his feet. Damn. He wobbled worse than a drunken looby.

"Are you all right?" Jane asked.

"Mostly," he answered. Big blow to his pride, but that didn't seem very important at the moment. He caught his breath several times, until finally the gray-speckled haze started to clean from his mind.

"You don't suppose we'll be fortunate enough that he'll stay down there?" he suggested.

"Not likely," said Trevenny. "But I expect he's down on his knees having a conversation with his Maker. 'Tis where a man oughta be when he finds blackness in his heart."

"I hope he listens. I'm damn tired of self-righteous Methodists."

"Best to watch your words, me lord, being as you're at sea with a boat full of Methodist tars. And I can't say any of us think too highly of either of ye."

As Jane cringed, Edenstorm cast a glance around him. He

knew their names. Smith, Wilson, Rawlins, Trevenny. Every one of those Methodist tars looked willing to put a knife in his belly.

"Being a Methodist don't mean a man's got no demons after his heart, sir. He's got his, like any man. He's just got to fight them harder."

His chest still heaving, Edenstorm put his arm around Jane's shoulder and led her to the cabin where they sat down on the deck, their backs against the cabin bulwark. At the moment, he wished Methodists believed in self-flagellation.

Jane straightened her shoulders and set her jaw like a man facing a duel. She dabbed the corner of her shawl to a sore spot on his cheek. "You're bruised all over, Edenstorm," she said.

"Some of them are left over from the cliff."

"I saw them. They must hurt, too."

"Bruises heal easily. No real damage. You weren't by chance planning to offer to be his mistress, were you?"

"Not anymore. Never."

"Never anyway, my love. I told you, you're mine."

She leaned her cheek on his shoulder, and he didn't care if the blasted evangelicals did think they were breaking some law of God. She was going to stay in his arms for now.

But those same self-righteous tars all turned their backs, making themselves busy with the business of the seas while their captain was below. For what seemed like hours, the deck was so quiet that the sea slapping against the boat was louder.

"I don't know what's come over Davy," she said, breaking the silence at last. "He's never been such a beast."

Damn, but he didn't understand any of them, most of all Polruhan. Even Edenstorm knew John Wesley had hated smuggling so much he'd decreed he'd never return to Cornwall if his Methodists didn't give up their favorite occupation. And his Cornish followers loved him so much, they promised never again to engage in the trade. But here was Polruhan, spouting his religion by day and free-trading by night. Preaching love thy neighbor with murder in his eye.

Oh, hell, he did too understand it. There wasn't a man alive who thought "love thy neighbor'" applied to his rival for a woman's affections. He'd be doing the same damn thing if he found the woman he planned to marry in another man's bed. He almost had once.

No, not almost. He had. He'd hit Kirkwood so hard, he'd broken the man's nose and sent him packing out the door without his breeches. Now he wished he'd killed him, because now he knew what the man had really done.

And it was a damned insult, what they'd done on his boat. Didn't really matter to Polruhan why they'd done it.

He angled his head toward her until it touched hers. "He's just jealous, love. Hurt, I'd say, except that no man ever admits to that. A man can be angry, but not hurt."

"That's silly."

"That's men."

"How can you defend him after what he's done?"

"I'm not. I just know how he's feeling. You told me once how people are so fond of him they just smile and give him whatever he wants."

"Well, he's not getting what he wants this time."

"That's what I mean. He never learned how to deal with not getting what he wants because he's always got it. He didn't mean for me to go overboard. I don't have the sea legs he does, and I slipped."

"You could have drowned."

"Now, think about it. Lines don't just dangle overboard on a boat as well maintained as this one. Someone threw me that line, and it had to be him." He hoped.

The hinges of the cabin door squealed as it opened, and Polruhan stepped up onto the deck. His black gaze knifed through them and he strode toward the bow. Edenstorm tightened his arm around Jane.

Up near the bow, Polruhan conferred quietly with his crew, his head lowered and occasionally nodding. It was Wilson doing the talking, and now and then Trevenny, but the words were too soft to hear. Maybe they were holding a prayer meeting or such.

Or maybe they were deciding the best way to dispose of their uncooperative passengers.

Abruptly, Polruhan looked up at Edenstorm. Eye to eye, they faced each other. Mentally, Edenstorm measured his adversary and promised himself if he went overboard again, Polruhan would go with him.

The man's gaze jumped to Jane, equally malevolent. "Lady Juliette, ye'll be going belowdecks. Like ye were told."

Jane jutted her chin, fear rounding her eyes. "I'm staying here."

"Ye'll do as I say. The captain is king at sea, and no man nor woman can say him nay."

She stood, clasping her hands together in a viselike grip. Edenstorm could see she meant to take a stand. He stood beside her. "Belowdecks, Jane. It'll be all right. I promise you."

She would be safe down there. That was all that mattered.

In the bright moonlight, he could see her swallow a lump he figured felt as big as a rock. She turned again and backed down the ladder into the cabin.

Edenstorm shifted his gaze to watch Polruhan, whose jaw jutted as he watched Jane close the door behind her. The dark eyes narrowed, but the frown was not one of anger. The man's Adam's apple rose, but only very slowly descended. With barely a glance at Edenstorm, he pivoted and walked to the bow, picked up his spyglass and studied the horizon as he had been doing before.

Edenstorm felt a tightening in his own throat as he watched.

He'd been there. He knew that pain. Polruhan might think it was the anger at betrayal that was tearing at him. But it wasn't. It was more like grief. He'd loved, he'd wanted, he'd dreamed... He'd lost.

The big question was, what would grief drive him to do?

Chapter Nineteen

For a while, Edenstorm braced his knees against the gunwale, as much for balance as for any desire to appear casual. He had no watch to check, but the moon continued in its arc high in the heavens as time passed. An hour, perhaps two. He was letting Jane sleep longer than he had said. Polruhan was hardly a man to need a watch to tell time when he had the moon and stars.

Every so often, the *Nightwind's* crew shifted the sails, tacking generally south, but they had little else to do. Trevenny ambled to the stern to watch the logline tossed out, then returned to the bow with a report.

Polruhan, on the other hand, constantly surveyed the horizon with his telescope, checked his sextant, then pulled out the silver chronograph from his waistcoat, frowning at it as if he had not just done the same thing ten minutes before. Then he went back to the spyglass again, moving it in a slow arc over the dark sea. Something off the forward starboard side had his attention, for he moved all the way to the bow and began his concentrated focusing again.

He turned back to Trevenny. "Lower topsails," he said. "'Tis too bright a moon."

"'Twill slow us down, Cap'n," Trevenny countered.

"Better to be slow than spotted. Only the divvil loves trouble so much he wants to borrow it."

Trevenny set the crew to the task, and both triangular topsails were quickly furled.

Something no bigger than a speck appeared on the horizon. Polruhan kept his spyglass fixed on that spot. At length,

Polruhan straightened, snapped the spyglass closed and handed it to Trevenny. “Frigate,” he said solemnly. “British. Portugal-bound, most likely. Set topsails.”

Trevenny and Wilson ambled toward the stern to hoist the topsails on both masts again.

Edenstorm moved in on Polruhan.

Polruhan turned to Edenstorm and fixed a glower on him. “Ye looking for a re-match?”

“No.”

“Good thing. Ye look like raw meat in a butcher shop.”

“I’m wondering if you might be a long-lost relative, considering we look so much alike.”

Polruhan snapped his gaze back to the sea, the side of his mouth twitching minutely. “Then what d’ye want?” he demanded.

“Curious,” said Edenstorm pleasantly.

“About what?”

“Our speed. Direction. Destination. What you’re looking for.”

“We’re making five and a half knots. I’d say ye’ve spent enough nights under the stars to know the rest.”

“Which makes our destination the Channel Islands or the west coast of France.”

“Clever lad.”

“And I’m curious why you call your split lugs Adam and Eve sails.”

“She told ye that? ’Tis not fit for a lady’s ears.”

“That being why you wouldn’t tell her.”

“Because it’s two parts ’at make the whole, the bigger and the smaller, but they only join at the crotch. That satisfy ye?”

Edenstorm nodded. He folded his arms.

“I’d say ye’re wanting to know something else.”

Edenstorm cocked an eyebrow. No point in responding to something they both knew.

Polruhan jerked his head sharply at the crewmen and they shuffled away toward the stern.

"All right, then, be out with it."

"Five thousand pounds to set us down on Guernsey."

Polruhan sneered.

"How much did you get from Harlton?"

"What makes ye think I took anything from him?"

"Sounded like you did."

"Two thousand. One to leave the precious lady floating in the Looe Pool with ye found dead, shot by your own gun. One more when the deed was done."

"Interesting. Considering there were no bodies left floating in the pool."

"But Harlton left Looe, so's not to be implicated."

"And then he wasn't around to see the *Nightwind* depart with its special guests. What are you really up to, Polruhan? You're an intelligent man. You have to know you can't get away with killing a peer."

The sharp black eyes narrowed until they were nearly hidden by the squint, and Polruhan diverted his attention back to the horizon. "Could be," he said.

"No 'could be' to it. You know you can't. Too many people know where I am. You have something else up your sleeve."

"Could be I just like watching ye squirm."

"Except that you know I'm not squirming. I've looked down the barrels of too many French muskets for that and you know it. The only thing I fear is what will happen to her."

The Cornishman's jaw worked from side to side, but he kept sweeping the telescope in a slow arc.

"That's what you fear, too. Don't deny it, Polruhan. No matter how angry you are, you don't want her hurt."

Polruhan said nothing, but his jaw didn't stop shifting around. He just glared into the sea through that bedamned spyglass.

"Five thousand to set her down on Guernsey, and you can do whatever you want with me."

Polruhan scraped his hand over the dark bristle on his chin and laughed harshly. "'Twould be interesting to collect. 'I have this draft, sir, in his lordship's own handwriting. Says I'm to feed him to the sharks, and ye're to pay me for doing the job.'"

"There might be a few problems to work out."

"D'ye think, maybe?" Polruhan's laugh became sharp, with the bitter downturn of his mouth. "I've had enough jawing with ye. Go below and wake her dainty ladyship. Ye're to take your turn now, with Wilson and Rawlins. Ye can have the bunk if ye can fit yourself into it. The men like the hammocks."

It hadn't seemed that long to Edenstorm, but then he no longer had a watch to check. And in some ways, it seemed an eternity of nights since Jane had gone below. "Someone else can take my turn. I don't need sleep."

Polruhan glanced at him, but kept his focus on the dark sea. "I heard that. They say ye're haunted."

"They'd be right."

"Folks in Looe are afrighted of ye. They don't like those pale eyes of yours."

"Can't help that."

Polruhan frowned at the sea. Edenstorm understood that. It wasn't easy for either man to look the other in the eye in any sort of peaceful way.

"And they say ye walk the streets nights and sit on the cliffs alone."

"Sometimes."

"Then what is't that keeps ye awake?"

"A drowning horse."

Polruhan cocked his head.

"A horse swimming after the ships sailing away from Corunna, trying to get to its master and too dumb to know its fate. And nobody can do anything because there's no ammunition left."

Polruhan gave a strangely cocked nod, his jaw jutting. "Aye, that'd keep me up nights. But that ain't what had ye haunting the cliffs."

"Guinea Jack."

"What would ye be wanting with him?"

"I'd want to know why a man would sell out his country."

"What makes ye think he does?"

"English guineas leave Looe and get to France, where they bring half again their value because Napoleon needs gold to pay for his war."

"Does it occur to ye the Corsican will bankrupt his coffers to pay for the gold?"

"So you're justifying smuggling as an act of loyalty."

Polruhan whirled about and snapped his telescope shut, eyes blazing. "Free trading's the right of every free man. 'Tis more'n a nob like ye would understand, considering the laws of England are made by the likes of ye and leave only the poor to starve. There's not a man in Cornwall that wouldn't die at sea or at the end of an exciseman's musket before he'd watch his family starve. What do taxes do but make rich men richer?"

"Taxes pay the wages of the soldiers in Spain that are keeping the French on their own side of the Channel."

"The divvil wi' ye. I'm tired of bantering. Belowdecks wi' ye, Edenstorm."

"Getting touchy, are you, Polruhan?"

"'Tis a foolish man that calls another a traitor when he's at that man's mercy. Ye could go overboard to the sharks for defying me on my own ship, and I'd be in the right of it."

Edenstorm folded his arms, feeling that dimple twitching in his cheek. "Yet here I stand. What are you really up to, Polruhan?"

"By God, man, ye're a foul idiot! I'm the captain here and ye'll do as I say! Belowdecks! Now!"

Edenstorm smirked, "Aye. Captain." The curt nod he gave was only half mocking, the other half respect. Whatever else he might be, Davy Polruhan was no traitor. Edenstorm strode across the deck toward the ladder, and reached out a hand to balance himself against the rough seas and save himself a bump on the noggin going down.

"Edenstorm!"

Edenstorm turned back to face the enigmatic Cornishman, whose jaw worked in furious flexing as his fists clenched and his chest heaved. Curious, he cocked one brow in a high arch.

"Ye couldn't have come knocking on me door at a worse time, damn ye."

"I figured that. The choice wasn't mine. A few more minutes and Harlton would have caught her."

Once more, Polruhan slid open his telescope and turned back to scanning the horizon. Edenstorm felt suddenly like an eagle swooping down on a defiant fox. Following his instinct, he crossed back over the deck and came up behind the Cornishman.

Without so much as glancing, Polruhan snarled. "Didn't I order ye belowdecks?"

Edenstorm folded his arms as he leaned against the gunwale to steady himself. He had to admire anyone who could walk steadily on a wobbling deck like this man.

"Aye. Captain," he said, returning the hint of snarl. "But then you dangled more bait before me. Must mean you have more to say."

The blocky hands fidgeted with the focus of the spyglass. Edenstorm stayed put, waiting.

"In *my bed*, damn ye."

That made him cringe. That was something that shouldn't happen to any man, not even a damned smuggler. "Sorry about that. But there wasn't another one available."

Polruhan's hand tightened on the spyglass.

"Easy, Polruhan. I'm laying that one right back on you. What did you think would happen when you put us down there together?"

"I'm trying not to think about it, ye damn fool idiot. Maybe I made the fool mistake of taking ye for a gentleman and her for a lady. Maybe I didn't think ye'd have the nerve."

Edenstorm only barely averted a wry grin. He supposed there was no good point to be made in explaining ladies and gentlemen were not all that different from commoners in that respect. "Now you know I do,"

Polruhan sidled a glare at him that should have sliced right through his head.

"She's very frightened, Polruhan. I know you're too much of a man to harm a woman, but I'm not sure she does."

"Ye couldn't give yer comfort like a moral, civilized man?"

"Not everything can be said with words."

"Damn ye."

"And you're too much of a man to be frightening her the way you are."

Polruhan ground his teeth. "You, I understand, Edenstorm. A man'll take what's there to be taken. But her..." The Cornishman dragged in a hard, deep breath, pinching his eyes closed. "A good woman doesn't give away her virtue."

The past slammed against Edenstorm like a rogue wave coming up from behind. He'd said the same thing. *I have no use for tainted beauty.*

He'd never given her a chance to explain, either.

"She gave a gift," he said. "A greatly treasured one."

Polruhan stared at the railing. "A woman's virtue is her greatest jewel."

"No. A woman's heart is her greatest jewel. When a woman gives hers to you, you'll understand."

The Cornishman dangled his spyglass in his hand, still looking out over the dark sea with its wave crests glinting from the silver moonlight. He squinted with pain.

"She's not even Jane. Turns out, all these years, Jane never even existed."

It was a look Edenstorm recognized, the way he knew he'd looked so many years before. It tugged at his heart, as if he were looking at himself for the first time.

"Jane or Juliette, she is the same woman," he replied. "Just stronger, kinder, more mature. Looe's been good for her."

"She's Lady Juliette Dalworthy. Jane Darrow I could've married."

"Yes, but she couldn't marry you. Telling you the truth would have condemned her."

"I hear ye talking with the wrong head. But I want to know. Are ye claiming her now? Or just using her?"

The sharp edge of Polruhan's words sliced like a knife. Was he? He owed her marriage, but how could he give it to her? She would spend her life in censure. Not to mention his family.

Jane was right about that.

"That's what I thought. Ye're no different from me. Maybe

worse. Yet ye're willing to give your life for her. Or is that just your bloody honor speaking?"

"I don't know."

Polruhan snapped the telescope closed. "Well, that's the first honest answer ye've given me."

"No, but it's not for you to know what's between us, Polruhan. That's what we've got to work out."

"And I've got to know. Did ye love her all this time?"

"No."

"Damn ye. D'ye think ye're too good for her?"

For a few moments, they both leaned their elbows on the gunwale, and the sound of their breathing was the only contrast with the lapping swells.

"She's not yours, Polruhan. She never can be. That's a hard thing for a man to accept when he's had his heart set on a woman for a long time. I know what that's like, too."

"Oh, and would the great lord condescend to know the little man's heart?"

"Cut line, you damn stubborn Cornishman. I'm speaking to you man to man, and you know it. In any case, you don't envy my life. You've got yours the way you want it."

"Except the reason."

"The reason's in yourself."

Polruhan studied the telescope in his hands, slowly slid it back open and trained it on the horizon. "Dawn's only a few hours off. Get below like ye're told, me high and fancy lord. And send the blanket up with her. It gets cold on deck, close to morning."

"Aye, Captain," Edenstorm said quietly.

In the cabin, he found Jane sitting on the bunk, rigid as a pole, holding the Conté pencil and her open sketchbook. The only thing she had drawn was the lantern on the peg that swung back and forth with each pitch and yaw.

He kissed her and chucked her under the chin. "I told you everything would be all right." He sent her up the ladder with the blanket wrapped around her shoulders, the sketchbook under her arm and the pencil clenched in her teeth. Just to be sure she made it in her awkward climb, he stood below to catch if she fell.

The night sky was paling when he woke and went back on deck. Polruhan went below with Smith for their two-hour turn in the cabin, and Trevenny took the watch.

Jane was huddled against the cabin bulwark, wrapped to the top of her head in the blanket, curled up in a tight ball with her precious pencil clutched in her hand. Edenstorm sat down beside her and picked up her little sketchbook. It looked like she had drawn every inch of the rigging before she had finally given in to sleep.

❧

"Sails off the starboard stern, Cap'n."

The swells made the small boat pitch, and Edenstorm found himself gripping the gunwale as he watched Polruhan home in on a target Edenstorm couldn't see. He squinted in the same direction but saw only clouds and blue sky and sea that seemed to go on to the ends of the earth.

"*Chasse maree,*" said Polruhan. "Divvil it. *Helios*, I'm thinking, but I don't see her red topsail."

As Edenstorm studied the distant waves, a tiny spot of red appeared and grew, blossoming into a triangle, set blood red against the sky.

"There 'tis. Trevenny. Set sails to run full to wind."

"Can we outrun her?" Edenstorm asked.

"No. She's a lugger like the *Nightwind*, but with three masts of sails instead of two. I'd build one like her if I could, but they're illegal in England. Too fast for the revenue cutters. Nor we can't out-shoot her."

"What's the point, then?"

"Ye never know, Edenstorm. I've outwitted her before and I have some surprises for her this time. I'm appointing ye in charge of that map ye found. It's not to fall into their hands, no matter what."

Edenstorm's mind raced, remembering the markings. So it was the French Polruhan was working against. He nodded his agreement.

"There's a weighted sack in the cabin. See to it the map and the small log are in it. Give it to the lady. She'll be the least of their worries when they board us because they'll be looking to the men for a fight. When ye know they're going to board us, ye give the signal. She's to back up to the rail and drop it. No hesitating, but don't toss it unless ye have to."

"Are you going to fight?"

Polruhan shook his head. "There's no point in dying for nothing when there's things worth dying for. But if I get a chance, I'll turn on her and shoot for her masts." He grinned. "The *Nightwind* can heave to faster'n any boat in the water. They don't know that, I'm thinking. Get at it. I've got things to do."

Polruhan yelled at the helmsman as Edenstorm dashed for the cabin, Jane running after him.

"What's he talking about?" she asked as she came down the ladder after him.

Edenstorm went straight for the sack. He'd seen the strange canvas bag and now understood its purpose. He grabbed the map off the table and rolled it into a tube to stuff into the bag. Then he picked up the odd little book with its strange codes and crammed it in.

"The troop movements," he replied. "I wondered why Polruhan knew so much about them and now I know. Wellington's greatest asset is the intelligence his exploring officers gather for him. The French would love to know everything in this book."

"But why does Davy have it?"

"He's gathering information. The French think he's a smuggler, all of Looe sees him as a smuggler and the British navy thinks he's a privateer. But he's a spy."

Edenstorm tightened and knotted the drawstring and handed the pouch to her. "Keep as far away from the French as you can, near the gunwale. You'll see my hand come down through the air if we have to do the deed. If anything happens to me, then you have to decide."

Her green eyes rounded. She nodded. Edenstorm pulled her into his arms and sought a kiss, his lips suddenly hungry for the taste of her. Too long yet too short. He dragged himself away with a groan, wishing to hell with Polruhan and the bloody French *chasse maree.*

"Up the ladder with you," he said, aiming a pat at her rear.

Topside, he sought out the *chasse maree*. It had gained on them. The *Nightwind* now flew a top sail on the mainmast and another like it was raising on the foremast. Edenstorm caught Polruhan's eye and a question flew between their gazes. Polruhan comprehended and pointed forward. Edenstorm raced to the bow where Trevenny handed him the line he was hauling, freeing the man for more vital tasks. The sail snapped into a billow, lurching the lugger forward. Other sails followed suit.

Polruhan stood back, hands planted on his hips and a wide grin on his face. He glanced back to Edenstorm, and Edenstorm nodded, acknowledging the triumph. But it was a shaky one, and everyone knew it. It was too much sail for the size of the *Nightwind*, and if the wind changed direction, they could capsize.

"Masterful," he told Polruhan. "Too bad you don't have a schooner."

"I'll have one someday. The *Nightwind* will do till then."

"She's no longer gaining on us."

"Oh, aye, she is. Just not so fast. The more time we buy, the better."

"You've changed direction."

"She was trying to out-flank us, but now we can run as close to the wind as the wind itself. Can ye handle a carronade, Edenstorm?"

"Light artillery. Easy."

"Good. I need ye on one. When they get close enough, we're going to come about sharply and stop. That's when ye fire. Aim for the masts. Trevenny's on the other gun. He'll give ye the trajectory."

"Think it'll work?"

Polruhan grinned, but there was no humor in his eyes. "Ye never know, do ye? Wilson, Smith, prepare to come about sharply. Trevenny, Edenstorm, prepare guns to fire."

"Jane!" Polruhan shouted. "Can ye swim?"

"Ye-e-sss," she squeaked.

"Good. Ye may have to. Kick off your shoes and take off your coat. Petticoats off, anything that'll drag ye down. When the firing starts, get down flat on the deck. Tuck your skirt up between your legs if ye have to jump."

Her green eyes as round as saucers, Jane took her place on the starboard deck as she clutched the map pouch.

They watched the *Helios* growing larger by the second.

Chapter Twenty

Her eyes fixed on the *Helios* with its blood red sails and Jane's hands trembled. Yet relief flooded through her. At least Davy wasn't passing them military secrets.

"Come about," said Davy in a calm tone, but he had the strong, direct focus and a certain wildness in his eyes that spoke of a coming battle.

Jane folded her arms, tucking her clenched fists into her armpits, hating the helpless feeling that engulfed her as she waited at the opposite gunwale, with nothing to do but watch as two men at each mast shifted the sails. The sails luffed, then caught the wind again, and the *Nightwind* turned sharply to run with the wind. Her feet slipped as the boat tipped, and she gripped the rail and started praying.

Trevenny called out numbers to Edenstorm, who was adjusting his carronade. The two little cannons were loaded, and the spark awaited.

"Heave to," called Davy.

The foresail shifted. The *Nightwind* suddenly stood dead still in the water. The *chasse maree* was coming on fast.

"Hold your fire," Davy said quietly.

"We're within their range now, Cap'n," said Trevenny. "I could send a perfect shot raking down their bow."

"No. Hold your fire."

Did Davy mean to give up the ship? Was it because she was on board?

"They're running up the Union Jack," said Smith.

"I see it. Don't believe it."

The carronades awaited as Davy squinted through his scope, twisting it for sharper focus.

"Cap'n!"

A small, striped pennant rose and spread above the *Helios'* red topsail.

"Blazes!" Davy swung around, snapping his scope closed, his eyes blazing in frustrated rage. "Stand down. It's that fool, Brainard."

"The divvil with him!" said Trevenny, and he pinched out the spark. "I say we blast him out of the water just for being a lunkhead."

"Aye," grumbled Smith. "T'would serve him right. How'd he get his hands on the *Helios*, anyway?"

"Aye, that snail of a cutter of his couldn't take it," said Wilson.

"Must've had help," said Trevenny.

"I take it this is not the enemy?" Edenstorm asked as he stood away from his post.

Davy slapped his forehead. "Divvil it! I can't let him see ye. Into the hold, Edenstorm, with your lady. Be quick about it. Jane, leave the map."

Edenstorm frowned, puzzled.

"Now, Edenstorm, and keep quiet."

Edenstorm's chin rose as he caught Jane's eye and he nodded sharply toward the hatch. She hurried after him, tossing the map pouch to Davy, and scurried down the ladder after Edenstorm. The hatch closed above them.

The hold was shallow, but down here the bobbing of the boat wasn't so pronounced. Behind them, a sliver of light slanted through a crack, and Edenstorm headed for it.

"Why didn't he want them to see us?" she asked.

"Who knows? I haven't figured out much of anything about him yet."

"Except that he's not spying for the French."

"Maybe. Could be he's spying for both. He wouldn't be the first."

"I don't believe it."

"Suit yourself. But we'll do it his way for now."

Jane found a place to sit among the crates and listened to the squeaks and rubs of two boats drawing alongside each other. Voice filtered through the deck planks, slowly becoming clear enough to understand.

"Brainard, ye idjit, why'd ye wait till the last minute to hoist your signal? We nearly blew ye off the water."

"You'd need a whole navy to do that, Jack," said a tenor voice. "You're late."

"A complication. How'd ye get your hands on the *Helios*? That old cutter of yours could never overtake her."

"Can when she's only got one sail. Storm ripped them off. We caught her dead in the water."

"Ye didn't have her last time we talked."

"I did. Just didn't mention her. She's been refitted since then."

Overhead, two sets of footsteps crossed the *Nightwind's* deck toward the cabin and made scraping sounds as they descended the ladder. Edenstorm pressed his ear to the rough wood of the bulwark separating the hold from the cabin. Jane did the same, but the clarity of their voices had become an indistinct mumble. With a sigh, she groped her way back to a crate and sat.

They waited, hearing nothing but scrapes and mumbles and Davy's occasional hearty laugh. Then finally the footfalls went back up the ladder and the voices became clear again.

"The contact has been signaling for two days. Can you make it tonight?"

"Tonight? How'll ye let him know so soon?"

"Pass the word by semaphore. If you can make it by midnight, they'll send a signal ashore right after dark."

"No privacy at all left in this world." He had a sneer in his tone.

"It'll be passed on in code. Nobody will know its meaning till it gets to the *Ajax*. It has to be tonight, Jack. They can't wait."

"Divvil it, that's dangerous water, Brainard. Why didn't ye do it yourself?"

"I'm not Guinea Jack. They don't trust me. Sorry. It's got to be you."

"I meant to go to Guernsey, then to Roscoff. Urgent business there."

"It'll have to wait."

"Ye don't even know what it is."

"You know the contact. Whatever it is, it'll be vital."

"Aye. The moon's full, and we can make good speed. But I don't like it, Brainard. Something's wrong."

"No trading this time. Just carry the packets. You've got to do it, Jack."

"Then ye'll take over once we get them out?"

The voices stopped as the footsteps continued. Dull thumps of heavy objects shook the deck. The boat yawed with the weight of men moving over the side.

"Keep yerself out of trouble, Brainard," Davy said. "The next lugger ye attack might not wait for your signal."

"It's only you, Jack. We're depending on you."

"He's running goods or secrets," Edenstorm whispered.

Several minutes more passed before the hatch opened again. Jane squinted as she climbed up into the light.

There stood Davy, frowning, with the rolled map of Spain tucked into the crook of his folded arms. He regarded them for a moment, then turned to his crew. "Set a course south by southeast," he said.

"Mind telling us what this is all about?" Edenstorm asked.

Polruhan threw him a dark look.

"Your usual cargo?"

"Not this time."

Davy stood by the gunwale, frowning at the red sail that was steadily becoming smaller. He glanced back at Jane, and she caught again that hostile spark in his eyes. "Find us something to eat, your ladyship. If it's not beneath ye, that is."

She jerked back, surprised. She'd thought he was beginning to mellow. Maybe that was only toward Edenstorm. But this time she'd had enough. As Edenstorm leaped forward, she stopped him with fury in her glare.

"There is only one thing beneath me, Davy Polruhan," she replied. "And that is men who behave like worms."

The elusive dimple formed on Edenstorm's cheek as he eased himself back to the gunwale where he had been leaning. One of the men behind her stifled a chuckle. The others became so silent, the sound of the sea lapping against the lugger sounded like slapping hands. Davy didn't move a muscle, except for the one that twitched in his jaw.

It was Smith who usually handled the food and kept most of it in the cabin where he prepared it. He sidled toward Jane as she moved toward the cabin.

"Leave it, Smith!" Davy growled.

Jane lifted her chin toward the sky and swept across the deck with the regality of a queen.

Chapter Twenty-one

The moon was one day past full and sailed high in the sky above a small, rocky cove in the Bay of St. Malo, on the Coast of France. The brisk wind chopped the high tide into little white peaks just as it was about to turn.

"Heave to," Polruhan called.

Edenstorm had heard the man say earlier that the tides on this coast could be extremely high and strong. He had seen rough storms at sea, and after the night he'd spent with Jane on the cliff, he had a new respect for wind and sea.

Polruhan studied the cove, combing it with his scope from sand and rocks to the low cliff surrounding it. Edenstorm squinted at the horizon with a soldier's eyes, looking for movement in the moon-cast shadows.

From the coastline came two faint flashes.

Polruhan snapped the spyglass closed. In silence, the smugglers slid over the gunwale into the dinghy from the *Nightwind's* stern. Polruhan gestured to Edenstorm to join them. It had taken Edenstorm a while to figure out the two unwilling passengers had meant Polruhan had to leave two crewmen behind, Edenstorm would have to substitute.

Trevenny took up position at the starboard swivel gun. To Jane, Polruhan pointed to the cabin. She shook her head. For a second, Edenstorm feared Polruhan's temper would explode like a mortar in the silent air. The man's jaw just tightened, and he turned away in silence.

Smith, Wilson, Rawlins and Edenstorm took the oars, and the dinghy bounced through the surf to the beach. Polruhan alighted first and sloshed through the shallow water to wet sand, while the others pulled the little boat ashore.

From the shadow of a tiny shack stepped a man of slender build who waited as Polruhan approached.

"Who is there?" asked the man in a thick French accent.

"Guinea Jack."

The shadowy man glanced back and beckoned. A dainty woman with a heavy shawl hiding her head and face stepped into the moonlight. Edenstorm recognized the distortion in her shape as being caused by a small child carried on her hip.

"Here you have your packets," the old man said, his English colored by his native French. "Here you have Madame Valérie Rouillet and here, her son. And here is the other packet." He handed Polruhan an elaborately carved walking stick. "Straight from Paris, carved especially for Lord Wellington. You must get it to his lordship right away."

"And the woman?" Polruhan asked.

"They will come looking for her and the babe. You must get them away from here quickly. There is much danger. She will tell you. You will find her very helpful, I think."

"Divvil. I didn't expect a woman," Polruhan said. "And a baby."

With a sharp jerk of his head, Davy stalked toward the dinghy at the strandline. Edenstorm took the woman's arm, and she glanced up with wide, dark eyes. He gave her hand a reassuring pat.

Jane must have been afraid like this when she ran from her brother. He had never really thought of it that way before. His teeth ground at the thought, and he resolved once more he would see her safe. She would never again be her brother's victim.

Nor his own. Polruhan had been right. He had been using her.

Well, then, it would have to be marriage. Whether she liked it or not. He'd take care of that as soon as they got back to the *Nightwind*.

"Maman," whimpered the child.

"Shhh." The woman bounced the child gently in her arms, hugging him at the same time.

A shot cracked the silence. The woman screamed. She whirled and pitched forward, moaning as her legs gave way.

Edenstorm grabbed the screaming baby in one arm and supported the woman with the other, all but dragging her as he ran toward the boat.

Horses galloped toward the beach.

"Divvil! Run, men!" Davy shouted, yanking the pistol from the waist of his breeches. He fired and hit the first horseman in the chest, throwing him from the saddle before the saber swung.

A second bang rang out as they crossed the beach, then another. Smith fell forward onto the sand, shot in the head.

Edenstorm pushed the woman and child into the bottom of the boat. "Get down!" he shouted as he pulled out his pistol to fire and nailed a second *cuirassier.*

Polruhan dove for Smith, retrieved the pistol from the dead man's breeches and fired. Rawlins reached the boat, then took out a fourth French rider, but fell, shot in the back, into the sea.

There was no time to reload as the *cuirassiers* rode down on them. All they could do was try to row out of range while the French were pulling back to reload. With Wilson and Polruhan, Edenstorm shoved the dinghy off the sandy beach into the water.

The riders came at them again.

From the *Nightwind*, the swivel gun roared. A shot whizzed past the dinghy into the galloping troops. Horses screamed, Hussars screamed. The louder boom of the carronade roared. A six-pound ball swooshed by them, tossing riders and horses where it hit.

"Row, damn your hides, row!" shouted Polruhan as he frantically rammed a ball down the muzzle of his pistol.

They rowed like madmen. In the bottom of the dinghy, the baby screamed, and every time the woman raised her head, Edenstorm pushed her back down with his foot. God, he hoped the baby hadn't been hit.

The French cavalrymen retreated. They would be reloading, too, and their muskets had a greater range than the Cornishmen's pistols, easily as far as the *Nightwind*, which sat less than fifty yards offshore. The *Nightwind's* guns could reach them, but Edenstorm guessed Trevenny would wait until they charged again because it would give the men in the dinghy more time to get closer to their boat.

He could hear Trevenny's voice from the deck. "Swab! Powder. Now the ball! Ram it! That's the way, me lady."

Edenstorm grinned. "That's our Jane," he said. He should have known she'd never sit by when her friends were in danger.

"Aye. She's a game one." Polruhan took up the other pistols, loading each one, to be ready for the next assault as Edenstorm rowed fiercely, in rhythm with Wilson. "Are ye a better shot than I am, Edenstorm?" he asked.

"Years of practice shooting Frenchmen," he replied. "But there's no time to switch now. How close are we?"

"Almost there. They're waiting till we're climbing aboard. We'll be easier targets then."

"How about the port side?"

"Take too long. We have to get out of here now. Edenstorm, go first and get the woman and baby aboard. Wilson, you next."

The dinghy pulled alongside the *Nightwind*, bumping against her with the bouncing waves. Edenstorm leaped up to the gunwale and pulled himself to the deck. He reached down and grabbed the baby, and laid the child on the deck. As he reached down for the woman, who Wilson hoisted up, the horsemen charged again toward the water.

"Fire!" said Trevenny. The carronade boomed and the ball plowed into the riders. The swivel gun fired and took out two more.

While Trevenny swabbed, Jane snatched up a rifle, slipped the strap beneath her elbow, and fired, taking out the foremost *cuirassier* as he reached the edge of the surf and raised his carbine.

But the next raised his carbine and fired. Polruhan yelled and crumpled into the dinghy, clutching the gunwale for support.

"Edenstorm!" Polruhan shouted.

Edenstorm swung a leg over the gunwale.

"No! Catch!"

The carved cane flew through the air. Edenstorm lunged and caught it.

"You're Guinea Jack!" Polruhan shouted, forcing himself to his knees. "Get it to Wellington!"

Before Edenstorm's horror-stricken eyes, Polruhan collapsed and toppled over the dinghy's side into the sea.

"The devil!" Edenstorm shouted back. He tossed the cane to the Frenchwoman and dove into the water toward the spot where Polruhan had disappeared into the blackness.

The cold darkness of the sea swallowed him, and he collided with the moving body. He lashed one arm around the man's chest and with the other arm stroked toward the surface until they broke through to air again.

"Let me go. Get them out," gasped the Cornishman.

"The hell I will. We stay together."

Over their heads, rifle shots from the *Nightwind* zinged, and once again Edenstorm sent up a prayer of praise for the man who had made the Baker rifle so accurate. On shore, the horsemen were falling beneath the rain of bullets and roundshot, none of them even struggling to their feet. Horses screamed with pain, but few men even moaned.

That was the part he hated most about war. Damned bad enough that men had to kill each other. Seemed like they ought to at least leave the innocent animals out of it.

Over the slapping water, he could hear voices above in the *Nightwind*, Trevenny calmly giving orders. Jane would be loading everything they had, along with Trevenny and Wilson, preparing for any new assault.

Wilson jumped down to the dinghy and hauled Polruhan onboard by his arms as Edenstorm shoved from behind, then Edenstorm climbed after him while Wilson secured the little boat against the *Nightwind*. Between them, they raised Polruhan up to the gunwale, where Trevenny pulled him aboard and they scrambled aboard, themselves.

"Damn ye, Edenstorm, ye're a fool," said Polruhan between coughs, as Wilson propped him against the cabin wall. "Last thing I want's to feel grateful to ye."

"Right. Now, how do we get out of here?" Quickly, he probed over Polruhan's arm and leg. "Looks like you've got some bad wounds. Broken collarbone."

"Not so bad. Leg's hit, too. Without Smith and Rawlins we're in trouble, but get me back to the tiller. I can handle it and watch the shore. Trevenny, the *Nightwind's* yours. Get us to Brainard. Set a course nor'west and stay away from the shoals around the south end of Jersey. Too treacherous for these English lubbers. Edenstorm, Jane, ye'll help with the lines."

"Let me take care of your wounds, Davy," said Jane, and she knelt down.

"No!" he growled.

Jane fell back as if slapped.

Polruhan sucked in a harsh breath. "Dammit, woman, ye've got to do a man's job now. Trevenny! Put this idle hand to work! Let's make sail before they find a way to blow us all to Kingdom Come!"

Jane stood abruptly. She raised the hem of her skirt, hauled up a handful of petticoat and bit down on the fabric. With a yank, she ripped off a wide strip of cloth, which she threw down at Polruhan. She stalked off toward the men struggling with the foresail.

Edenstorm released the deep breath he had been holding. Oddly, he wanted them to work it out. There was something about Polruhan she needed. He was the brother she couldn't have in Harlton. Not that the stubborn Cornishman would ever accept that.

He gritted his teeth. Like the soldier he was, he left others to their duties and set his mind to his own. The foresail shifted. Both sails caught the wind. Trevenny called for topsails raised as the boat slipped away from the little cove into the sea, catching the turning tide.

"Nor' by nor'west," said Trevenny. "Lord Edenstorm, sir, if ye don't mind, would ye see to the rifles and pistols?"

"Aye. Aye, sir," he corrected himself.

"Lady Juliette, mind your guns."

"Carronades and swivel loaded and ready, sir," Jane replied. "Then see to the passenger."

Jane scurried down the ladder to the cabin.

"I'd like to check on the captain," Edenstorm said. "I know war wounds, and his could be dangerous."

"Aye, then, me lord, but hurry. If they was looking for us at the rendezvous, they'll likely be looking to trap us at sea. If ye need, bring him up here and put her ladyship on the tiller."

Edenstorm dashed to the stern where Polruhan leaned over the tiller, holding it beneath his armpit while balancing his spyglass in the same hand. The other arm was dropped into a makeshift sling from the strip of Jane's petticoat like the one she had made for Lady Beck a few weeks before.

"You'd make a great infantryman, Polruhan," he said as he dropped into a squat to check the leg.

"Got better plans for me life. Not a sign from the beach. Thank the Lord someone taught that woman how to shoot."

"Her father, I think. Harlton complained about that once."

"No feeling's lost between those two, I'm thinking. I'm fine, Edenstorm."

Edenstorm probed the wound that went through Polruhan's upper inner thigh. He smiled as he realized the real reason Polruhan didn't want Jane tending his wound. Too near the groin.

"So," he said, for a shade of distraction from the pain, "the gold was a cover. Smuggling to cover spying."

Polruhan winced, but gave no groans or cries. "They'll do anything for gold," he replied. "Even look the other way. I figure that's over now."

"I'd say so. But where did the gold come from?"

"Ye'd have never traced it. It's all done at sea. From the Admiralty through Brainard."

"Ah. And I suppose the Home Office knows nothing about it."

Polruhan chuckled, then gasped as Edenstorm pulled a fragment of cloth out of the wound. He caught is breath then laughed more heartily. "Your friend Rokeby works for the Home Office. That was when we knew we had a problem. Had to get ye out of the way, but as ye say, can't go around bumping off nobs wi'out someone noticing."

"Not that you would have. How did you find that out?"

"My aunt, Lady Launceston. She's an amazing woman."

"Quite surprising," Edenstorm agreed. "Ha, you're a damned lucky man, Polruhan. Still bleeding, but not bad. You'll be fathering children after all, and no bone smashed. That'll save you from the surgeon."

"Maybe. I'm not afraid of dying, Edenstorm," said the Cornishman, flashing a grin that showed a bit too many teeth. "Hurts like the divvil, though."

Edenstorm padded the wound and wrapped strips of the petticoat tightly as he could around Polruhan's upper thigh to hold the bandages in place. "Now, let's see that shoulder."

"Get back to your post. I'll be fine."

Edenstorm ignored him. He tore more strips from the petticoat fabric to tie on a bandage, but it didn't hold in place as well. "Looks like a shot through the back that hit your collarbone. Broken, but maybe not shattered. Ball is probably lodged against the bone. How the devil did you manage to tie this sling?"

"I've got teeth, ye know." His laugh faded, and Polruhan sighed. "Ye got to thank her for me, Edenstorm. I didn't mean to yell at her. We can't waste the time when we've got to get out of here."

"Apologize to her, not to me."

"Aye. When I can. Ye're right, ye know. I can't blame you for what ye've done, and I can't blame her, either. But ye'd better make it right."

"That's for her and me to work out, Polruhan. Trust us to do it." Edenstorm stood. "What's in that cane?"

"Something worth dying for. No time to look now, but treat it like the map. If we're about to be taken, it goes overboard. Understand? And if anything happens to me, ye make sure it gets where it's got to go. I want your word, Edenstorm."

"It is the Grand Cipher, Monsieur," said a quiet woman's voice. The Frenchwoman stood behind them, a strip of white cloth, barely visible beneath the edge of her black shawl, bound around her upper arm.

The Grand Cipher! When he'd left the Peninsula in January, one of Wellington's exploring officers was still hard at work deciphering the immensely complicated code. He'd been warned never to speak of the cipher, for Wellington didn't want word leaking out that they even knew it existed.

"How do you know it's the cipher?" he asked.

"I wrote it, Monsieur. It is not complete. Only the new changes."

"How did you manage to copy it, then, without anyone seeing it?"

"I have to write the messages to the commanders in Spain. My husband is a proud man and he does not want anyone to know his eyes fail him, so he says it is beneath him to write the letters. I memorize the numbers and every night I write them down because I know I want to leave. But there is no safe place to put my notes. So I buy him a beautiful cane, and the man makes it hollow in the center for me. That is where I keep the notes. Then when I go, I steal the cane. I do not think anyone would help me unless I have something important to give them."

Edenstorm laughed. "It's important, all right. Do they know you've taken the code with you?"

"I do not know, Monsieur. But I think they would wonder why a woman steals a man's cane, no?"

That made it even more important. No way to tell if the code would be changed or not, but either way, Lt. Scovell could make use of the information. Some of it might be in use right now, so it had to get to Wellington right away.

"We've got company," Trevenny called.

"Divvil!"

Polruhan raised his scope in the direction Trevenny was searching, behind and to port. But it wasn't necessary. Edenstorm could see the sails of two *chasses marées*, blooming like white roses in the moonlight.

Chapter Twenty-two

"Set sails, wing and wing," called Trevenny. The Cornishmen scrambled.

Jane grasped her line as Wilson unlashed the cleat, and they shifted the mainsail. It fluttered like a frightened hen, then ballooned again. The *Nightwind* took on the appearance of a great white bird soaring across the sea in the moonlight.

"Trevenny," called Davy from his position at the stern, juggling between the tiller with his spyglass aimed at the advancing vessels. "Make for Jersey, due north. 'Tis time to pull out the new mizzen sail. The wind's right. Get us some distance from the French and then we'll change our course again."

"Aye, Cap'n. Wilson, fetch the mizzens sail from the hold."

"Devil it, Polruhan, you've got another sail? Can this craft take it without capsizing?"

"If I could hang out me nightshirt, I would. Don't question me, Edenstorm. Get it rigged."

In minutes, the crew had the new white triangle in place and trimmed over the stern.

For a moment, at least, Jane could catch her breath. She tied her shawl around her hips to keep her skirt from whipping in the stiffening wind and re-braided her hair to catch up the loose curls and keep them out of her eyes. She felt helpless, waiting. At least when someone gave her an order, she could do something. She shuddered, thinking of the Frenchwoman in the cabin, helpless to do anything to save herself or her baby. Yet despite the woman's wide brown eyes, she hadn't looked so helpless.

"It is not so bad," Madame Rouillet had said as Jane had

patched the slight wound on her arm. “We shall be free now.” She had told Jane of her violent husband who had recently taken to hitting their tiny son as well as his wife.

It had taken courage to steal the cipher and flee with her baby. Jane knew what it was like to run from everything she had ever known.

She looked toward the stern where Davy struggled, trying to balance the spyglass while holding the tiller steady. The strong wind coming from the southwest pushed the *Nightwind* faster than she had ever sailed before. The boat behind them had the same advantage and it had three masts full of sails to catch the wind. But the *Nightwind* had nearly the same sail power with the new sheets, and they were a lighter boat.

Davy’s gaze caught hers. She looked away.

“Jane,” he called, beckoning with his head. “Come hold the tiller so I can watch.”

She nodded and walked around the side of the cabin. Was he growing weak? What if they lost him?

At the thought, she winced. She listened to Davy’s instructions as she studied the wood of its shaft, and looked anywhere but at him. Why should it bother her what Davy thought of her? But it did.

Davy balanced himself, sitting on one hip with his injured leg extended and his elbows on the rail as he peered through his spyglass.

“Are they gaining on us?” she asked.

“Don’t think so. Likely we can’t outrun ’em, though. If we can make open sea, they might not follow. But the blockade’s stretched thin here in the bay, so they might dare it.”

“I think Madame Rouillet is very important.”

“More like the husband wants the son and the Cipher. They’ll kill her if they catch her.”

“You can’t let them get her, Davy.”

“I won’t let them get her. Nor ye, either, darlin’.”

Jane hung her head.

“Jane, look at me.”

She cringed, for in her mind she could see the hot rage in his eyes, the disgust. It would be like this now for anyone who learned her secret. Now all of Looe would know, and she could never stand the looks in their eyes. She'd have to find a new place to live. Someplace where no one knew her. But even there— If there even was such a place.

"Look at me."

"No."

Davy tucked his spyglass into his armpit. He took her chin in his good hand and forced her face to turn, but he couldn't force her eyes to meet his. She blinked hard.

"Jane— Lady Juliette— I'm sorry for yelling at ye. I'm ashamed of meself."

"It's Edenstorm who should have your apology."

"We've dealt with that, Jane. But ye're the one I've hurt. I'm sorry for yelling, and I'm sorry for not ever listening to ye when ye kept telling me what I didn't want to hear. And I'm sorry, lass, but I can't marry ye. I couldn't marry ye now even if ye were really Jane."

Her face screwed up into a grimace. So now he was turning it around. How was that for humiliation, to be rejected by the man she'd been rejecting for years, as if she'd suddenly come begging to him?

"I couldn't marry you, Davy, can't you see that? I couldn't, knowing how angry you'd be when you found out."

"Oh, aye, I'd've been angry. But I'm thinking, Jane, if ye'd loved me, ye'd've found a way."

Jane jerked her head away from the hold he had on her chin. Maybe that was why she felt so guilty, because she couldn't love him. She'd wanted that safe life in Looe, the life Davy could have given her, but she'd known all along she couldn't give him what he really wanted. She couldn't give him her heart.

"Jane, I'm angry with ye, I'll admit that. But can't ye see, I'm just a fool of a jealous man? Edenstorm's right, ye're a good woman. Why ye'd want a bloody nob when ye could have a fine Cornishman, I can't see, but even if he died right now, I couldn't marry ye. I could never have it that ye loved him instead of me."

"It's not—" She blinked again, not understanding, not knowing what to say.

"Oh, aye, ye do, darlin', and he's in love with ye, too. Don't waste it, lass. It's too hard to come by."

"I'm sorry, Davy. I never wanted to hurt you."

"It's the way the Lord made ye, darlin', to love the right man, and him only. Who am I to tell the Lord His business?"

He wanted her to marry Edenstorm? Confused, she looked up at him, finally facing his dark eyes and seeing kindness where there had been only rage for days.

"No, I can't. I can't marry anyone. I can't ever go back to the life he leads. You don't know them, Davy. They won't let a woman disappear for years without asking questions about where she's been, what she's been doing all that time, and none of her answers will ever be good enough. His family prides itself in the purity of its name, and they'll be humiliated.

"And I can't go back to Looe now, either, because everyone will know everything. You remember how it was with Annie's mother. They wouldn't even let her be buried in the churchyard. I've got to go somewhere that nobody knows me."

Davy shook his head. "Ye're afraid. I can't believe it. Ye fought off French cavalry with a cannon, but ye'd run from old tabbies wi' more pearls than teeth. Lass, ye're giving 'em too much credit. Ye could go back to Looe, I'm bound. 'Tis not the same as it was with Annie's mama. But Looe's not the place for ye now. Edenstorm's a powerful man, darlin'. He can save ye from anything your brother could do. Ye got to have faith in him."

"You don't know how much the cut direct can hurt, Davy."

"Much as a musket shot through the leg?"

She winced at that. Well, maybe not that much. "He wants to do the right thing, I know, but it can't be. He'd come to hate me for it someday. I couldn't stand that."

Davy leaned down and dropped a kiss on the mess that was her hair. "Ye always said ye wanted love, Jane. And here ye are running from it. I'm thinking ye've been running from it all along. But ye've got courage, darlin'. There's nothing ye can't survive. Ye just got to give it a chance. Give yourself a chance. Give him a chance."

His words made her feel like a wad of cloth had been shoved down her throat. She turned away.

Jane looked back at the white sails behind them. "You sure they're not gaining on us, Davy? Maybe it's not going to matter."

"There ye go again, darlin'. Running from it. Don't ye worry. It's going to matter. A lot."

She watched the open sea in silence. She turned back and looked toward the bow where Edenstorm talked with Trevenny, both of them studying the sea to the north. He glanced back to her as if he felt her watching him, the shadow of the foresail falling across his face and making his expression unreadable.

She had known the moment she had seen Edenstorm's face break through the roiling sea on Colliver's Cove that she loved him. She would give anything for him, including her life. But she couldn't marry him. She couldn't face that life. Davy just couldn't understand.

She just wanted to be loved. But maybe she didn't want it enough. Maybe she didn't have the courage to actually live her dream. Maybe she was only good at dreaming it, the way she used to stand on the cliff and dream of sailing off on some great adventure, knowing she'd never actually do it.

Deliberately, that is. She hadn't quite counted on Edenstorm showing up or her brother's wrath catching up with her. Or Davy absconding with them the way he had.

Had she loved Edenstorm when they first met? No, she knew she had not. He had frightened her too much. But what had she really been frightened of? Suddenly, she wasn't as sure as she had been.

Even though the bright moon was heading toward the horizon and lines of clouds were bunching up to dim its light, Jane could see a line in the distance that looked pale against the dark sea and even darker night sky.

"Here, darlin', see for yourself," Davy said, handing her the spyglass. "That's Jersey, broad on the port bow. We'll be upon it within an hour. I'm thinking we'll set into St. Helier on the south coast. It'll be hard navigating the shoals there with the tide going out. 'Twould be hard even with a crew full of good Cornish tars, but I think we can do it. But I want more distance from those fellows on our tail first."

"But that means we have to stay close to France," she replied.

“Aye. We’re running along the coast, about ten miles to sea. We’re in British-held waters, but this is the Bay of Saint Malo and we have France on all sides but one. Thin as the blockade is here, they’ll follow us all the way into the harbor if they can. But the closer we get to Jersey, the more likely we’ll meet a British ship.”

“Davy,” she said, lowering the spyglass. “I think you’d better take this back. There’s more out there than an island.”

“Cap’n,” called Trevenny. “Broad on the port side. More sails.”

Trapped.

Chapter Twenty-three

"Call the crew to the stern," Davy said to Jane. "The Frenchwoman, too."

Jane nodded and rushed between cabin and gunwale to Trevenny with the message, then scurried down the ladder to bring Madame Rouillet on deck. Davy was already discussing the situation with the men when the women arrived.

"They're blocking our route to St. Helier's," Davy said. "If we can head into the channel between Jersey and France, they'll have to sail south to get around the shoals to sou' and east of the island. We'll still have the two *chasses marées* on our tail, but we might make port at Gorey before they catch us. And the east side of the island is lined with watch towers about every half mile."

"Why not make for Le Roq?" asked Trevenny. "Isn't it closer?"

Davy shook his head. "No real harbor there. The shoals are too dangerous, especially at night. We could have our belly ripped out and still be miles from land."

"Then let's make for Gorey," said Edenstorm.

Davy pulled out his silver chronograph and frowned. "It's not that simple. The tides range up to forty feet in the channel with hidden shoals everywhere, almost as bad as the south coast. We're already over three hours past high tide. Ye figure the rate—the sea drops five, six, feet an hour, so fast ye can see it pulling back. We could run aground and be sitting ducks."

Edenstorm frowned. "Do you know the way through?"

"Been there only once. No sailor worth his salt navigates the shoals when the tide's going out unless he has to. We've got a chart and we've got Lady Moonlight to guide us, but we can't take the time to sound the depth. The shoals have a lighter color to them, though, even by moonlight."

"I'd like to say the same could happen to them as to us, but they'll be marking our course, and if we make it, we'll be showing them the way."

"Unless they have a deeper draft," Trevenny replied. "Or the tide goes out a wee bit more."

"Aye, there's that," Davy said.

"Can you do it?" Edenstorm asked.

"Short two crewman, wi' a one-armed, pegleg captain, two English lubbers and a woman with a baby?"

"Same question. Can you do it?"

"Maybe. Everyone gets a vote. It's your lives we're risking."

"I say trust to Lady Moonlight, Cap'n," said Wilson. "I'm longing to be back home and let me wife know how much I love her. Can't do that from a French prison."

"Or a watery grave," agreed Trevenny. "Aye, Cap'n. I ain't ready for me last prayers yet. We got to give it a try. Lubbers or no. They ain't so bad."

"Then let's hear from the lubbers. Edenstorm? It's a big risk."

Edenstorm glanced at Jane, but she could see his decision in his eyes. "We'll never know till we try. Besides, we English lubbers are being trained by Cornishmen."

"Jane?"

"I'm with Guinea Jack. What do I have to fear? And I'm not as much a lubber as you think. Aye."

"One more. Madame?"

"I die if they capture you. They take my son even if they don't kill me. *Non, Monsieur,* it is more. We all die because of what I brought you. If I must die, I wish it to be on the rocks. It is my baby's vote, too."

Davy stood and hobbled along beside the cabin. "Trevenny, set a course nor'east. Keep a good two miles off the island. Jane, ye'll take the tiller. I'll have to navigate. Wilson, as soon as the sails are set, be sure all guns are in order. Edenstorm, fetch me the chart and the lantern, then gather everything from the cabin that might have to go overboard, and Madame, you're to drop what Lord Edenstorm gives ye into the sea if he gives ye the signal. Wilson, ye'll be in charge of getting the rifles ashore without getting the powder soaked."

"Give me the tiller, *Monsieur*," said Madame Rouillet.

"Ye know how to do it?"

"A small boat, but it is the same. I can take orders. My baby will stay at my feet."

"Then Jane, take the guns. Ye've shown us ye can do it."

Davy started to wobble. Edenstorm grabbed him by the arm.

"You're getting a bit green around the gills, Polruhan. Maybe—"

"I'm fine!" Davy growled, and Jane saw the spark flash in his dark eyes the way it had been a day before. "Ye may be a fancy lord on land, but ye're on my boat and ye'll do as you're told."

"Aye, sir," Edenstorm replied. He grinned.

Her chest grew so tight, Jane had to force in a breath. It seemed strange, but Edenstorm was a military man, accustomed to accepting commands.

This, too, was war. Any or all of them could be dead by tomorrow, but she couldn't think about that. She assessed her guns and ammunition. The carronades could pivot to cover almost any direction. But there weren't very many six-pound balls, and the four swivel guns had very limited range. She was hardly an experienced gunner, having fired exactly three shots. Any of the men could do better, but their greater strength was needed handling the rigging and sails. She'd have to do.

Edenstorm fetched a crate for Davy which he placed by the portside gunwale, with a second crate to serve as a table for the chart, giving Davy a place to scope the distant island and watch for shoals by their pale color reflecting in the moonlight.

Now, it was a waiting game.

From the *chasse marée* to their left, Jane spotted a flash, then a boom bellowed through the silent air.

Jane's heart sped as she sprawled on the deck beneath Edenstorm's protective arm. She looked up to see Davy still sitting on his crate. The shot fell short into the sea.

She could hear Edenstorm's loud exhale. It matched her own.

He dropped a kiss on her cheek. "They're testing their range. They have a ways to go yet."

That wouldn't last long. And the two *chasses marées* behind them were also catching up to them

"Maybe we should pull out those nightshirts now, Polruhan," Edenstorm called out.

"Aye, and maybe we'll just let your long wind blow us there. Steady, Trevenny. Get us into the passage."

"Aye, Cap'n," came Trevenny's calm voice. "I have the Bay in me sights now. Can't be five, six miles."

"Take her to starboard a little. Color of the sea's too light here."

The minutes passed in agony as the French boats drew closer. Davy looked weaker by the minute and he was whispering things in Edenstorm's ear. That couldn't be good. It meant he didn't think he was going to make it and needed Edenstorm to fill in with Trevenny and Wilson.

To their left, a scattering of rocks jutted out of the water, and wet sand gleamed not far beyond. The water had a lighter color now, beneath the choppy surface. That had to be the dreaded shoals just beneath their keel, lying in wait to rip open the *Nightwind's* belly. The passage lay ahead, with shore and safety perhaps a mere five miles to their left.

Again the cannon flashed in the darkness. Then the boom.

Jane shouted, "Fire, broad on the port!"

She crouched by her gun, waiting and watching, as a ball crashed into the gunwale between her and the bow. The *chasse marée* had turned broadside for the shot and was beginning to turn back to the chase.

Time to fight back.

She lit the match from Davy's lantern.

"'Ware the powder, me lady," said Trevenny.

Oh, yes, she would beware. She aimed the carronade, elevating it as Trevenny had taught her, and touched spark to the touch hole.

With a boom, the carronade recoiled against its restraining ropes, as the shot sailed through the air. She watched as she stowed the match and swabbed out the barrel. It looked like the shot fell short, setting up a tall splash.

"Glory be!" said Wilson.

A third flash and roar from the boat on their port side. A ball tore through the foresail rigging, sending it flapping. Edenstorm and Trevenny dove for the sail while Wilson grabbed up spare line, and Trevenny stabbed a hole in the canvas for a makeshift fix.

"Aim for their sails, me lady!" shouted Trevenny.

Nice thought. But how could she aim at all, with everything, including the deck, moving up and down?

She raised the elevation a little more and again touched fire to hole. The carronade roared and bucked back against its ropes. Her heart sank as the shot again fell short.

"Glory be, the lady's a miracle!" shouted Wilson.

A miracle? "But it's short!" she replied.

"Not if ye keep cutting 'em off at the waterline, darlin'," said Davy.

Jane fired again, quickly before something changed. She watched in awe as the small cannonball pounded into the French boat's side once again. Edenstorm freed himself from the sails and took up the other carronade beside her. Two more balls slammed the French boat and it wasn't firing back.

It was turning away instead.

No, it wasn't. It was sinking!

Jane stood up, staring. Her jaw hung open. She'd sunk a ship? Well, a boat. She gulped, as it suddenly dawned on her there were sailors aboard that lugger. A big knot of guilt lodged itself in her throat. She sent up a prayer that they could all swim, for at least they weren't far off shore.

The Frenchwoman juggled her crying baby and the tiller at the same time, her great solemn eyes glowing with respect. And there was Davy, showing off that wide, white-toothed grin she'd feared he had lost. Trevenny and Wilson, cheering.

And Edenstorm stood, laughing, and grabbed her into a crushing hug. "Damn, woman, I think you could shoot the eyes out of a bullfrog."

"A French bullfrog, anyway," said Trevenny.

A boom from behind. A cannonball crashed into the stern, through the cabin and slid across the deck.

Wilson screamed.

"No!" she cried.

Wilson clutched his arm where a giant splinter of wood protruded. "'Tis nothing, me lady. A splinter is all," he gasped out. But he was as white as the moonlit sails above him.

Edenstorm grabbed the fragment of wood and yanked it out, and blood gushed from Wilson's arm. He picked at what Jane thought would be a few smaller ones.

"Edenstorm, to the bow! Trevenny, steer to nor'west! Jane, see to Wilson's arm if ye can."

Northwest? Toward the island? Jane glanced around hurriedly and saw they'd passed the shoals on the island's south side, and the beacon on the southeast point was nearly directly west of them. She'd seen the chart and knew they had to dodge around the shoals directly ahead of them. But that would also bring them into better position to fire at the French behind them.

Wilson scrambled back to the port gunwale where Jane awaited, both loading the carronades and tearing another hunk of cloth from her ruined petticoat. Gritting her teeth, she used Wilson's knife to dig out fragments from the splintered gunwale and quickly tied a tight bandage around the bigger wound.

"I can fire, ma'am," he said.

"But I don't think you can load. All right, let's work together."

As the *Nightwind* turned, aimed almost toward the island's eastern shore, Jane realigned the carronade, and aimed at her new target.

"There," she said to Wilson, and handed him the match.

As he fired, she was making ready the second carronade. Wilson lit it off while Jane swabbed out the first. He seemed to be recovering from his shock, and helped load, one-handed.

French fire kept coming, some short, some off to the right. The next slammed into the side of the cabin, then another followed it. Another went right between the masts, whizzing by Jane so close she felt its wind.

Her shots were going wide or low. Her luck seemed to be leaving her. She looked at the stack of balls. Two left.

"I need more ammunition!" she shouted.

"No good, ma'am," said Wilson. "We've already taken all the starboard balls."

"We'll use the swivel gun."

"'Twouldn't reach, ma'am," he replied. "Nor we've only got a few balls for it."

The moon was almost gone, and dawn was not yet showing. The two French boats behind them grew larger, running with confidence directly in the *Nightwind's* track. They needed more time. She had to buy it for them, and she couldn't do it with the puny swivel gun, not against cannon fire.

A cannonball tore through the mainsail, blowing the yardarm in two, and Edenstorm was behind the sail. Jane's racing heart screeched to a halt. The shredded sail flapped like a tattered flag, burying Edenstorm beneath it and its heavy yardarm. She wanted to scream, to run to him as she watched his body movements flailing under the heavy canvas.

Wilson stopped her. "Do yer duty, me lady," he said, and he ran to help untangle the sail instead.

Her duty! Her heart was screaming at her, again racing and pounding like drums. It was her love trapped, maybe mortally wounded beneath the sails and rigging. But she wouldn't be strong enough to help. She knew that. She had to stay out of the way. Trembling, she watched, unable to tear her eyes away.

Trevenny sliced away the tangles of cloth and line, and Wilson one-handedly helped lift the fractured wood. Edenstorm emerged slowly. She watched, her breathing almost stopped. Blood spattered his face and over his coat. But it didn't flow and grow in big red blotches, as it had on Wilson.

"I'm all right," he said, his light eyes fixed on her, telling her what words couldn't say, reaffirming his promise that she would survive. For him, it was always about her and her survival, never about himself. "Let's get this mess out of our way."

Above them, the topsail flew its lonely white triangle high in the air.

Jane gulped. Well, she'd never thought fighting a war could be easy. For the first time in her life, vengeance sounded like a good idea. "Let's do it, Wilson," she said. "Go for their masts."

Jane loaded and Wilson aimed his carronade on the forward French lugger. Jane turned hers on the one slightly trailing.

"Fire!"

Both carronades boomed, shaking the *Nightwind*. The baby screamed. One shot ripped through the sails and the second...

She watched, astonished as slowly, like a tree being felled, the mast went down.

A cheer went up around her. She turned back to grin and saw Edenstorm trying to lash a rifle like a splint on the broken boom. He was yelling and laughing as loud as the others. He halted for a second and blew her a kiss. Right in front of everyone.

"To divvil with ye, Edenstorm," Davy shouted, and he blew her a kiss, too.

Wilson laughed. Jane did, too, something inside her niggling at the odd notion that anything could be funny at a time like this. Yet wild exhilaration pumped her heart in an overwhelming madness. She couldn't think of what might be on the far end of her shots, only of what was on this end, the ones she had to protect. Her friends, a woman, a baby. Her love.

He was. She'd better live long enough to tell him so.

But the night wasn't over, and the *Nightwind* was as crippled as the boats chasing it.

"Damn, they're stubborn," Edenstorm said.

"The divvil with 'em, so are we," said Davy. "Run her aground, Trevenny!"

"But Cap'n—"

"Do it! Drive her onto the sand, full speed! It's our only chance. They won't do the same or the tide'll strand 'em on British soil. Nor they can't anchor within a mile of us if they don't want to run aground when the tide's out."

"He's right, Trevenny," Edenstorm said. "They won't dare, not with watch towers on either side of us."

"What if the men in the towers think we're the frogs, Cap'n?"

"The damn fools ought to know the difference between a two-master and a three."

"Not if Jane keeps blowing their masts off."

The Cornish men laughed and cheered again.

"Jane!" Davy shouted. "Fire the carronades."

"But there's no more ammunition."

"There's powder. Fire it! Make a lot of noise."

"Aye, me lady," Trevenny said. "There's watch towers all along the shore. Let 'em know there's a battle out here. And a battle means more'n just French boats."

Trevenny pointed the *Nightwind* straight at the beach. The dark sea gleamed a lighter blue in the moonlight as the boat raced toward the golden sand. Behind them the two French boats began to slow.

Jane fired the starboard carronade, almost forgetting to get out of the way of the recoil.

"I could fire faster if I don't swab it," she yelled to Trevenny.

"And have it blow up in ye face? Take ye time, me lady."

On the other hand, it didn't matter which gun she used now. She fired the second starboard carronade. Then she dashed across the deck and prepared the two on the port side.

"They're thinking it over," Edenstorm said.

"Thinking about the towers. There's big guns there, not the little six pounders we carry. If they fire even one shot toward the island, they'll be fired upon, and if they follow us in, well, they've got a deeper draft."

Jane fired the two port carronades.

"That's enough, me lady," said Trevenny. "Don't want the towers to think we're firing on them now."

Closer, the *Nightwind* ran. The sand gleamed pale beneath the water. With a dull thud, the keel struck sand. The boat jolted to a halt.

"Abandon ship!"

Trevenny jumped into the shallow water, and Edenstorm lowered the Frenchwoman then the baby to Trevenny, followed by Jane. Wilson passed down rifles, powder and shot, then jumped down, himself. Jane sloshed through the water, her eyes on where she put her feet but her ears trained to the argument behind her on the *Nightwind's* bow.

"All right, Polruhan, your turn."

"Go on without me. I'll hold 'em off."

"We stick together. Over you go. It'll hurt less if you work with me. Keep your leg up. We're jumping together."

She turned back. She couldn't leave without either of them.

Behind the boat, a thin line of light showed on the horizon, and she could see the two French boats hovering out in the channel. They'd be easy to spot from the towers soon.

"Take a rifle, me lady," said Wilson.

She slipped the sling over her shoulder, and glanced back where Trevenny waited and Madame Rouillet scurried over the firm wet sand. She turned back to the boat.

Behind it, she saw a dinghy boat set out from the *chasse maree*. The French ship would pull back now, out of range of the towers, but the men in the dinghy would row to shore and be shooting even before they reached the sand.

Edenstorm grabbed Davy around the chest. Davy braced his good arm around Edenstorm's neck. They climbed over the gunwale, and jumped.

Davy roared with pain as they landed.

Edenstorm ignored the cry and made himself into Davy's crutch on his good side. They sloshed through the water to the sand where Jane stood, her rifle slung over her shoulder as if somehow she might shoot away the oncoming dinghies.

"Ye can't keep up with me hanging on ye like this," Davy complained. "Leave me. Help the others."

"Notice what's beneath your feet now, Polruhan? It's sand, not deck. I'm in charge now and we stick together. Trevenny, head up onto that outcrop with the women, then wait for us. Find places with cover where you can fire if you need. We'll catch up."

"Aye, sir. Good vantage point."

"Here, Jane," Edenstorm said, tossing her the cane and the weighted sack. "Now you're Guinea Jack. Get it to Wellington."

Sudden panic surged through her. Her heart drummed a rapid pulse in her ears. No. She couldn't leave him. He'd be killed. "Merritt, no. I can't."

"Go," he said. "We need you up there, covering our retreat. We can move faster than you think. Go. Don't argue with me."

She bit her lip. It was a lie. She could cover them better at closer range.

But they were men. They had to be men, and she had to accept them that way. No man, least of all these two, could live with himself if he let her life be risked when he could do something about it. They needed to depend on her doing her job.

"Go. Run. Trust me."

Jane spun around, tears rushing her eyes, and dashed across the wet sand after Trevenny, Wilson and the Frenchwoman. They were counting on her. She had to keep the documents safe. And the Frenchwoman and her baby.

The sand turned dry, trapping their feet, but she trudged on, catching Madame Rouillet by the arm when she stumbled. They reached the sedge lining the edge of the beach and picked up speed behind Trevenny. Over the rocks they scrambled, up the slope.

Madame Rouillet had to stop and catch her breath on the steep slope of the granite outcrop. Jane took the baby and they passed him up in stages. Jane, too, was gasping by the time Trevenny and Wilson pulled them up the last gap.

She looked down, seeing Edenstorm still struggling with Davy through the dry sand. She remembered how her feet had sunk into it.

Hurry! Hurry, my love!

As the two men reached the grass, the French dinghy grounded on the sand. The Frenchmen leaped out and shouldered their muskets.

"They're in range. Let 'em have it!" Trevenny yelled.

Jane anchored the rifle strap beneath her elbow, the way her father had taught her so long ago. She picked the second man and fired. Two men dropped. More kept coming. Davy stumbled, taking Edenstorm down with him. Had they been hit?

Wilson traded her spent rifle for his, and he forced his wounded arm to reload. Trevenny grabbed the spare rifle and fired. A third man dropped his musket, grabbing his arm.

On the shore below, Merritt turned with his pistol, firing before Jane could bring her rifle into play, and another Frenchman cried out, crumpling to the sand. Wilson switched rifles with her. Jane fired. A second pistol from below fired. She couldn't tell which shot caught that man. Perhaps both. Trevenny fired again.

The French sailors drew back to their dinghy for shelter, just beyond rifle range, some of them stumbling or in a crouch as they moved. Edenstorm got Davy back to something resembling upright walking, and they limped over the grassy slope toward the granite knoll.

"Wilson, get them up here!" she shouted. "We'll hold them off."

"Aye, me lady." Tossing the freshly loaded rifle toward Trevenny, Wilson jumped down to the ledge below and scrambled down the rock.

Jane lost sight of Edenstorm and Davy as they climbed, but kept her rifle aimed toward the Frenchmen in the dinghy. All they had to do was advance about twenty yards, and she'd nail them again.

"I figure there are only about three of 'em that can still come at us, me lady," Trevenny said. "We can take 'em."

"That we can, Trevenny. We have five rifles loaded."

But Merritt and Davy were still within range of the muskets. Why didn't the French fire? Maybe they were hidden enough within the rocky ledges that they no longer made good targets.

Jane's heart started racing again as two men jumped out of the dinghy, but they grabbed its gunwales, shoved off and leaped in. Oars came out.

From the watchtower to the north of them, a cannon roared. So, the sleepy watch had finally noticed there was a battle raging at their feet.

"We done it, me lady," said Trevenny solemnly. "We done it."

Behind her, the dark shape of a man scrabbled up onto the

knoll.. Wilson stood on the granite, then with his one good arm reached down to help the next man. Davy came into view, and scrabbled over the edge until he rested atop the gray granite. Jane held her breath. Waiting.

"Come on, me lord," said Wilson. "Just a little bit more."

Was he hurt? Jane held her breath, praying. Her heart was going to explode from fear. She ran to Davy as she waited, watching for Edenstorm as she sought out Davy's condition.

"Davy, are you all right?"

Davy grinned, but she could see his chest was pumping for breath and there was a funny twist in his smile that spoke of pain. An awkward stab of guilt hit her as she realized her relief was for Edenstorm, that he was still alive. How horrible of her. Yet she thought she'd die of pain in her heart if Edenstorm had been the one shot. Or if he died.

"What're ye doing with me, Jane? There's the man who loves ye. Don't waste your worrying on me."

Wilson bent down and reached over the edge of the knoll. Edenstorm's head appeared from below, then the rest of him, clasping Wilson's hand.

And then he stood on the knoll. The sunrise turned golden.

There he was, safe. Whole. His chest heaving from the exertion of carrying a man as heavy as himself across a quarter mile of slippery sand and up the rocks.

He was so beautiful. So wonderful. He filled up the entire world and nothing else mattered.

"I think I'm afraid, Davy," she said breathily.

Davy laughed in his old, familiar, warm-hearted way.

"Being afraid's nothing, darlin'. We all are. Just make that first step."

Being afraid was nothing. Yes, he was right. There was the man she loved, standing on the cliff in front of a sunrise that caught the color in his hair and made it gleam like a golden halo. For him, she would face anything, go through any trial. Including old biddies with wagging tongues.

But did he really want her? She couldn't tell what it was in his face. Uncertainty? What did he think of a woman who acted like a man?

Jane rose from her knees and smoothed the unsalvageable fabric of her dress. She ran her hand over her hair, which must look as awful as she had that night they had spent on the cliff. Why he would want her, she couldn't imagine. But she wanted him. Forever.

She took the one step. It led her to take another. And another. Her fear made the air feel thick. But the sky brightened behind him, glowing with the crimson and gold beauty of a new dawn. A new beginning.

She lifted her face to look in those marvelous silver eyes that had come to mean more than she had ever dreamed possible.

"Will you have me?" she asked.

The dimple formed in his cheek. The one thing that always told her the truth about him.

"Will I?" The dimple deepened and folded into the crease of his smile. The silver in his eyes sparkled. "You are a scandal, Lady Juliette. You eloped with an adventurer and you ran away from home to become a lady's companion where you hang about cliffs in wild storms."

She gulped. "I didn't—" Was this yes, when it sounded like no? Or no when it maybe sounded like yes?

"You consort with pirates."

"Pirates!" She stiffened in protest.

"And smugglers and spies."

"Free traders, if ye please, your fancy lordship," Davy said with a chuckle.

Jane suspected she might be the target of a bit of male humor, of which she'd had rather a lot, recently.

"You shoot a cannon like an artilleryman and a rifle like a sharpshooter. A woman could hardly be more improper."

Jane huffed. "This from the hero who is really a spy, when he's not falling off cliffs in a storm and helping pirates run their gold to the French and stealing their secrets."

"Making us a perfect match. A scandalous lady for a scandalous lord. The lady who gave me back my life when I was so near dead I didn't even know I was almost gone. Aye, you're scandalous, and whether you're Juliette or Jane, I don't care.

I'll have no other."

One more step and she was there. As he pulled her into his embrace, she slipped her arms around his chest, reveling in the wonderful feel of his hard body, and she leaned her cheek against his chest.

"None of this propriety," he said. "We're too scandalous for that." He took her chin in his hand, lifted her face and his mouth descended to capture her lips.

"Aye, that's some scandalous lady," came Davy's voice from behind them. "Look at her, kissing a man in public."

Epilogue

Rokeby House, London

June 1813

"I still think you should have called him out."

Edenstorm glanced back at Rokeby, who stood beside one of the many huge potted palms that had been brought in from the Rokeby conservatory to decorate the ballroom. He tried to avoid rolling his eyes.

"No point in calling out a coward," he replied belatedly. "He'd just run. Besides, he's still her brother. I wouldn't want her feeling responsible for his death."

"But do you think this will work? Sort of chancy."

It was risky. It was a very fashionable waltzing party, and he had made sure it would be the very best, if nearly the last one of the Season. The dancing had not yet begun, and the orchestra played light chamber music that melded with the silks and velvets and the scents of lavender and candle wax. People milled about in their gay summer dress, murmuring about the hot weather and laughing with excitement about their plans to return home for the remainder of the summer.

"With your mother and my mother in charge, how can it fail? They're so good at raising their armies, Wellington should have made colonels of both of them."

"It'll cost me, though, if it works," Rokeby said.

Edenstorm raised one eyebrow slightly, the most emotion he was willing to demonstrate in this tightly scripted situation. "Meaning that you are about to turn thirty, and your mother will have expectations?"

Rokeby sighed. "I have until the spring, when I am to attend every fashionable occasion to which a young, eligible man can be involved, and I shall find a wife."

"Marry for love, Rokeby. There's no other way to go."

Another sigh.

"It will find you. Just give it a chance."

Rokeby shrugged and headed off toward the bachelors clinging to the sides of the ballroom to urge them into circulation.

Edenstorm turned back to run a last check of his chosen battle site. On the far side of the huge ballroom, Juliette walked on his brother-in-law Lord Cadridge's arm, with Edenstorm's sister on the other arm as they skimmed about the ballroom in a flurry of graceful introductions.

His mother and Rokeby's mother circulated through the gathering, quietly managing the gathering with their superb skills. The two elder ladies had paired together earlier to pave the way for Juliette with carefully engineered waves of gossip, and shortly afterward, Lady Beck and Lady Launceston had arrived in Town creating another wave of their own.

It was a formidable army the four ladies had created, and it looked like Juliette would be accepted into its ranks. Everyone in the room knew the Winslows and the Rokebys never allowed scandals in their midst, and Lady Beck and Lady Launceston commanded the highest regard. Everyone knew they would never have sheltered a tainted woman. So if ears cocked up at the peculiar stories circulating, they were colored with an unusual amount of compassion.

It was the explanation itself that had to be so carefully contrived, a tricky tightrope to walk, for some truth had to be laid bare, favorable to Juliette, with nothing flattering to Harlton. It could easily go wrong.

Fortunately, Harlton had not yet caught on. They hoped. And timing was everything.

Edenstorm circulated about the large room, accepting greetings and congratulations on his good fortune in finding such a lovely wife, all the while smiling broader than he had in many years, for it was every bit the truth. She was more than lovely. She was his life.

The chatter buzzed about them, the sound of bees pouncing on freshly blooming lavender. He smiled as he picked up snippets. It sounded like things were going their way.

"My Harvey says he intends to become prime minister someday."

"Well, I make it a point never to interfere in the affairs of men, Amanda., but I must not say aloud what I would do to my George if he should ever consider supporting such an odious creature. Good heavens, a man who tried to kill his own sister?"

"And for money. How gauche."

Edenstorm ambled on past one of the huge red marble columns that supported the vaulted ceiling above him. As he neared a potted palm so large it really should be growing at the edge of some desert, the voices from the other side carried to him.

"And I lay it all on Edenstorm."

"Oh, I cannot see how."

"I should like to know. He was to marry her years ago, wasn't he? Why didn't he do it then?"

He stopped, concealed behind the palm's dangling fronds. Lay what? Was scandal about to erupt despite their careful plans? He'd stick with her no matter what, but this was a gift he wanted desperately to give to her.

"Quite the question, is it not? Well, I have deduced the whole thing."

He could almost hear the women moving in closer for the secret. He craned an ear in that direction, his heart racing ruthlessly.

"Why didn't he marry her? Because she disappeared. And how can a man marry a woman who cannot be found?"

He sucked in a breath. Please, God.

"Now," continued the authoritative voice," you may recall some many years back, one of the Harlton women made a marriage quite outside the family's hopes and was disgraced. However, the young man eventually redeemed himself by making quite a fortune, and you may be sure the Harltons suddenly found him quite useful. They are that sort, you know. She was left quite wealthy on her husband's passing, but she was not as generous to her family as he had been. The present Harlton, I have it on good authority, presumed her fortune would come to him when his great-aunt passed on, he being the titular head of the family, and she without direct issue."

Oohs and ahs came from the far side of the column. Edenstorm held his breath.

"Imagine his surprise, then, when he learned his sister, not he, was the beneficiary. Unfortunately, he had already made plans to marry off lovely little Juliette to the younger Winslow. But if he did, all that money would pass out of the family. And not only that, he was not even the trustee, so he could not possibly get his hands on it."

The oohs became louder.

"Well, what was he to do? Just how could he get his hands on all that marvelous money? So he locked up our lovely Juliette and told the young Winslow his sweetheart had jilted him.

"Broken-hearted, our young man returned to the war, where he stayed until the deaths of his father and brother brought him home. But he still mourned his lost love, who Harlton viciously told him had died. Drowned, of all things! I know that to be true, for I heard him say it once, myself."

Sad moaning sounds came forth, encouraging the speaker to continue her story. Edenstorm continued to hold his breath.

"Now I have deduced how Edenstorm unraveled the truth. In his great sadness and desire to know of his love's last days, he sought out her neighbor, Lady Beck, who had been her friend. But learning Lady Beck has returned to her native Cornwall upon being widowed, he followed her there. And there, kept safe from her odious, venomous brother by Lady Beck and her mother and the marvelous people of that lovely little village, Edenstorm found his lost love, and married her."

Accompanied by a collection of female sighs, Edenstorm chuckled. He left the concealment of the palm fronds and headed back to the center of the ballroom where his wife was happily chatting. That was nearly as good as the story his mother was passing around. He wouldn't bother to point out a few of the details that didn't line up quite right.

He caught Rokeby's sharp nod toward the ballroom

entrance. There stood Harlton, a goat being led to slaughter. Unaware of his lost sister standing not twenty feet from him.

Harlton, tall and arrogantly resplendent in pristine black, strutted up to Lady Rokeby and bowed, as elegant a bow as Edenstorm had ever seen, for it had been hinted he might find supporters amidst those who had gathered to appreciate the waltz. Harlton reached for Lady Rokeby's hand.

Her eyes widened, she jerked it back, staring, saying nothing.

The music stopped. The babble of a hundred voices ceased as if chopped clean. Every person in the room began a slow turn like the graceful movements of a minuet, and all came to a stop at precisely the same moment. Facing Harlton. It was just at this time he spotted Juliette, who stood directly in front of him.

Harlton's jaw dropped open.

The company of the Ton moved like the slowly flowing water, a sea of colored cloths and sparkling gems, resplendent with the scents of lavender and the burning wax of the finest candles, like the turning of the tide on a windless day. The tide that was the Ton oozed around Juliette, an arc of protection aimed at Harlton.

No one saw the man. They looked not at him, but through him, seeing the pale blue watered silk wall, seeing the golden sconces, each with two slim candles beside a tall, gilt-framed mirror reflecting those who studied it. Before Edenstorm's very eyes, the man between them and the wall actually seemed to fade.

Although he had never seen it, Edenstorm had always known this was how it was done. They all did. They were the Ton. They knew from birth the gruesome magic of the Cut Direct.

They turned again, the Ton. This time not in unison, but each at his own pace, as if propelled by individual whim, turning their backs to the white-faced man in black who stood alone. They sought out the intricate jacquard weave of the golden, blue-fringed draperies that were swagged in a most intriguingly unusual fashion, or admired the mahogany brownness of Lady Aston's curls, and they chattered gaily about the delights of summer that awaited them at home in their country seats. Harlton became so pale he really did look as if he would fade away.

It was a shame, in a way, for, turned away as they were, none of them could see the last of the hearty blood drain from Harlton until his face was as ashen as death. None saw him grab a gilded table for support, but then they did not care. Only Edenstorm saw the horror on the man's face as he perceived his public career crashing to ruin.

Only Edenstorm was left to confront him, eye to eye.

Harlton gulped as if he could not breathe. He pivoted awkwardly and staggered from the room. He was gone, perhaps forever. Who knew? Or cared? That was the way of the Ton.

Harlton would never bother Juliette again.

The music resumed, not with the whimsical chamber music that had been little more than a part of the scenery, but with the first waltz of the evening. Edenstorm turned to find his wife, and there she was, holding out her hand to him with a smile that lit his heart.

"Thank you," she said, so quietly it was almost a like a soughing breeze.

She smiled. The violet of her dress somehow turned her eyes to the greenest of emeralds, and he was lost in them. He put his hand at her waist and they were lost together like a boat rocking on gentle waves of the sea.

"Psst. Merritt."

He stepped out of his reverie, back to the ballroom where he held the most beautiful woman in the world in his arms.

"I love you," she whispered, and licked her lips.

He missed his step.

He chuckled. She still had that effect on him. With just a gesture she could turn the world-weary man into the infatuated, bumbling, tongue-tied schoolboy. He whispered back the same and heard his hushed words echoing like a cannon's boom throughout the ballroom. Someone snickered behind him.

But he was proud of his words. He was proud of the woman in his arms. She was not plain Jane Darrow. Nor was she any longer Lady Juliette Dalworthy. All of that was gone.

She was Juliette, Countess of Edenstorm, his scandalous lady, his wife.

And Jane when the lights went out at night.

Author's Note

I didn't make it up—the story about the horse swimming after the ship when the British evacuated Corunna in January, 1809. Men have always loved their horses, perhaps even more did the cavalrymen whose lives had depended on their animals. I think we all understand why one man would disobey the order to shoot his beloved mount, even knowing it would likely starve in the desolate winter. But no one could have predicted the horse would jump into the sea, desperately trying to reach its master. There was nothing anyone could do to save it. Nothing. I knew when I read this story that my hero had stood aboard this ship, tears streaming down his face as they did with every man aboard. This was what war was about then. It still is.

Delle Jacobs

About the Author

To learn more about Delle Jacobs, please visit www.dellejacobs.com. Send an email to Delle at delle@dellejacobs.com. Delle blogs with the Wet Noodle Posse at wetnoodleposse.blogspot.com, Rose City Romance Writers at http://rosecityromancewriters.blogspot.com/ and her own blog, BluestockingChronicles, at:

bluestockingchronicles.blogspot.com.

It's only a restorative tonic for women.
So why are the bachelors of the Ton *running scared?*

Aphrodite's Brew

© 2008 Delle Jacobs

The Earl of Vailmont, a confirmed bachelor who laughs at superstition, scoffs at the rumors that a love potion is behind the recent string of improbable marriages, and he vows to expose the charlatan behind the fraud. But when Val meets Sylvia, Lady Ashbroughton, her silver-green eyes set his soul spinning as if he has just encountered a witch.

Sylvia needs no handsome earls prying into her life. If Val learns of her secret trade in potions, she will be ruined and her beloved stepdaughter will be deprived of her Season. Worse, the earl could uncover Sylvia's most shameful secret—her penchant for handsome men. To ward him off, she protects her fragile heart from unwanted new passion by wearing her family recipe in a locket.

But neither logic nor charms can combat the stubborn love that sweeps them into a whirl of unbridled passion.

And, from somewhere in the mists of time, a forgotten, nameless god is laughing.

Warning, this title contains the following: explicit sex and unexpected bursts of side-splitting humor.

Printed in the United States
141881LV00003B/4/P

9 781605 041759